Also by Yvonne Lindsay

Honor-Bound Groom
Stand-In Bride's Seduction
For the Sake of the Secret Child
Arranged Marriage, Bedroom Secrets
Contract Wedding, Expectant Bride
Tangled Vows

Also by Yahrah St. John

Cappuccino Kisses
Taming Her Tycoon
Miami After Hours
Taming Her Billionaire
His San Diego Sweetheart

INCONVENIENTLY WED

YVONNE LINDSAY

AT THE CEO'S PLEASURE

YAHRAH ST. JOHN

MILLS & BOON

First Published in Great Britain 2019
by Mills & Boon, an imprint of HarperCollinsPublishers,
1 London Bridge Street, London, SE1 9GF

ISBN: 978-0-263-27169-0

0119

MIX
Paper from responsible sources
FSC™ C007454

This book is produced from independently certified FSC™ paper to ensure responsible forest management.

For more information visit: www.harpercollins.co.uk/green

Printed and bound in Spain
by CPI, Barcelona

INCONVENIENTLY WED

YVONNE LINDSAY

I wouldn't be here without my wonderful readers, so this story is for you. Thank you for all your support and kind words through the years.

One

"It's going to be okay, Mom." Imogene hastened to reassure her mother for the thousandth time.

She had no doubt her mom remembered all too well the broken woman Imogene had been when she'd returned from volunteering in Africa with her first marriage and all her hopes and dreams in tatters. But as she'd told her mom several times, things were going to be completely different this time around. This marriage would be based on mutual compatibility after an intense clinical assessment by a team of relationship counselors and psychologists—absolutely nothing impractical about that. She'd done the passionate love thing. Experienced the soaring highs of love at first sight and barely made it through the devastating lows of discovering it had all been a lie. This way, at least, nothing would go wrong.

"Ready?" the wedding planner asked in her perfectly calming and well-modulated voice.

Imogene smoothed a hand down her gown, the silk-and-organza creation a far cry from the borrowed cocktail dress she'd worn to her last wedding, and nodded. "Absolutely."

The wedding planner gave her a wide smile, then indicated to the pianist to change his music for the bride's entrance. Imogene hesitated at the door. Then, taking her mother's hand, she began to walk slowly and confidently toward the man she was going to build a future and create a much-longed-for family with. A serene smile wreathed her face as she briefly made eye contact with her friends and the sprinkling of extended family who'd made the trip to the West Coast from New York. The formality of signing the license application could be done separately here in Washington, which kept to the Match Made in Marriage rules of meeting at the altar. This was the right thing for an old-fashioned girl with old-fashioned values to do, she assured herself. This time she wasn't leaving anything to chance. This time, she was getting it right.

The last time Imogene had married, she'd been filled with excitement together with a crazy-mad dose of lust. *And look how that turned out*, the little voice inside her head reminded her. She grimaced slightly. Today was different. There was no bubbling excitement, beyond a quiet curiosity as to exactly what her groom would be like, and there was certainly no lust. At least not yet.

No, this time she was not a victim of the dizzying heights of passion—a passion that had blurred her sensibilities, not to mention her common sense. This time she had a specific goal in mind. A family of her own. Yes, she knew she could take steps to be a parent by herself, but she didn't want to do it alone. She truly wanted a like-minded companion. Someone she could grow to love over time. Someone with whom she could be sure that love would have longevity, if only because of the time it took to grow. And if love didn't come? Could she live without it? Of course she could. She'd done the impulsive marriage before, and it had left her shattered when it all fell apart. This time she'd taken every precaution to ensure there would be none of that. With care and mutual respect, anything was possible.

But was marrying at first sight taking things a step too far? Her parents obviously thought so. Her father hadn't even come to Port Ludlow, here in Washington, for the ceremony, citing an important human rights case he was working on. But his distaste for her entering into an agreement with the exclusive matchmaking agency, which discreetly boasted a 100 percent success rate, had been clear. To him the very prospect of meeting your husband or wife at the altar was a recipe for disaster, but the dictates of Match Made in Marriage were clear. There was no chance to meet your intended prior to the ceremony and both participants had to put their trust completely in the matchmaking process. Imogene took a quick look at her mom, who had agreed to accompany her only daughter down the aisle to marry a stranger. Caroline O'Connor looked back, her gaze meeting and melding with her daughter's—concern for what Imogene was doing clearly reflected there.

Her eyes were glued to her groom waiting at the altar with his back turned, a man whose posture showed he was the kind of person used to being in command. A frisson of awareness tickled at the back of her neck. As they neared the front row, her mom hesitated and bestowed a swift kiss on Imogene's cheek before taking her seat. Imogene took a deep breath and focused anew on the stranger standing there. Waiting for her. There was something about the set of his shoulders and the shape of his head that prodded at her memory. Something that wasn't right.

As he turned around, disbelief flooded every cell in her body and she stopped a few feet from the altar.

Recognition dawned.

"No," she breathed out in shock. "Not you."

Imogene barely heard the groan of "Not again" that came from the groom's side of the room. Instead, her gaze was fixed on the man who'd finally turned to face her.

Valentin Horvath.

The man she'd divorced seven years ago.

There should have been some satisfaction that his expression was equally as stunned as her own must be, but there was none. In fact, satisfaction took a back seat while anger and confusion vied for supremacy. Imogene stood rooted to the spot, staring at the man she'd shared more intimacies with than any other human being in existence. The man who had not only broken her heart, but crushed it so completely that it had taken her all this time to even contemplate marriage again.

And yet, beneath the anger, beneath the implacable certainty that there was no way this marriage could go ahead, was that all-too-familiar flicker of sexual recognition that had led to their first hasty, fiery and oh-so-short union. Imogene did her best to quell the sensations that bloomed to life inside her traitorous body, to ignore the sudden flush of heat that simmered from deep inside and radiated outward. To pay no heed to the way her nipples had grown tight and hypersensitive in the French lace bustier she wore beneath her strapless gown. It was merely a physiological response to a healthy male, she told herself. It meant nothing.

He meant nothing.

Valentin reached a hand toward her.

"No," she repeated. "This is not happening."

"I couldn't agree more," said her ex-husband very firmly. "Let's get out of here."

He took her by the elbow and she reluctantly allowed him to lead her toward a side room—all the while fighting to disregard the realization that they might have been apart all these years but the fire that always burned so fiercely between them had reignited just like that. Her skin warmed where his hand lightly cupped her elbow, her senses keenly attuned to the size of him, to the heat that emanated from his large form, to the scent he still wore. A scent that she'd tried her hardest to forget but that seemed to be indelibly imprinted on her limbic system.

An older woman with a cloud of silver hair and alert blue eyes rose from her seat in the front row of the groom's side of the room.

"Valentin?"

"Nagy," he said in acknowledgment. "I think you need to come with us. You have some explaining to do."

Some explaining to do? Imogene's brow creased in ever-growing confusion. She recognized the diminutive of the Hungarian word for *grandmother* from back when Valentin used to talk about his family. But how could his grandmother have anything to do with this?

"Yes, I believe I do," replied the old woman in a firm voice. She turned to appease the assembled guests with a reassuring smile. "Don't worry, everyone, we'll be back shortly."

Back shortly? Imogene doubted that very much, but

she allowed Valentin to guide her along in his grandmother's wake as she walked purposefully ahead of them.

"Explain yourself," Valentin demanded, rounding on his grandmother the moment she closed the door behind them.

"I did exactly what you asked me to do. I found you a wife."

"I don't understand," Imogene interjected.

Valentin didn't understand, either. The brief he'd given Alice had been pretty straightforward. He wanted a wife and he wanted a family. After his first failed attempt seven years ago, when he'd thrown his usual logic to the four corners of the world and leaped before looking, he'd decided to take a more rational approach. He did not—in any way, shape or form—expect to see his ex-wife approach him here today. No matter how much more beautiful she'd grown in the years since he'd last seen her.

He took a moment to fill his gaze with the vision of loveliness that was his ex. She hadn't changed that much. Not her dark auburn hair that so richly adorned her head or her green-gray eyes that snapped angrily at him now or her smooth alabaster skin that had always shown every mark from his five o'clock shadow—making it necessary for him to shave twice a day when they were together. He'd have done anything for her, once—shaving twice a day was the least of it. But all that was in the past, and would remain there.

He transferred his attention to his grandmother, who composed herself with her usual grace and instinctive air of command before speaking.

"Imogene, let me explain a little. But first, please,

take a seat. And, Valentin, that means you, too. You know I can't tolerate your pacing. You always did have ants in your pants, even as a child."

Valentin bit back the retort that in this case, he had every right to pace. Instead, he gestured to Imogene to take a chair in the small side office and took another for himself. They were close enough that he could smell her fragrance. It was something different from what she used to wear but no less potent when it came to his senses. He used his customarily rigid control to ignore the way the scent teased at him, inviting him to lean a little nearer, to inhale more deeply, and instead focused on watching his grandmother.

Alice settled herself behind the desk and rested her age-spotted hands on the blotter in front of her. She took her time to speak, obviously choosing her words carefully.

"I would like to remind you both that you have signed a contract to marry today."

"Not him!"

"Not her!"

Their responses were simultaneous and equally emphatic.

"I don't recall either of you stating any exclusions when you approached Match Made in Marriage. Do you?" She arched one silver brow and gave them each a pointed look. "No, of course not. Because when you signed the contracts with Match Made in Marriage, you gave us an undertaking to find you your ideal life partner. Which I—" she hesitated and corrected herself "—*we* did."

"What?" Imogene gasped and turned her gaze on Valentin. "Your grandmother is a part of all this?"

He nodded. "She is. And she's usually very good at it, but in our case, she's clearly made a mistake."

Alice sighed and rolled her eyes. "I do not make mistakes, Valentin. Never, and especially not in this case."

"You can't seriously begin to expect me to believe that," he responded, his voice rising in frustration. "We ended our marriage seven years ago due to irreconcilable differences."

"Infidelity," Imogene injected into the conversation. "Yours."

Valentin held on to his temper by a thread. "As I said, irreconcilable differences. As far as I am aware nothing else has changed between us, so I fail to see how Imogene became my perfect match. Your instincts have failed you this time."

"Instincts?" Imogene's voice ran cold. "I was of the understanding matches are made using specialists, not mumbo jumbo. Doesn't that put *you* in breach of contract, Mrs. Horvath?"

Valentin watched his grandmother level a considering look at his ex-wife.

"You will find that the 'mumbo jumbo' as you so dismissively call it is well-defined under clause 24.2.9 subparagraph *a*. I believe the term has been set out as 'subjective assessment by Match Made in Marriage.'"

"That's ridiculous," Imogene protested.

"May I remind you that no one forced you to sign the contract," Alice said in a voice that dripped icicles.

"Either way," Valentin interrupted before Imogene could let fly a volley of words that he imagined were hovering on the edge of her tongue, "what you have done is gross manipulation of us both. This doesn't need to become uncivil. Contracts can be broken. I think I speak for both Imogene and myself when I say this marriage will go not ahead."

"And I speak for Match Made in Marriage when I say it definitely will. You are right for each other."

"Impossible!" Imogene snorted inelegantly. "I specifically said that infidelity was a deal breaker. If my prospective partner could not promise to remain faithful to me, I could not contemplate marriage with him. What about that was not clear?"

"I was not unfaithful," Valentin protested in frustration.

They'd gone over this already seven years ago. But Imogene's refusal to accept his word, and his promise to her, had seen her walk out on him without so much as a backward glance. In fact, for her, at least, it had been all too easy to call an end to their life together. To the dreams they'd shared, let alone the passion. Still, he'd reminded himself often in those early days, it was better he'd found out her lack of staying power then, rather than later when there may have been children to consider, as well.

"Stop behaving like a pair of squabbling children!" Alice admonished them both. "Your pairing was ascertained after rigorous testing. There is no one else more perfect for each of you than each other. Now, Valentin, do you trust me?"

"I'm not so sure about that anymore, to be completely honest with you, Nagy." He rubbed a hand over his jaw.

"Well, that's regrettable," Alice said on a sniff of disapproval. "But perhaps you will realize the error of your ways. You can have a successful marriage despite how unfortunately your last attempt at being a couple ended."

"A-attempt?" Imogene spluttered. "You say that as

if I made the decision to leave Valentin lightly, when I can assure you I did not."

Alice waved a slender hand in the air as if Imogene's words were of no consequence. "The facts here today remain that you each requested a life partner when you contracted Match Made in Marriage. All the data gleaned during your screening process supports my—*our*—decision to match you. I'm aware you two have issues—"

"I-issues?" It was Valentin's turn to splutter now.

"Hear me out, please," Alice commanded with a quelling glare at him. "Can you both honestly say that seeing each other again leaves you totally cold?"

Valentin shifted a little in his chair, all too aware that his physical reaction to Imogene when he'd seen her today had been as fierce and as instant as it had ever been. He still remembered the first time he'd met her, when she'd brought a child from her primary school into the ER where he was a trauma specialist. Even as he'd switched into his clinician's role seamlessly, he hadn't remained unmoved by her presence. Now, with her seated beside him, studiously avoiding his gaze when he turned to look at her again, he observed the proud posture of her slender body and the surprisingly determined line of her jaw. A jaw he'd traced with kisses. His body clenched on a surge of desire—his instinctive need for her as overwhelming as it had ever been—and he turned his stare back to his grandmother.

"No, I cannot," he said with great reluctance.

"And, Imogene? When you realized it was Valentin waiting at the altar for you today? How did you feel when you saw him?"

"Confused," she said bluntly.

"And?" Alice prompted.

"Fine, I was attracted to him. But attraction isn't the only thing necessary to make a marriage work. We proved that already."

"Yes, you did," Alice conceded. "But since that attraction still burns between you, don't you think you owe it to yourselves to find out if, under different circumstances from those in which you originally met, you can make an honest attempt at a good marriage?"

"I believed I was making more than an attempt at the time," Imogene protested. "I loved Valentin with all my heart. A heart he subsequently broke."

Alice sighed and leaned back in her chair, settling her hands in a loose clasp in her lap. "I see," she acknowledged. "And it still hurts, doesn't it?"

Imogene gave Alice a stiff nod.

"Then you still have unresolved feelings for my grandson, don't you?"

Valentin made a sound of protest. "Nagy, that's not fair. She made her decision a long time ago. You can't make us do this. It's cruel and unnecessary."

"It's never easy facing your failures," Alice said, slowly and stiffly rising from her seat. "I will leave you two for a few minutes to discuss this further. I strongly urge you to give your marriage one more chance. Your circumstances have changed dramatically since then. Neither of you is as young or as volatile as you were and, I might point out, neither of you has found a more suitable mate since. Please, discuss this as rational adults. Be certain that you won't spend the rest of your lives wondering if you should have given each other another chance. I will wait outside for your decision. Don't make me wait too long."

Two

The door closed as Alice left them alone in the room.

"She's a piece of work, your grandmother," Imogene said harshly. "How dare she do this?"

"She dares because it's what she does."

Imogene rose from her chair, her gown whispering with her rapid movement and her breasts heaving above the jeweled neckline.

"What she does? Seriously? You're condoning her behavior?" Imogene forced a short laugh from her throat. It was either that or scream.

"No, I'm not condoning it. I'm as angry and as shocked as you are. I never thought in a million years..."

She stared at Valentin as he rose to his feet and faced her. Always a big man, he dwarfed the room, but she wasn't scared of him. She knew all too well how gentle he could be—how tender his touch was. Her pulse kicked up a beat and she fiercely quelled the direction of her thoughts. This wasn't what she'd signed up for.

"A million years wouldn't be long enough," she murmured, and turned her face from his piercing blue-eyed gaze.

No, she thought. The end of time wouldn't be long enough to undo the ravages of their first union. He'd taken her love, her adoration, her heart. Then he'd thrown it all away. She'd never forget that moment she'd walked into their small house and smelled the distinctive heady perfume one of his colleagues at the hospital had always worn. Nor would she forget walking on legs that had become stiff and wooden toward the bedroom where she'd discovered said colleague, still naked and drowsy in her and Valentin's bed.

The sheets of the bed had been tumbled in disarray. The combined scents of fresh sweat and sex had been heavy on the air. Imogene had heard the sound of the shower running in the tiny bathroom down the hall but she hadn't waited to see her husband. When his colleague Carla had asked if she was looking for Valentin and gestured to the bathroom, she'd turned on her heel and marched straight back through town and stopped at the first law office she'd seen.

Numbly she'd gone through the motions of filing to dissolve the marriage that had obviously meant so little to Valentin and yet had meant the world to her. *He* had meant the world to her. Until she'd been faced with his infidelity.

She'd been in such a state of shock. Was it possible she'd misunderstood Carla? But then again, if she had, why had Valentin so easily given her up? If he was as innocent as he protested himself to be, why—at any time in the next few weeks—didn't he find her at the hotel she moved her things into until she could be released from her teaching contract and get the next flight back to the States? Instead, he'd simply let her go, which smacked of a guilty conscience to her—both then and now. Besides, she didn't want to think for a minute that she'd made a mistake, or that she'd behaved rashly in the heat of the moment. Carla had had no reason to lie, and Imogene knew the other woman and Valentin had been an item before her own arrival in Africa. Valentin himself had told her. More fool her, she'd believed him when he'd said it was over—that Imogene was the only woman for him.

She was dragged back into the present by the sound of Valentin clearing his throat.

"So I'm guessing you're a no, then?"

"You're guessing right," she answered adamantly.

"Not even prepared to think about it?" he coaxed.

"Not even," she said firmly. "I will not marry a philanderer ever again."

"Imogene." He said her name softly, with a tone of regret lacing the three syllables together in a way that struck her at her core. "I was never unfaithful to you."

"I know what I saw, Valentin. Don't take me for a complete idiot."

He shoved a hand through his hair in a gesture of frustration. "What you saw was—"

"Your mistress, curled up in my sheets, in my bed, and stinking of you!" she answered viciously.

"It wasn't what you thought it was."

"Oh, so now you're going to tell me you never slept with her?"

"You know I can't tell you that, but I told you the truth when I said that had all been in the past. I was never unfaithful to you," he affirmed.

"You say one thing. I saw another."

Valentin took a step toward her and she took a step

back, but her motion was halted by the wall behind her. She looked up at him, her nostrils flaring, her mouth drying as she studied his oh-so-familiar features. Involuntarily, she stared at the lines that had deepened around his eyes, the new ones on his forehead, the stubble that persistently made its presence felt even though he would have shaved only a short time ago. His face had been so dear to her once. If she closed her eyes now she could recall every aspect of it—the color of his eyes in exquisite detail, the short dark lashes that intently framed those eyes, the way that special shade of blue darkened and deepened when he was aroused. The way they were doing now.

A bolt of desire hit her. There had never been any other man who had this effect on her. Ever. Only Valentin. No one had ever come close to him, nor, she admitted ruefully, would again. Which left her between the devil and the deep blue sea, didn't it? Go against everything she'd promised herself she would never accept, or settle for less than what she knew Valentin could give her.

"Can we call a truce?" Valentin asked, his voice husky.

She knew that sound, knew he was gripped by the same intense need for her that she suffered for him. But in her case it was only for him. Could he say the same? She doubted it.

"Maybe," she answered reluctantly.

"What brought you here today?" he asked.

"You tell me first," she insisted, unwilling to show any weakness to this man who'd had the power to love her forever or destroy her, yet had chosen the latter.

"Fine," he said abruptly. "When I asked Nagy to find me a wife, I had a clear picture in mind. I wanted a companion, someone to come home to at the end of the day who I can share my innermost thoughts with. Someone, most of all, who wants a child, or children. After you left me, I thought I could live my life without a family of my own, but as I grow older I find I can't see a future without a wife and children in it, nor do I want to be alone for the balance of my days. I guess it's part of the human condition to want to be a part of something, to know a part of you will continue long after you're gone."

Imogene felt unexpected tears prick at her eyes. The words he'd chosen, his reasons for being here today, they were so similar to her own. How could they have this in common and yet be so wrong for each other at the same time?

Valentin continued, "Is that why you approached Nagy's company, too?"

"If I'd known it was your grandmother's company, I would have run in the other direction as fast as I could," she said defiantly. But then she softened, the fight spilling out of her. "Yes," she said simply. "That's exactly why I signed my contract. I want children in my life. Not just other people's children. My own. To love. Unconditionally. But more than that, I want a partner. Someone I can rely on. Someone I can trust."

Trust.

The word hung on the air between them. Valentin drew in a deep breath. Trust had been in short supply back in Africa, and not just within his marriage. All around them had been the constant threat of danger as a struggling government fought against corruption on every level. Even within the hospital there had been those he knew he could not rely on.

"Trust is a two-way street, is it not?" he asked gently.

"Always. You never had any reason not to trust me, Valentin. Ever."

"Whereas you feel you cannot trust me. That's what you're saying?"

"Based on past experience, what else can I say? You broke our marriage vows, not I."

The old frustration and anger bubbled from deep inside. She wouldn't listen to him back then; he doubted she'd listen to him now.

"So that leaves us at a stalemate, doesn't it? Unless you're prepared to put the past aside."

Imogene looked at him incredulously. "You think I should just forget you screwed another woman in our bed?" She deliberately chose strong language, not prepared to soften what he'd done by describing it with any moniker associated with the word *love*. "Just *put it aside* as if it didn't matter?"

"It doesn't matter because it never happened. Did you see me that day, Imogene? No, because I wasn't there. You wouldn't give me a chance to talk to you before having that lawyer serve papers on me. Perhaps you will at least do me that courtesy now." He pressed on, knowing he had a captive audience. It had bothered him intensely that Imogene never allowed him the opportunity to present his side of what she thought she'd seen. If anything it had underscored how wrong they'd been for each other that she'd been prepared to cast him in the villain's role so immediately. "Look, I know you were shocked to discover Carla in our house, let alone our bed. When I gave her the key to the place it was supposed to be so she could get some sleep between shifts because the doctors' lounge had been appropriated for more patient beds. You know the crazy hours we were working and the volume of patients we had to deal with. Carla was overdue a break and I said she could use our place because it was close to the hospital. I didn't know she planned to have company. Imogene, I barely got to see you. If I had free time, why would I have spent it with her?"

"Why indeed," Imogene answered with an arch of her brow and a lift of her chin.

He let go a huff of irritation. "I wasn't the one with her that day."

"That's not what she led me to believe."

"She told you I was there?"

Imogene hesitated. Replayed the words in her head as she'd done so very many times before.

"Not in so many words," Imogene conceded.

"And yet you still don't believe me."

"I don't. I can't."

Hearing the underlying pain in her words made Valentin think again. She sounded as though she were in an internal battle. That maybe, just maybe, she wanted to believe him. He wondered how he'd feel in the same situation. Torn. Confused. And facing the realization that if she believed him, then that would have made the past seven years of loneliness and sorrow, the end of their marriage, all her fault. But it wasn't. While he had never been unfaithful to Imogene, he knew he should have done more at the time to fight for their marriage—followed after her, insisted she see him instead of letting her hide in the only decent hotel in town until she flew out.

He knew Carla could be intimidating. The woman had a confidence many women he'd met lacked. She'd set her sights on Valentin as soon as he'd arrived on his volunteer service and they'd had a brief, intense fling.

It wasn't until Imogene came on the scene that Carla had begun to eye him again, and she'd made it clear to everyone, Imogene included, that he was hers for the taking. But Carla had been wrong. From the minute Valentin had seen Imogene there had been only one woman for him.

She still was that woman.

Admitting that didn't come easily. Pride had always been an issue for him. A child prodigy, he wasn't used to making mistakes. His world had been filled with successes, each more glowing than the last. His failed marriage to Imogene had been the one black mark on the pristine blotter of his life. It was something he felt bound to rectify. If he could persuade her to give him, *them*, another chance, then maybe they could make things work.

His grandmother's words repeated in the back of his mind. *Be certain that you won't spend the rest of your lives wondering if you should have given each other another chance.* Would he regret it if he didn't try again? Looking at Imogene now, resplendent in her bridal gown—the same woman who'd stood with him in a hurried civil ceremony all that time ago, and yet different in subtle ways he ached to explore—he knew the answer to that was a solid, unequivocal yes.

He chose his next words carefully. "So is there nothing I can do to persuade you to consider marrying me again?"

"I can't believe you even want to think about us marrying again," she shot back.

"Why not? Let's remove emotion from the equation and try to look at this logically. We both approached marriage this time in a more clinical fashion, and yet look at us. Here together again. Let's not discount the science that went into our pairing."

"Science!" She snorted in disbelief. "More like your grandmother's tampering with the results."

"And why would she do that if it would only make us unhappy?"

He knew he had made his point when she conceded.

"So what are you suggesting? That we give this a go? I'll be honest with you, Valentin. I don't hold hopes for things being any different than they were the first time. We may have gotten along in bed, but we had very little in common outside of it. Carla aside, and as difficult as it is to admit, I don't think we'd have lasted the distance. We met in a hothouse of extreme circumstances. It wasn't a normal relationship in any sense of the word."

"Then why not give it a chance and see how we do in a more traditional setting? We're unlikely to find another match that can make us both feel like this," he said, before reaching out one finger and tracing the line of her lower lip.

Shock and desire warred with each other as he felt her softness. Her warmth. The gasp of heated breath as her lips parted. Every muscle in his body clenched in anticipation of closing the distance between them. Of tasting that tender flesh and discovering if she was still as sweet, and as tart, as she used to be. Valentin watched as a light flush colored Imogene's cheeks and as her pupils dilated to almost consume her irises.

While she battled with her emotions, Valentin pressed on. "Imogene, look at it this way. We have a rock-solid prenup in force. We have a three-month out clause. What have we got to lose?"

He saw her internal battle reflected in her eyes.

Heard it in her every ragged breath. Sensed the moment of weakness, the chink in her armor, and took the opportunity to drive straight through it.

"And children, Imogene. Think about the kids we would have together if it all worked out. The family we always wanted. I promise you, if you agree to marry me again, you won't regret it. I will be faithful to you. I will see to it that I meet your every need as your husband and your life partner. I failed you last time. I never fought for you the way I should have, so I'm fighting for you now. I realize that I had tunnel vision when it came to my work, which left very little beyond the physical for you. I never saw the cracks when they appeared in our marriage. Never saw how vulnerable you had become. If I had been a better husband, you would never have jumped to the conclusion that I had been unfaithful. I won't let that happen again if you give us another chance. What will your answer be? Will you marry me?"

Three

She said yes.

Alice Horvath couldn't even begin to describe the sense of relief that overtook her when Valentin came out of the office and informed her the wedding would go ahead. She hadn't wanted to believe it wouldn't—she did, after all, trust her instincts wholeheartedly—and persuading others she was never wrong was rarely the issue, but it seemed that when it came to her grandsons, she was two for two, so far, on having her judgment questioned.

Valentin had gone to rejoin his brother, Galen, and a handful of cousins, who had congregated at the front of the function room. Alice took a moment to find her medication in her handbag before resuming her seat. This darned pain in her chest was becoming tiresome. She certainly didn't have time for it now. She fought the urge to rub at it. It never did anything anyway. Ah, there was her pillbox. She popped a tablet under her tongue just as Imogene came out of the office.

"Are you all right, Mrs. Horvath?" she asked.

"I'm fine, my dear. And let me say that I'm so glad you've decided to go ahead with the wedding."

"Let's just say your grandson can be very persuasive."

Alice looked at the younger woman carefully. It was easy to see why Valentin had been attracted to her in the first place. The dark auburn hair and delightful figure aside, Imogene O'Connor had a rare exquisite beauty that was very clearly underlined with a strong personality and bright intelligence. During her background checks, Alice had discovered that over the past seven years, Imogene had grown her early-childhood centers into a business that had just been franchised nationwide. She was a strong and independent young woman with a good head on her shoulders, but it was the emotional side of Imogene that intrigued Alice most. She knew Imogene had rarely dated after her return from Africa. Whether it was because she was too busy for a new relationship or that she simply wasn't emotionally ready, Alice was glad the other woman hadn't rushed headlong into someone and something else.

When Alice looked at Valentin, with his aloof and slightly dark nature, together with the bright flame of light this woman epitomized, she knew Imogene was unquestionably the yin to his yang. The computer data and her specialists had backed up her instincts completely. She would never have taken a risk with either of these young people's happiness otherwise. Life was just too precious, as she was becoming all too well aware.

The tablet continued to dissolve under her tongue, and incrementally the angina that had become such a plague in recent months began to ease. Alice inhaled carefully, relieved to feel the last of the tightness disappear, and directed a smile at the beautiful bride in front of her.

"Shall we return to the ceremony?" she asked.

"Perhaps you could ask my mom to join me again," Imogene said in a voice that was just a little indecisive. "I'd feel better with her beside me."

"Certainly." Alice turned to leave, then hesitated and looked back to Imogene before reaching out to take her hand and squeeze it lightly. "You won't regret this, you know. It may not be an easy road back to loving each other the way you did before. In fact, I hope the two of you discover a different kind of love this time. Something stronger, something that will endure. That's my wish for you and Valentin."

"It remains to be seen."

"Yes, it does. And it will take hard work from both of you."

Imogene gave her a nod and Alice turned away. These two were going to have an interesting time of it—of that she was certain.

Imogene went through the motions, repeating the words uttered by the celebrant standing before her and listening to Valentin do the same. The service was simple, without the personal touches that it might have had if they'd planned this day together. In many ways it was about as detached as their first wedding had been, although the celebrant today tried to invest the ceremony with a great deal more joy than the slightly bored local official who'd performed their ceremony back in Africa.

Africa. She had to stop thinking about that time and comparing it to now. It was another world ago.

Today was a new beginning. One she'd agreed to pursue. She still wasn't even certain how Valentin had persuaded her to go ahead with it. All she knew was that with that one touch of his fingertip to her lips, he'd reminded her of the incendiary attraction they'd shared. Just one fingertip and she'd made a decision that would affect her for the rest of her life. Her entire body had reacted, concentrated on that mere touch. No one else had ever had the ability to set her alight with the brush of a finger the way he did. Which was a good thing, she'd always told herself as she'd pointed her attentions into her career and into establishing, then expanding, her business. Dating had been, for lack of a better word, a bland experience once she'd decided to test the waters again. But that very blandness was what had put her in search of a matchmaking service that would find her something better than bland. Had she been unconsciously searching for a relationship like what she had with Valentin all along? The idea was as terrifying as it was exhilarating.

And more important, now that she had agreed to go ahead, where would they go from here?

"You may now kiss your bride."

The celebrant's words penetrated her thoughts, dragging her back to the reality that was her wedding day. Her eyes flared wide as she caught Valentin's smile and she froze in place. His eyes locked with hers, a serious expression reflecting back at her as he lifted her left hand to his lips and placed a kiss on her wedding finger.

"This is the ring you deserved all along," he murmured before leaning closer.

She barely caught her breath before she felt the pressure of his lips against hers. Sensation bloomed through her like a starburst, radiating to the tips of her fingers and the soles of her feet, not to mention everywhere in between. She parted her lips in response, kissing him back instinctively. Her hand rested on his chest for a brief moment before sliding up to his neck. The texture of his slightly long hair against her fingers sent another jolt of awareness surging through her and she lifted slightly upward. Valentin's arm curled around her waist, holding her to him.

It had always been like this between them. This intensity. This overwhelming need to be close. Closer still. As if the world began and ended with each other.

"Um, guys?" Valentin's brother, Galen, interrupted them. "Care to leave something for the honeymoon?"

The gathered crowd laughed at his words and Valentin slowly drew away, leaving Imogene feeling more than a little stunned by what had just happened between them. Seven years. Actually, to be precise, seven years, three months, two weeks and five days since she'd walked out of his life. And still she was as hopelessly overcome by him.

"Are you okay?" Valentin asked gently, his arm still around her waist and his blue eyes searching her face for any signs of distress.

"Well, aside from my lipstick, which is probably demolished right now, I'm fine," she said as coolly as she could manage given the rapid beat of her pulse and the tingling shocks that still lingered in parts of her body that hadn't tingled in far too long.

He gave her a smile, took her hand again, and together they turned to face the assembly.

"I give you Mr. and Mrs. Horvath!" the celebrant triumphantly declared before surreptitiously wiping at his brow with a handkerchief.

They were married. Imogene couldn't quite believe it. Her synapses were still somewhat fried by that kiss. But there was no mistaking the strong fingers that were wrapped around her own, nor the steady presence of the dark-suited man standing beside her. Her mother rushed forward, her cheeks still wet with tears, to congratulate them both. But as she drew back again she fixed Valentin with a stern eye.

"Don't mess it up this time, young man. You're lucky to get a second chance with my girl. Look after her."

"I will," Valentin promised.

Imogene felt a sting of embarrassment at her mother's words, but the gentle pressure of Valentin's hand signaled he'd taken no offense. She knew her mother would never understand why she'd made her choice to go ahead today. But then again, maybe she would. After all, her own husband had conducted many, albeit discreet, affairs during their marriage. Which was another reason Imogene had felt so strongly about infidelity. She'd always wondered why her mother had agreed to settle for less than 100 percent from her husband. Why she'd allowed other women to fill his life, where she rightly belonged. But then again her mother accepted a lot of things in the pursuit of her ordered life. Heavily involved in charity work, she enjoyed the distinction of being married to a leading international human rights lawyer. Of being perceived as calm and unflappable and the perfect hostess at all times. Imogene had learned early in her life that she wanted far more than that when she married. And she'd thought she had it with Valentin when they'd fallen so instantly and passionately in love.

Could they achieve that together again? She thought of the words Alice had spoken to her just before the ceremony, about it not being an easy road back to loving each other again. Could they even hope to love each other again? she wondered. When she'd agreed to go ahead with this, the only thing she'd locked her mind onto was her main goal in this entire venture. A child, or children, of her own to love. But to love her husband, too? She flickered a glance up at Valentin. She wasn't sure if she could trust herself to trust him again, let alone love him.

Her insides clenched at the idea of making a baby. He'd made it patently clear he wanted children, too. Would that be enough to be the glue that would hold them together?

He also told you he was never unfaithful to you, a snide voice whispered in the back of her mind. In fact, he'd been adamant on that point, promising she had nothing to fear on that score. She wished she could believe him. Her eyes had told her a different story seven years ago. But she couldn't think about that now. She'd made her choice. She'd agreed to marry him and agreed that once their three-month trial period was up, if they were still together, they'd start trying for their family. And until then, she could only wait and see.

Valentin fought his frustration. He was never good with crowds, and this crowd was too happy, too noisy and very much too in his face. He had to concede that everyone here was celebrating his wedding, but it didn't mean he had to like it. Not when every cell in his body urged him to take Imogene by the hand again and whisk her to where the helicopter waited on the expansive lawn outside so they could head to SeaTac, and then in one of the Horvath private jets to Rarotonga for their honeymoon. He couldn't wait for that part, but even though that kiss to seal their marriage had been better than everything he'd remembered, he knew that this time he and Imogene needed to tread carefully if they were going to make their union work.

He had no intention of creating a family without a strong foundation based on love and genuine trust in each other, no matter how well they survived the initial three-month trial period of their marriage. He wouldn't do that to her, nor would he do that to any child they might have. Their future happiness hinged on one thing: rebuilding Imogene's trust in him as her life partner. He had to do whatever it took if this was going to work. But it couldn't all be one way. He needed to be certain she was working just as hard on their future as he was. That she wouldn't run out on him again.

Losing her the first time had been crippling. He'd coped the only way he knew how, by throwing himself into things he could control, to a degree anyway. He'd signed on for another volunteer contract and did longer clinics, more surgeries and, even under the growing threat of civil war, more visits out into the bush. Some might say he'd had a death wish, because the political climate in the nation had become wildly volatile—driving many volunteers out—but for Valentin it allowed him to focus on what needed to be done and to tuck away the pain of distrust and abandonment that Imogene had left in her wake.

He looked across the room, to where she circulated among her friends. God, she was beautiful. But physical beauty aside, he knew she had depths he had yet to discover. Depths they'd never imagined of each other the first time around. And now they had another opportunity. When he'd seen her today he'd been shocked, but instinct had taken over. And while logic had protested, his body had rejoiced.

All of which brought him back to his thoughts of

only a moment ago. He couldn't give in to that powerful pull they had between them. If he kissed her again, the way he truly wanted to, there was no way he'd be capable of pulling away.

Imogene's face lit up on a burst of laughter as one of her friends said something amusing. Again he felt the knot deep in his gut. He was going to have to do some serious workouts to burn off the sexual energy that had taken his body hostage since seeing Imogene again, because they had to take things slowly this time—to truly begin to know and understand each other better before losing themselves in physical sensations.

"So, having second thoughts?"

Valentin turned to face his brother, Galen. "No, should I?"

"I have to say I was worried there for a while at the beginning. I'd have laid odds that today wasn't about to go ahead and that my staff would be eating cake for the rest of the week."

Galen was head of the Horvath chain of resorts and was based here in Washington. Valentin allowed himself a small smile.

"Well, I'm glad I didn't have to inflict that on them."

Galen looked at him. "Something's different. Are you okay?"

"Why?"

"I don't know exactly. You were looking forward to this marriage, I know that much. But I was certain that when Imogene came down the aisle you would put a stop to it. You both seemed so adamant about it not going ahead. What changed your mind? Don't tell me Nagy put a spell on you both," Galen finished with a laugh.

Valentin paused for a moment. With his brother, he'd

always been honest. With his cousin Ilya, too. The three men had grown up close. But for some reason he didn't want to put into actual words what had come over him when he'd made the decision to try to persuade Imogene to go ahead with the wedding.

"Maybe she did." It was all he would concede. "But it's early days yet. We have our three-month trial period to get through."

"You say that as if you don't believe it'll be easy."

"Nothing worthwhile ever is. We both know that, right? And Imogene and I have a lot of work to do. Deep down she still believes I was unfaithful to her."

Galen spluttered his disbelief. "As if. You are the most loyal man I've ever known. So, who does she think you had an affair with?"

"One of the doctors I worked with."

"Was she hot?"

"Oh, yes, she's hot."

Galen stiffened beside him. "As in present-tense hot?"

He could always rely on his brother to be quick to pick up an unspoken thread. "Yes. As in she works for me now as head of research and development in New York."

Galen let out a slow whistle. "That could prove to be an issue. Have you told Imogene yet?"

"No, and I'm hoping we can overcome that before it becomes a problem."

"Well, if anyone can, you can, my brother. You deserve to be happy. I just hope that Imogene is the one you can find that happiness with."

"As do I. As do I."

Four

The jet was impressive; it even had its own master suite complete with luxury bathroom. Imogene wondered about the wisdom of having a bubble bath at thirty-six thousand feet but then pushed the idea aside. Right now, weariness dragged at every cell in her body and her mind. All she wanted to do was rest. She looked at the wide bed in the master bedroom and the expanse of fine Egyptian cotton that covered it. She knew it was fine because she'd touched it, her fingertips sliding over the silky softness of the high-thread-count fabric in absolute delight.

Valentin entered the room behind her.

"Tired?" he asked as he tugged his cravat loose from his throat.

"Shattered," she replied, feeling herself physically wilt.

It had been a tough day on so many levels, not least

of which was discovering she was still powerfully attracted to her ex-husband. Well, new husband. She would never have believed he could talk her into agreeing to go ahead, but he'd been so convincing, almost making her believe that maybe she'd made a mistake all those years ago. That maybe she should have waited and listened before reacting. But then, given her own family situation, and her vehemence about never being in the same position as her mom, was it any surprise she'd reacted the way she had? Faced with the same situation, heaven forbid, wouldn't she do the same again?

She looked up at Valentin and saw the lines of strain on his face.

"You must be worn-out, too. I remember you never were one for grand social occasions."

"You remember correctly. Look, we have just over fourteen hours before we get to Rarotonga. We should get some sleep. Try to be fresh when we arrive at the Cook Islands."

"Did you want to take the bed?" she offered. "I can sleep in the main cabin."

"No, you take the bed. While you remember my discomfort with large social gatherings, I remember how you need to be comfortable to sleep."

Imogene felt her cheeks color at his words and the images that rapidly filled her mind. Of the two of them in a narrow double bed doing anything but sleeping. Or when they did, and despite the intense heat of equatorial Africa, they curled so close together it was hard to tell where one ended and the other began. She'd grown used to sleeping with him so quickly after they'd met, and it had taken her months before she'd stopped reaching for him in the dark after she'd returned to New York.

She averted her gaze before she suggested something

stupid, like sleeping together again. After all, they were married and had a common goal of creating a family together. But even as she thought it, she knew she wasn't ready to take that step. Not yet anyway.

"Thank you," she finally managed. "Would you like to use the bathroom first?"

Valentin laughed.

"What's so funny?" she asked.

"Us. We sound so damned civilized."

She giggled. "Yes, we do. Surprising under the circumstances, when you think about it."

"Shows we're better people than we were before." His eyes grew dark and serious. "I meant what I said back in that office, Imogene. Even more than the vows we exchanged. You won't regret this."

Imogene swallowed against the lump in her throat and gave him a small nod. She was beyond words, but she wasn't beyond feeling, she discovered as he strode through to the well-appointed bathroom and closed the door behind him. After a few minutes she heard the shower begin to run. She groaned at the knowledge that he was naked, that water now coursed in strong rivulets over his body. A body she'd once known perhaps even better than her own. She slumped onto the bed and kicked off her shoes before tugging at the invisible side zipper on her gown. She stood again and let the gown drop to the floor before stepping out of it and picking it up again to gently fold it and lay it on an easy chair.

As she did so, she caught a glimpse of herself in the mirror. Dressed in a white lace-covered bustier and matching panties, together with white lace garters and sheer white stockings, she looked the epitome of bridal innocence. She touched the top of her thighs where her skin was exposed and felt a shiver course through her.

Looks were one thing, but the actuality was quite another. Her entire body was attuned to every sound she could make out from the bathroom and it responded to the visual effects that her mind so willingly supplied.

The water snapped off and the sound propelled her into action. She grabbed her carry-on case and yanked out the robe she'd packed in there earlier. Had it only been this morning? It felt like a lifetime ago. She shook out the robe and gasped when she saw a shower of rose petals fall from the folds. The only person who could have sabotaged her things was her mom—she was the one Imogene had wanted with her all morning. And despite the lack of romance in her own marriage and her trepidation about the way Imogene had approached this one, Caroline had attempted to inject a little romance into her daughter's day.

The door to the bathroom opened.

"You okay? I thought I heard you make a noise," Valentin said, stepping through the doorway with a white towel wrapped around his hips.

All rational thought fled. The perfect lines of his body could have been carved by Michelangelo, except she knew that if she touched him he wouldn't feel like cold marble. No, his skin would be hot, pliable and highly responsive to her caress. Every feminine instinct in her body clamored to be reacquainted with him. Intimately.

"Are those rose petals?" he asked, snapping her out of the seductive trance that threatened to take over her weary mind.

He drew closer and Imogene quickly shoved her arms in the sleeves of the robe and dragged it closed at her waist.

"Don't rush on my account," Valentin teased, the gleam in his eyes showing his appreciation of her attire.

"I'm sorry, I'll clean them up. Mom must have—"

"Hey, don't panic. It's okay." He reached out a steadying hand to her and clasped her forearm before she could bend down. "Relax, okay? I think a few rose petals are only to be expected with a bride and groom aboard, don't you?"

Heat flared along her arm. Heat that tantalized and teased her already overwrought senses. Imogene pressed her lips together before answering, "But we're not your typical bride and groom, are we?"

"We never were typical," he agreed.

His words sent another rush of color to her cheeks. She groaned inwardly. Why did she continually blush around him? No one else had ever had the capacity to wring that kind of reaction from her before. She gestured to his towel.

"Are you planning to sleep in that?"

"It might give our cabin crew a bit of a shock if I did. No, I have some pajamas in my case. When you go to the bathroom I'll change in here, if that's okay."

Ah, so they were back to being polite again. That suited her just fine. Right now she didn't know what to think or say or do. All she knew was that she needed to create a bit of space between herself and Valentin before she did something stupid, like press her lips to the small brown discs of his nipples, or lick off that tiny droplet of water that followed the indentation of his abdomen.

"I'll say good-night now, then," she said stiffly and gathered up her toilet bag.

"Good night, Imogene," Valentin replied.

His voice was gentle and deep and almost her undoing. It would take only a second to lift her face to his. To claim a good-night kiss. But if she did, she knew exactly where that would lead and she knew she definitely wasn't ready for the ramifications of what would follow. Not mentally. Not yet.

Valentin looked out the aircraft window at the glorious coastline that appeared beneath them. Turquoise waters edged by foaming waves crashed against a reef that appeared to encircle the island they were approaching. As the plane drew lower still, he could make out white-sand beaches and towering palm trees that waved their fronds in the onshore breeze.

"Look at that," he said to Imogene, gesturing outside.

"It's beautiful," she answered, leaning across him to get a better look. "And it's certainly not like the New York winter we've left behind. Still, I guess, being in the southern hemisphere, it's summer down here, right?"

He grunted in response, barely able to speak right now. Did she know her breast was pressed against his arm, he wondered, or realize what her closeness was doing to him? How her subtle fragrance invaded his mind and made him think all kinds of inappropriate things he'd rather be doing with her right now? Her very nearness was going to be a major test of his ability to practice abstinence while they worked toward understanding each other better. It was something they were going to need to discuss very soon or he'd go crazy.

He moved slightly and Imogene immediately pulled away.

"Sorry," she murmured.

She fiddled with her seat belt, tugging at the strap and ensuring it was firmly done up.

"No problem," he responded, even though her touch had rapidly become a problem for him, indeed. He gestured out the window again. "Looks like we're coming in to land."

Imogene reached for his hand. "Do you mind? I always get nervous."

He curled his fingers around hers and was surprised at how tight her grip became as they descended through the clouds. "I never knew that about you."

"Well, we've never flown together before, so I guess you never got the chance to find out."

Her words came out lightly but he knew there was a lot more behind them.

"You're right," he conceded. "We didn't get to know a lot about each other at all, did we?"

The wheels touched the tarmac and her grip tightened even more. The plane felt like it was fighting the brakes as they eventually began to slow down and taxied toward the terminal building. One of the cabin crew came toward them, a warm smile wreathing her pretty face.

"We'll be disembarking soon," she informed them. "Once the stairs are down I'll come and get you and direct you to customs and immigration. It should only be a few minutes."

"Thanks, Jenny," Valentin acknowledged.

He felt Imogene disengage her fingers from his hand one by one.

"She's attractive, isn't she?" Imogene commented. "Do you know her well?"

Valentin shrugged, suddenly aware that any comment right now could be a potential minefield. "As well as I know any of the Horvath Aviation crews. I fly a lot with my work and I've gotten to know a few of them. Jenny's husband, Ash, is one of our pilots. It's company policy that if staff are a couple, they be assigned together whenever practical."

He felt Imogene relax a little. Was it because she now knew that Jenny was married? Until that supposed incident with Carla, jealousy had never been an issue, but was it going to be an issue now? Obviously Imogene felt vulnerable—she'd taken a major leap of faith in marrying him again, but then again so had he.

As soon as they were settled into their accommodations they'd be having a serious discussion about the boundaries of this new marriage of theirs and what they each expected out of it. Failure wasn't something that Valentin accepted, which was what had made him an excellent student, a brilliant doctor and an astute businessman. The fact that his first marriage had failed had always been a thorn in his side. He knew he'd been the innocent party all along but his failure in not being able to make Imogene see that had been hard to bear. Her insecurity had driven her away from him, which, in turn, meant he'd failed her. Now it was up to him to make sure she never felt that way again.

Before long they were descending the stairs of the aircraft and stepping onto the steaming-hot tarmac at the airport. It was a short walk to the small terminal building, and clearing customs and immigration took only a few minutes since they'd landed at a quiet time at the airport with no commercial airliners arriving or departing. The air around them was thick with humidity but a steady breeze blew off the nearby ocean and tugged at their clothing as they exited the terminal building to find a driver waiting for them with a sign.

"*Kia orana!*" the woman said in greeting as she slipped a lei of fragrant blooms around each of their necks. "Welcome to the Cook Islands. I'm Kimi and I'll be your contact and your driver during your stay with us. Please, come with me."

Valentin put a hand to Imogene's elbow as they followed Kimi to a van. Their luggage was loaded in the back and in a few moments they were off. After twenty minutes they were at their destination: a secluded villa just back from the sand on a private lagoon.

"Everything here is at your disposal," Kimi said expansively. "You have your own pool and you'll find water toys to use in the lagoon in the shed behind those bushes. There's an outdoor shower for you to use in complete privacy when you come back from the beach and if you need anything else here at the house, please just lift the phone over there and someone will handle your query. I'm available to drive you anywhere you want to go.

"There's fruit and drinks in your kitchen, together with a few breakfast items, and you're welcome to use the neighboring resort restaurants for breakfast and lunch and just charge it back to the villa. Tonight, dinner will be brought to you at seven. We can serve it here on the patio or down on the sand if you'd prefer, although we're expecting a bit of a storm tonight. Oh, and there's a car or scooters for you to use if you want to drive around the island yourselves. Just remember to keep left and watch your speed. It's only thirty-two kilometers round-trip to get around the island, but you can take as long as you like. You're on island time now."

"Thank you, Kimi. This is lovely," Imogene said with a genuine smile.

He realized that beneath the smile, though, she still looked tightly drawn and tired. Obviously having that great big bed to herself during the flight hadn't ensured a good enough rest for her. Or maybe she was worried about something else. They'd essentially be alone here for the better part of seven days—was that what was bugging her?

Kimi bade them farewell and left.

"Well," said Imogene, with her hands on her hips and looking out to the tranquil lagoon. "Here we are. It's certainly beautiful."

"As are you," Valentin said softly. "You're going to need to be careful with that fair skin of yours."

"I brought plenty of sunblock," she said nervously as if she suddenly realized that he would be the one applying it in the areas she couldn't reach. "What time is it?"

"Just after 8:00 a.m.," he commented after glancing at his watch.

"Wow, it's going to feel like a long day, isn't it?"

"You can rest anytime you need. Our honeymoon is going to be all about doing what we want to do. And getting to know each other all over again. In fact, there's something we need to discuss."

She stiffened and drew away from him slightly. "Oh? And what's that?"

"Sex," he answered.

To his delight, color shot through her cheeks and her eyes flared in shock at his bluntness.

"S-sex?" she said on a wobbly note.

"I don't think we should do it."

Her eyes widened even farther. "You don't?"

He swallowed. This was all coming out wrong and even though it went against every male instinct in his body, it had to be said. "Obviously I want to…y'know. But last time we leaped into a sexual relationship so quickly it blurred everything else out of existence for us. We met, we married and we separated all within the space of only a few months. I think we should take our time this time. In fact, I'd like to…"

"You'd like to…?" she coaxed.

"I'd like to court you this time."

"Court me? Isn't that kind of like locking a stable door after the horse has bolted? We're already married."

"That doesn't mean we can't take the time now, this week at the very least, to get to know each other better." He took a step toward her and put his hands gently on her shoulders. "Imogene, this is important to me. I don't want anything to go wrong this time."

Five

Imogene looked at Valentin in surprise. There was a note to his voice she'd never heard before. He'd always been strong and decisive, and yet at this moment he sounded unsure. And for someone who was very much a take-charge kind of guy, he'd definitely put the ball in her court. Had he noticed how nervous she was? She'd never known him to be terribly observant of her before. His patients usually were the ones who got all of his focused attention and rightly so, but somewhere along the line, he'd changed. Either he'd expanded his powers of observation or he was truly making an effort for her. A warm kernel of hope lit deep inside. A hope that they'd be able to make this work this time around. She made her decision.

"Yes, I'd like you to court me," she replied with a shyness she hadn't expected to feel.

"Okay." Valentin exhaled on a long breath. "So,

today—shall we go for a swim first, or would you like something to eat?"

"A swim sounds divine. We were fed so well on the flight I don't think I'm going to need to eat again for a while."

"Beach or pool?"

"Oh, beach, definitely."

Imogene walked off the patio and through the sliding doors into the house. Fans turned lazily on the ceiling, and she carried on walking until she found the master bedroom where their luggage had been put. There was another room on the other side of the hallway.

"I'll take this other room and leave you the master," she said, making a decision there and then.

To her relief, Valentin didn't protest. Instead he grabbed her cases and rolled them across the tiled floor to her bedroom.

"I'll knock on your door when I'm ready," he said with a grin. "It'll be like coming to pick you up on a date."

She smiled automatically in return. He really was taking this seriously. "Sure," she answered and closed the door behind him.

A flutter of nerves started low in her belly. It felt weird, yet exciting at the same time. Being courted by her husband? What a novel idea. She quickly opened her case and lifted a filmy beach wrap out together with a bikini. She eyed the bikini with a little trepidation. Was this going to be too revealing? She hadn't worn one in such a long time she'd even felt uncomfortable trying it on in the store, but the sales assistant had been effusive in her compliments, saying the emerald green of the fabric worked brilliantly with her skin tone and brought out the color in her eyes. Well, Imogene decided as she began to shed her clothes, even if they were merely courting this week, no one said anything about not being tempting at the same time. In fact, wouldn't that just be normal?

A knock a few minutes later saw her tie the beach wrap firmly around her hips before opening the door.

"I'm ready," she said breathlessly. "I just need sun-block on my back, if that's okay."

"Yeah, sure," Valentin answered, taking the tube of lotion from her. "And if you can do the same for me, too?"

"Oh, yes," Imogene replied, hoping her fear at having to touch him, at having him touch her, wasn't clearly evident.

She was so attuned to his every movement, and while she'd agreed in principle to their no-sex agreement, actually living that agreement was going to be a challenge. But she, like Valentin, didn't want to muddy this chance at a new beginning by making the same mistakes they'd made before.

Mistakes? Had loving each other so absolutely been a total mistake? Unbidden, her body rode a wave of remembered pleasure. She fought her scattered nerves back into submission. This was going to be a whole lot more challenging than she'd ever expected.

"Turn around," Valentin instructed.

She heard him squeeze a liberal dose of lotion into his hand, then felt the cold shock of it as he stroked it across her skin. The cold shock was rapidly replaced by the warmth of his palms as he firmly rubbed the lotion over her back and shoulders. When he got to the small of her back she drew in a sharp breath. That area had always been particularly sensitive for her and judging by the way his fingers lingered there, he remembered just what it did to her inside. After several taut minutes, he passed the tube over her shoulder.

"My turn," he said.

She swiveled around and took the tube from him, reluctantly meeting his gaze. There was an imp of mischief gleaming behind his blue eyes that tugged at her. He'd never shown a playful side of himself before. Everything about their last relationship, from their dangerous location and the risks involved with that, to the seriousness of his work and their own massive emotional highs followed by the deepest low of her life, had been borne on a power of emotion that had been exhausting at times. There'd been no time, no chance in that very different world, for flirtatiousness or fun. Given the contrast in their circumstances now, she found herself beginning to look forward to the rest of this week and dreading it a little at the same time. What if they failed again? What if this week simply proved the only thing they had in common was sex? That wasn't basis enough for marriage or a family. They'd already proved that.

Imogene gestured for Valentin to turn around, hoping he wouldn't see the turmoil that churned inside her. The moment he presented his back to her she went to work, squeezing lotion into her hands and then massaging it into his broad, strong back. Her palms tingled at the touch. It had been so long, too long, since she'd touched anyone else like this and that it should be him… Well, that just made the experience all the more acute. Even though she thought she'd pushed all those memories into a dark place in the back of her mind, never to be taken into the light again, she still remembered him so well. Every line of his body. The dips, the hollows.

Where he liked to be touched. Where he was ticklish. It was too much.

She gave him a slap on the shoulder. "That's it. I think we're covered."

"Thanks," he said, his voice rough.

"You okay?" she asked.

"Just a little uncomfortable," he admitted. "Only to be expected."

He turned to face her and her eyes dropped immediately below his waist where evidence of his discomfort disturbed the line of his swim shorts.

"Oh, I see," Imogene said, feeling an answering surge of need swell through her body.

"It's okay, Imogene. Just because I said we shouldn't have sex while we work this out doesn't mean I won't desire you. It also doesn't mean there's any pressure on either of us. Just think of it as a normal healthy response."

"Normal, huh?" She looked down again, then back up to his face. "If you say so."

For a moment he looked surprised, then his face split in a grin before a chuckle rose from deep inside. Imogene felt her lips pull into an answering smile before she slipped past him and out to the covered patio, where she grabbed a couple of towels and headed down toward the gleaming white sand. That laugh, and the pleasure of seeing the sheer joy on his face, reminded her starkly of all they had missed together, of all that they had never had. Her eyes blurring with unexpected tears, she dropped the towels and her wrap on a hammock conveniently strung between two tall palms and carried on to the water's edge.

It was just tiredness that was causing this stupid reaction, she told herself as she looked across the lagoon.

Behind her, she heard Valentin's rapid approach. She didn't have time to think before strong arms lifted her in the air and his forward motion propelled them both into the sea. She squealed just before they went under, feeling a brief moment of panic before she realized the water was warm and clear and she could easily touch the sandy floor.

Pushing herself upward, she let the water course from her face as she eyed her laughing husband.

"You looked like you needed a bit of help getting in," he said by way of explanation, but that mischief she'd spied earlier belied his so-called helpfulness.

"Thanks," she said wryly. "Sometimes I guess you just need to take a leap of faith, right?"

His eyes grew serious. "Yes," he answered. "Like we did yesterday. A leap of faith is exactly what we need, Imogene. Faith in each other."

With that, he turned away from her and struck out with strong strokes toward the reef. Imogene watched him swim. Powerful, purposeful. Pretty much how he'd always done everything in his life when she'd known him. He seemed to believe they'd be okay, but as she started a gentle breaststroke through the water, staying nearer to the shore, where she felt comfortable, she still wasn't convinced. The specter of their past still stood like an unresolved invisible wall between them. Until she could believe him, wholeheartedly, it would always remain.

For the rest of the day they swam, ate and napped. The threatened storm hadn't yet appeared, so when it was time for dinner they elected to eat down on the sand by candlelight with the night breeze blowing past them and sand at their bare feet. The scent of frangipani wafted down from the garden and the palm fronds whispered constantly on the wind.

"What would you like to do tomorrow?" Valentin asked as he topped up Imogene's glass of champagne.

"I wouldn't mind seeing around the island. You know, get our bearings. What about you?"

"Sounds fun. I'm happy doing whatever you want."

"Valentin, this isn't just about what I want."

There was a note to Imogene's voice that struck a warning—some of that he put down to the sheer exhaustion she had to be feeling in the aftermath of their wedding and the travel. And even though they'd had a pretty easy day so far, he, too, felt tired tonight. But for the rest, he recognized immediately that she didn't want to be pandered to. He chose his next words carefully.

"No, I understand that," he answered with a smile. "Don't think you're going to get everything your way."

He got the response he'd hoped for when she gave a small laugh.

"Well, that's good to know, I think."

After dinner they got out one of the island maps that was tucked in a visitor guide on the coffee table inside the house and pored over it. After some discussion, they chose a few places they wanted to stop during their circuit of the island and marked others to visit on another day. They both agreed a week was probably not long enough for them to see everything they wanted, but they'd hit the highlights and play the rest by ear. By the time Valentin saw her to her room, and to bed, they were both dragging their feet.

"Sleep well, Imogene," he said, leaning forward and placing a gentle kiss on her cheek.

"You, too."

He waited until she closed her bedroom door behind

her and turned to his own room. He stood in the center of the floor for a moment, his hands fisted at his sides, willing his body to release the sexual tension that had gripped him all day. Today had been an exercise in torment. Whether it had been applying sunblock to Imogene's back or simply watching her swim or snooze in a hammock, he'd wanted her with an ache that verged on desperation. No other woman had ever had this effect on him and, he was certain, no other woman would. He had to earn her wholehearted trust back. He'd been given this second chance to make it work and he'd better not screw it up.

Which brought him back to the conversation he'd had with Galen about Carla. He'd have to tell Imogene at some stage about the other woman being on his staff, but he didn't think his honeymoon was the right place or time. No, he'd wait until they were home and in a routine. When they were feeling more comfortable together again instead of walking on eggshells and rediscovering their way with each other.

Which in turn brought him back to the one thing that had remained constant between him and Imogene through the seven-year absence they'd had from each other. The one thing that had brought them together in an incendiary conflagration to begin with—the overpowering strength of their attraction. Was it any wonder their relationship had burned up the way it did? Emotions had been high, passion for each other even higher. In some ways he'd resented that at inopportune moments in his workday, his thoughts would turn to Imogene, or what they'd done together the previous night. Their relationship had been a puzzle to him and his ordered mind from day one, but he'd been unable to resist the attraction despite every logical part of his mind urging him to take things slowly and to tread with care. It didn't matter which way he dressed it up or tried to ignore it, then or now. He wanted her on a level that even he, with all his education and experience in life to date, could not quantify or explain. The only thing he could do was accept it and roll with it. No matter how much discomfort it left him in.

The next morning they elected to use the scooter to get around the island. Despite the heat that already stuck their clothes to their bodies, Valentin couldn't help feeling scooters were a vastly underrated method of travel because having Imogene plastered to his back, with her arms tightly wrapped around his waist as they drove on the island roads, was something he decided he'd like to get used to. Even with the cloying humidity that hung in the air after a heavy morning shower, he relished the feeling of her body pressed firmly against his. He was equally glad the low speed limit on the island ensured their trip took longer than he'd expected.

After a short ride, they strolled around the main center and a large colorful market before stopping for lunch at a restaurant overlooking the harbor. The place thronged with people from all over the world, judging by the accents and languages they heard on the air, but overlaying everything was a sense of relaxation and casualness that left them both unwinding by degrees.

"This is some place, isn't it?" Imogene said as she watched a bunch of kids playing in the water.

"It sure is. Are you enjoying yourself so far?"

"Yeah," she said after a minute. "I am. It's been good to relax and kick back. I guess I didn't realize how tense I was before the wedding. Things have been really busy at work. I decided to take a step back from the active management of my company and get back to my roots as a teacher, but it's meant a huge amount of work. More than I imagined, to be honest. And when we get home it'll ramp up again when I start interviewing for my replacement as CEO."

"I heard you'd remodeled your company to create a franchise-based operation."

He watched as her eyes brightened and her face became animated as she explained the reasons behind what she'd done and how she'd put the new structure in place. It only increased his admiration for her. He'd never really understood her on this level before, but now, hearing her talk about her work like this opened up another window on the woman he'd remarried.

"My mother can't understand why I'd want to go back to teaching. She sees it as less important than being in charge of a company."

"Education, especially early education, is vital. If we can't teach kids a love of learning from their early days, it makes life more challenging for everyone as they grow up."

"Exactly. It's why my centers focus on finding out the best way for individuals to learn. Not everyone responds to the same style. And that's something I've really missed since I've been out of the classroom. Plus, I want a better work-life balance. I don't want my kids being raised by strangers while I pursue the next dollar. That's not what's important to me."

He loved listening to her speak so animatedly and wanted to know more.

"And your family? Are they excited for you with the changes? They must be proud of all you've achieved."

"Oh, they don't care one way or the other. Dad's attention is pretty much solely on his work and Mom is very busy with her charity committees. My work is peripheral to their interests."

She said the words lightly but he could hear the pain that lay beneath them. Valentin sensed the disconnect in her family was far wider than she'd let on. Her father hadn't even been there for their wedding, and while her mother had made the effort to be supportive, Caroline O'Connor had clearly thought the whole concept of marrying at first sight to be a ridiculous way to approach a marriage. She certainly hadn't looked any happier when she'd realized her daughter wasn't marrying a stranger after all, and had remained coolly civil when conversing with him at the reception.

"You're not close?" he probed.

"I'm closer to my mom, but not to my dad. Oh, don't get me wrong, I'm sure he loves me in his way, but he's never been a hands-on parent. That's something I am determined to be and it's one of the reasons I restructured my company. I want to be there for my kids. For everything."

"We agree one hundred percent on that," he said, reaching across the table to take her hand.

The idea of them starting a family together filled him with a hope and excitement he hadn't expected.

"Good to know," she answered, tugging her hand free after a moment. "You lost your dad a while back. Do you have many memories of him?"

"I do, and good ones. He made an effort to be there for Galen and me. I get the impression that Mom was the rule maker on that issue because his work could easily have consumed him. Either way, until his heart attack he was a constant in our lives, even if he did struggle a bit with my incessant need to learn and understand the why of everything."

She laughed. "I've had kids like that from time to time. They're a challenge, all right. But they push you to be a better teacher in the long run."

Valentin looked across the table at her and smiled again. "Your classroom kids will be very lucky to have you back teaching."

"Thank you," she said. "That's one of the nicest things you've ever said to me."

He felt a jolt of shock. "Is it? Then it's something I definitely need to work on. You've a special talent, Imogene. I'm glad you're chasing your dream."

She looked a little flustered by his compliment and swiftly turned the attention back on him. "And you? Is Horvath Pharmaceuticals your dream or do you miss practicing medicine?"

"Yes and no. Working as a trauma surgeon was rewarding most of the time but there was always a disconnect between me and the people I treated. While I was saving lives, I was only the first port of call in what was often a long journey for them. It didn't bother me so much at first but as I've grown older I guess I've been looking for something different, something *more*, in my life. And when I looked at the work I was doing in Africa and the things that so often prevented us from making a lasting difference, I began to see where I might make a significant contribution. We were always hamstrung by a lack of supplies and medications to treat even the simplest of issues. Things that we take for granted that we can and will be treated for here. I went there to make a difference but what I did barely scratched the surface.

"When I returned home it only felt natural to go into the company business and work to try to make those vital medications more accessible for others. Not just overseas but at home, as well. The red tape can be suffocating at times but I like to remind myself that I'm making a difference in improving people's lives and life expectancies."

The waiter chose that moment to bring their orders to the table, interrupting him. As soon as the guy had left Valentin felt as though the closeness that he and Imogene had begun to share had changed. Had it been his mention of Africa? Probably. He gave himself a mental kick and slowly turned their conversation to more general matters, exhorting himself to be more careful in the future. This relationship of theirs was a fragile thing and needed careful tending.

And the more time he spent with Imogene, the more he knew just how much he wanted their marriage to succeed. The thing was, did she? Was she as invested in trying to make this work and going past their three-month trial period, or was she simply marking off the days on the calendar? She wasn't as easy to read as she used to be and the realization troubled him more than he wanted to admit.

Six

Imogene lay in her tangled sheets fighting to get to sleep. The past six days had been incredible. Fun, even. It wasn't what she'd been expecting. Oh, sure, the physical attraction they'd always shared had simmered between them constantly. Even flared up a time or two in a way that had made her wish that one of them, at least, would do something to relieve it. Should she be the one to take the initiative? she wondered as she flopped onto her back and stared at the ceiling.

Of course not, she told herself. They had an agreement. They'd get to know each other better before taking that step. But then why did her body continually ache for his touch? Why did she wish he'd take her hand as they strolled along the beach, that he'd kiss her as the sun set so gloriously, painting the sky with shades of purple and apricot and blush pink until the dark velvet of night consumed it all? Aside from those times when he helped her with her sunblock, he barely touched her at all.

She rolled onto her side and sighed heavily. Even though they were trying to get to know each other, they only hovered on the surface. It was as if they were each so determined not to cross any lines that they were almost being too careful, too respectful of each other's space. She sat up with a growl of frustration and pushed her sheets off. Maybe a nice cool swim in their pool would help, she decided.

She reached for a bikini, then looked at the glowing face of the digital clock at her bedside. It was 2:00 a.m. She was hardly likely to be observed by anybody else at this time of night, and with her nerves stretched to breaking point the idea of the silky soft glide of the pool water against her naked skin sounded like just the balm she needed.

Imogene grabbed her beach wrap and tied it around her before letting herself out of her room and padding on bare feet over the tiled floor. The humidity was higher than usual tonight; the air felt thick and cloying against her skin, making her scalp prickle and her hair cling to her face. The pool was looking better and better.

Outside, she heard the patter of a gentle rain on the patio. The night sky was obscured by clouds. She unwrapped the sheet of fabric from her body and walked toward the pool, gasping a little as the rain hit her overheated skin. She stood there for a moment, lifting her face to the sky and simply letting the rain fall on her.

There was something elemental about the night, about standing here alone, naked. With nothing between her and the rest of the world. No secrets, no shadows.

She walked the rest of the distance to the pool and dived cleanly into the water, staying below the surface for as long as she could hold her breath. Eventually, she popped up and drew in some air. She felt fantastic. The water slid around her, caressing her skin and soothing her fractured nerves. Maybe she needed to do this every night. She struck out for the end of the pool, determined to do some laps and to wear herself out so she could sleep, but the sensation of the water against her body only served to heighten the tension that had kept her awake. Yes, it felt divine, but at the same time it teased and tantalized. In fact, right now she felt more aroused than she had lying in bed thinking about Valentin.

She pushed herself harder, completing the laps more quickly, and once her muscles began to burn she slowed down again. Each lap got slower until she flipped onto her back and simply floated there on the surface while her heart rate and her breathing returned to normal. A gap in the clouds above revealed the twinkle of stars, and for the first time in a long time, Imogene simply allowed herself to be present in the moment. To empty her mind and to listen to the night sounds around her, to feel the occasional drop of rain from the last of the stubborn clouds hanging overhead and to enjoy the steady *shush* of the waves on the beach not far away.

That was when she heard the shuffle of bare feet on the patio beside her. She looked across. It could only be one person. Valentin.

"Couldn't sleep?" he asked, squatting down beside the pool for a moment before sitting on the edge and letting his legs dangle in the water.

"No," she said, letting her feet drop down so her nakedness was not quite so obvious. "You, either?"

"Must be our night for it," he said before lowering himself into the pool.

He dropped down until his head was covered and then bobbed back up again.

"I'll, um, I'll leave you to it, then," she said, striking for the edge farthest from him.

"Don't leave on my account," he said. "In fact, stay. Please?"

It was the *please* that was her undoing. Even though every ounce of inner caution urged her to create distance between them, to avoid any chance of accidentally exposing her nakedness, she stayed right where she was. She knew it was risky but right now a part of her discovered that risk was looking pretty darned appealing.

"Sure, but could we turn off the pool lights?"

"Turn off..." Valentin's voice trailed to a halt as understanding dawned. "Ah," he said eventually. "I see. How about I even the stakes?"

Before she could answer she saw him reach for his swimming trunks and seconds later they flew through the air to land on the poolside with a wet slap. Excitement buzzed in her veins along with a fair serving of trepidation. She knew how this was going to end. It was like watching a train wreck that you knew you couldn't halt. And in their case they already knew what the outcome would be like. They'd already traveled that road together. The one where passion ruled every waking moment of their lives, leading inexorably to their destruction. But they were better than that now, she told herself. They'd spent almost an entire week together without so much more than a chaste good-night kiss. They'd slept apart—well, *sleep* being a relative term given how many nights she'd tossed and turned alone in her bed.

Was this to be a turning point for them?

"Meet me halfway," Valentin coaxed from his end of the pool.

"And then?" she asked, her voice suddenly husky as a surge of desire dragged through her body.

"And then we'll see what happens next."

She didn't bother answering. In fact, she doubted she could form a cohesive sentence right now. Her blood fizzed in her veins as she pushed away from the edge of the pool and floated across to the middle. Valentin was already there, waiting with an expression on his face that drew the breath from her body. Even in the pool light she could see a flush of need on his cheeks, a glitter in his eyes that told her far more than words ever could. He wanted her as much as she wanted him.

Without another thought she slid straight into his arms, wrapped her legs around his waist and felt like she'd finally found home.

"I've missed you," Valentin said as he supported Imogene in the water.

"Let's not talk about it, not when we have so many better things to do," Imogene said breathlessly before pressing her lips to his in a kiss that silenced them both.

She wasn't subtle. There was a carnality in her kiss that quite simply took his breath away. She made her position abundantly clear by silencing him as she had, but even as his body erupted with heat, and lust threatened to cloud his mind, he knew he wanted more than a physical release. Yes, she'd come to him willingly, without any hesitation, but he found himself wanting more than that. They'd only just begun the journey to understanding each other better this week and he was no closer to knowing why she'd been so quick to believe he'd been the wrongdoer in their first marriage. Why she'd been so adamant about not listening to his side of the story.

But then the heat of her body wiped thought from his mind. What was he doing thinking so darn hard when he had this beautiful, willing woman in his arms? A woman he'd once loved with a force that had frightened him so much that when she'd walked away he'd immured his emotions—throwing himself into his work with scant regard for his safety on several occasions. He'd never understood, until he'd been served with the divorce papers, that one human being could hurt another so deeply without actually causing a physical injury. It had been an eye-opening shock. One he hadn't wanted to repeat, ever. His logical, quantitative mind had rejected the pain, told himself it wasn't reasonable, but reason took a hike in the face of what he'd experienced.

Imogene's tongue swept across his lips and reason took a hike all over again. His body responded in kind and tightened on a new energy that focused solely on the sensations that coursed through him, on the rightness of having her here in his arms, skin to skin, mouth fused to mouth, her inner heat poised over that part of him that ached with need. He kissed her back with a fervor that spoke of the years of denial he'd gone through, of how much he'd missed her, of how much he wanted her right here and now.

She shifted her body and the tip of his penis brushed the heated core of her. He shuddered and groaned, tightening his hold on her. In response her nails dug into his shoulders and she pressed her body more firmly against his, the tight points of her nipples imprinting on his chest. Valentin let one hand drift down her back, farther to the curve of her buttocks and farther still until he lightly caressed her opening. She moaned into his mouth and let her head drop back. Her long hair swirled around them in the water, the tendrils brushing against him and setting off small electric charges with each touch.

He lowered his mouth to the smooth, pale column of her neck, licked against the pulse that fluttered there, nipped at the hollow beneath her earlobe and felt a tremor run through her from tip to toe. As delightful as this was, it wasn't enough. He wanted access to all of her and he couldn't do that here. He propelled them across the pool to the edge where he lifted her from the water and took a moment to enjoy the sight of the water coursing off her body, relishing how it skimmed over her pert, high breasts and shimmered over the lean muscles of her stomach and thighs.

"Had enough already?" she teased from her superior vantage point.

"Never enough," he growled and nudged her knees apart.

He heard her sharply indrawn breath as she realized his intentions. But she didn't pull away. Valentin trailed his fingers softly along her inner thighs. She was trembling now as she anticipated his next move but he took his time, letting his fingers drift closer to their eventual goal before skimming back down toward her knees.

"You never used to be this mean to me," she protested, as he let his fingers drift past her center again.

"This isn't mean," he assured her and bent his head to kiss her creamy skin and follow the path his fingers had just taken. "This is merely taking my time."

Her legs tensed beneath his touch. He nuzzled against her, drawing in the scent that was a combination of her and the saltwater pool. And then he was there at her center. She leaned back and braced her arms behind her, spreading her legs wider to give him access to her sweet spot. He'd always loved this with her.

Loved the taste of her, the sounds she made when he made love to her body the way he was doing now. He let his tongue trace around the bud he knew was super-sensitive, not quite touching it but edging closer with each sweep. Her whole body shook now and he looked up, seeing her gaze on him, watching his every move. Without breaking their eye contact he pressed his lips to her clitoris and applied pressure with his tongue and his lips until her body grew so tightly strung he thought she might shatter into a million pieces. And then she did. Her climax hit in huge waves that left her limp with satisfaction.

So much had changed between them in the past seven years but this, this one incredibly special thing, remained the same. Valentin hauled himself out of the water and bent to lift Imogene into his arms. Holding her close to his body, he strode through to the house and into his bedroom. He took Imogene into his en suite, turned on the multihead shower and held her upright as water coursed over their bodies.

"You expect me to stand on my own after that?" she asked, with a light, teasing note to her voice that had been missing for much of the past week.

"You can always lean against the wall," he said, smiling as he lathered up his hands and began to stroke them over her body.

She did as he suggested, murmuring her approval as he smoothed his hands over her breasts. He loved how neatly they fitted against the palms of his hands, how her pale pink nipples darkened as they tightened into peaks that begged to be kissed and sucked and lightly bitten. She let out a moan of pleasure as he did exactly that. Her hands came to rest on his shoulders, clinging as if he was all that stood between her remaining upright and collapsing into a heap on the floor of the shower. He finished washing her body, then rinsed her thoroughly. When her hands released their grip on his shoulders and began to move over his chest, he felt a swell of pleasure pour through him. If it was even possible, his erection grew harder, more demanding, as she stepped closer to him. His rigid flesh was trapped between them. The heat of her body on his sensitive skin was a delight and a torment.

Imogene reached for the shower gel and poured it over his chest, her free hand working it into a lather that slid down his body, teasing him further. She put the gel back on the shelf and then focused her attention on caressing his body. Across his chest, over his abdomen, then back up again to his shoulders, his arms, his back. Then finally, finally, she reached for his aching flesh. Her slender fingers curled around him, her thumb gently rubbing his sensitive tip. He dropped his head into the crook of her neck and shoulder, and groaned out loud as she increased the pressure of her fingers, stroking up and down. In the end he couldn't take it anymore. He wrapped his fingers around hers to stop her.

"Let's take this to the bedroom," he said unevenly.

He reached for a towel and roughly dried her before scraping it quickly across his body. Then he took Imogene by the hand and led her to the sheet-tossed bed he'd left not so long ago. He'd gone in search of surcease. Instead, he'd found his wife.

While Imogene lay down on the bed, he reached for the bedside table drawer and pulled out a condom. He sheathed himself and in seconds they lay on the bed together—hands reaching, legs tangling, mouths meshing until there was no clear delineation between where he ended and she began. He rolled her under his body.

Her legs shifted to allow him to settle between them and then he was nudging at her entrance. The head of his penis bathed in the heat of her body. He surged forward, his rhythm uneven at first as he fought to stay in control. But then their synchronicity of old reasserted itself.

Valentin felt Imogene's body tighten around him, heard the keening cry that spilled from her lips as her second orgasm flooded her body. Then and only then did he let go. Pleasure shot through every inch of his body and his mind. This perfection was what he'd been missing for far too long—this, and the incredible woman in his arms.

His woman.

Seven

Imogene sat next to Valentin in the Horvath jet as they flew back over the Pacific and away from their island paradise idyll. Waking in his bed this morning had felt all kinds of right and all kinds of wrong at the same time. Her entire body still hummed with the aftermath of his lovemaking. A part of her had wanted to start their day with a reenactment of their middle-of-the-night passion, but logic had dictated she slip from his bed and go to her room to shower and dress before their flight home.

They'd barely spoken. As if both of them were too lost in their thoughts about what they'd shared and where they should go next. Their physical compatibility was a given. He'd only had to touch her and she'd gone up in flames and, she suspected, it was much the same for him, too. Beneath all of that, however, was a deep sense of disappointment in herself. They'd both allowed physical needs to overwhelm the agreement they'd made to take things slowly. Oh, sure, they'd waited—what—six days before acting on the simmering tension that hovered between them? That was hardly admirable. And while she knew she could argue with herself until she was blue in the face about the fact that they were adults with needs and were perfectly entitled to have incredibly amazing sex if they wanted to, deep down she knew it was wrong.

There was still so much unresolved between them. So much left unsaid. And while they had no trouble communicating with their bodies, their ability to open up to each other verbally continued to be an issue. In this entire week together, they'd stuck to peripheral topics, barely skimming the surface of who they really were or what they each truly wanted—out of their remarriage or out of life in general. And she was mad at herself. This week had been her opportunity to reach out and discover if Valentin really had changed from the man she'd left back in Africa. Whether she honestly could trust him again. All she'd discovered was that she couldn't trust herself around him. Hormones, it seemed, ruled over her head whenever she was around him.

Even now, seated next to him on the plane. The seats were large enough that they weren't even touching and yet she could feel the imprint of his body next to her as if they were. The heat of him, his scent, the sound of his steady breathing. Every little thing about him. She shifted in her seat and looked out the window beside her. Nothing but clouds. A bit like how her brain felt right now. She sighed.

"Everything okay?" Valentin asked, leaning closer.

A gentle waft of his cologne invaded her senses and sent a shaft of longing through her body. She clenched her inner muscles on an involuntary wave of need and fought the urge to close the distance between them. To assure him with her lips and her hands that everything was just peachy.

"I'm fine," she muttered through clenched teeth.

"Forgive me for saying this but you neither look nor sound fine."

She turned to face him and caught the twinkle of humor in his eyes. "It's not a laughing matter," she said sharply.

His humor dimmed immediately. "No, you're right, it's not. But it's done. We went against our own edicts. I hope you're not going to sulk about that all the way home."

"Sulk? You think this is sulking?" Outrage fired every nerve in her body. "I'm angry, if you must know."

"Thank you for communicating that," he answered calmly.

His calm only served to fuel her irritation. "Angry at you," she spit.

"I accept that."

She rode the wave of tension in her body for a split second longer before it ran out of her in a rush of helplessness. Sagging into her seat, she added, "And angry at myself."

"And that's the problem, isn't it?"

"Yes. What are we going to do, Valentin?"

He sighed. "Exercise more restraint in the future, I imagine. I'm equally annoyed with myself, but you can't say it wasn't a memorable experience. In fact, given the same opportunity, I would do it all again. Do you have any idea how alluring you looked swimming in the water naked?" His voice dropped, grew deeper, thicker. "Your hair spread out around you. The pool lights illuminating your ivory skin. You were otherworldly. A water nymph set to ensnare me. I was in your thrall. Seeing you like that brought back every memory of our life together before. Every kiss, every caress—every time we made love until we could barely breathe anymore. And I wanted you. I'm not ashamed of that. I still want you, Imogene."

Imogene felt her eyes fill with tears at the depth of emotion in Valentin's voice. He'd never spoken to her like this before. Never been this honest about his feelings for her.

"But we both know where wanting will lead," he continued. "And it's not enough, is it?"

Sorrow pierced her heart. "No, it wasn't before… It isn't now."

"We have more work to do before we allow ourselves the pleasure of each other again. Agreed?"

She nodded solemnly. "Agreed."

Even though she knew he was right, it didn't prevent regret from filling every empty space inside. She'd missed the physical side of a relationship, and the physical side of anything to do with Valentin had always been the pinnacle of perfection. It was just everything else that had destroyed her. That was what she had to remember. That was what she had to work on.

"Imogene?" he prompted when she fell silent again.

"Hmm?"

"We can do this. I want to understand you better. I want you to understand me. And I want the physical aspect of our marriage, too. I'm prepared to wait so we can get the rest right this time."

"Thank you," she said softly in response. "It means a lot to me."

"You mean a lot to me. You always did."

He'd hurt her so very badly. Had expected her to simply believe him when he said he hadn't slept with Carla since their marriage. Hadn't understood what she'd seen, what she'd been told, and had made no effort to. He'd made his statement, he'd stood by that and he'd expected her to believe him. But she couldn't believe him. Not when she'd seen what she'd seen. And not when he exhibited every last trait of her father's, a man made more attractive by his devotion to his duty, by his single-minded focus on what was right. Add into the mix his physical attributes and the adoration of the people around him and you had a dangerous mix. She'd always sworn she'd never marry a man like her father. Not for her, the life her mom had chosen—being a token wife while he pursued his calling and dallied in multiple sycophantic relationships.

Was it too much to expect devotion from your partner? To be married to a man who saw fidelity as necessary in a successful marriage? No. Not in her book. And until she could be certain that Valentin was capable of that, she had to ensure she kept her guard very firmly up. Yes, she'd agreed to give this marriage a second chance, with the hope that one day she could have the children she dearly wanted. But she wasn't going to put her heart on the chopping block for Valentin Horvath to destroy again.

She had to be certain.

By the time they landed in New York they were both shattered. The layover time in Los Angeles had seemed to go on forever but at least they'd been able to sleep while in the air. Valentin thanked their driver after they pulled up outside his apartment building on Fifth Avenue. Light flurries swirled around them and across the road Central Park was shrouded in ice and snow. The wintry January climate was a vast change from the warm, humid air of Rarotonga.

"I'll take care of our cases, Anton. You head on home to your wife and kids," he said as the man removed their cases from the trunk of the limousine.

"Not a problem, Mr. Horvath."

"Seriously. It's already past eight o'clock and I know how much you love reading to your girls."

"Then thank you, sir. I'll pick you up at seven for work?"

"Make it a little later tomorrow. Maybe eight?"

"Whatever you say," Anton said with a smile. "Enjoy your night, sir. Ma'am."

Imogene gave Anton a distracted smile and reached for the handle on her case as the car pulled away from the curb.

"How could I forget how cold it is here?" she grumbled.

"It's not Rarotonga, that's for sure. Here, let me take that," Valentin offered.

"Thanks," she replied and looked skyward at the Neo-Italian Renaissance–style exterior of the building. "I had no idea you lived on the Upper East Side. Have you been here long?"

"Since coming back from Africa. I love looking over the park."

"I bet the view is stunning."

"It is, although we'll have to wait for a clear day for you to fully appreciate it. Let's go up."

After a nod to the doorman and the concierge, they traveled up in a mirrored and wood-lined elevator that looked as if it was original to the building but ran as if it had been built yesterday. Smooth and silent. The doors slid open on the top floor.

"Penthouse, no less," she commented.

Valentin wondered if she was regretting subletting her brownstone apartment in Brooklyn about now. Or if she was wishing that they'd kept separate homes while they found their way back into a lasting relationship.

"I saw it and couldn't resist." He gestured, dragging their cases onto the parquet floor of the vestibule.

"Wait, this is it? We're here? No corridor, no separate entry?"

Valentin chuckled, the first time he'd felt any sense of humor for a while. He gestured back to the elevator. "This not enough of an entry point for you?"

"Oh, it is. I just..." She seemed at a loss for words as she peeked from the vestibule into the main foyer that led to his formal rooms. "This is huge. You have the whole floor?"

He shrugged. "Should I apologize for that?"

"N-n-no," she stammered. "I'm just a bit surprised, to be honest."

"Surprised?"

"You were such a minimalist back in Africa, and let's face it, this is hardly a bachelor pad." She looked to the rooms beyond the entranceway. "It's a real home."

"Is that a problem?"

"No, of course not, but it's very different from what we had before. I don't know what I expected—I just never pictured you in a setting like this." She seemed flustered as she stepped through the foyer and into his library, moving straight to the windows that overlooked the park. "Wow, this is beautiful. It's like stepping back into the thirties."

He followed close behind, leaving their cases in the

foyer. "Close. Mid-1920s, to be precise. I had the choice to renovate extensively, or preserve the special character of the apartment. It had been in the same family for years before I bought it and it seemed a shame to wipe all that history out and replace it with something with less soul. Less heart."

She looked at him in surprise.

"What?" he asked. "You don't think I have a heart?"

A tinge of pink touched her cheeks and she busied herself undoing the buttons on her cashmere coat. "No, it's not that. It's just that every now and then I realize how much I don't know you."

He reached a hand out and touched her forearm. "That's what this is about for us now, Imogene—rediscovering each other. We can do this. Day by day, okay?"

She put her hand over his and squeezed. It was the first time she'd voluntarily touched him since last night. Or was it the night before? They'd been traveling so long he'd grown confused with all the time zones.

"I'll show you to your room, let you freshen up and then show you around the apartment, okay?"

"Sounds like a good idea," she said, letting him go.

He felt the loss instantly and wished he could simply take her hand, like a normal couple, and tug her down the hallway to *their* bedroom, not hers and not his. He closed his eyes briefly and took in a steadying breath. All in good time. Back in the foyer he snagged their cases and then led Imogene down the hallway toward the larger of the guest bedrooms.

"This is yours and you'll find the bathroom through there. It connects to the next room but there's no one in there. My room is farther down the hall and Dion's room is on the other side of the apartment."

"Dion?"

"My butler-slash-maid. But don't let him hear me call him that. He prefers the term *general factotum*." Valentin forced a smile. "He came with the property and takes his role very seriously. His family served the family who owned the apartment before I did. He's also a darn fine cook, so there was no way I was encouraging him to retire after he fed me the first week after I moved in."

"Where is he now?"

"I sent him to visit his daughter while we were on honeymoon. She lives in Vermont. He'll be back tomorrow."

"And his wife?"

"He's a widower." Valentin put her case on one side of the room. "When you're ready, come down the hall to the master bedroom to get me and I'll take you on a tour."

"Okay, I'll do that."

Valentin turned to go but hesitated at the door for a moment before turning back to face her again. "We're going to make it this time," he said with more force than he intended.

Imogene locked gazes with him and they stood there like that for several seconds. She was about to say something when his mobile phone chimed. He slid it from his pocket and looked at the display.

"It's Galen. I probably ought to take this."

"Please, go ahead."

He went down the hall, answering as he entered his bedroom.

"Galen, good timing. We just got back."

But it was his brother's next words that drove him to his knees. "Nick and Sarah, they're dead."

Galen's college buddy and his wife had been instrumental in helping Galen build the Port Ludlow resort into the successful business it was today. They were his best friends and, together with their nine-year-old daughter, Ellie, had spent a lot of time with the Horvath family over the years. So much so, they were like honorary members of the extended clan. But dead?

Valentin listened as Galen outlined the details of the accident that had taken his best friends' lives. Felt his brother's grief in every syllable.

"And Ellie?" He was almost too afraid to ask.

"She's devastated, poor kid. I've got her staying with me. Her class was on a school trip, thank God, otherwise she might have—" Galen's voice broke off.

Valentin filled the gap instantly. "What's going to happen to her? They didn't have much in the way of family, did they?"

"No," his brother answered brokenly. "Just us, really. Nick asked me years ago if I'd agree to be Ellie's guardian if something like this happened and of course I said yes. I just never thought..."

"You're not alone, Galen. And neither is Ellie. We'll all help where we can. In fact, I'll come tomorrow," Valentin offered.

"No, don't do that. You're just back from your honeymoon. I wouldn't ask it of you even if you weren't. There's nothing anyone can do."

"The funeral, then. We'll both come."

"Thank you, I'd appreciate it. So would Ellie. You know how much she adores you."

"As I do her," Valentin said grimly. The poor kid. Alone now. No, he told himself. Not alone. She had Galen and she had the rest of his family to buoy her through this awful time. "I'll call you again tomorrow, okay?"

"Yeah, thanks. I should have more details then. In the morning I have meetings with the lawyers regarding guardianship and Nick's and Sarah's effects."

"It's not going to be easy, but you'll get through it. They're counting on you now. Remember I'm here if you need me. For anything, okay?"

He hung up the phone and sat with his back against his bed. The news was sobering, proof that life could change in a split second.

"Valentin? Bad news?"

He looked up to see Imogene hovering in the doorway. He gestured for her to come in and explained what had happened. Instantly compassion flooded her features.

"That poor girl. Poor Galen. Is he going to be okay?"

"I guess, but he certainly didn't ever count on becoming an instant parent."

"Kind of makes our problems dim in comparison, doesn't it?" she said with an empathy he heartily appreciated.

"It certainly does. We'll go for the funeral. I'll let you know when I have the details."

"Of course," she said. "Look, you've had a shock, can I get you something? Make you some hot chocolate, maybe?"

He looked up at her and nodded. "Yeah, I'd like that."

"Then you better show me where the kitchen is," she said with a gentle smile.

She held out her hand and he grasped it firmly, allowing her to help him to his feet. And he made himself a silent promise. This would work between them, come what may. He didn't want a life of regret—to look back and wish he'd done things differently or better. Through their match made in marriage his grandmother had given them a second chance at love. It was up to him to ensure it didn't get messed up.

Eight

It was hard to believe they'd been married a month already. That week in Rarotonga, that magical night—those memories had been shoved firmly in the past by a New York winter and both her and Valentin's getting back to work. But tonight, she wanted to mark the occasion and she'd asked Dion to help her create a delicious taste sensation as a special dinner. Dion had been only too happy to help.

If only it had been summer, she thought, even spring. Then they could have dined on the garden terrace upstairs. Of course it was covered with snow right now and still bitterly cold, so the dining room would have to do. Or maybe a picnic in front of the fireplace in the library—now, there was an idea. She nibbled at her lip as she pondered the logistics. Beef Wellington served off a plate on the floor? Probably not the best plan.

Despite their agreement to get to know each other better, they'd both been shoved straight back into the demands of their jobs from the day they'd returned to work. Weekends had been busy, too. Their first weekend home they'd flown back to Seattle to attend the funeral of Galen's best friends. It had been a terribly sad experience, but the way Galen had supported Ellie, and the way all the Horvaths had shown their support for them both, had been balm for the soul.

There was no doubt Galen loved that little girl as if she were his own and he was doing everything in his power to assure her of that fact. It had been an eye-opener for Imogene, too, to see that Valentin was equally protective of the child. It had shown a new facet of his character that gave her some inkling as to what he'd be like as a father.

She flickered a glance at the calendar on the wall. Two more months until they'd have to make a decision about whether their marriage would go ahead. While she hadn't seen any evidence to support her fears that he shared her father's attitude to marriage, she still felt as though Valentin was holding something back. Sure, they'd spent the past few weeks sharing their evenings, debating politics, discussing aspects of their work, but she still sensed something was missing. She'd learned more about Valentin's childhood—a challenging one for all concerned, given his high intelligence and burning need to learn. Even now he spent a lot of his free time poring over textbooks or scientific essays, all in the pursuit of being better educated and well-informed so that nothing would surprise him in the course of his work. That need in him to know all fascinated and amused her. It seemed that to Valentin everything was quantifiable and, she supposed, in his world it probably was. A smile tugged at her lips as she considered how he'd cope in one of her day cares for a week. With varying age groups of children in various stages of willfulness. One thing was consistent in childcare and early education—no two days were ever the same.

Imogene sighed wistfully. She'd missed that. The color and noise of the classrooms. The bright eager minds as yet unformed by societal pressures or the idea that there was anything they should not or could not do. She looked forward to being back in that environment. Next month would see the appointment of her replacement as CEO. Only a few months ago that had been a topic under discussion and now it was happening. Change was constant. That was never truer, she realized as she considered her own position. So on that basis, it was logical to assume that *if* Valentin *had* cheated on her seven years ago, he was capable of change now. She had to learn to let go of that dark place in their past. To put it in a box in the back of her memory and fully embrace this fresh new start that they were both skirting every day.

The timer beeped on the oven, distracting her from the direction of her thoughts. She was just about to check on the beef Wellington when her phone rang. She recognized the chime instantly. Valentin. She couldn't help the tiny flutter of excitement that struck when she answered and heard the timbre of his voice in her ear.

"Imogene? How are you?"

"Looking forward to seeing you," she said, deciding to take the bull by the horns and to stop denying the fact that hearing from her husband thrilled her. "I have something special planned for when you get home."

There was a long pause as he obviously digested her words, and Imogene felt her stomach drop by degrees.

"Oh, Genie," he sighed across the phone line, regret heavy in his voice. "I'm so sorry. Something has come up at work that requires all my attention right now. I won't be home until late. It's why I was calling."

She realized that for the first time since she'd walked out on him, he'd called her by the nickname only he had ever used. The sound of it falling so easily from his lips was a balm to her soul. A reminder that even though they were still treading so carefully with each other, there was emotion between them and a growing trust. She fought back her disappointment that he was working late and focused instead on him. He sounded tired, frustrated. And she wanted to resolve that for him—to take away the guilt that reverberated in every word.

"Don't worry, Valentin. I'll be here when you get home. We can do something special another time."

"I'm really sorry," he repeated. "If I could get out of it, I would. We're so close to closing this deal but there's been a hiccup in the development budget that requires urgent work."

"It's okay. I understand. Things happen. Please, don't worry."

"I feel bad. Since we've been back I've been working all hours. That wasn't my plan."

She had to admit that she felt a little as though they'd slid immediately back into their old roles. Him working all the hours while she waited at home for him. Except this time around she'd been busy, too. There'd been days when he'd beaten her home because she'd been interviewing candidates for the CEO role or tied up in other matters that couldn't be taken care of during business hours. She got it. When you were in charge the buck stopped with you and you had to deal with it. She could hardly complain when something came up that he hadn't anticipated.

"Valentin, please, don't worry. It can wait."

"I'll make it up to you, I promise."

"I'll look forward to that," she said, smiling.

They said their goodbyes and she turned to survey the kitchen and her preparations to make tonight special for them. Yes, she was disappointed but at least she'd matured enough now not to take that out on him. Not like she used to before. It was a sobering realization and she was still lost in thought when Dion entered the kitchen.

"Was that Mr. Horvath?" he asked.

"Yes, it seems he has to work late tonight."

"That's a shame. Would you like me to finish up in here and put things away?"

Imogene thought for a moment, then shook her head. "No, I want you to help me find a way to take all this to him. If the mountain won't come home for dinner, then I'll just have to take dinner to the mountain."

Dion's wrinkled face creased into a smile. "That sounds like a perfect solution, madam. I have just the equipment you'll need. You go and get ready and leave the rest to me. I'll order the car to be out front for you in half an hour."

"Excellent, thank you, Dion. I appreciate your help."

"It's what I'm here for, madam," the older man said with a twinkle in his eyes.

Imogene fled for her bedroom. Suddenly tonight was looking a whole lot more interesting after all.

From the moment he'd ended his call with Imogene he hadn't been able to concentrate. The spreadsheets on his computer had begun to blur and all he could focus on was the hastily disguised disappointment that had been in her voice when he'd said he wasn't coming home for dinner. He looked at the date at the bottom of his computer screen and understanding dawned. He was such an idiot. How could he have overlooked that today was a month since their wedding? And it augured well for their marriage that she'd wanted to mark the occasion. Not so great was the fact that he hadn't even noticed.

Guilt slashed across his mind. His obsession with work had been a major player in the discontent in their first marriage. His hours had led to more than one argument at home. Arguments that had ended with passionate lovemaking and promises to try harder but that hadn't saved his marriage in the end. Nor would they now if he didn't improve his awareness.

He was torn. Instinct told him to get up from his desk and head home to his waiting wife. Logic told him that one more pass of the spreadsheets would allow him to see exactly where the problem lay. It wasn't like Carla to make a mistake in her budgets, but the flaw in the calculations that he'd been provided with could derail this whole deal by ballooning the costs.

A sound at the door made him look up. As if he'd conjured her up with his imagination, there was his wife. She wore her cashmere coat buttoned up to the neck and a pair of sinfully high pumps that highlighted her slender ankles and finely muscled calves. Her hair was up in one of those twists that looked entirely feminine and exposed the delicious sweep of her slender neck. A pair of diamond studs glinted in her earlobes. Valentin felt a jolt of sexual awareness, but as had become his habit since their return from their honeymoon, he quelled it just as quickly as it arose.

"Imogene?" he said, pushing up out of his chair and going to meet her. "This is a surprise."

"A good one, I hope," she said, holding the door open

with her foot and maneuvering a small cart through the door from behind her.

A delicious scent permeated the air in his office and Valentin stood, rooted in shock. “You brought me dinner?”

“Happy monthiversary,” she replied with a satisfied smile on her face. “Now, where would you like me to put this?”

When he was too stunned to reply she carried on as if his response wasn’t necessary.

“Okay, how about over by the window? Dion assures me that this folds out into a little table, so maybe if you could bring a couple of chairs over…?”

She gestured to the two guest chairs sitting opposite his desk and he hastened to comply. While he did so, Imogene undid the buttons on her coat and shrugged it off her shoulders. Any and all attempts at controlling his libido were moot at that point as she revealed a figure-hugging dress that ended high above her knees. Long-sleeved, it gave the impression of demureness—the boat neckline skimming across her collarbones modestly and the rich purple fabric making her skin appear to glow. But when she turned around to fold out two sides on the cart and apply the brake, she exposed her back—bare from nape to just below her waist with a drapey thing of fabric that hung like a shawl around the edges. His mouth dried and his hands clenched on the back of the chair he was carrying. The rest of his body? Well, that just went up in flames.

Imogene continued to set up her surprise for him, shaking a pristine white tablecloth over the makeshift table. Then she reached underneath the trolley, pulled out several dishes together with plates and cutlery and set it all on the table. She even had a small posy of flowers in a crystal bowl in the center. Throughout, she remained oblivious to the torment she was inadvertently putting him through. Or was it inadvertent? They'd been married a month. They'd been "dating" when time permitted. They'd observed all the rules they themselves had set in place. Was it too much to wish that they—no, *she*—was ready to take it up to the next level?

"I was going to bring candles, too," she said, straightening a knife beside one of the plates. "But I wasn't sure what the regulations were in your building regarding open flames."

He was speechless. She'd gone to all this trouble for him. No, he corrected himself again, for *them*. Which only served to make it all the more special. He carried the second chair over to the table and the moment his hands were free he reached for her, pulling her close.

"You are an incredible woman," he said. "Thank you."

"If there's anything I've learned in the past seven years, it's that if I want something, I have to reach for it myself. I can't just sit around waiting for things to happen or expect other people to do things for me."

He looked into her eyes, more green than gray tonight, and felt himself fall a whole lot in love with her all over again. This was it. The real thing. He had been an idiot to let her go before, and he wasn't going to let that happen ever again.

"Shall we eat?" Imogene said, interrupting his intention to show her exactly how he was feeling right now.

"Sure," he replied, releasing her and turning to the table. "You did all this yourself?"

"I had a little help from Dion but he mostly just supervised. Seems he's quite the romantic beneath that hoary exterior."

Valentin suspected it had a lot more to do with the nature of the beautiful woman in front of him and how she brought light into every place she went rather than Dion's romantic side. He held her chair out for her, bending over her slightly as she settled herself. Her scent wafted up to him. Fresh and clean and with that little something spicy underlying it—the spiciness a reminder of Imogene's hidden depths. His fingers tightened on the back of her chair as he pushed it in. If they were a normal couple he'd have kissed the exposed nape of her neck just now. But, he reminded himself, they weren't like other couples. Instead, they were a couple working their way back to where they ought to be, from a past fraught with suspicion and misconceptions. They had both been immature about relationships that first time. Obeying the demands of their bodies over any semblance of rational thought. It was no wonder they'd crashed and burned. But this, tonight, it was a symbol of what they were building together. Something with strong bones, a joint purpose. Hope.

Before they ate, Valentin adjusted the lighting in the office, dimming the overheads and leaving just one lamp on in a corner. The action increased the sense of intimacy in a way he wouldn't have dreamed possible in his workplace. And so, with the Manhattan skyline twinkling outside the window, they dined together and sipped one of the very good bottles of red wine from his well-stocked wine racks that she'd brought to complement her cooking. And Valentin felt his desire for his wife grow by steady increments.

"I never knew you had this hidden talent for great cooking," Valentin said, toasting her with his glass. "Kudos to the chef."

"Thank you," she answered, accepting his compliment with an inclination of her head. "I surprised even myself."

"Oh, come now," he said, putting down his glass. A tendril of hair had slipped from its twist to frame her face. He reached across to gently twirl it around his forefinger. "Don't tell me you're not adept at everything you put your mind to. I know that much about you. In that regard, you're a lot like me. Neither of us accepts failure."

He let the piece of hair drop from his finger and saw the light tremor that traveled through her as it drifted back across the responsive skin at the side of her neck. She was so sensitive to touch. Always had been. He picked up his wine again and took a generous sip. Anything to avoid touching her again and potentially breaking the spell that had surreptitiously wrapped around them in the cocoon of his office. Tonight it felt as if the rest of the world had ceased to exist—as if there were only the two of them. Oh, how he wished he could touch her. Properly touch her.

"Valentin?" Her voice had grown husky.

"Hmm?" He looked up and saw raw hunger reflected back at him. Desire punched through him and his voice was less than steady when he spoke. "Please tell me you're thinking what I'm thinking?"

A playful look stole across her face. "Well, that depends. Maybe you should tell me what you're thinking?"

"I've always preferred actions over words."

"Show me, then."

Nine

Valentin didn't need telling twice. He rose from his seat and reached for Imogene, pulling her up into his arms and against his body. Her do-me heels brought her almost to his height. She hooked her arms around his neck and her lips parted on a short intake of air.

"I didn't make dessert," she whispered. "I kind of hoped…" Her voice trailed away.

"For this?" he asked.

He took her lips with his. There was no finesse to the kiss. It was hard. It was hot. It was wet. It was everything he hoped for, wanted and needed and, judging by the way she responded in kind, it was everything she wanted, too. He could taste the red wine on her lips, her tongue, and the flavor blended with the essential flavor of her. It was something he knew deep on an instinctive level, something he'd missed without realizing it. But she was here now. In his arms. Against his body. Heat flaring between them so they were aware only of each other.

His hands splayed across her bare back. Her skin was heated, as if she burned with a fever. He knew he burned with one. A fever for her. He reached one hand beneath the bottom edge of the dip at her lower back, lower still until he felt the bare curve of her buttocks beneath his touch. His arousal grew painfully hard as skin met skin. She'd sat there, opposite him, in that deceptively prim dress—eating dinner, sipping wine—and all the time with no underwear? Perhaps it was just as well he hadn't known or he might not have been answerable for his actions. But he planned to be answerable for them now.

His fingers flexed against the lush fullness of her, pressing her hard against his straining erection. She sighed into his mouth, running her hands through his hair, her nails scraping lightly against his scalp.

"Yes," she murmured softly. "Do that again."

She ground her hips against him as he did her bidding and cursed gently beneath her breath before she kissed him with a need that screamed how much she wanted him right now. Her tongue swept his mouth, her teeth grazed his lips, her fingers now tightened almost painfully in his hair, tugging him closer to her with each desperate mesh of their lips.

"The couch," he managed to say, pulling her with him as he backed up toward that blessedly close piece of furniture.

He almost fell to the cushions and watched in awe as Imogene spread her legs and moved to straddle his lap. She tugged at his belt, deftly undoing his button and zipper and delving beneath his boxer briefs to release him into her hands. He groaned as her fingers closed around his length and stroked him from base to tip.

"Were you hiding this from me all through dinner?"

she asked with a teasing note to her voice that made him want her all the more.

"Uh-huh."

It was all he could manage as she chose that moment to squeeze him just that little bit tighter. Sensation swamped him, making him tip his head against the back of the couch and groan again. She leaned forward and kissed him, more sweetly this time than before.

"I've missed this," she said softly against his mouth. "I've missed *you*."

He felt her shift and opened his eyes in time to watch her shimmy her dress up over her hips, exposing the cleft of skin at the apex of her thighs and the neatly trimmed thatch of dark red hair above it. She pulled the garment up over her head and let it fall behind her somewhere on the floor. Valentin's fingers ached to reach out for her, to cup her pink-tipped breasts and to roll her nipples between his fingertips. He continued to watch her as she positioned her knees on either side of him on the couch and rose up. He could feel the heat of her body as she hovered over his engorged length. If she didn't do something soon he thought he might be forced to take control. To pull her down onto him until he was buried so deeply he might never want to be separated from her again. To bury his face against her breasts and lave them with the attention they deserved. He licked his lips in anticipation.

"Uh-uh," she cautioned. "I know what you're thinking. You're about to go all he-man on me, aren't you?"

"It's under discussion with my self-control right now," he admitted.

"Well, then, you'll just have to be patient. I've forgotten one very important step."

Imogene gracefully removed herself from straddling

his lap and walked, naked and still in her high heels, to her bag. He cursed himself for being an idiot the second he saw her remove a foil packet. How could he have forgotten contraception? *Because of her, that's how*, he thought, watching her walk back toward him and reassume her position. She quickly sheathed him, her touch a torment as she slid the condom over his length.

"Now, just in case you think you need to take control, I think we'll do this," she murmured as she reached for his hands and pinned them against the back of the couch. "You might be the big boss here, but right now, I'm the boss of you."

And with that she took him inside her body. Her inner muscles tightened almost unbearably around him.

"Oh."

It was all she said before she began to move, her hips tilting and rolling, lifting and dropping until all Valentin could think about was the pleasure that coiled and tightened at that point where they joined. He wouldn't have dreamed it humanly possible but he grew even harder. And try as he might, he couldn't remain an inert recipient of her attention. His hips began to thrust each time she dropped or tilted toward him. He watched her move, saw that moment her climax stole her breath and forced her to close her eyes and ride out the deep-seated rolling paroxysms of pleasure that rippled through her body. And then he saw nothing as he was gripped by his own orgasm, his body jerking and thrusting in unison with the clasp and release of hers. Satisfaction pumping from his center and through to his outer extremities.

Imogene collapsed against him, her breathing harsh, her heart racing and sweat soaking her back. Through the front of his shirt she felt the answering beat of his heart and it occurred to her that while she was completely naked, he was still essentially fully dressed. The concept made her laugh and squeeze against him.

"Well, that's a new take on the concept of office romance, isn't it?" she said lightly.

"Hey, the boss isn't complaining at all," Valentin answered as he nuzzled her neck and nipped her skin lightly with his teeth.

A shiver ran through her body, desire climbing again hard on the heels of what they'd just done together. She rocked against him and an aftershock of pleasure jolted her anew.

"It seems I can't get quite enough of you tonight," she observed, pulling away from him and reaching to loosen his tie. "And it would also seem that I dispensed with a few of the necessaries."

"Such as?"

"Such as ensuring you're as naked as I am. I want to see you, Valentin. I want to touch all of you."

"I'm yours, Imogene," he answered. His voice was deep and steady and there was a look in his eyes that promised that and so much more. "Touch me. Do whatever you want with me on one condition."

"And that is?" She paused in undoing his buttons and chewed her lower lip as she thoughtfully regarded the skin she'd already exposed on his chest.

"You allow me to do exactly what I want with you, too."

"Hmm," she said and cocked her head as if she was giving serious consideration to his words. Ridiculous, really, she thought, when he was still buried deep inside her body. She gave him another squeeze just because she could and just because she really, really wanted to. "I think that sounds reasonable."

A smile spread across his handsome face and Imogene felt herself smiling back in return. Their lovemaking had always been impassioned but sometimes it had been fun, too. She loved that they could banter even in a situation like this.

"Does that mean I can touch you now?" Valentin growled. His eyes were hooded by half-closed lids and if anything it made him look even sexier than before.

"Please do," she said primly, and let her hands fall from his shirt.

She gasped as his palms cupped her breasts, their heat searing the sensitive undersides. His fingers and thumbs closed around the taut peaks of her nipples, squeezing them gently.

"Do you know how much I wanted to do this before?" he demanded.

"Show me," she whispered, barely capable of breathing.

The contrast between the fabric of his trousers beneath her bare legs and the warmth of his skin where he touched her was driving her to distraction. Rough and smooth, man-made and man. Everything collided together to coalesce in a feast of feeling that jumbled through her. Valentin leaned forward, his mouth closing around one nipple while he let one hand slide down to where their bodies met. His fingers brushed over her clitoris, sweeping the already oversensitized bud again and again, driving her upward toward another climax. Just before she rolled over that point and into oblivion, his teeth caught her nipple and he bit lightly against the tender skin. It sent her flying, soaring, her body no longer her own but his to command. She was sobbing when she returned to reality, to the awareness that he'd grown hard inside her again.

And to the knowledge that they were no longer alone.

"Valentin, I have those new figures you wanted."

It was a female voice. One she recognized.

Carla Rogers.

The woman who'd wrecked their marriage. Ice-cold reality doused any lingering remnants of closeness that had existed all too briefly between her and her husband.

"Oh, I'm sorry. I didn't know you had company."

Imogene didn't mistake the vague sneer in the other woman's voice.

"Get out!" Valentin's words were clipped and vehement and laced with a fury that vibrated through him.

His arms closed around Imogene even as she tried to pull away. But he couldn't protect her from the very obvious fact that she was naked, sprawled across her husband's lap, with the tears of emotion wrought from her last orgasm still lingering on her cheeks.

"I said get out!" he repeated.

Behind them, Imogene heard a muffled apology swiftly followed by the sound of his office door closing. Imogene didn't waste any time. She yanked herself off him, bent to grab her dress off the floor and dragged it back over her again. Shock coursed through her veins. *Carla Rogers? Here? Working with Valentin?*

Had he expected she'd never find out? Anger billowed through her, hazing her vision and twisting her mind into a dark and ugly place. She looked across the room toward the makeshift table she'd brought. To the remnants of the meal she'd so lovingly prepared. Bitterness flooded her mouth. She'd been such a bloody fool.

"It's not what you think."

Valentin had straightened his clothing and come up behind her. He rested his hands on her shoulders and started to turn her to face him.

"Don't touch me!" she spit, revulsion filling her as her mind worked overtime.

"Imogene, I can explain."

"Don't you think it's a bit late for that? Seriously, Valentin. Your old mistress? Working here? With you? How long has she been here? How long did you think you could keep that from me? Or maybe I've got it all wrong. Maybe she's not your *old* mistress after all. Maybe you never ended your affair with her." She closed her eyes and swallowed hard against the lump in her throat that threatened to choke her. When she could speak again, she opened her eyes and fixed Valentin with a fierce glare. She swept her hands out to encompass all the hard work she'd done to make the evening special for them. "Well, I hope the two of you get a damn good laugh about all this. I'm sure you must think I'm pathetic."

"Pathetic? That's the furthest thing from what I think about you. And Carla? She's not my mistress. She wasn't seven years ago and she's not now. Believe me, Genie."

Not so much as a *please* in there, she noted as fury gripped her, leaving her shaking from head to foot.

"You want me to believe you? To trust you? That's rich," she sneered, her words dripping with revulsion and scorn. "That woman walked in on us having sex on your office couch. Have you any idea how that makes me feel? How can you possibly expect me to believe you? You had contact with her every day back then and it seems you still have contact with her every day now. Excuse me if I find it a little hard to put any confidence in what you say."

She reached for her coat and yanked it on, trying to ignore the fact that her entire body was trembling. She couldn't believe she'd been such a fool. That she'd fallen for his earnest promise back at their wedding that he'd never been unfaithful to her. She'd wanted to believe him—to believe *in* him. And all along he and his mistress had been laughing at her behind her back.

Three-month trial or not, as far as she was concerned, this marriage was well and truly on the way to being over. She headed for the door, her bag clutched in one hand. Come morning she'd contact her lawyer and see how quickly she could break the lease and return to her brownstone. She wanted to be out from under Valentin's roof as soon as possible. And then she'd see about untangling this mess that was their marriage.

"Stop, Imogene. Don't go. Not like this."

His words came out as commands, putting her back up even more. Right now he should be groveling. Begging her forgiveness. Instead, he stood there, perfectly composed. Tall and aloof as always. And so darn handsome her heart broke all over again at his betrayal.

"Don't tell me what to do," she retorted. She made a sound of absolute disgust. "For goodness' sake, she probably even sees more of you than I do! Clearly we should have obeyed our first instincts back in Port Ludlow. Remarrying was a mistake."

"Look, I'm sorry. It came out wrong. I never lied to you about Carla. That much is true."

"But you didn't exactly rush to tell me you two continue to be work colleagues. Did she come back with you from Africa? Have you been nice and cozy together all this time?"

Even as she said the words she began to recognize them for the knee-jerk shock reaction they were. If he was so comfortable with Carla, then why had he put himself in the hands of Alice Horvath and the team at Match Made in Marriage? Why had he tried so hard to convince her to go through with their wedding when both of them hadn't initially wanted it?

Valentin's face grew bleak. "I know you won't believe me—I probably wouldn't believe me, either—but I did mean to tell you about her. When the time was right."

She barked a harsh laugh. "Right? And when would that have been, I wonder?"

Her anger, and the adrenaline that had coursed through her only moments ago, had completely faded now, replaced with overwhelming sorrow laced with exhaustion, both physical and mental.

"I'm going home," she said, dejected. "I can't deal with this right now."

"I'm taking you."

"I'll take a cab."

"I'm taking you home. No argument."

"And the food cart? We should—"

"Forget the damn food cart! I'll get someone to take care of it."

Imogene watched him as he slammed his laptop closed and shoved it in the sinfully soft leather satchel she'd bought for him only last week. Bought with love on her mind and him in her heart. She turned and stared out the window. At the sparkling skyline that had only a short time ago seemed so deliciously romantic. Again, bitterness flooded her mouth along with a deep sense of bereavement for what she thought they'd begun to build together. His voice cut through her thoughts.

"Let's go."

He stood by the door, waiting for her to come to him. His face was like granite, his posture stiff and unyielding. It reminded her very much of the last time she'd confronted him about the ever-present Ms. Rogers. He'd rarely expressed his feelings to her without some kind of shield. The only time she'd ever felt like they'd experienced true honesty with each other was when they'd made love. But now she wondered whether even that had been just another facade after all. She buttoned up the top button of her coat and headed for the door.

Ten

The ride home was completed in utter silence. Valentin hazarded a look at Imogene but her gaze was firmly focused out the side window. When they arrived at their apartment building she didn't wait for him to come around and open her door. She was on the sidewalk and heading to the entrance of the building before he'd even said thank you and good-night to Anton. At least she'd waited for him in the elevator, he conceded to himself reluctantly.

He could feel anger and disappointment pouring off her in waves. He guessed anger was better than tears and recriminations, which was what he thought he'd be forced to bear. A flicker of irritation hovered on the edge of his mind. In fact, it was more than irritation, it was burning up into an anger of his own. At himself. He should never have allowed a situation like that to happen. If he hadn't had the presence of mind to lock his office door, he could at least have had the presence of mind to whisk his wife home before they'd made love so they could have indulged in each other without fear of being interrupted.

His body tightened on the memory of seeing her straddle him. Of watching her strip away her dress and reveal her beautiful body to his gaze. Of hearing the sounds she made, the expression on her face.

And it had all been destroyed in a careless moment that was entirely his fault.

"I'm sorry that I put you through that," he said stiffly as the elevator car traveled to the top floor. "It was unnecessary."

She looked at him incredulously. *"Unnecessary?"* she repeated. "Your mistress walks in on us and you say it was unnecessary? Wow. You really have some gall."

The elevator doors slid open and Imogene strode into the foyer and turned immediately down the hall toward her bedroom.

"Imogene, wait. Please, we need to discuss this."

He heard her mutter, "Now he says please?"

It took her a few seconds, but she stopped and turned around.

"Honestly, Valentin. If you want this marriage to stand any chance of success—*any*—she has to go."

"Look, you're jealous, I understand that."

Imogene's face took on a scary expression as she marched back toward him. "*Jealous?* You think that's what it is? That woman deliberately destroyed our marriage seven years ago. What part of that don't you understand? Or maybe it's that you won't understand it. Maybe you can't do without her in your life. Well, I have news for you. It's her, or it's me. You cannot have us both."

"You're being childish," he responded, giving his

anger a voice. "She's an integral part of Horvath Pharmaceuticals."

"Well, then, she'll have no trouble finding another job somewhere else. I'm sure you'll give her a glowing reference on all aspects of her apparently unique talents. Now, if you'll excuse me—I desperately need a shower. I feel disgusting."

She spun on one exquisitely turned heel and stalked to her room. Valentin started to follow her but realized it would be futile. Why did she have to continue to beat that old drum as far as Carla was concerned? He had no feelings for the other woman beyond those of one colleague to another. Carla had a sharp mind, and her medical background and ability to problem solve made her excellent in her role as head of research and development. And her ability to do her job well was what made their teamwork so cohesive, and that was great for Horvath Pharmaceuticals, period. It had nothing to do with the very brief sexual relationship they'd had in Africa before Imogene even arrived on the continent.

And once she had... Well, no one else had existed for him after that. Then or since. But despite that, as he went to bed, he was left wondering if the perceived sins of the past could not be forgiven or forgotten after all.

When he rose the next morning Imogene had already left for work. Valentin was in a less-than-good mood when he went to the kitchen for his morning coffee. Dion took one look at his face and immediately poured one for him and put the mug in front of him at the breakfast bar.

"Last night not go so well?" he tentatively asked.

"The meal was fantastic. Thank you for helping Imogene organize it," Valentin managed in a civil tongue.

Dion hovered, obviously waiting in case Valentin

had more to add. For a moment Valentin felt tempted to confide in the older man, who he knew had enjoyed more than forty years of marital happiness before his wife passed away, but he wasn't used to sharing personal challenges with anyone and this was more personal than most. Instead, he ate the breakfast provided to him, thanked Dion, then went on his way to work. The problems he'd been working on last night still required his urgent attention.

And his relationship with Imogene? Didn't that require his urgent attention, too? he asked himself in the car on the way to work. Of course it did, but maybe he needed help. An impartial observer to bounce ideas off. Maybe he should call Alice and let her know she'd made a monumental mistake by matching them. But then again, things had remained strained between them and he wasn't in the mood for a lecture à la Alice. Nor, after having convinced Imogene to go ahead with the wedding a month ago, was he in the mood to admit to his grandmother that he was the one who had failed. Again. His mind rejected the idea completely. He wasn't the type to go to others for help. He solved everything himself. And he'd solve this, too.

Eventually.

Imogene fumed at her desk, furious with herself for not being able to compartmentalize her brain enough to focus on the work in front of her. She should have waited at home this morning and confronted Valentin. Cleared the air. Made her position abundantly clear as to what she wanted and expected of him. She understood that he probably didn't see an issue. It was who and how he was. She knew he didn't easily engage in relationships with people outside his immediate family. But not being prepared to let go the one person who had made Imogene's life absolute hell? That, she couldn't understand.

Last night she'd begun to feel as if they'd established a bridge between their old life and their new one. That they'd created a stable foundation upon which to move forward and to enjoy a normal marriage with all the ups and downs that might bring. But it seemed their foundations remained weak and unstable. Built on sand ready to be washed away by the first storm to roll through and, as far as she was concerned, Carla Rogers was in the ballpark of a Category 5 hurricane.

A message pinged on her computer screen and she hastened to open it. Anything to steer her thoughts from the boiling anger that continued to distract her from what she should be doing. Her eyes widened when she saw the message and she picked up her phone and dialed through to reception.

"Send Ms. Rogers in," she managed to say in a steady voice, resisting the temptation to add, *and put security on standby in case there's a full-on fight.*

She got up from her desk and smoothed the front of her dress, glad she'd chosen severe black with a statement piece of turquoise and silver to wear around her neck. She looked formidable, which was exactly how she wanted to feel when facing her nemesis. Even so, her heart began to hammer in her chest as the door to her office opened, admitting Carla Rogers.

The woman was dressed in a two-piece ensemble that wouldn't have looked out of place on Audrey Hepburn. Her black hair was caught in a chignon and her jewelry was minimal. She looked all business, but Imogene saw the cattiness in her eyes before she composed her expression. It was clear Carla thought Imogene was no more than a mouse to be played with, then discarded at will. Well, if she thought that, she had another think coming, Imogene decided, firming her lips and staring the other woman down.

She remained silent as she gestured for Carla to take a seat opposite her desk and waited for Carla to speak. She didn't have to wait long. After elegantly folding her legs, Carla clasped her hands on her lap and leaned forward slightly.

"I felt I needed to come and apologize," she said with what most people would assume was genuine emotion.

"Is that right?" Imogene refused to give her an inch.

Carla smiled but it failed to reach her eyes. "I'm sorry I walked in on you and Valentin last night. I wasn't expecting to find you there."

"Get to the point, Carla. We both know there's no love lost between us."

"Well, that's a shame, don't you think? We both have such strong links to Valentin. It's a shame we can't work something out like rational adults."

"So you're implying that if I don't want to share my husband with you, I'm the one being irrational?" Imogene allowed a small pitying smile to play around her lips.

"I think we can come to some arrangement. I thought he'd gotten you out of his system but it's clear he can't let either of us go."

Imogene fought the urge to leap over her desk and claw the other woman's eyes out. Instead, she leaned back in her chair, rested her elbows on the armrests and steepled her fingers. She impaled Carla with a baleful glare. "Is that all you came here to say?"

Carla inclined her head, and for the first time some

of the confidence she wore like a carapace around her began to slip.

"I'd like you leave now," Imogene stated bluntly.

"Leave? But we—"

"You've said your piece. I listened. That's all I owe you. Before you go, though, there is one thing. I will *never* share my husband with another woman. If you'd ever truly loved someone, you'd know that and feel exactly the same way. Now, do I need to call security or are you happy to leave under your own steam?"

With a sniff of annoyance, Carla rose from her chair. "You're making a mistake."

"No, *you're* making a mistake. You're assuming I'm still the same scared and insecure young woman you managed to frighten away seven years ago. Well, I have news for you. I'm not. Now, to quote my husband from last night, get out."

"This isn't over, Imogene. Don't think I'm giving up on him that easily—not after all this time."

"Giving up? Well, first of all he would have had to be invested in a relationship with you, wouldn't he? Seems to me that he wouldn't have married me, *again*—" she paused for emphasis "—if he was."

"You don't know anything," the other woman said bitterly before heading for the office door. "You'll be sorry you did this."

After she'd left, Imogene forced herself upright on legs that shook with the aftermath of emotion and headed out to her next meeting. She wasn't sure how she managed to get through the rest of her day, but by the time she'd picked up her laptop case and headed out the office she'd achieved a lot. Maybe she should run on a postconfrontation anger-adrenaline high more often, she told herself as she headed downstairs and hailed a cab. While she'd been in a mild state of shock after Carla left, she felt incredibly empowered. For the first time she felt like she'd taken the upper hand and held on to it, and she was proud of herself for that. Whether Valentin would be so proud was another thing. He'd better not be working late tonight, she quietly seethed, or she'd have no hesitation in bowling up to him at work and having this out there.

It turned out she needn't have worried. He was already home when she entered the apartment, and working in the library. She walked straight in and waited for him to look up.

"I had a visitor today," she began.

"Clearly they did not improve your mood," he observed dryly.

"No, never let it be said that Carla Rogers improves anything," she replied.

She was rewarded with a look of shock on his face.

"Carla came to see you today? I didn't expect that."

"Nor did I, but yes. She said she came to apologize. But then she got to her real agenda. She thought it might be nice if we came to some agreement together."

"An agreement. That sounds reasonable," he said with caution.

"Whereby we *share* you," Imogene enunciated clearly.

The look of shock hardened to granite. "And you said?"

"I told her I didn't share my husband with anyone."

His eyes gleamed; he looked impressed and not a little relieved. "Well, I'm pleased to hear it."

"You don't understand, Valentin. She seems to think she has rights to you and that it's okay to bully me. I set her straight on both counts. However, if you don't support me in this, whatever I say won't carry any weight. She's vicious and she's manipulative. She tore us apart once before and she will do anything in her power to do it again.

"You need to believe me. I said it last night and I'll say it again. Either she goes, or I will. I will not have a ménage marriage."

"I'm not suggesting anything of the kind. I want this to work as much as you do." He got up from his desk and crossed the floor toward her to take her hands in his. "Imogene, last night was incredibly special to me. *You* are incredibly special to me. I want this to be forever."

She tugged her hands free. "Words are easy enough to say, Valentin. It's action I need to see. I don't want her working with you. That's it."

"So my promise to you, to remain faithful only unto you—that isn't enough?"

Imogene only wished it were. She knew that he saw her as unnecessarily obsessed with the other woman but was it too much to ask him to see things from her side?

"Not when she's around."

"So you expect me to let go a member of staff who is not only a valuable team leader but instrumental in the current talks we're having for a global supply contract with an international aid organization."

Imogene held her ground and nodded. "I most certainly do."

"Even if I told you that I love you? That I've only ever loved you?"

Eleven

She stood there in shock. She'd wished to hear those words from his lips again, but had feared it would never happen. And now, while they were fighting over someone else, he threw them into the conversation, just like that? She didn't know what to do. She'd imagined when they exchanged these words it would be over something special, something meaningful to them both. Not that they'd be used as ammunition so he didn't have to disrupt the impeccably smooth running of his workplace. She blinked back unexpected tears.

"That's not fair. You can't use love against me like that," she said in a voice that was barely above a whisper.

"Not fair? It's the truth. I've always loved you, Imogene. Remarrying you has only served to underscore that for me all over again. I don't want anyone else. Only you. Always you."

Imogene felt as if her chest were being torn open. She would have given anything for these words seven years ago. She would have had the strength to stay and fight for her husband, for their marriage, instead of running away. But she was the one who'd found Carla in her bed while someone showered in their bathroom. She'd assumed it was Valentin and, shouldering all the deeply embedded damage of a child of an unfaithful parent, she'd run from the hurt and injustice of what she thought she'd seen.

A month ago, at their wedding, he'd emphatically reiterated to her that the person in the bathroom hadn't been him, and she'd wanted so much to believe him. To believe they had a second chance. But if he was being honest and he truly thought he loved her, then it wasn't enough. He needed to show her this time. To prove he meant it. She would settle for absolutely nothing less.

Valentin lifted one hand to her face and gently cupped her cheek, forcing her to look directly at him. "Imogene, I mean every word. But if we are to make this work, you have to trust me. I have no feelings for Carla other than the respect of one colleague for another—that's basically all there has ever been between us. I can't jeopardize everything we've been working for by releasing her from her employment contract right now."

His touch was tender but his words were like bullets to her soul.

"So basically you're telling me you're not prepared to do anything," she said, fighting to keep her voice even.

"I will talk to her tomorrow. Discuss what you've told me."

Imogene pulled away from him. "Discuss all you want. It won't change a thing as far as she's concerned. And until you can see that, too, we don't stand a chance." She started to head out the library but then stopped in the doorway. "Valentin, tell me this. What do you think she stood to gain when, back in Africa, she one hundred percent led me to believe it was you in the bathroom showering off the sweat of your lovemaking with her? Why would she have lied about that then if it wasn't her intention all along to have you to herself? Anyone else would have given up and moved on when we married for a second time, but for some reason she can't let you go. Carla Rogers is a predator and she has you very firmly in her sights. If you can't see that, then I'm sorry but you must be completely blind."

Valentin rubbed at his eyes. He'd endured another sleepless night, in the end going into the home gym and pounding out some miles on the treadmill to wear himself out. With every stride, one question continued to repeat in his head and had been there again at the forefront of his thoughts on waking. Why wasn't his love enough for Imogene? Maybe she was right after all. Maybe they didn't have a future together. As far as he saw it he was doing everything reasonably possible to rebuild their relationship, but her preoccupation with Carla Rogers made her appear slightly unhinged. So he was going to the source—Carla Rogers—who would be here in his office at any moment.

A sound at the door made him turn away from the window.

"You wanted to see me?" Carla said as she walked toward his desk.

She looked, as ever, perfectly composed. He'd seen this woman in the most dire and urgent of trauma circumstances when a gang war had blown up in the African city they'd been assigned to work in, and through all the blood and the chaos she'd been a rock of calm and reason. She was, like him, a person dedicated to their work, whether it be a hands-on situation like multiple patients with horrendous injuries or the development of a new product that would have far-reaching implications in developing countries. He'd come to rely on her—then as much as now—and he couldn't see his working life without her. Correction, he didn't want to see his working life without her, a voice that sounded suspiciously like Imogene's chided in his head. He pushed the thought aside and smiled at Carla.

"Thank you for coming. I know you're busy."

"I always have time for you, Valentin. You know that."

He hated that he suddenly couldn't take her words at face value. That the things Imogene had said to him last night, and the night before, made him twist what Carla said and look at it from a different angle. Did she have another agenda? Was that innuendo in her tone? He looked carefully at her perfectly made-up face and into the dark eyes that were the window to her brilliant mind, and saw nothing but the familiar features he'd known now for more than eight years. He sucked in a deep breath and chose his words carefully. No point in sugarcoating them. Carla was the kind of woman who came straight to the point, and he owed it to her to be equally up-front.

"I understand you went to visit Imogene at her office yesterday," he started.

To his surprise, Carla laughed.

"Oh, so she told you about that, did she?"

"Did you expect she wouldn't? We don't keep secrets from each other."

"Oh, I don't expect you think you do."

He was affronted by her choice of words. "What do you mean by that?"

"I suppose she told you I surprised her with my visit." Carla paused, looking at him for a response. When none was forthcoming, she carried on. "She summoned me to her office. I was quite surprised. But she's your wife, and even though it took me away from precious hours here at work, I thought it must be important. So I went. I have to say, I was shocked. She was extremely rude to me. Told me I should start looking for another job because she didn't want me anywhere near you. It's ridiculous really, when we both know you have no possible grounds to rescind my employment contract. Your wife has a serious problem with jealousy, Valentin. She acted crazy. And to think she's involved in the childcare industry? It's all bit scary, to be honest."

Valentin hid his shock with a great deal of effort. Which woman was telling the truth? The behavior Carla had described didn't sound like the Imogene he knew, but then again, how well did he really know her? Their first marriage had been conducted after only a few short weeks of knowing each other. And those weeks had been driven by lust and passion and a heightened sense of drama in a city that was under constant threat. It had hardly been a normal courtship. And nor had their marriage been, either. The time they'd managed to spend together was short and sweet, and there'd been little room for long and meaningful discussions. Not when they couldn't keep their hands off each other. Until Imogene had believed he'd rekindled his relationship with Carla. At that point, yes, she'd been unreasonable.

His heart told him he needed to believe his wife, but logic—his fallback in any situation—told him to stand by his employee. Someone he'd worked with and whom he trusted implicitly. Neither answer sat comfortably on his shoulders but there had to be a middle ground there somewhere. Surely.

"It's not the story she gave you, is it?" Carla asked with one arched brow.

"There are some differences, yes," he reluctantly admitted. "I will discuss it with her further."

"Don't bother. Honestly, if you were my husband and the situation were reversed, I'd probably be staking my claim, too."

There was a note of truth that rang loud and clear in her words.

"Staking your claim?" He forced a laugh. "Kind of makes it sound like I don't have a choice in all this. I have to say, I feel a bit like a bone caught between two dogs."

"Don't you mean two bitches?" Carla asked impishly.

This time his humor didn't have to be forced. "Well, since you put it that way. Not that either of you are, of course."

"Of course not," Carla all but purred.

For some reason, her manner brushed his nerves the wrong way. Like fingers running against a velvet pile.

"Now that I have you here, let's finalize the budget predictions we've been working on," he said, determined to change the subject.

In an instant she was all business, something he was grateful for, because throughout their discussion he'd found himself wanting to believe her, yet not quite managing to. Could it be that Imogene had told him the truth, or had it simply been her version of the truth? Somehow, he had to figure it out.

That night Valentin made certain he was home on time because they were expected for dinner at Imogene's parents' house. After a day mulling over what Imogene and Carla had said, he was no closer to working out which woman had given him the real turn of events in Imogene's office, and things remained strained between him and his wife as they were driven to her parents' apartment building.

"You didn't tell me your mom and dad lived so close to us," Valentin commented as they pulled up at the prestigious Fifth Avenue address.

Imogene merely shrugged. "Is it important?"

"They are your parents."

"Yes, but we don't spend a lot of time together. Dad's always busy. Mom, too."

"Your dad's a human rights lawyer, isn't he?"

"Yes, one of the best. It puts him in demand. So much so, I'm surprised tonight wasn't postponed, like things like this usually are."

Valentin heard a note of weary resignation in her voice that pricked at him unexpectedly. In their first marriage he'd rarely been home when he said he would. Every day, emergencies had arisen that had required his immediate attention. His, or his ego's? a little voice asked from the back of his mind. He had been part of a team. Not the only trauma surgeon in the hospital. And always on call if he'd been needed. But he had to admit, he'd enjoyed the urgency of the ER. Excelled under the pressure of time-sensitive situations. A lot of people accused surgeons of having a God complex, but the truth was they did literally hold the life of another human being in their hands at times. It had been an adrenaline rush, he couldn't deny it. And he'd loved his work wholeheartedly. Still did, although what he did now was so different.

As much as he professed to love his wife?

It was not the same, he argued internally as they entered the building on Fifth and took the elevator to her parents' apartment. Beside him, he felt Imogene stiffen.

"Everything okay?"

"About as okay as it gets, I suppose."

She appeared to brace herself as the elevator doors slid open and they walked together down the paneled hall to a set of wooden double doors. She'd no sooner pressed the buzzer than her mother swung the door open for them. Caroline O'Connor was a beautiful woman. In her early fifties, she clearly had been able to enjoy the best of everything when it came to personal grooming. Her hair was a few shades lighter than her daughter's, but her clear gray-green eyes were the same.

"Mrs. O'Connor," Valentin said, as they entered the vestibule and he put out his hand. "It's a pleasure to see you again."

"Oh, I don't think we need to stand on ceremony, do you?" The older woman gave him a smile and, ignoring his outstretched hand, reached up to plant a swift kiss near his cheek. "After all, we're family now. Call me Caroline, please."

"Caroline," he repeated with a quick smile.

"Is Dad home yet?" Imogene asked, looking past her mother into the large empty sitting room beyond.

"Not yet. There's been a little holdup. You know what he's like," her mother said smoothly but with a look of censure at her daughter.

Imogene ignored the silent caution. "Honestly, Mom, he could have made an effort for us. It's the first time he's getting to meet Valentin. Anyone would think he didn't care we've gotten married."

Caroline started to protest but Valentin stepped smoothly in, touching Imogene on the shoulder. "Don't worry. I know what it's like when you get caught up at work."

"Yes, you do, don't you?" Imogene said pointedly before stepping away and shrugging off her coat to hang it in a cupboard off to one side.

Valentin bit back the retort that sprang to his lips. He wasn't going to point out to his wife that lately she'd been home at erratic hours herself and he certainly wasn't going to enter into a debate in front of her mother. Caroline stood looking from her daughter to him and back again, a small worried frown creasing her almost impossibly smooth brow.

"You have a lovely home," Valentin said to her in an attempt to break the growing tension. "Have you lived here long?"

"Our entire married life," Caroline said with an ease he was sure was well practiced. "When Howard and I moved in here we only had this floor, but when another apartment came available above us, he bought that also and converted this into a duplex. Would you like me to show you around? Dinner won't be for another hour. We'll still have time for a nice drink before we dine."

Valentin looked across at Imogene, who shrugged again much as she'd done in the elevator before. "Do what you want," she said. "I'm going to check on what Susan's preparing for us."

The tour of the seven-bedroom apartment took longer than he expected, or maybe it was just because Caroline was very clearly stalling to mask the absence of her husband. By the time they returned to the sitting room, Imogene was seated in one of the expensively upholstered easy chairs with an almost empty glass of wine in her hand.

"I was beginning to think I'd have to send out a

search party," she said, rising to her feet. "Shall I get you each a drink?"

"Thank you, darling," her mother said, allowing Imogene to assume hostess duties.

Once their aperitifs were finished a uniformed maid called them to the dining room. Still no sign of Mr. O'Connor, Valentin noted with sympathy for his new mother-in-law, who'd done her best to fill the void left by her husband by steering the conversation seamlessly before dinner. They'd just begun their appetizers when the sound of the front door banging shut echoed through the apartment.

In moments the energy of the room changed with both women sitting just a little straighter. There was an expression of hopeful relief on Caroline's face and one of annoyance on her daughter's.

"Be nice," Caroline had time to hiss across the table to Imogene before Howard O'Connor entered the room.

"Sorry I'm late, people. Couldn't be avoided. I'm sorry. You must be my new son-in-law," he said smoothly, as if meeting the man his only daughter had married was a frequent occurrence. Valentin stood and offered his hand. "Or should I say recycled son-in-law," Howard added with a hearty laugh at his own attempt at humor.

Valentin tried not to bristle. For someone who ought to be adept at diplomacy, the man was trying far too hard. "It's good to meet you at last, sir."

"And you, Horvath. And you."

Howard turned his attention to Imogene, who sat quietly at the table, but not before Valentin noticed a lingering hint of a woman's fragrance around his host. His nostrils flared as he analyzed it and came to a rapid conclusion. He'd smelled the subtle scent Caroline O'Connor wore as she'd shown him around the apartment. This was entirely different. The man had obviously not been tied up at work—unless work entailed being in very close, possibly intimate, contact with another woman. At the table, Caroline laughed brittlely at something her husband said, her eyes not leaving him for a second. Her daughter, on the other hand, stared at her plate.

Was that what lay behind Imogene's insecurity around him? Was Howard O'Connor an unfaithful husband and all-too-absent father? Suddenly Imogene's obsession with fidelity and her issues with trust were coming into very clear focus indeed.

Twelve

They'd just had their main dishes brought to the table when Howard's cell phone began to chime insistently. Excusing himself, he rose from his chair and left the room. Valentin heard his voice recede down the hallway, then grow more muffled as he closed a door behind him.

"Sorry about that," Caroline said. "We've had to learn to share him with his work. Well, it's more of a vocation, really. A calling. You must feel the same with your medical background, Valentin."

Valentin looked across at Imogene, who stared evenly back at him. He could usually read his wife, who was becoming accustomed to the nuances in her expression. But right now she was a blank canvas.

"I don't know why you keep apologizing for him, Mom," she said, not taking her eyes from Valentin's. "You know we play second fiddle to Dad's other…interests."

The words were crushing but Valentin could hear

the pain behind them. And the warning. She'd grown up with this. She was not going to tolerate it in her own marriage. Dessert became an exercise in diplomacy as Valentin attempted to temper his wife's darkening mood with her mother's overeager attempts to cover the glaring absence of her husband. It was a relief when it was all over.

By the time they returned home, Valentin knew they had to talk this out before it grew into a black hole between them.

"Have you got time for a nightcap?" he asked as he helped her out of her coat. "I'd like to talk."

"I thought you might," she said. "Make mine a brandy. I think I'm going to need it."

There was an attitude about her now, as if nothing and no one could break her. But he knew only too well how fragile she was and how shaky the barriers she'd erected around her.

"Brandy it is," he agreed.

By silent mutual consent they went into the library and Valentin poured them each a measure of brandy before joining her on the sofa.

"That was a tough night for you," he said without preamble.

"You think that was tough? Sadly, that was normal. At least, that's what my mother thinks. I don't know why she puts up with it." She shook her head before taking a sip of her drink. "No, that's not true. I know exactly why she puts up with it. I don't think she loves my father any more than he loves her. They both, however, love the illusion of a stable marriage and the lifestyle my father's income allows them to enjoy."

She sounded so bitter. So damaged. It made his chest ache to hear her speak that way. He decided to get straight to the point. "Has your father always been unfaithful?"

She looked at him and raised her brows. "You noticed that already, did you?"

"Well, kind of hard not to when he came home smelling of some other woman's perfume."

"He used to shower before coming home. Now he doesn't care enough to hide it. Mom just turns the other cheek. She's fought long and hard for her position in society and her home. She's not about to rock that boat for the sake of his mistress of the hour."

What kind of upbringing had Imogene had for this kind of behavior to be so accepted, so normal? He felt sorry for her having had to grow up with that. His own father had been a workaholic but he'd loved his wife fiercely and protected what family time he could carve out.

"I'm sorry, Imogene. You deserve better."

"Yes, I do," she agreed emphatically. "Look, it might be a situation that my mother is happy to tolerate, but I've seen what it's done to her over the years. She might have loved my father in the beginning, but bit by bit that's slowly died. When something isn't nurtured, shared and encouraged, what else can it do? They have nothing in common anymore aside from their desire to present the perfect facade to the world. Mom acts as hostess when he entertains foreign visitors and he acts the devoted husband when anybody else is watching."

"He was hardly the devoted husband this evening," Valentin felt obliged to point out.

"That's because he stands to gain nothing from his association with you. You're merely my husband, and in my father's eyes his family comes a very solid last in any bid for his attention. I learned that from the cradle, Valentin. I will not subject my children to the same thing."

The warning in her voice was loud and clear.

"I will be here for our children, Imogene. And for you."

"You're making the assumption that our marriage will last."

He bristled slightly. "There's no reason why it won't."

"There is one," she answered sharply. "One you either won't see, or refuse to admit to."

"Look, let me make it absolutely clear to you. I am not your father. I'm nothing like him. I am and have always been faithful to you. I know you believe you saw evidence to the contrary and I know you were left hurt and bewildered. I acted selfishly when we were in Africa. I put my work ahead of you because I didn't realize how tenuous our relationship was. That was my fault. Giving Carla the keys to our place so she could sleep was my fault. I had no idea she'd use the opportunity for some tryst and I'm sorry you were led to believe I was involved in that tryst. I don't know how much more often I have to tell you that before you believe me."

Imogene stared into his eyes, her face softening. "I want to believe you, Valentin. If I didn't think I could believe you I wouldn't have married you. But she's still in your life. Still making trouble between us. As long as she's there, there will always be trouble. Can't you see that? Look, my father has had several mistresses during his marriage to my mom. Because he doesn't love them, he doesn't see that as being unfaithful. In fact, he's convinced himself that he's not. But fidelity is everything to me. *Everything.*"

"You have my promise, Imogene. There is no one else but you for me. I really want you to believe that. I love you and I want a life with you, children with you."

"Like I said, I want to believe you, Valentin—" she began.

"Then believe me. That's all it takes," he urged.

"I wish it were as simple as that."

"We can make it that simple."

He reached across and took her glass from her and put it on the coffee table beside his own. Then, cupping her face gently, he kissed her. There was no heat in the kiss, nothing like the passion that had overwhelmed them the other night. Nothing but a steadfast reassurance that he was here for her. Her man. No one else's. Her lips trembled beneath his, parting as his tongue traced the fullness of them. As he ended the kiss and pulled back, he looked into her eyes and made a silent promise. Come what may, he would convince her of his love for her. They would succeed on this rocky journey of theirs and they'd come out stronger at the end as a result of it.

He got to his feet, holding out a hand to her. "Sleep with me tonight."

"I don't know, Valentin."

"Just sleep. Nothing more. I want you in my arms, in my bed. With me and beside me."

"Okay," she agreed.

She took his hand and together they walked down the hallway to the master suite. While she used the bathroom, he turned down the bed, and on her return he helped her undress.

"Hop into bed, I'll only be a minute," he said, heading for the bathroom himself.

He heard the rustle of the sheets as she did as he suggested. When he returned to the bedroom she was lying back on a pillow, sheets tucked up to her chin and her body rigid with tension. He shucked off his clothes and slid into the bed beside her, reaching for her and pulling her against him. He pressed a kiss against her nape, inhaling the scent of her hair, her skin.

"Good night, Imogene. We'll work this out."

She didn't respond and for a while he began to wonder if she would, but then he heard a softly uttered "G'night."

He smiled in the darkness. He understood now why she was so adamant about the situation with Carla. After what had happened in Africa and with her own father's less-than-stellar example, Imogene felt vulnerable. Afraid to trust. Well, he had to earn that back from her—somehow, someway. He felt her begin to relax incrementally in his arms and listened as her breathing slowed until she was finally asleep.

Valentin lay there for ages, wondering if she'd ever feel secure with him. She said she wanted to believe him but in light of the conditioning she'd had growing up, could she ever really trust anyone? He hoped so, because he wasn't fooling himself about fidelity like Howard O'Connor was. But given how Imogene felt, could she be rational about the subject? Their first attempt at marriage had been anything but rational, and now, thinking about it, he was reminded of the conversation he'd had with Carla earlier today and of what she'd said about Imogene. Tonight had hardly been the time to bring that up with his wife, but how on earth was he going to get to the root of the issue without discussing it with her?

If he could be certain Carla was the one who lied, then he would obviously not be able to trust her again. It would be much easier to insist on her exit from Horvath Pharmaceuticals. But if she'd been telling the truth… what then?

* * *

Imogene woke the next morning to find herself alone in bed. In Valentin's bed, she realized sleepily. She hadn't slept that deeply in a long time. She stretched out, then started in surprise as Valentin strode naked from the bathroom. Her eyes hungrily roamed his body. For someone who put in long hours in what was essentially a sedentary job, he still managed to find time to work out. His body was beautiful, from the breadth of his powerful shoulders all the way past his hips and lower. She felt her mouth go dry and swallowed, hard.

"Good morning," he said with a smile that told her he hadn't missed her detailed perusal of his body and that he also didn't mind one little bit. "Sleep well?"

"Really well, thank you."

She struggled to sit up against the pillows and tugged the bedsheets up with her.

"Don't bother on my account," he teased as he walked to an antique tallboy and pulled out a drawer.

A flush of color heated her cheeks at his words. They were hardly strangers to each other and yet she felt uncomfortable being naked in front of him this morning, as if it left her feeling too exposed. In light of their conversation last night, it was no wonder. She'd shared truths with him she'd never shared with anyone else. Growing up, all her friends had envied her the fact her parents had the perfect marriage. It was an ironic analogy, she thought, that here she was, hiding beneath the sheets, much as she hid so much of herself, while her husband strode confident and naked about the bedroom. Could she take that to mean that he was being as open and honest about everything, his feelings for her included, as he was with his body?

"Which one?" Valentin said abruptly, turning to face her and holding a silk tie in each hand.

For a second her mind wandered, thinking of a suggestion she could make to him for using both ties, but she quickly pushed it away. "Depends on your suit, I guess. And your shirt."

"Navy and plain white."

"Then the red and navy broad stripes."

"Thanks."

With that he pushed the other tie back in the drawer and went through to the bathroom. She heard the dressing room door on the other side of the bathroom close. Imogene lay back in the bed and realized her heart was racing. What had just happened? Their exchange had been so normal and yet here she was as nervous as a mouse in a room full of cats. She got up from the bed and wrapped the sheet around her before picking up her clothes and heading down the hall to her bedroom. After a quick shower and getting dressed in a tailored pantsuit for work, she went through to the kitchen. Valentin was already there, sipping his coffee at the breakfast bar.

"I'll be late home tonight. My new CEO is shadowing me for the day and we're visiting our New York centers before spending the rest of the afternoon in the office."

"Thanks for the heads-up," Valentin replied before getting up and taking his cup to the sink. "I'll wait up for you."

"You don't need to do that," she said. "I don't know how late I'll be."

"Yes, I do. I'll see you tonight."

He kissed her on the lips, hard and swift, and then he was gone. Imogene stared in his wake, wondering what the heck had just happened. She was interrupted by Dion coming through from the butler's pantry.

"An omelet this morning, Mrs. Horvath?"

"No, thank you, Dion. Just coffee this morning."

He tsk-tsked under his breath as he poured her coffee with cream, just the way she liked it. She downed the coffee, only barely tasting it, then collected her computer case and headed out the door.

She was early to the office but even so her new CEO had beaten her in. She smiled as she walked toward him, knowing that the board of directors had made an excellent choice in Eric Grafton. A Columbia graduate, he'd gained a strong reputation across a range of businesses—every last one of them becoming more successful than they'd been before he took charge. She couldn't complain about that. And he was a genuinely nice guy. Married to his high school sweetheart, with two daughters of his own, he seemed to have found the perfect balance between life and career. She envied him that, she realized.

"Eric, good to see you," she said, walking toward him with her hand outstretched.

His clasp was warm and strong, much like the image he portrayed.

As they discussed their plans for the weeks ahead her mind kept drifting back to Valentin and last night. It had been comforting to sleep in his arms and had given her hope they were on the right track together. They had better be, she thought as she glanced at the man who was taking over her role here in the company she'd created. In this, at least, she was confident she was leaving her business in good hands. If only she could be as confident about her private life.

The next few weeks became a blur of center visits

across the country, traveling with Eric and introducing him to the franchise holders nationwide. She hated being away from Valentin, but it couldn't be avoided. They hadn't slept together again since that night after dinner at her parents', and she found herself missing him at unexpected moments. Still, it wouldn't be for much longer, she told herself. Once she was back in the classroom her hours would be more regular.

And the three-month trial period of their marriage would be looming, she realized. The thought of walking away from Valentin made her feel physically ill, but as far as she was aware he was still working with Carla. Of course she understood that if he was to let the other woman go, there would have to be an exit strategy. As much as she disliked and distrusted Carla, she knew she couldn't simply be turned out of her job and onto the streets. Due process needed to be followed. But was Valentin even doing anything about it, or was he simply allowing things to continue as they had before? She knew she needed to discuss it with him, but the opportunity hadn't arisen and with her hours lately they'd become ships in the night. Much like they had in the early days of their marriage before she'd taken the bull by the horns and taken dinner to him in his office.

She made an involuntary sound as her body clenched tight in response to the memory of that night.

"Everything okay?" Eric asked from beside her in the cab as they headed from the airport back to their office.

"Fine, thanks," she managed smoothly.

It was hard to think about that night without thinking about what had happened next. And her confrontation with Valentin over Carla. They remained at an impasse and she didn't like it one bit. She was going to have a make a decision in the next few weeks, whether she liked it or not. Stay, and potentially put herself in the same position her mother lived in—because she had no doubt that Carla Rogers would not retract her claws from what she saw as her proprietary interest in Valentin—or walk away. Imogene felt her stomach flip uncomfortably as she accepted that if she was to be true to herself, she really only had one option, and it just about broke her heart to admit it.

Thirteen

He missed her.

Seeing Imogene work such long hours, coming home late at night and worn-out, gave him a new appreciation for how hard she worked and also reminded him of what she'd had to put up with from him in the early days of their marriage. He didn't like it, not one bit, but having some understanding of what she had gone through made him vow to strive to keep more regular hours at the office, and to encourage his staff to do the same. But on a personal basis, the days of separation were creating their own issues—widening the gulf that had developed between them even further. They didn't even have an opportunity to talk to each other beyond the basics of common courtesy. They'd gone from trying to build a marriage to living like a pair of roommates and it made him feel a difficult combination of emotions. He, who had always been the calm in a storm, had become short-tempered at work and taciturn here at home. Even with Dion, who had done nothing wrong, Valentin had snapped unnecessarily—like when he'd very reasonably asked him if Imogene would be home for dinner.

He walked over to the window overlooking the park and took in a deep breath. This unreasonable, moody behavior wasn't him. Worse, he knew precisely why he was behaving this way. He was afraid his marriage was dying before it even had a chance to live. He had to do something, but what? How did a man woo back his woman when they barely spent any time together?

Make time for each other, a little voice in the back of his head prodded him none too gently. A light bulb went off. She'd brought him dinner at work when he was working late; the least he could do for her was the very same thing.

"Dion!" he shouted as he strode out of his office.

"Yes, Mr. Horvath?" Dion said, wiping his hands on an apron as he came into the hall from the kitchen.

"First, I need to apologize to you for being a bear this evening…well, every evening these past few weeks."

"That's all right, sir. I know you're missing Mrs. Horvath."

"You do?"

"Of course, it's only natural. She's missing you, too. But if you'll excuse me for being forward, neither of you seem to know what to do about it."

"You're right," Valentin agreed. "We've been married before, to each other, and it all blew up in our faces. Now I think we're both too wary to fully commit again."

"Understandable, sir. No one enters into these things expecting or wanting to be hurt again. But love brings vulnerability and at a certain point you need to surrender to that to give love a chance."

His words sank deep. "You're very wise, Dion. You must miss your wife a lot."

"With every breath, sir. Now, what else was it that you wanted?"

"I thought I might return the favor to Imogene and take dinner to her at work."

A large smile split Dion's lined face. "That's an excellent idea, sir. I'll get on it straightaway."

Dion was as good as his word. Within an hour he had a fragrant meal of spaghetti Bolognese together with salad and a wrapped loaf of warm, fresh bread.

"Did you want to use the trolley, sir, or the thermal picnic pack?"

Valentin thought about the night Imogene had brought dinner to him and how special it had been dining by his office window. But this time he wanted to make it different, and hopefully achieve an ending that was far less traumatic than the last one had been.

"No, I think I'll just wing it and use the pack, but perhaps take a tablecloth or blanket, as well?"

"I have just the things, sir."

Fifteen minutes later Valentin was in the elevator of Imogene's building and heading to her floor. The doors pinged open, revealing a large open-plan office space with several individual offices lining the outside edge. Not a soul was around, and most of the lighting was dimmed, but over in a far corner, Valentin made out a glow of light. He struck out toward it, realizing he really should have shown more interest in Imogene's work and workplace before now. In fact, coming here, not knowing exactly where he was going, was like holding up a mirror to how he'd been treating his marriage so far.

He had to do better. All along he'd been saying he was invested in making their union work when he'd really only been going through the motions, not taking an active part in making things work. He'd slid back into his old habits and had made few changes to his life to accommodate the fact that he was, once again, married.

With the promise of doing better echoing in his mind, he reached the door of the lit office and looked inside. Two heads were bent close together at the large desk over by the window. Very close together. Suddenly Valentin had an all-too-vivid realization of what Imogene had been going through with him continuing to work with Carla, because a vicious surge of jealousy cut through him like a hot knife through butter. He must have made some kind of noise because simultaneously, the two heads looked up and straight at him. Imogene seemed at first shocked, then overjoyed to see him there.

"Valentin, this is a lovely surprise," she said, coming around from the desk and walking quickly toward him.

But when she reached him, she hesitated, as if unsure of what she ought to do next. Given the estrangement they were suffering, it was no wonder, he told himself, and he put down the pack and reached for her, kissing her on the cheek briefly before letting her go.

"I thought I'd bring you dinner," he said, looking straight into her eyes and trying to tell her with so many words unsaid that he was doing his best to take steps to rebuild the bridge that had broken down between them.

"That's so thoughtful of you. Eric and I were just saying we needed to finish what we were doing. Eric, come and meet my husband."

She gestured to the man, now standing beside her desk, and he came forward, hand outstretched. Valentin did his best to remain courteous but it wasn't easy. This was the man Imogene had been spending hours with, traveling overnight with. A man she'd been spending more time with than she'd been spending at home. It was hard not to feel some pangs of envy, especially when they were obviously already close.

"Your wife is quite a woman," Eric said after their initial introductions had been performed. "I'm stunned by what she's achieved with her business and honored I was chosen to fill her shoes as CEO."

"She's quite a woman, all right," Valentin agreed, silently adding, *my woman.*

Eric seemed to pick up on the invisible tension and turned to Imogene. "I'll leave you to it and we can get back to work in the morning. My wife and girls will be waiting for me."

He added the last with a pointed look at Valentin, as if assuring him that he wasn't poaching on his property in any way. Valentin gave him a short nod in acknowledgment.

"Thanks, Eric," Imogene said, looking from one man to the other as if realizing she'd just missed some kind of silent male communication between them.

Once Eric was gone Imogene turned to face Valentin. "What the heck was that all about?"

"You never told me your new CEO is tall, dark, handsome and charming," he said before he could stop himself.

To his surprise, Imogene laughed. "You're kidding me, right? He's also married and a devoted father and not interested in me in that way at all. In fact, he's been a breath of fresh air because he doesn't see me purely as a woman but as a business equal."

Valentin reached for her again, encircling her in his

arms. "He doesn't see you as a woman? Then there is something very seriously wrong with him because you're beautiful."

He bent his head and captured her lips before she could speak and in that brief instant he knew he'd done the right thing in coming here tonight. He needed this, but more than that, he needed her to know—to be sure—that he was here for her, for them. He ended the kiss and reluctantly released her.

"Are you hungry?" he asked, bending to retrieve the picnic pack from the floor.

"Starving. I can't remember when I last ate."

Valentin tsk-tsked under his breath. "You need to look after yourself better," he said, then stopped and corrected himself. "No, *I* need to look after you better."

"I'm a grown woman, Valentin. I can look after myself."

"But that's the thing," he said. "You don't need to do it all yourself. I'm here for you."

"Are you?" she asked, a wary look in her eyes. "I know you're here now, but are you really there for me 24/7?"

She had every right to ask that question. He knew that. And in all honesty, he couldn't tell her he had been.

"Look, we both have work to do in our relationship. You need to trust me but more than that, I need to make it clearer to you that you can." He sucked in a harsh breath and decided to come out with complete honesty. "I hated seeing you here with Eric like that this evening."

"Valen—"

"No, please, hear me out. I refused to understand how you felt about Carla, and that's on me. I've been an idiot. It wasn't until the shoe was on the other foot that I began to get an inkling as to how you've been feeling all this time."

A frown drew lines on her forehead and her eyes reflected her concern. "I don't think you can understand, Valentin. Seeing me working with my replacement, a man who won't be a big part of my life once I've fully stepped down, is nothing compared to you continuing to work with a woman you once were intimate with. A woman who is doing her best to undermine me."

Valentin swallowed. She was right. If Eric had been a part of her past, Valentin would likely have stepped into her office and then engaged in a very unattractive brawl right here with her new CEO. Some Neanderthal part of his brain had gone into overdrive when he'd seen the two of them together, quite without reason. But then reason always had fled when it came to him and Imogene, hadn't it?

"You're right," he said, swallowing the last of his pride. "I may not ever understand fully how much I've hurt you, but I want it to be clear that I never want to hurt you like that ever again. I'll be talking to the Horvath legal department in the morning to see what I can do in terms of letting Carla go or moving her to another office away from New York. Beyond all else, you are the most important person to me and your happiness is my goal."

He saw tears swim in her eyes before pooling and spilling down her cheeks. If she'd cut him with a knife it couldn't have hurt any more than realizing just how much this meant to her and how little attention he'd really paid to it. He'd assumed she was jealous, and, yes, she probably was, but she'd had a valid point. And he'd ignored that, putting his company's interests ahead of his wife's.

"I love you, Imogene. Believe me."

"I believe you," she whispered.

He kissed her again, pulling her close to his body where she fitted against him so perfectly. Their embrace was tender, an affirmation of their commitment to each other. When they parted, Valentin felt like they had forged a new link between them. One that was stronger than before, one that would stand the test of time.

Imogene looked at her husband, seeing his sincerity and feeling a new sense of hope fill the dark empty place that had taken up residence where her heart should be ever since Carla Rogers had walked in on them weeks ago. Maybe they really could make this work. Before she could say anything, her stomach rumbled loudly. Valentin laughed.

"I guess that's my cue to serve dinner," he said.

"I guess it is," she answered, feeling lighter than she had in a long time.

"Where shall we set up?"

"There's the meeting table over there, or we could just sit on the floor by the coffee table." She gestured toward a long sofa that faced a coffee table and two easy chairs.

"Coffee table it is," he said and moved away.

She watched as he set everything up and fell a little more in love with him as he laid their meal out.

"Dion's hard work?" she asked as she settled beside him on the couch and accepted a glass of red wine.

"You really don't want to try my cooking," he replied with a grimace. "So, yeah, it's Dion to the rescue again."

"Thank goodness for Dion," she murmured. "So, shall we make a toast?"

"To us?"

"To us," she affirmed as they clinked glasses and each took a sip of wine.

"Let me look after you," Valentin said, putting his glass back on the table.

"I certainly won't object to that," she said. "It's been a long day."

"Tell me about it," he encouraged. "You don't often talk about your work."

"You don't often ask," she answered simply.

"I'm sorry about that. I will try harder in the future, Imogene. I promise. I want to be the husband you deserve."

"You are right now," she said, accepting a plate of steaming spaghetti from him.

"No," he corrected her. "But I will be. Just you wait and see."

She had no answer for that but again, that sense of light and joy filled her inside. Maybe they could make this work after all.

While they dined she let Valentin coax the details of her day from her, and bit by bit she found herself relaxing more and more. When it came to discussing business, he was so easy to talk to, she noted. A shame they'd struggled so much about other things. But that was changing, wasn't it?

Partway through dinner, Valentin had risen and played with her iPod dock, which sat on a credenza behind her desk. He'd chosen an easy listening playlist and once they'd eaten their fill, he put out one hand to her.

"I want to dance with you, Imogene," he said in a voice that brooked no argument.

She smiled her response. They hadn't danced since the stiff formal wedding dance almost three months ago. "I'd like that."

He pulled her to her feet and into his arms and they began to move together, swaying gently to the music, not dancing quite so much as simply being together. It was beautiful, and it lit a familiar slow-burning need deep inside her. But even so, her insecurities still hovered on the edge of her thoughts. She loved Valentin and she loved being with him, but until he'd fully resolved the situation with Carla she didn't feel as though they could confidently move forward together. But he was taking steps to do that now, she reminded herself as he nuzzled the curve of her neck, sending a shiver of liquid fire to burn through her body. And was it that she didn't trust him, or didn't trust Carla Rogers?

Definitely the latter, she decided. But that didn't mean that Valentin was completely out of the woods in that department. He'd made promises to her tonight, promises that were likely going to be a challenge to keep. The proof would be in what came next, she decided, giving herself over to the man holding her in his arms. The only man who'd ever had the ability to make her blood sing with desire. The only man she'd ever loved.

When Valentin's hands began to move over her back, his fingers playing with the zipper that ran the length of her back, she whispered a soft "Yes" in his ear before biting gently on his earlobe. It was all the encouragement he needed to undo her dress. The sensation of his hot, broad hands on her bare skin was temptation and bliss rolled into one. With the fingers of one hand he unsnapped her bra, then reached up to push the fabric of her dress down off her shoulders, easing her arms out of the long sleeves and letting her bra and dress fall to the floor in a pool around her feet. Her whole body hummed with need. Need for him to take her, to touch her, to taste her—everywhere.

"Lock my door," she instructed, stepping out of the puddle of fabric.

He did so, quickly, and returned to face her.

"You are so beautiful," Valentin said gently as he looked at her.

His eyes roamed every inch of her exposed skin, his fingers now tracing the edges of her garter belt, then the edges of her panties. She could barely swallow, such was the intensity of the wave of desire that hit her.

"I want you, Valentin," she said on a voice that shook with emotion. "Make love to me."

"Your wish is my absolute command."

He lifted her into his arms and carried her over to the couch they'd only recently vacated, and laid her there before reaching for his clothing and shedding it with an economy of motion that impressed her.

"I never knew you could move so fast," she teased from her recumbent position.

"With the right incentive, I can do anything." He grinned, settling over her.

"Anytime, anywhere?"

"For you, always."

And then he showed her. His hands skimmed her breasts, his touch light as a feather and making her skin prick into goose bumps and her nipples draw into tight beads. Lower and lower he let his fingers drift down her body, unsnapping the catches on her garter belt and, one by one, rolling her stockings down her legs. As he reached each foot, he massaged the instep, his touch sending wild jolts of pleasure through her. Then he worked his way back up again—his touch sure and strong this time. He gently massaged her calves, her thighs, and then reached to tug her panties down and expose her to him completely. She shivered in anticipation as his hands cupped her buttocks and he bent to flick his tongue against her thigh, then to the curve that indented at the top, before doing the same to the other leg.

"Valentin, you're driving me crazy."

"You want me to stop?"

"No, don't stop. Whatever you do, don't stop." She heard him laugh and lifted her head to look at him. His eyes had darkened to indigo and they shimmered with desire and love and just a sprinkling of mischief. Oh, how she loved this man. Loved how he made her feel, loved what he did to her. "Please, don't stop," she reiterated in a voice that could barely be heard.

Without taking his gaze from hers, he lowered his mouth to her and she gasped as he flicked his tongue against her sensitive bud. "Like this?" he asked.

"Like that," she managed.

"Or maybe more like this?" he asked before closing his mouth around her and sucking gently and rhythmically at her.

Her eyes closed involuntarily, her head fell back on the cushions, as sensation overtook her body and she climbed to the apex of pleasure and then tipped over into the abyss, her body lifting on the waves of pleasure that threatened to rob her very consciousness. When the pleasure began to slowly seep away, she felt him move again, heard the sound of him opening a condom packet and covering himself. Then she felt the blunt tip of his penis pressing into her swollen slick flesh, felt herself stretch and mold to accommodate him. She lifted legs that felt weak, like jelly, and buried her heels into his buttocks, lifting her hips and letting him slide deeper inside her. She groaned on a new wave of pleasure as he pressed against her.

"And like that," she said on a moan. "Just like that."

Valentin kissed her deeply, his tongue sweeping her mouth as his hips began to move, at first slowly, then more quickly as the momentum of their joining overtook them both.

"I can't hold back," he groaned against his mouth.

"I don't want you to," she replied, her hands tightening on his shoulders as she began to feel her second orgasm build deep inside her. Different from before. Stronger, deeper.

She felt his body surge, then surge again. A cry tore from his throat as his entire body tensed and shook and pulsed with the power of his climax. And as he shuddered against her she went over the edge again, soaring on a physical joy so intense, so incomprehensible in its strength, that she knew she was bonded to Valentin forever.

Fourteen

Tonight they were joining Alice Horvath for dinner. Imogene was a little worried about how it would go. Valentin had been very annoyed at being manipulated by his grandmother into their marriage, but Imogene had to admit, even though she'd been angry at first herself and while they'd had a rocky time of it, they were working things out. It was something they'd never have done on their own. And the longer Imogene was with Valentin, the more she knew he was the only man for her. She only wished she could be 100 percent certain he felt the same way.

He said and did all the right things—she knew he'd had meetings with his legal team and Human Resources regarding the situation with Carla—but as far as she knew, the woman was still very firmly entrenched in his day-to-day life. And after that stunt when Carla had come to Imogene's office, Imogene didn't trust her one little bit. With a sigh of resignation, she turned away from the walk-in closet, two dresses in her hands.

"Which one?" she asked Valentin, holding them both up for his perusal.

One was the purple dress she'd worn to his office the night they'd made love there, the other, something new she'd spied on a rare shopping trip with her mother the other day. Valentin nodded toward the new dress.

"That greeny-colored one. I like what it does to your eyes."

She laughed. "You haven't seen it on, so how do you know what it does to my eyes?"

"Trust me, I'm a man. I know these things," he said calmly before kissing her firmly on the lips. "By the way, I wanted to tell you that we had a meeting at work today. My legal team and a representative from HR and me, together with Carla and her legal representative. She has accepted a very healthy severance package and will be leaving Horvath Pharmaceuticals immediately. I thought you would want to know that everything's been taken care of."

Emotion threatened to overwhelm her. He'd done it. For her. For them. "Oh, Valentin, I don't know what to say."

"'Thank you' will suffice. And maybe a kiss to embellish your thanks?" he suggested with a wry smile.

She did both, tossing both dresses on the bed and rushing across the room to jump at him.

"Thank you," she said again as they drew apart.

"I'm sorry it took me so long. Maybe now we can carry on with a clean slate, yes?"

"Yes, I'd like that," Imogene replied vehemently.

"Good, then let's finish getting ready. If there's one

thing my grandmother can't stand it's a lack of punctuality."

He went through to the bathroom and Imogene recovered her dresses from the bed, holding each one in front of her in turn, as she stood opposite the full-length mirror. He was right, she realized. The teal gown did make her eyes sparkle and glow. Or maybe it was just him, she thought as she hung the purple dress back in the closet. It had been two weeks since that night he'd come to her office. Two weeks of the kind of marriage she'd always wanted with him. Two weeks filled with hope and love and plans for a future she'd begun to think she'd never achieve. And now she knew her hope hadn't been misplaced. Without the shadow of Carla in their lives, she knew they would make it.

When they got to the restaurant at the Waldorf, Alice was already seated at their table. As they approached, she rose from her chair, offering her cheek first to her grandson and then to Imogene.

"You two look happy," she said with a genuine smile.

"We are," Imogene said as Valentin helped his grandmother to be seated again. "But it remains a work in progress."

"Marriage is always a work in progress. It never stops being one, nor should it," Alice said sagely before focusing her attention on Valentin. "You look better, my boy. Less strained."

"Thank you, Nagy. And you look as beautiful as ever."

His grandmother blushed at the compliment but Imogene noticed Alice wasn't looking quite as well as she had nearly three months ago.

They turned their conversation to more general things, Valentin's brother, Galen, included.

"He's coping better with fatherhood than I expected," Alice admitted after taking a sip of the champagne she'd ordered for the table. "Ellie is a charming child. Missing her parents, obviously, but she loves Galen. She has a fear, though, that he'll be taken from her unexpectedly, like her parents were."

"Understandable, I suppose," Valentin said. "No one could have predicted her losing both of them like that."

"Yes, but Galen's taking it seriously. He's asked me to find him a wife. One who wants a ready-made family."

Imogene looked as her husband sat back and stared at his grandmother in shock. "A wife? Oh, no, not Galen. Not through Match Made in Marriage anyway."

"And why not?" Alice bristled visibly, bright spots of color rising to her cheeks.

"Not for Galen. Not with everything else he's dealing with. You have to admit, both your pairings for family members didn't start out so well."

Imogene knew he was referring to his cousin Ilya's rocky start to marriage with his business rival Yasmin Carter. Yasmin had left her husband early on in the marriage, but they'd worked things out in the end and had appeared to be very much in love at her and Valentin's ceremony. But she knew Valentin had a point and she watched as Alice's expression set in stone, much as it probably did back in the days when she ran the entire Horvath Corporation—an iron hand in a velvet glove, she'd heard it described as—and no one had dared go against her.

Alice looked at her grandson. "Are you saying the two of you are in crisis?"

She watched as Valentin and Imogene exchanged a glance.

"It hasn't been smooth sailing."

She sniffed audibly. "As I said before, marriage is a constant work in progress. Are you two giving up?"

"No, definitely not," Valentin hastened to assure her.

"Then why should Galen not find his perfect match?" she pressed, irritated beyond belief that Valentin had the gall to suggest she not find Galen's future bride.

The all-too-familiar pain in her chest asserted itself again. She didn't have time for this now, she thought angrily, and she was equally annoyed that this dinner, which was supposed to be a happy celebration, had started on the wrong foot.

"I just don't think Match Made in Marriage is the right vehicle for Galen to find long-term happiness," Valentin said, sticking to his guns as he always had, even as a child.

"Well, it's a good thing he feels differently. I'm already screening our database for a suitable applicant. Now," she said, indicating an end to the subject, "let's concentrate on the purpose of this evening."

"And that is?" Valentin asked with one of his disdainful looks down his perfectly straight nose.

A nose that had looked equally handsome on the dear face of her late husband, Eduard. It was moments like this, when she caught glimpses of her late husband in the wonderfully large and growing family they'd created, that she missed him so very, very much. The niggle in her chest grew a little tighter.

"To celebrate your impending three-month milestone, of course. Unless you've come here tonight to tell me you're separating at that juncture?"

She gave them both her most supercilious stare, daring them to refute the evidence she'd seen with her own eyes as they'd entered the restaurant together. She'd observed the solicitous way Valentin had taken his wife's coat. Watched as his hand had lingered on her shoulder and how Imogene had smiled at him, her eyes never leaving his for a moment. This was not a couple on the verge of separating.

"Of course not, Mrs. Horvath," Imogene hastened to assure her.

"Imogene, call me Alice or Nagy. We're family now," she instructed her granddaughter-in-law with a benevolent smile. "So, we're celebrating, yes?"

To her great relief, the two of them exchanged another of their deep and meaningful glances, then both nodded. The sensation in her chest eased a little, allowing her to draw in a deeper breath.

"Good," she said. "Then I propose a toast. To Imogene and Valentin and their long and happy and, dare I say it, fruitful marriage."

"Well, isn't all this just darling?"

Alice stopped midsip as another woman came to stand by their table. She looked up at the petite creature. Pretty enough, but with a hardness about her face that was distinctly off-putting. And there was something else about her, an energy that bordered on frenzy. Whatever it was, it made her feel very uncomfortable. Alice glanced across the table to see whether Valentin or Imogene had any inkling as to who the creature was. Imogene's features had frozen into a mask of disbelief while Valentin looked angrier than she'd ever seen him.

"I'm sorry," Alice said, when the others failed to speak. "You have me at a disadvantage. I'm Alice Horvath, and you are?"

"Carla Rogers," the other woman said. "Ask Valentin, he knows me. Well."

"Carla, please leave. This is a private family function," Valentin said sternly. "We said all we needed to say in the meeting today."

"You may have. However, there is one little detail I think your wife ought to know," Carla said firmly. Then, placing the palm of one hand over her lower belly, she looked at Imogene. "Please, do the right thing. His child deserves to know its father, not be banished into oblivion."

The pain in Alice's chest increased tenfold as the dreadful woman's words sank in. Valentin's child? With this creature?

Imogene rose abruptly to her feet, her chair toppling behind her as she did so. "No," she said in a voice that shook with horror and emotion. She turned to Valentin, who looked equally shocked. "She's pregnant? With your baby? So this is how you *take care of things*? I believed you when you said it was over. I *won't* stand for this. It's the final straw. I can't stay in a marriage riddled with lies!"

"She's the one lying, Imogene. I told you the truth." Valentin rose also and reached for his wife, but she was already moving out of range.

Alice stood, too, her legs unsteady and her breathing becoming more and more difficult as the pressure in her chest built.

"Imogene, please, wait." Alice caught Imogene's arm as she made to brush past, halting her in her tracks. She then directed her attention to the interloper. "And you, Ms. Rogers, leave us this instant. You're not welcome here."

That was all she managed before the pain became overwhelming. She could no longer draw a breath and the faces in front of her began to swim and blur before disappearing altogether as she collapsed slowly to the restaurant floor.

* * *

Imogene did her best to catch Alice as she crumpled, but caught unawares, she could do little but break her fall. She looked back as she heard Valentin cry out, "Nagy!"

He moved quickly to his grandmother's side. Imogene remained rooted where she was, recognizing instantly that her husband's beloved grandmother was possibly dying of a heart attack before his very eyes. Valentin looked up at Carla, who stood to one side, staring at the tableau before her with a strangely blank expression on her face.

"Carla, I need your assistance. I'll do compressions and you breathe for her," he said abruptly.

Without looking to see if Carla had followed his directive, he straightened Alice on the restaurant floor, checking her vital signs as he did so. Then he began compressions, at the same time looking up for Carla. It was only logical that he would, Imogene told herself. Carla was a doctor after all. They'd worked together in the ER in Africa. They were experienced with this high-need urgent-action situation. But Carla turned her back on them all and started toward the door. Imogene moved to intercept her.

"Help him," she urged. "He needs you."

"He doesn't need me. He chose you," she said bitterly and continued walking.

"You're a doctor. You can't just walk away!" Imogene cried out to Carla's retreating back.

Carla looked over her shoulder. "Watch me," she said coldly and continued for the door.

Imogene looked back at Valentin, who kept up compressions on Alice's tiny frail chest, keeping her heart beating for her when it had given up on itself. There was no time for hesitation. She pushed through the growing crowd that had formed around them and knelt on the floor opposite Valentin.

"I've done CPR training, but only ever on a dummy," she said with a faint tremor in her voice. "Tell me exactly what you need me to do."

Without breaking his rhythm on his grandmother's chest, he gave Imogene clear instructions.

"Where's Carla? I asked for her help," he said, briefly looking up and around to see where she was.

"I saw her walk out the restaurant soon after Alice collapsed," Imogene said between breaths. "It doesn't matter. You don't need her here."

Imogene forced back the instinctive sense of being second choice in her husband's life. The woman might be carrying his baby, but she wasn't here for him when he needed her most.

They worked in tandem until a commotion behind them announced the arrival of an emergency team. Valentin gave the details to the lead paramedic and only sat back as the highly trained EMTs, armed with a defibrillator, took over. He didn't relax until he heard the magic words. "We've got a pulse."

Imogene went to Valentin's side. Despite everything, she still wanted to comfort him. "She's going to be okay, Valentin."

"I can't lose her. Not because of this," he said brokenly as the paramedics began transferring Alice to a gurney.

"You won't. Go now. Go with her."

Even though the paramedics were beginning to wheel Alice away, he hesitated, his hands grasping Imogene's. He looked feverishly into her eyes. "Imogene, Carla was lying. She's not carrying my baby. It's impossible. I promise you."

"It's not important now."

"It is important that you believe me. Please, say you'll wait for me, that you won't do anything rash until we've spoken properly."

"I won't go anywhere. Not yet."

"Sir, are you coming with us in the ambulance?" one of the emergency team asked.

"Yes, I'm a doctor. I'll travel with my grandmother." He turned back to Imogene one more time. "Please, wait for me," he pleaded before pressing an urgent kiss against her lips and then moving quickly through the restaurant to follow the gurney.

Imogene stood there, oblivious to the people milling around her asking her if she was okay. She finally sat down in a vacant chair at what had been their table and began to shake as the reality of what had just happened sank in. Carla's arrival. Her bald statement. Alice's heart attack. Working with Valentin to save her life. It was all too much.

"Ma'am, can we assist you with a ride home?" the restaurant manager asked. "Or perhaps to the hospital?"

"I… I'm not sure where they're taking her, to be honest. But, yes, our driver can be reached at this number." She fumbled in her bag for a card and gave it to the manager.

"Perhaps you'd like to wait downstairs in the hotel lobby? It will be a little more private for you than here, I suspect," he suggested. "I can arrange for someone to sit with you until your car arrives."

"That won't be necessary. Just the car, please."

Imogene nodded her thanks and rose to her feet to follow him. While he called for her driver, she retrieved her coat from the coat check, then headed down to the lobby. Suddenly desperate for the cool fresh night air and to get away from the heat and chatter that had surrounded her inside, Imogene went out through the front doors of the hotel. A movement in the shadows to one side startled her and she stifled a groan of disbelief as Carla materialized beside her.

"Haven't you done enough damage?" she growled at the other woman.

"You're one to talk. Your marriage is nothing but a sham. Valentin loves me. Always has and always will. We'd still be together if you hadn't come along again and distracted him. You have no idea how hard I've worked to get him back. How patient I've been."

"Perhaps the fact that you had to work so hard at it was an indication that your feelings for him weren't reciprocated?"

"It doesn't matter what you say. He loves me. I know he does. And now with the baby, I think it's time you step aside and leave him, this time for good."

Imogene looked at Carla and was shocked at the unnatural brightness in her eyes. Her words were those of a madwoman, not the calm, cool, collected doctor she'd met in Africa and certainly not the intelligent and gifted head of research and development that she'd heard Carla described as. Perhaps losing her position at Horvath Pharmaceuticals had unhinged her completely.

But no matter how she felt about her, the woman was pregnant and out here in the cold night without a coat and, judging by the way she was hanging around, without a ride home. Clearly she needed help. Pushing aside her own feelings of anger and betrayal toward her husband and her definite dislike and distrust of Carla, Imogene made an offer.

"I can get you help, Carla. I really think you need it. But first of all, let me see you home."

"Why?" Carla retorted, looking at Imogene as if she were the one who'd gone completely crazy. "I've slept with your husband. I'm doing my best to break up your marriage again. Why would you be nice to me?"

Imogene looked at Carla and spoke quietly and steadily, seeing her car draw near. "Because you need help and because," she said as an alternate spin on the situation began to bloom in her mind, "I'm not entirely sure I believe you right now. Look, let me give you a ride home."

To her shock Carla dissolved into tears. The doorman looked at the two women with concern and began to walk toward them, but Imogene gestured for him to stay back.

"Come on, Carla. My driver is here. Let's go."

Wrapping one arm around the other woman's waist, she guided her into the back seat of the car.

"A slight detour today, Anton. We'll be seeing Ms. Rogers home first."

"And Mr. Horvath?"

"There's been an incident with his grandmother. He's gone to the hospital with her."

Anton expressed his regrets before steering the car into traffic.

"Carla, give Anton your address."

"It's all right, Mrs. Horvath. I already know it," Anton replied smoothly before Carla could answer.

Imogene's body felt as though it had been cast in stone. She could barely breathe as the ramifications and possibilities of that one statement surged through her. Did that mean that Valentin was frequently driven to Carla's home? That every word from his mouth had been a lie? That he wouldn't, or couldn't, let Carla go from his life? That he was just like her father after all?

She tried to swallow against the lump that threatened to block her throat and felt her eyes burn with unshed tears. She'd be damned before she'd cry in front of this woman. No matter that she'd chosen to help her, there was no way she would show weakness in front of her, too.

On the other side of the back seat, Carla sat huddled against her door. Her crying had slowed to an occasional sob, and in the dark interior she eventually lifted her head and looked at Imogene.

"I'm sorry," she said brokenly.

"Are you?" Imogene tried to keep her voice neutral. Not easy given the shock she'd just received. "What for, precisely?"

"All of it. Africa. Here. Tonight."

Imogene held her silence, hoping it might prompt Carla to continue. Even in the dark she could see what a mess Carla had been reduced to after her crying jag. Imogene reached into her bag for a small pack of tissues and silently handed them across. Carla accepted them with a small thank-you. After a few more minutes, she finished mopping her face and blowing her nose and straightened in her seat.

"I'm not pregnant," she said bluntly.

A massive wave of relief flooded through every inch of Imogene's body. She'd begun to suspect that Carla had been staging it all in a last-ditch effort to drive her away. Not trusting herself to speak, she held her silence. Besides, there was still the issue of Valentin's visits to Carla's home to be worked out.

"And I lied about Valentin being my lover that day in Africa. He was still at work. I'd brought one of the new doctors back to your house with me. I knew you'd likely show up at some point and I wanted to use that to my advantage."

"What do you expect me to say?" Imogene blurted out, anger beginning to boil just beneath the surface.

Carla had manipulated them all—Imogene, Valentin and her poor unsuspecting lover, who'd been showering when Imogene had arrived home that day.

"I don't know. I hope that one day you might be able to forgive me."

"I don't know if I can do that," Imogene said through lips that felt frozen and immobile.

All those years wasted. All that unhappiness. All for a lie.

"I understand. I wouldn't if the situation was reversed." She shifted in her seat and plucked at the seat belt that crossed her body with a listless hand. "Valentin was the only man to ever end a relationship with me. It only made me want him all the more. Of course there have been others since him, but no one has ever matched Valentin. He was always my end goal."

"You speak about him as if he had no choice in the matter. As if he were something to acquire, not a flesh and blood man to love and care for."

Carla looked away from Imogene and out the window. "You love him, don't you?" Without waiting for an answer, she continued, "He never stopped loving you, you know. Through all these years he's constantly rebuffed my attentions, and those of anyone else who dared make an advance on him. You were always the only one for him. It drove me crazy. I'm not very gracious in loss, as you've probably gathered. I hope you'll believe me when I say I am truly sorry, to you both."

Imogene let Carla's words wash over her and slowly

penetrate the frozen shell that had locked her in place. Slowly she became aware that Anton had pulled up to the curb in front of an apartment building in Greenwich Village.

"I won't trouble you again," Carla said. "Thanks for the ride home."

Before Imogene could say another word, Carla had let herself out and was walking toward the entrance. Once she was gone from view, Imogene met Anton's gaze in the rearview mirror.

"Do you think she'll be all right?" she asked.

"She's a tough one. She'll get through it," he said. "And, since I couldn't help overhearing—I just want to clear something up for you. Mr. Horvath never accompanied Ms. Rogers to her apartment."

"I know that," Imogene conceded.

Now all she had to do was work this out with her husband.

Fifteen

Imogene entered their apartment and was struck by its emptiness. Every night these past few weeks Valentin had greeted her on her arrival home. Now, of course, he was at the hospital, no doubt worried sick about Alice. She checked her phone to see if he'd messaged or called her yet. Nothing. At least that had to be good news, right? she told herself as she shrugged out of her coat and hung it in the closet off the foyer. Her stomach rumbled. They hadn't even had the chance to place an order tonight, let alone eat anything. But even though she was hungry, she didn't know if she could stomach anything right now.

She wandered to their bedroom and kicked off her shoes, sitting on the bed for a while and pondering what she should do. She felt restless, her mind still in turmoil over Carla's sudden about-face and her apologies. It made Imogene want to turn it all over in her mind again.

To examine every step of her journey with Valentin and to see where she allowed herself to be so badly duped.

Had it all been Carla's manipulation, or had she been an easy victim because of her own preconceptions? She admitted she'd gone into her whirlwind relationship with Valentin starry-eyed but holding back a piece of herself all the way. Yes, she'd been wooed by Valentin's attentions, had fallen hard and fast in love. But had she given him her all? If she had, would she have felt more secure?

She got up from the bed and walked through the apartment to the bedroom that had been converted into a den for their private use. Cozier than the formal lounge and perhaps a little more inviting than the library, it contained comfortable furniture and shelves filled with knickknacks and books, as well as Valentin's enviable movie collection. Entering the room, Imogene made a beeline for the shelves that housed Valentin's old photo albums. She'd teased him about them, telling him he was archaic because didn't everyone store everything digitally these days? But he'd remained staunch in his old-school values and reiterated to her the pleasure he found in thumbing through the albums, reliving highlights of the past.

She knew exactly which one she wanted and slid it from the stack. The date on the spine was seven years ago, the title, quite simply, *Africa*.

Opening the album to the beginning, she was instantly cast back to the central African nation where they'd been volunteering—to the heat, the smells, the sounds, the people. Her contract had only been supposed to be a short one, filling in for another teacher who had been called home to an emergency. But she'd talked of extending her stay to tie in with the completion of Valentin's contract. Until Carla.

Imogene's eyes blurred and she blinked away the unexpected moisture before turning the page. She felt a jolt of shock as she studied the photos there and her gaze locked on a younger, happier version of herself, caught midlaugh by Valentin's lens as she attempted to drink from a gourd for the first—and last—time. The expression in her eyes as she stared into the lens struck her, reminding her of how very much she'd loved him then.

But it was nothing compared to how she felt about him now. Her emotions were so much deeper. Stronger, even. Shrouded, yes, with the fear of being hurt again, but deeper nonetheless. She stared at the younger version of herself and then turned the page, this time to a photo of the two of them, oblivious to the person taking the shot, with eyes only for each other. He'd been her first real love and, she realized, he was her only real love, too. Now or ever. But had she ever really told him that? Shown him? No, she'd never allowed herself to love him as fully as he deserved.

Her entire first marriage with Valentin had been based on her waiting and watching for him to show signs of her father's behavior. Of him disengaging from her and pursuing other women while maintaining the facade of a happy union. She'd basically handed him to Carla on a platter, she realized in retrospect. She'd gone through the motions of being his wife, of trusting him and loving him, but she'd never really trusted him at all. Instead she'd been waiting for him to show he had feet of clay, unable to believe that he could love her as she so desperately wanted to be loved. Waiting for him to be the man her father was. Charming, yes. Dedicated to his work, definitely. Dedicated to his family? Well, when it suited. She hadn't wanted that, and by making that her focus, that was exactly what she'd ended up with.

Instead of looking for the differences between Valentin and her father, she'd looked only for the similarities and where she'd found them, they'd derailed her confidence, derailed her conviction that their love was forever and that their marriage was a perfect match.

Imogene turned the pages on the album more swiftly now, noticed the changes in herself—her expression, her posture. She could track the outgoing nature she'd exhibited in the early days of their relationship slowly being snuffed out by her own paranoia about having married a man like her dad.

She gently closed the album and filed it back in the stack, certain now of what she needed to do. It was time to be there for Valentin at the hospital, as a wife ought to be, comforting him through the worry he must be feeling about his grandmother. And then, when he was ready, to tell Valentin the truth about her love for him.

Valentin slumped in the uncomfortable chair in the waiting area while a cardiac team worked hard to stabilize his grandmother behind the curtains in the ER. Every harsh word he'd ever said to her came back to haunt him, making him wish them all unsaid. No matter how angry he'd been at her three months ago, she had his best interests at heart. He should have given her more credit. The problems he and Imogene faced were of their own making, not Nagy's, and it was up to them to make them right again.

If Imogene would still consider it after tonight's debacle, he thought ruefully.

He knew Carla had been lying but he'd never forget

the look of raw pain and unadulterated shock that had ripped across Imogene's face, exposing her vulnerability for all to see. He hated that she'd had to be hurt like that again, and by a woman he'd been deaf, dumb and blind about for far too long. But most of all, he hated that even with the rebuilding they'd been doing in the past fortnight, hell, the past three months, she'd believed Carla's lies in an instant.

It wasn't so impossible, he rationalized. Her father was a class A jerk when it came to marriage, and if that was the best example she'd ever had before her, it was no wonder that she'd believed Carla's lies. Which meant if this was to work between them, he had to work harder.

He closed his eyes and tipped his head back against the wall, frustration making his body tense. He wished he could be on the other side of that curtain, helping the specialists with his grandmother. Be there for her, if nothing else. Not for the first time, he missed being actively involved in medicine. No matter how good and how meaningful the work he was doing now, he would never quite get over the rush of being hands-on in critical situations. Of saving lives. Of making a difference. But that lifestyle had taken its own toll. On him and on his marriage. He hadn't been able to see the cracks forming until it was too late. And once the damage was done, things were too far gone.

And now? Was it too late? Would Imogene ever let him back into her heart, her life?

The gentle touch of a soft hand on his and a hint of the fragrance Imogene always wore swam through the myriad smells around him and made his eyes fly open.

"Valentin, is she okay?"

"I don't know yet," he said, putting his other hand

on top of hers as if by doing so he could stop her from pulling away from him again.

She was here, beside him, and he was determined to anchor her to him and not let her get away if he had anything to do about it. Time ticked past ever so slowly and they sat together with so many unspoken words between them. He took strength from her presence, from the fact that she'd come here, to him. And that she stayed, physically connected and assuring him of her nearness. He would never take her for granted again like he had seven years ago. Back then he'd expected everything to simply flow in a natural current of life. But he hadn't taken into account the rocks and boulders and changes in direction that life and other people could throw at a relationship.

He knew why he'd been so darn naive about marriage. As a child prodigy, his life focus had been on learning, on being the best. And once he'd conquered one educational mountain, he'd tackled another. When his peers and cousins had been attending high school dances and dating, he'd been in premed. When they started college, he was already an intern and dealing with the disbelief and distrust of the patients on the wards when they realized how young he was. So he'd worked harder, longer hours, with everything he had in him. And that was how he'd coped when the link between him and Imogene had begun to falter. When she'd made accusations he'd believed were baseless. When she'd had enough and had her lawyer draw up the papers to dissolve their marriage—signing them and sending them to him for his signature even as she boarded the plane to return to the States.

He felt her fingers tighten around his hand.

"Valentin? They're asking for you," she said.

Fear gripped him.

"Dr. Horvath?"

"Yes," he said, rising to his feet.

"We've managed to stabilize your grandmother and we'll be moving her up to the ICU now. We'll run more tests in the morning, but she will need surgery, sooner rather than later. We'll discuss that with her in the morning and hope to schedule her in for surgery later tomorrow if we can. I'm sure you understand the need to act quickly."

"Yes, I do. Thank you. Can I see her now?"

"Briefly. Understandably, she's very tired."

He was torn: afraid to abandon Imogene in case she left while he was gone, but fearful that if he didn't see Nagy now, his last memory of her would be of her being wheeled away from him when they'd arrived here at the hospital.

"Go," Imogene urged him. "I'll be waiting right here for you."

He wanted to kiss her but with all the drama of what happened at the restaurant still unresolved between them, he didn't know how well it would be received.

"Dr. Horvath?" the other doctor prompted.

"Yes, I'm coming now."

With one last glance at Imogene, who nodded at him encouragingly, he followed the doctor behind the curtains. As a trauma surgeon, seeing a patient hooked up to monitors and having tubes running in and out of their body had been an everyday thing for him. Seeing his grandmother like that was quite another matter. He felt as if he'd abandoned all his medical experience on the other side of the curtain, leaving just the anxious grandson here in the cubicle with her. He hastened forward and took her hand, automatically checking the pulse at her wrist. Not as strong and steady as it should be, but there. He looked down on his grandmother's wrinkled face and felt her mortality hit him square in the chest. They had to do everything to make her well again.

She'd persevered through so much—fleeing Hungary with her parents before the outbreak of World War II, settling into a new and foreign life in the States. Supporting her husband, Eduard, through the establishment of Horvath Aviation and subsequently expanding into the Horvath Corporation. Losing her beloved husband too early to a heart attack. Then losing two of her sons to the same congenital affliction soon after—his own father one of them. Through it all she'd done everything she could to hold her family together. And her family had a lot to be grateful for. They'd rally around to support her now that she needed them most. If she could just hang on.

Her eyes flickered open. "Valentin?"

"You're in the hospital, Nagy. You've had a heart attack."

"Stupid heart pills didn't work," she grumbled behind her oxygen mask.

Heart pills? He wondered how long she'd been taking medication and if anyone in the family knew. Likely not, he reasoned. Nagy was nothing if not fiercely proud and independent. A trait he'd exhibited himself a time or two.

"We'll get you better, don't worry."

"Imogene?" There was a querulous note to her voice that concerned him. The last thing she needed now was any anxiety.

"She's outside, waiting. Don't worry. We'll sort everything out."

"Something I needed to tell you both," she said weakly. "Important."

Behind him he heard the arrival of the orderlies, ready to take her up to the ICU. "Later, Nagy. They need to get you settled on the ward now. We'll talk later, okay? I promise."

Her eyes slid closed and he stepped aside as the team gathered around his grandmother, attaching and reattaching monitors, before moving her out the cubicle and down the hall to the elevator.

"Excuse me, sir," a nurse said as she bustled into the area. "We need to set up for our next patient."

"Certainly, sorry," he said and walked back toward the waiting area—to Imogene.

Would she still be there? He didn't realize how tense he was until he saw her beautiful but pale face turn toward him. She rose and walked to meet him halfway. A symbol of their future? He hoped so with every cell in his body.

Sixteen

When they returned to the apartment, Imogene felt as if she'd been away from it for days, not merely a few hours. And if she felt that way, how did Valentin feel? she wondered.

"Can I get you something?" she said, moving toward the kitchen. "Dion's bound to have some magical creation in the fridge if you're hungry."

"Maybe a sandwich," he said, following her. "I'll help."

Despite their familiarity with each other and despite their proximity in the kitchen, Imogene couldn't help feeling there was a massive gulf yawning between them. They needed to talk. She needed to tell him she was ready to accept a great deal of the blame that had led to their initial separation, not to mention the difficulties they'd faced since.

"Shall we take these through to the den?" she suggested as she cut the bread diagonally in halves.

"Good idea," Valentin replied, picking up the tray with the plates on them and carrying it through.

They settled side by side on the massive sofa, each reaching for a sandwich and chewing in a continued awkward silence.

"So, they're—"

"Imogene, I—"

They both started simultaneously, then laughed awkwardly.

"You first," he said.

"I just wanted to ask about Alice. They're doing surgery tomorrow?"

"She'll have an angiography first, I imagine, to confirm their suspicions. Then surgery."

"She's strong, Valentin. She'll pull through."

"A lot of that will depend on the damage to her heart muscle but, yeah, she's strong. Which reminds me. Before we talk, and I mean really talk, I need to let the family know what's happened."

"Of course," Imogene said.

She watched as he scrolled through his phone, calling his eldest cousin, Ilya, first, then his brother, Galen. The other men agreed to let the rest of the family, mostly based on the West Coast, know about their matriarch. Valentin slid his phone onto the coffee table and leaned back on the sofa.

"Well, that went more easily than I anticipated."

"It's good that they're all there for you. Families should always be like that."

"Yes, but you didn't have that growing up, did you?" Valentin said, obviously seizing the opportunity to turn the conversation toward the subject they'd both been so carefully stepping around.

"No, I didn't. I admit, I didn't realize until tonight

exactly how much that altered my perception of everything. Of everyone. Including you."

"Do you want to explain?" he prompted.

She pulled one leg up underneath her and turned to face him on the sofa. "I *need* to explain it to you. You've seen what my family is like. Isolated satellites, orbiting around each other. Occasionally living the same life in the same room, but that's no life at all. Not for me, at least. If I were more like them, maybe I could handle that. But—"

"But you're not like that at all," Valentin interrupted. "You have too much heart. And I was too stupid to see that. Imogene, you have to believe me, I haven't been conducting an affair with Carla under your nose or while we were apart. I didn't do it in Africa. I didn't do it here. In fact, since you, there's been no one else—which has been mighty uncomfortable at times," he said with an attempt at humor.

Imogene looked at him and knew he was telling her the truth. This proud, intense, focused man had more honor in his little finger than her father had in his entire body. Why had she been so reluctant to see that?

"Same," she said softly. "I couldn't bear the thought of someone else touching me, being with me. I knew I'd have to get over it eventually. I was prepared to push myself. I thought if I entered into a Match Made in Marriage I'd be paired with someone so compatible that the sexual side of the marriage would be a natural progression."

"And it was," he commented wryly.

"Yes, it was. It *is*," she affirmed. "I know you weren't unfaithful to me. I'm sorry I ever thought that you were capable of being so cruel and cavalier about the vows we made to each other. It's easy to blame my parents but the fault lies with me. Rather than see the truth before my eyes, I went looking for trouble. Carla, it seems, was only too happy to provide it."

"I wish I'd listened to you then. Properly listened. Understood how she made you feel."

"How I allowed myself to feel," Imogene corrected. "I need to own up to this. To take my life and my feelings and reactions back under my control. I gave her power over me back in Africa. And she made the most of it. Did you know you're the only man ever to refuse her? That's part of why she wanted you so badly."

"We went out briefly, but like I said to you a long time ago, it burned out quickly. At least it did for me. I didn't understand it, but she obviously never took my breaking things off with any finality, more as an abeyance—something to be resumed later."

Imogene nodded in understanding. "I couldn't believe it when she turned up tonight, especially after what you'd told me here at home. But I'm so sorry I believed her when she said she was pregnant with your baby. I just—" Her voice broke off and it took her a few moments to get her emotions under control. "I just felt so betrayed. I want children—our children—so very much, and to have her stand there and baldly announce she was having your baby? It just cut me in two. I would never stand in the way of anyone and their child the way my father's mistresses have with me. I would have left you for that reason alone, so you could create a family with her and your baby."

Imogene's voice had grown thicker with every word until she was beyond speech. Tears began to roll down her cheeks and she swiped them away angrily. She didn't want to be the kind of woman who used tears as a weapon or to manipulate a situation. She needed to be strong, for herself and for Valentin. Her distrust of him was a serious issue. One she needed to overcome. If she couldn't, then what hope did they have?

"And that's a part of what makes you so special, Genie," Valentin said, moving closer and pulling her into his arms. "It's one of the reasons I love you so much. You're my everything. Did you know that? Since the day I met you, you've never been far from my thoughts. I admit I wasn't the best husband the first time around, and I'm probably not doing such a great job this time around, either. I've needed to learn to put you first, before my work. It hasn't been easy but I know we can do it. We can make our life together a rich one and we can build that family we both want together.

"Tonight consolidated that for me. When Nagy collapsed at the restaurant I was terrified that I was going to lose her. How on earth would I be able to explain that to my family? Me, a doctor, unable to do anything to save my own grandmother? I guess what they say about having a God complex is kind of true. So many times I've held people's lives, literally, in my hands. But I've never been frightened about my ability to do what I've been trained to do until tonight, and going through that reminded me of how I felt when you left me. I didn't know what to do. Logic should have told me to follow you home, to fight for you, but I did the only thing I knew I could be a success at—work. So I signed another contract, stayed in Africa another year, and when I got home I threw myself into Horvath Pharmaceuticals, doing everything I could to forget you. To forget my failure with you. But I failed at that as much as I had failed you in our marriage. I couldn't forget you and I found I didn't want to."

He took in a deep breath before continuing. "Yes, I

was angry when I saw that Nagy had paired us up at Port Ludlow. But most of all I was angry with myself because I had failed where she had succeeded. Despite how I felt about you, I never reached out to you, I never visited you here at home even though I knew you were most likely still here in New York. I made no effort and for that I am truly, deeply sorry. I wouldn't blame you if you wanted to leave me now.

"Imogene, know this—I love you and I want you to be happy, but if you can't bring yourself to trust me I know you'll never be happy in our marriage. I know what love is now. And I know that I'm prepared to let you walk away from me again, rather than hold you to vows that neither of us were probably ready to make in the first place. I should have put you first then, too. Should have let you walk away from Nagy and her pressure on us, if that's what you wanted. Instead, seeing you again reminded me all too viscerally of how much I still wanted you. I was prepared to do anything to persuade you to give us another chance, but I did that without considering what it would do to you if we failed again."

"Valentin, I agreed to go ahead with our marriage. It was a mutual decision that day. Yes, my initial instinct was to run like hell in the opposite direction, but when push came to shove, I couldn't do it. The moment I saw you, my body recognized you and was drawn to you. It's always been that way between us, but that's worked to our detriment, too."

Valentin buried his face in her hair and inhaled the scent that always served to calm and incite him at the same time. It was that very juxtaposition that lay at the base of their union. Could they manage to work through that? Could they honestly make this a solid, tangible thing and move forward stronger than before? Or would they implode all over again?

"If you choose to stay with me, Imogene, I want you to know it's forever this time. I won't let you go again and I will spend the rest of my life proving that to you. If you can only love me in return and trust me to cherish and protect that love, I will ensure you never regret your decision for a moment. But if you can't forgive me for the mistakes I've made in the past, for not listening to you, especially when it came to Carla, I will understand. I never really knew what love meant, aside from the family sense or from the physical side of things the first time we married. Not until I lost you. I don't want to lose you again."

Imogene shifted until she was facing Valentin. She could see the worry in his eyes that tonight's episode had pushed her away—had exposed a yawning chasm in their relationship. And she could see his fear that they had no coming back after that. Her heart ached for all the unsaid words between them. For all the love she'd borne for him all these years but never been able to adequately express. She looked him deeply in the eyes.

"Leaving you was a dreadful mistake, I know that now, but not believing you was far, far worse. I am so desperately sorry that I didn't trust you. Carla delivered a few truths to me tonight. She said she had deliberately tried to break us up. I guess she thought that if she couldn't have you, then no one should, especially not me. I think seeing us together again drove her over the edge. She told me you hadn't touched her from the day you met me. And I find myself wondering why I can believe her, when she spilled her lies or when she admitted them like she did tonight, and not you. It's a flaw in my character that I didn't believe you, not a flaw in yours. Can you forgive me for being so distrustful? For allowing my own experience with my family to create the blueprint for our life together? I have so much to unlearn, but I really want to succeed with you. I love you, Valentin Horvath, with all my heart, but is my love going to be enough?"

"Enough? You love me—that's all I need," Valentin replied.

He cupped her cheeks with his warm hands and kissed her. Not a kiss of passion or of need, but one of affirmation, of promise. Deep in her heart, Imogene began to feel hope for the two of them. When he released her, she chose her words carefully.

"So, you think we can take a chance on each other again? Get it right this time?"

His blue eyes never left hers as he took both her hands in his and kissed each one as if making a vow. His voice, when he spoke, was firm and unequivocal. "Yes."

Imogene clasped his hands tight and got to her feet, pulling him up with her. She led him to the bedroom. *Their* bedroom, she corrected herself. There would be no more his and hers if they were to make a success of this. There would only be what was theirs. In the semi-darkness of their room, she reached for his clothes and began to undress him. Her hands made swift work of the tie at his throat, the buttons of his shirt, the belt at his waist. As she bared more of his skin, she allowed herself the simple pleasure of touching him, with her hands, with her lips, with her tongue. Imprinting the memory of his body indelibly onto her mind and into her heart. When he was naked, she pushed him toward the bed and swiftly stripped off her clothing and followed him onto the mattress.

"I love you, Valentin," she repeated. "I never want to lose you again."

"You won't," he replied, reaching for her. "Because I love you, too, and I'm never letting you go."

She smiled at him in the darkness before kissing him, her lips claiming his and pressing upon him the weight of her emotions, her need for him. And he kissed her back, returning his love and accepting her need, giving of his own.

When they joined together it was with a gentleness and promise they'd never allowed themselves before. Gone was the urgency. Gone was the desperation. Instead, in their place was a solid affirmation of constancy. And as they moved together, climbing the rungs of passion, their movements became a promise—of intention, of love, of stability and the future.

Afterward, they slept together, legs entwined, arms around each other, hearts beating in total sync.

Valentin's mobile phone woke them as the gray of morning slid through the bedroom window. He and Imogene sprang apart and he felt his heart race with fear as he leaped from the bed and grabbed his trousers from the floor to find the phone. It was the hospital.

"Hello," he said, his heart hammering in his chest. Was it good news, or bad?

"Dr. Horvath. Sorry to call you so early but we wanted to inform you that your grandmother has been scheduled for surgery midafternoon."

"That's great."

"Well, yes," the woman on the other end said before pausing. "But we're having a small issue."

"Issue?"

"She refuses to sign the consent forms unless she sees you and your wife first."

"But why?"

"She hasn't seen fit to inform us of that, sir."

Valentin heard the note of irritation in the woman's voice. "I'm sorry. She's always been strong-minded."

"Well, strong-minded or not, she needs that operation today. Can I take it you'll be in to see her so we can get her to surgery on time? I'm sure I don't need to impress upon you the urgency in her case."

"We'll be there as soon as we can." He ended the call and turned to Imogene. "I'm sorry, we have to go into the hospital. Nagy is asking for us."

"Of course," Imogene said, slipping from the bed and into a robe. "I'll put the coffee on while you shower. Do you want anything to eat before we go?"

"A slice of toast, maybe?"

"I'm on it. Now, go shower," she said, shooing him in the direction of their bathroom.

He hesitated.

"Are you okay?" Imogene asked, moving to his side quickly.

He wrapped his arms around her and kissed her hard. "I'm glad you're here," he said before kissing her again.

"She'll pull through this, Valentin. They're going to look after her."

She gave him a small smile, then hurried from the room. By the time he was showered she had a light breakfast and coffee ready. She was nowhere to be seen and he assumed she'd gone to shower in her old bathroom. He realized he was right on the money when she reentered the kitchen, ready to leave.

"I've never known a woman to get ready as quickly as you do," he said, his eyes roaming her appreciatively.

"As someone who has always loved her sleep, it was a matter of necessity. Otherwise, I'd arrive everywhere looking like a hag."

"Hag? Impossible, but I appreciate it. Shall we go?"

"Yes, I called Anton. He'll be waiting downstairs. I thought it would be easier than using a cab."

"Good thinking."

When Anton dropped them off at the hospital they went straight up to the ICU. A nurse at the station directed them to Alice's room. The tension gripping Valentin's body eased when he saw his grandmother propped up in her bed. Yes, she was still seriously ill, but there was a fire in her eyes that he recognized immediately.

"You took your time."

Her voice was weak but he heard the indomitable spirit that underpinned everything that Alice Horvath was and every decision she'd made her entire life.

"We're here now," he replied, choosing not to point out that it was still ridiculously early. "How about you tell us what you need to say so you can get better again."

She snorted inelegantly. "Better. There's nothing wrong with me that some good news wouldn't cure. Have you got some good news for me?" Alice looked from one of them to the other. "Well?"

"If you mean have we sorted things out after last night," Imogene said, coming forward and gently taking his grandmother's hand, "then, yes, we have."

"And that woman? Did you get rid of her?"

Valentin bit back the instinctive urge to defend Carla. After all, he'd worked with her for a long time, both here and in Africa. But, he reminded himself, she didn't deserve his loyalty. She'd done her level best to drive his only love away from him. Not once, but twice.

"Yes, she's gone," he said simply.

Alice looked at him. “She’s not pregnant, is she?”

“If she is, it certainly isn’t my child,” he reassured her.

“Last night, when I saw her home, Carla admitted to me that she lied about being pregnant,” Imogene informed them both.

“Good.” Alice nodded, then turned her gaze back on Imogene. “And you, you’ve decided to stay with this grandson of mine?”

“Since I’m lucky enough that he can forgive me for believing someone else over him, yes, I am.”

“Good,” she said again.

“Nagy, stop beating around the bush. What is it that you wanted to tell us?” Valentin pressed.

“I’m not beating around the bush at all, I’m merely ascertaining what the situation is between you two today. I trust you are both equally invested in your marriage now?”

Valentin and Imogene exchanged a glance and in her eyes he could see her love for him reflected clearly.

“Yes, we are,” he said firmly.

Alice drew in a deep breath. “Thank goodness, because what I have to tell you two may come as a shock.”

That got both their attention.

“In fact,” Alice continued, her voice getting stronger now. “One day you might even see the humor in the situation. All I can say is that it was a good thing neither of you married anyone else after Africa.”

“And why not?” Valentin pressed.

“Because it would have been bigamy.”

Imogene gasped in shock. “Bigamy? But how? I signed the divorce papers. My lawyer was instructed to send them to Valentin immediately and to file them appropriately on their return.”

“I signed the papers. Against my better judgment, I

have to say. But I did it because it was clear to me that you wanted out. I sent them back to your lawyer immediately." Valentin looked at his grandmother. "Get to the point, Nagy. Why would it have been bigamy when we did everything we needed to?"

"The papers were never filed," she said with a smile of genuine satisfaction on her pale face. "I'm only sorry it's taken this long to get confirmation of it. We instigated an investigation before your marriage but with communication between the two countries being slow, at best, we decided to take the risk of going ahead before we got confirmation back from Africa. You were both convinced you were free to marry again and, since you were marrying each other, I didn't see the harm.

"Imogene's lawyer was apparently involved in several fraudulent activities with a local warlord. Once that was discovered he was shut down. It seems several local businessmen were angered by his involvement and before another law firm could retrieve the active files being held at his office, the building was firebombed and burned to the ground. All client information and documents were destroyed."

She looked tired now, but relieved she'd finally managed to tell them the news.

"You mean to say we've been married all along?" Imogene asked incredulously.

"Just think of the Port Ludlow ceremony as an affirmation of your vows," Alice said, her voice growing weaker again.

"You know what this means?" Valentin said, reaching for Imogene's hand and raising it to his mouth to kiss her knuckles. "We get to celebrate two anniversaries."

"For the rest of our lives," Imogene affirmed and reached up to kiss him.

* * *

Alice lay in her bed and looked at the happy couple standing beside her and smiled. Not everyone would agree she'd done the right thing pairing them, but she knew, to the depths of her soul, that they belonged together. Always had, always would. They hadn't had the smoothest path to their current happiness but she knew herself that sometimes the hardest road led to the greatest joys. And now that whatever troubles had kept these two apart had been resolved, it had only served to make them stronger than before.

"Mrs. Horvath? Are you ready to sign the consent forms now?"

There was that dratted woman again with her blasted clipboard. "If I must," she acceded.

"Nagy, you must. We want you better again. You still have Galen's wedding to plan," Valentin reminded her as he bent to kiss her on the cheek.

A smile crept across Alice's face. Yes, thank heavens for Galen. He would be her focus now. She could go into this operation, no matter how much it terrified her, secure in the knowledge that she'd effected yet another successful match made in marriage. And when she was well again—and after she was done with Galen—she had plenty more grandchildren to take care of.

Everyone deserved happiness. Everyone deserved a lifetime of love. And it was up to her to make sure they had it.

* * * * *

AT THE CEO'S PLEASURE

YAHRAH ST. JOHN

To my agent, Christine Witthohn,
for her hard work in helping me move
to the Desire line.

One

Ayden Stewart stared out at the Austin city skyline from the fiftieth floor of Stewart Investments. It had taken him fifteen years since graduating from Harvard to build his company, but at thirty-six, he'd finally achieved his goal. And he'd done it all on his own. Without the help of his father, Henry Stewart, a rich man who'd never bothered to acknowledge his eldest son's existence, not after his second wife had given him two heirs for his own company, Stewart Technologies. It was just as well. He'd long ago stopped looking for love and acceptance from his old man.

Knock. Knock. Knock.

"Come in." His office door opened and his assistant, Carolyn Foster, walked in. The statuesque blonde wore pregnancy well; barely a baby bump could be seen in the smart attire she wore.

"Do you have a minute?"

"Of course," Ayden responded, moving away from the window. "What can I do for you?"

"I have some not so pleasant news to deliver," Carolyn said.

"Oh, yeah? Whatever it is, just give it to me straight, no chaser."

"Very well..." She paused for several beats. "I won't be coming back after my maternity leave in a few months."

"Excuse me?" This couldn't be happening to him *again.*

"I'm sorry, Ayden—really, I am—but my husband and I have been trying for some time to start a family. And, well, I just want to enjoy the time with our first child because I'm not sure when we might have another."

Carolyn would make a fantastic mother because she was already putting her child first. It made Ayden think of the only person who'd ever cared one iota about him, who was gone, taken away too soon. His mother Lillian Stewart-Johnson, God rest her soul, had passed away several years ago from a heart attack. He suspected his mother's illness had been caused by years of stress and abuse at the hands of his stepfather Jack Johnson. Jack was a habitual smoker and a mean drunk.

Ayden had focused hard on his studies, so he could get the hell out of the house. And he'd been lucky. In junior high, his teachers recognized his high IQ and had helped Ayden receive a scholarship to a prestigious boarding school in the East. From there, his grades helped him get into Harvard and he'd never looked back.

Growing up, Ayden had developed a thick skin. He'd had to in order to live in the Johnson household, and not just because of the bruises, but because of the lack of love or affection. He'd learned he didn't need either. If he hadn't met his roommate, Luke Williams, in boarding school in the ninth grade, who knows how long Ayden would have gone without any real feelings. Ayden's goal had been to save his mama from working two jobs to support Jack's pack-and-bottle-a-day habit, but it had been useless. By the time he'd finally started making enough money, his mother was gone and he was all alone in the world except for Luke, his closest friend. Why had his mother let men bully her all her life? First, Henry had intimidated her into a small settlement, cutting her out of her rightful shares in Stewart Technologies. Then, Jack spent the little money she had received. Why hadn't she fought for the child support she was entitled to?

"I imagine there's nothing I could do to change your mind?" Ayden inquired. He knew it was a long shot, but he couldn't understand why anyone would throw away a good-paying job in order to stay home and change poopy diapers. Carolyn's departure was going to leave him in quite a pickle. One he hadn't been in since a certain uptight but beautiful assistant had left him five years ago.

"No, there isn't," Carolyn said, "but we can find a replacement. You always said you never thought you'd find someone as good as Maya and look what happened—you hired me."

He would never forget the day, ten years ago, when Maya Richardson had walked through his door looking for a job. She'd been a godsend, helping Ayden grow Stewart Investments into the company it was today. Thinking of her brought a smile to Ayden's face. How could it not? Not only was she the best assistant he'd ever had, Maya had fascinated him. Utterly and completely. Maya had hidden an exceptional figure beneath professional clothing and kept her hair in a tight bun. But Ayden had often wondered what it would be like to throw her over his desk and muss her up. Five years ago, he hadn't gone quite that far, but he had crossed a boundary.

Maya had been devastated over her breakup with her boyfriend. She'd come to him for comfort, and, instead, Ayden had made love to her. Years of wondering what it would be like to be with Maya had erupted into a passionate encounter. Their one night together had been so explosive the next morning Ayden had needed to take a step back to regain his perspective. He'd had to put up his guard; otherwise, he would have hurt her badly. He thought he'd been doing the right thing, but Maya hadn't thought so. In retrospect, Ayden wished he'd never given in to temptation. But he had, and he'd lost a damn good assistant. Maya had quit, and Ayden hadn't seen or heard from her since.

Shaking his head, Ayden strode to his desk and picked up the phone, dialing the recruiter who'd helped him find Carolyn. He wasn't looking forward to this process. It had taken a long time to find and train Carolyn. Before her, Ayden had dealt with several candidates walking into his office thinking they could ensnare him.

No, he had someone else in mind. A hardworking, dedicated professional who could read his mind without him saying a word and who knew how to handle a situation in his absence. Someone who knew about the big client he'd always wanted to capture but never could attain. She also had a penchant for numbers and research like no one he'd ever seen, not even Carolyn.

Ayden knew exactly who he wanted. He just needed to find out where she'd escaped to.

"Aren't you tired yet?" Callie Lewis asked Maya Richardson after they'd jogged nearly five miles in the muggy San Antonio weather. They'd met up at 6:00 a.m. after Maya had stumbled out of bed, placed her shoulder-length black hair in a ponytail, and put on her favorite sports tank with built-in bra and running shorts.

"No. Not yet." Maya hazarded a glance at Callie. Her friend was five foot two and nearly two hundred pounds, and had been following an intense exercise routine to lose weight. She'd already lost fifty pounds and Maya was trying to encourage her. They'd been best friends ever since Callie had defended Maya from bullies in the fifth grade, so Callie's well-being was important to her.

"Well, I need to stop a sec," Callie paused midstride. She limped over to a nearby bench and began a series of stretches.

"Okay, no problem." Maya jogged in place while she stretched.

"What's got you all riled up?" Callie asked. "You've been on edge for a couple of days."

Maya stopped jogging and stood still. She'd been trying to outrun the past, which was impossible, but she was giving it the old college try. "I received an invitation from Raven and Thomas for Nysha's baptism."

"You received what?" Callie's brown eyes grew large with amazement.

"You heard me."

"I just can't believe your sister and that sleazy husband of hers had the nerve to send it. Not after what they did to you."

Maya shrugged. It had been five long years since she'd felt the sting of Raven's betrayal with her boyfriend, Thomas. If anyone had told her that her baby sister would steal her man and marry him, she would have called them a liar. Maya and Raven had always been so close. When their father had left their mother, it had broken up their family, leaving her mom Sophia alone to support them. It hadn't been easy especially because her mother favored Raven.

"How can you be silent about this?"

"Because… I've made my peace, Callie," Maya replied. "I had to. They got *married*, for Christ's sake. I didn't have much choice."

"You didn't go to their wedding."

"How could I? Back then it was all too fresh."

"Including what happened between you and Ayden?"

Maya rolled her eyes. "Let's not talk about him, okay?"

"Why not? If I recall what you said back then, it was the best sex you'd ever had in your life," Callie said, making air quotes. "Yet after your night with him and his failure to acknowledge what happened, you quit your dream job."

Maya sighed heavily. She wished she'd kept that secret to herself. Five years ago, for better or for worse, her life had changed. She'd accepted it and moved on.

She began running in place again. "C'mon, my muscles are starting to tense up. We have to finish our run."

"You go on ahead," Callie stated. "I'm going to sit this one out. I'll call you later."

"Sure thing." Maya jogged off in the opposite direction. As she did, she thought back to that horrible night.

She'd been working late because Ayden needed a presentation for the following day. She'd picked up takeout to bring to her boyfriend, Thomas. Using the key he'd given her, she'd opened the door to his town house and found it dark. It was surprising, given his car was sitting in the driveway. After placing the bags on the kitchen counter, she'd heard voices.

Who was visiting Thomas? It was well after eight o'clock, so Maya had walked upstairs to investigate. She'd never forget the sight that greeted her: her baby sister, Raven, on top of Thomas as they writhed on the bed. Maya had screamed bloody murder. Raven had rushed off the bed to the bathroom while Thomas tried to cover himself with a sheet as he'd attempted to explain. What was there to discuss? She'd caught him banging her sister. Maya had rushed out of the room, damn near falling down the stairs and losing a great shoe in the process to make it to her car. Fumbling with the key, she'd eventually started it up and was pulling off when Raven came running out the door in Thomas's shirt calling after her. The whole incident had been humiliating.

How long had their affair been going on?

How long had both of them been laughing behind her back?

Maya ran harder. Faster. But she couldn't outrun the memories. They must have really thought she was a fool for believing his lies that she was the kind of girl he wanted to marry. Her mother was right. Raven was the beauty in the family.

That was the state she'd been in when she'd arrived on Ayden's doorstep. Maya hadn't known where else to go. Callie lived in San Antonio and Maya had just lost her sister to a man she thought she loved. Over the five years of their working relationship, she and Ayden had shared some personal stories, especially when he'd told her about his past; she'd hoped he could lend her an ear now when she needed someone to listen.

Ah, Ayden. He'd been her secret crush for years before she'd met Thomas. When she'd started working for him, Maya had thought the sun and moon hung on the green-eyed devil, but Ayden hadn't seen her like that, like a woman. All he saw was a smart, efficient PA who did his bidding—which included making reservations for his dates with beautiful women, and sending them expensive flowers or trinkets as a parting gift when he was done with them. And yet, she'd chosen to go to Ayden, the man who didn't believe in love and thought it was a hoax meant to sell greeting cards.

That night, he'd offered her comfort. A shoulder to cry on. Comfort in ways she'd never been able to forget. Initially, he'd been shocked by her disheveled presence on his doorstep, but as soon as he'd seen her puffy, red-rimmed eyes, Ayden had immediately taken her into his embrace and closed the door behind him. He'd sat her down on the couch and listened as she'd told him of Raven and Tom's betrayal, of her failure. No one was ever going to love her, *want* her. She was a nothing. A nobody. A plain Jane that no man would ever be compelled to marry. Ayden had refused to hear of it. Had told her she was wrong. He'd stroked her hair and told her everything was going to be all right. With tears in her eyes, she'd glanced up at him, and then she'd done something desperate. She'd kissed him.

The surprising thing was he hadn't pushed her away. Instead, he'd kissed her back. One thing had led to another and the next moment, she and Ayden were making love on his bear skin rug on the floor of his living room. To this day, Maya had never been able to fully understand what had happened. One minute, he'd been consoling her and telling her she was beautiful and worthy of love, and the next, she'd been wrapped in his arms having wild, passionate sex.

It had literally been the most exciting sexual encounter of her life. Maya had experienced true bliss and one hell of an orgasm, but as soon as it was over, Ayden had pulled away. What she'd thought was heaven on earth had soon turned into a nightmare. Ayden told her he hadn't meant for it to happen. Maya had been crushed for the second time in one night. She'd dressed as fast as she could and had left to lick her wounds in private.

She'd relived that moment many nights since, wondering how their relationship had taken such a turn. Maya had always harbored feelings for Ayden in the past, but she'd never thought for a second that they were reciprocated. She'd eventually come to the conclusion that he'd made love to her out of pity because she'd been so pathetic. Knowing how he felt, Maya couldn't face Ayden again and had tendered her resignation.

Looking back, Maya realized that she'd been more upset over Ayden's rejection than Thomas's. Sure, she'd been hurt by Thomas because she'd loved him, but it had been her sister stealing her man that hurt the most. She'd never forgiven Raven, and they hadn't spoken in five years. It was Ayden who'd really broken her heart.

Once Maya had pushed herself to the limit with ten miles, she stopped running. It was time she faced the past with her sister so she could move forward with her life. And there was no better time than the present.

"Do you think she'll come back?" Ayden asked his best friend on a transatlantic call later that evening. It was before 7:00 a.m. in London, but he knew Luke Williams would already be up. How did he know? Because they were alike—notorious workaholics and driven to succeed. Luke was a financial analyst making millions.

"After the way you treated her when she left?" Luke said. "I wouldn't."

Ayden frowned. "Was I really that bad?"

"Hmm, I don't know, let me think," Luke paused for dramatic effect. "You were a slave driver at the office, rarely giving the poor girl a day off. And at a moment of weakness, you shag her and then tell her to kick rocks. I dunno, I might have a problem with that."

"Thanks a lot, Luke."

"You did call me, you know," Luke responded. "If you

didn't want me to keep it one hundred with you then you should have called another mate."

"You're my only *mate*." Ayden replied. He didn't have many friends. He'd never had the time to make any because he was too busy pushing himself to excel, to make something of himself despite Henry Stewart turning his back and leaving him and his mom with an abusive stepfather.

"Yeah, that's true. No one else can tolerate you. Except maybe Maya, and you made a royal mess of that relationship."

"I know I messed up, but I can fix it."

Luke snorted. "By offering Maya her job back? Why on earth would she ever agree? What does she get out of it?"

"I'm prepared to offer her a generous salary."

"And if she wants more?"

"What do you mean?"

"C'mon, man, don't be an idiot. Maya left because you two slept together. If you offer her a job, she might be thinking there's more on the table."

Ayden had never thought Maya might want more. "I'm not prepared to give her anything else. You know how I feel about love, marriage, the whole white-picket-fence thing."

"Yeah, yeah, sing to the choir. I've already heard this bit before," Luke stated. "Poor you, your dad left your mom to marry a hot tart, leaving you and your mom with nothing."

"That's right. Love is for other poor dumb schmucks."

"Like me, you mean," Luke countered.

Darn. He'd stuck his foot in his mouth. Luke had just married a beautiful redhead named Helena and they were head over heels in love. But if anyone could make a go of marriage, it was Luke. "Present company excluded," Ayden stated.

Luke chuckled. "You've never minced words before, Ayden, so don't start now."

"Helena is lovely," Ayden replied. "And she's madly in love with you. She can't wait to have a mess of babies with you."

"That's right, my friend. I'll have Helena knocked up before the year is out," Luke said, laughing. "That way she can't leave me for another man when she realizes she married a dumb schmuck like me."

Ayden laughed. That's what he loved about Luke. He could be self-deprecating and still be the life of the party. "So let's return to my original point for this call."

"What was that again?"

"Maya. And what it would take for her to agree to come back to me, I mean, the position of executive assistant at Stewart Investments."

"You would have to find the right incentive that doesn't include becoming a notch on your bedpost."

"That's not going to happen again," Ayden said. "Bedding Maya was a one-time thing. Plus, I doubt she's been carrying a torch for me. For Christ's sake, it was only one night!"

"If you say so, my friend. I've given my advice, for what it's worth. Good luck, and let me know how it turns out."

"Will do." Ayden ended the call and stared down at the folder in his lap. It held the address of where Maya was staying in Austin. He'd hired a private investigator to research her whereabouts. His timing was perfect because she was back in town for her niece's baptism and staying at a downtown hotel.

Ayden had to admit he was shocked by what he'd read in the file. He recalled how devastated Maya had been the night she'd come to him after discovering her sister in bed with her boyfriend. If she was returning, it had to mean she'd forgiven them. Surely that meant good news for him? He could ask her to come back to Stewart Investments, and things would be different between them now. After all, it had been years since Ayden had seen her. Although he might have had the odd fantasy about her, on his part, any residual feelings from their night together five years ago were long gone. Ayden had been with many women since Maya. More beautiful. More stunning.

He and Maya had always enjoyed an excellent working relationship. He was certain they could get past this if she was willing to forgive him for his lack of sensitivity and give them another chance. He knew it was a long shot, but there was only one way to find out. He had to go to her, and he wasn't leaving until her answer was yes.

From the bathroom of the Baptist church, Maya fretted as she smoothed down the dress she'd chosen to wear to Nysha's baptism. Should she have come?

Throughout the years, Raven had tried to extend an olive branch, but Maya had rebuffed each and every effort. Why? Because Maya was jealous. Raven was living the life that should have been hers. If she was honest, Maya would have loved that life with Ayden, but he hadn't wanted her five years ago. Or not in the way she'd hoped.

So why come back?

Because she couldn't go on living this way, holding on to past hurts and hiding away from the world. It was time to move on with her life. She'd come to make peace with her sister.

She glanced at herself in the mirror. The sleeveless plum dress had a deep V showing a swell of cleavage, thanks to the push-up bra she'd spent a fortune on in the hopes it would give her a bosom. Her long black hair, her best feature, was coiffed and hung in big curls down her back. She'd even allowed her hair stylist, who doubled as a makeup artist, to do her face. After all these years, she had to look her best because, Lord knows, her mother would be in full diva mode. Raven, of course, wouldn't have to try hard because she was naturally beautiful.

And now it was time to face the music. She couldn't very well hang out in the church bathroom forever. Grabbing her clutch purse, she made for the door. Sophia Richardson was greeting guests at the church entrance. From where Maya stood, she noted her mother's stylish salt-and-pepper updo and what looked like her Sunday-best suit, complete with pumps. But rather than looking the picture of a radiant grandma, her mother had lost weight and appeared a bit gaunt with sunken cheeks. Her normal caramel skin looked sallow.

Maya braced herself as she walked toward her. "Mother."

"Maya?" On cue, Sophia looked her over from head to toe—from the designer sandals to the simple Marc Jacobs sheath to the designer handbag. Apparently she passed muster, because her mother said, "I'm happy you've finally chosen to put the past behind you and return to the fold."

She held open her arms and Maya reluctantly walked into them. As expected, the embrace was brief. Maya suspected she'd received it because several guests had walked in and her mother wouldn't dare make a scene.

"Raven and Thomas will be so happy to see you," Sophia whispered in her ear. "Please go in." She motioned Maya toward the pews.

Would they be happy to see her? Or would her presence be a reminder of their past transgressions? Maya forced herself to put one foot in front of the other and enter the hall. Raven and Thomas were at the end of the aisle talking with the pastor. Her sister looked as stunning as ever even though she'd just had the baby two months ago. She was wearing a cream suit and had her hair in a French roll. Raven was already back to her svelte size-six figure. Thomas wore a suit and striped tie and beamed by her side, holding the baby.

Maya walked toward them. When Raven turned around and saw Maya, Maya felt her heart constrict. It had hurt being estranged from her baby sister.

"Maya?" Raven said as she drew near.

Maya glanced at Thomas and gave him a nod, stepping toward Raven. "Yes, I'm here."

Tears welled in her sister's eyes. "Oh, thank God, our prayers were answered. I've asked God for forgiveness every day for what we—" she glanced at her husband "—did to you. And now, I'm blessed to have you back in my life, in our daughter's life."

"Don't get carried away, Raven," Maya responded. "All is not swept under the rug."

"Of course not," Raven said. "I owe you a long overdue apology." She reached for Maya's hands and grasped them in her own. "I'm so sorry for hurting you, Maya. Can you please find it in your heart to forgive me?"

Maya stared at her in stunned disbelief. She had never expected an apology. Least of all, from Raven, who'd always been self-centered. But then again she'd never given her the chance.

"We're both sorry," Thomas said from Raven's side. "You deserved better than how we treated you. You deserved the truth. We should never have sneaked behind your back. It was wrong and I'm sorry."

Maya swallowed and nodded. She was too overcome to speak. She didn't know what she'd thought would happen during the visit, but clearly Raven and Thomas had matured enough to admit their mistakes.

"Would you like to meet your niece?" Raven asked, tears brimming in her eyes.

"Y-yes, I'd like that very much."

Raven walked over to Thomas, took their daughter out of his arms and placed the sleeping baby in Maya's. Her niece was the most beautiful little girl Maya had ever seen, with her smooth brown skin and shock of hair surrounded by a white headband with a bow. She was outfitted in the cutest white lace baptism dress. "She's beautiful." Maya grasped her niece's little finger in her hand.

"Can you believe I'm a mom?" Raven asked in wonder.

"Actually, I can't," Maya said, glancing her way, "but you are."

Raven gave a halfhearted smile. "You were always supposed to be the stay-at-home wife while I was supposed to be the career girl. It's funny how the tide changes."

"Yes, it's funny." Maya leaned over and returned Nysha into her sister's arms. "She's really beautiful. Congratulations to you both."

Maya stepped away as fast as humanly possible. It didn't hurt that guests were already headed toward them to greet the happy family. She needed some air. She couldn't breathe; it felt like she was suffocating. Maya sidestepped several guests entering the church and rushed outside.

Leaning against the building, she took in large gulps of air and forced the rising tide of emotions overwhelming her to calm. Had she honestly thought it would be easy seeing Raven and Thomas with their daughter? Maya glanced at the door. It should have been her. She should be the one who was a wife and mother; it's what she'd always wanted. Maya had always known she would make a good mom because she'd cared for Raven her entire life. Sophia Richardson had been too busy working two or, sometimes, three jobs to be there for them. Maya had been left to care for Raven, make her dinner, help with her homework and pick out her school clothes. So much so that Raven once had called her Mommy. Sophia had been livid and had yelled at Raven that *she* was her mommy.

Maternal instinct ran through Maya's veins, while Raven had never cared for another human being beside herself until now. But it was clear to Maya that Raven loved her daughter and was happy. Maya didn't begrudge her sister happiness, but did it have to come at her expense? Perhaps she'd made a mistake in attending? She could sneak off with no one being the wiser. She'd made an appearance. Surely that had to count for something?

Maya was just about to head down the church steps when her mother's voice rang out. "Maya, dear, we're about to begin."

Darn. She'd missed her chance to use her get-out-of-jail-free card.

Inhaling, Maya spun around to face her mother and walked inside the church.

Hours later, Maya was looking for her handbag in one of the many bedrooms of Nysha's godparents' home. She was ready to leave. After the baptism ceremony, the entire group had adjourned here for a light meal. True to form, Sophia had gushed over their home, how beautiful it was and what great godparents they would make. It made Maya ill to see that nothing had changed; her mother was just as superficial as she'd been before.

Maya had done her part by showing up and making polite pleasantries. It was time for her to leave.

"Ah, there it is," she said aloud when she discovered her purse.

"Do you have a minute?" a male voice said from behind her.

Maya didn't need to turn around to know who it belonged to. They'd once been lovers. She whirled on her heel to face Thomas. If looks could kill, he would have been struck down on the spot. "What do you want?"

Thomas held up his hands in a defensive posture. "I'm sorry. I didn't mean to scare you."

"You didn't."

"I was hoping I could speak to you for a few minutes."

"I don't wish to discuss the past," Maya responded. Just being with her family had conjured enough of her old insecurities.

Thomas lowered his eyes. "Quite frankly, neither do I. It wasn't my finest moment."

"Then what is it that you want? I don't have all day."

Thomas glanced up and Maya hated to see the regret in his eyes. But she wasn't prepared for his next words. "It's about Sophia."

Maya's ears perked up. "What about my mother?"

"You may have noticed she's lost some weight?"

"Yes, I did, but I figured maybe she was dieting for the big event," Maya offered. It wasn't completely out of the realm of possibility. Her mother believed in looking her best, especially when the spotlight was on her.

"She's not dieting, Maya. Your mother is sick."

"Sick?" Maya clutched her purse to her chest. "How sick?"

"She has pancreatic cancer."

"Cancer?" The words felt like an anchor around her heart, but she managed to ask, "What stage?"

"Stage three. Sophia has been undergoing treatments the last month and, needless to say, it's taken its toll."

"Months? How long have you known about her condition?"

"Maya…"

"How long?" How long had her family had been keeping her in the dark? Why they hadn't told her Sophia was dying?

"Two months."

"And you didn't think to inform me sooner? She's my mother."

"Whom you've been estranged from for five years," Thomas retorted with a huff, "along with the rest of this family."

"You're *not* my family."

"I may not be a blood relation, but I care about Sophia. Raven and I have been carrying the load because her treatments are expensive even with insurance, not to mention the laboratory visits, PET scans and medications. And besides, it's been tearing Raven up seeing Sophia like this and not having anyone to talk to beside me. She needs you."

"She's always *needed* me," Maya responded tightly, "and I've always been there, but what do I get out of it? The short end of the stick."

"I—I thought you were going to let go of the past, Maya. You came today."

Guilt surged through her. Her mother was sick and this wasn't the time or place to take score on who'd harmed who. "Thank you for telling me." She started toward the door.

"What are you going to do?" Thomas inquired.

Maya had no idea. Today had been hard enough as it was. She needed a few minutes to digest everything he'd told her and come up with a plan. "I don't know, but I'll be in touch."

When Maya finally made it back to her hotel room, she was mentally and emotionally exhausted. Confronting the members of her family who'd hurt her and feigning to be the happy aunt had been hard enough. But finding out her mother had cancer was the straw that broke the camel's back. Not only did she have a splitting headache, but her feet were aching from the new designer sandals she'd bought to ensure she measured up to her mother's scrutiny. All she wanted to do was run a hot bath, take some ibuprofen and go to bed. In that exact order.

Maya had kicked off her shoes and was unzipping her dress when there was a knock on her door. She glanced down at her watch. It was seven o'clock. She was in no mood for company after the bomb Thomas dropped on her. And who knew she was in town anyway?

Padding to the door in her bare feet, Maya swung it open in frustration. The person on the other side was someone she never thought she'd see again, not after the one night they'd shared.

"Ayden?"

"Hello, Maya."

Two

At six foot three, weighing about 210 pounds of solid muscle, Ayden looked as yummy as he ever had. Maya was dumbfounded to see the man she'd once adored standing in the flesh in front of her. How could she not be enthralled by those hazel eyes, his strong nose and the light stubble surrounding the best mouth and cleft chin in Texas? He was impeccably dressed in a dark suit with a purple-and-white-striped tie.

"Wh-what are you doing here?" She pulled back her shoulder blades to project that she wasn't taken aback by seeing him after all this time, when she definitely was.

"I came to see you." He rewarded her with one of his sexy smiles. "May I come in?"

"I don't think so..." Maya responded, and began to close the door. What did you say to the man you'd once slept with, but hadn't seen in five years?

"Maya, please." Ayden stuck a foot in the door to prevent her from shutting it. "I wouldn't have come if it wasn't important."

"All right, but only for a few minutes. It's late and I've had a trying day."

"Thank you." Ayden brushed past Maya, and she caught a hint of his cologne that was so uniquely him. Her stomach clenched in knots like it always did whenever she was around him. And her nipples puckered to attention underneath her dress.

Maya closed the door and turned around to face him. "I repeat, what are you doing here?"

"Is that any way to greet an old friend?" Ayden teased.

Maya folded her arms across her chest because, with Ayden's radar, he might see he'd aroused her, and she'd be mortified if he knew she was still attracted to him. "We were never friends, Ayden."

"Weren't we?" he asked, stepping toward her. "You knew all my secrets. I told you everything."

"And you knew nothing about me."

"That's not true," Ayden said. "I know your favorite color is green. I know *Pretty Woman* is your favorite movie because you're a closet romantic. I know you write in a journal when you think no one is looking. I know you run when you need an outlet to ease tension."

Maya chuckled inwardly. She was surprised he knew that much, but she supposed he would have had to pick up on something. She'd been his executive assistant for half a decade. "All right, you know a few things about me."

Ayden raised a brow. "A few? I think I know a lot more than that."

His implication was clear. He'd known her in the biblical sense and there was no getting around that. But why bring it up? It was over and done with. Finito. He'd made sure of that.

"Why are you here? Clearly, you sought me out. How else would you know I'm back in Austin?"

"I admit I had an investigator try to find you. They informed me you were back for your niece's baptism," Ayden replied. "How did that go? Have you ever been back since…"

He stopped. *Have you ever been back since the night we slept together?* That was the question he couldn't bring himself to finish. At least he had the grace to stop before he embarrassed them both.

"Why would you have an investigator look for me? I don't appreciate you treating me like one of your females," Maya stated.

Ayden was notorious for having the women in his love life investigated to be sure they had no ulterior motives. But Maya, why her? It wasn't like she was one of them. All she'd wanted out of today was to make peace with her family and move on with her life, but now that wasn't possible. First, because of her mother's illness and now Ayden's surprise visit. He wanted something, and despite her anger at his invasion of her privacy she was curious to find out what it was.

"I'm sorry about that, but I didn't know where you were or how to find you. When you left five years ago, you disappeared without a trace."

"Yet, you didn't come looking for me."

"No, I didn't, and I think we both know why. I'm here now and we can talk about that. But first, you mentioned having a bad day. I can't imagine seeing your sister and your ex-boyfriend, now married with a child, was easy, especially when you thought you were headed down the aisle to matrimonial bliss with him yourself."

Maya laughed bitterly to avoid the pain of hearing him say out loud what she'd already thought so many times today. “Apparently, he didn’t get the memo, so no, today wasn’t a pleasant experience.”

Ayden began removing the jacket he was wearing.

“What are you doing?” she asked with a frown. “I didn’t ask you to stay. I only agreed to talk for a few minutes.” He had no right to make himself comfortable in her hotel room. Not after the way he’d dismissed her so long ago.

Ayden paused. “I’m sorry yet again. I keep apologizing to you tonight.” He held up his jacket. “May I?”

“I suppose you can stay a few minutes longer.” Ayden draped the jacket across the sofa and sank down into its plushness.

He sat forward on the couch and rested his very large forearms on those powerfully muscled thighs of his. *Jesus!* Why couldn’t she think straight when she was around him? Sure, he’d always had this effect on her, but she would have thought his treatment of her five years ago would have cooled any physical response she might have to him now. Apparently, she’d been wrong.

“I’m sorry for what you went through with your sister. It’s truly a shame because you’re worth a thousand Ravens.”

Maya couldn’t resist a small smile forming on her lips. Ayden didn’t compliment people often. “You don’t have to say that.”

“You don’t think I mean it?”

She spun away and shrugged. It didn’t matter. None of it mattered. Ayden, Raven, Thomas—they were all in her rearview. She’d only come back to Austin to get closure and move on with her life. She’d done that. Her mother having cancer had certainly put a wrinkle in her plans to go back to San Antonio and her new life.

When she didn’t answer him, Ayden must have risen

from the sofa, because Maya felt rather than saw him behind her. "What? What is it that you want from me?"

His large hands grasped her shoulders and guided her around to look at him. "Don't hide from me, Maya. Aren't you tired of it?"

Maya jerked out of his hands. "Don't presume to think you know me, Ayden, just because you can spit out a few obvious facts about me."

"All right. Then how about this. I want you back."

Maya sucked in a deep breath and reminded herself that Ayden was a master at getting his way, especially with women. Over the years, she'd seen him bring the most intelligent and independent women to their knees and have them beg him to take them back. He never did. Instead, he'd have Maya send a farewell gift with his regards. *His regards!*

It must have crushed his ego when she'd chosen not to stay working for him after he bid her adieu after their night together. She wasn't about to go backward even though her heart yearned for more. Still, she was curious and found herself asking, "Why do you want me back?"

"You're the best assistant I ever had. You know how Stewart Investments is run. Hell, how I work. I can count on you to make decisions whether I'm there or not. I trust you implicitly. And remember the Kincaid Corporation deal that I've always wanted a crack at?"

She nodded.

"I have the opportunity to pitch Stewart Investments to them again. You remember how important it was for me to land that account. He's one of my father's largest suppliers. You remember how hard we worked on that first pitch only for him to go to a larger firm. Times have changed and Stewart Investments is in better shape than ever to compete with the big boys."

Ayden didn't want *her* back. He wanted his trusty workaholic assistant back under his grip. "I see."

"You see what?"

"You want me back so I can be your shadow, following you around, being at your beck and call. Well, I'm not your pet, Ayden."

"I never thought you were." He sounded offended. "And I've never treated you like one. You were always a valuable employee."

Maya shook her head. So he was just going to act like it never happened. That they'd never seen each other naked? That they'd hadn't slept together on the bear skin rug in front of his fireplace? "You should go, Ayden." She pushed at his rock-hard chest, which was darn near impenetrable, and walked to the door.

"Why?" He grasped her wrist. His eyes were fire when he said, "You haven't even heard me out."

"Why should I, Ayden, when you refuse to even acknowledge the elephant in the room? I left for a reason and you damn well know why."

Ayden sighed heavily and slowly released her as if she'd struck him. He leaned backward against the door and his intense gaze rested on her. "I'd hoped we wouldn't have to discuss it."

Maya rolled her eyes upward, not wanting him to know how hurt she was by his words. Yet again, Ayden was bruising her already fragile ego. But try as she might, she couldn't ignore the tears that trickled down her cheeks. She wiped at them with the back of her hands.

Ayden swore when he saw her tears. "Christ! I'm sorry, Maya. I didn't mean to hurt you. Not again."

"But yet you continue to do it."

"Not on purpose," Ayden said. "Never on purpose. I care for you, Maya. I always have. I suppose that's why I allowed our relationship to become—" he paused for the right word "—*complicated.* And I take all the blame for what happened. You were destroyed when you came to me, but rather than comforting you, I took advantage of you, and for that I'm terribly sorry. I should never have let things go as far as they did."

Maya glanced up at him through her tears. He was apologizing for making love to her? Was he mad? He was making the situation so much worse, because to her that night had been one of the most sensual encounters she'd ever experienced. But why should she be surprised? He'd only been with her out of pity. He could never find her, Maya Richardson, attractive like he did the many beautiful women he frequently bedded.

Much to her chagrin, Ayden kept going. "The next morning I was so mortified by my actions that I sought to sweep it under the rug like it never happened, which I know wasn't fair to you. But I didn't know what else to do, Maya. Clearly, I'd compromised our working relationship so much that you couldn't come back to work for me. It's why I gave you such a generous termination package. I was sorry for taking advantage of you. I'm still sorry, but I promise, should you choose to work for me again, I will never cross that line and take advantage of you again. I promise I will respect you and your right to have a life of your own without me taking up every minute of your free time."

"Why are you saying all of this?"

"Because I *need* you, Maya. My assistant, Carolyn, is leaving in a couple of months to be a stay-at-home wife and mother, and I need you back."

The desperation in Ayden's tone stunned Maya. She

watched him reach into the jacket pocket of his suit and pull out a thin envelope. He handed it to her. “Read it. I’m offering you an extremely generous salary and benefit package to return to Stewart Investments.”

Slowly Maya ripped open the envelope and pulled out the single sheet of paper. The offer letter was nothing short of impressive. The salary was more than generous, it was astronomical. And the benefits of increased 401(k), profit sharing and an abundance of time off was staggering. “Ayden…”

“Listen, I’ll make this worth your while. I’m willing to offer you a signing bonus of twenty-five thousand dollars if you’ll agree to come back *right now*.”

She looked in his direction and saw the worry that she would say no etched all over his face. And she should. She had every right to turn him down. He wasn’t good for her. And she’d made a good life in San Antonio. She should go back where it was safe, but when had she ever used her head when it came to this man? The bonus he was offering her was too great a sum to turn down, not when the funds could help her ailing mother. When he looked at her with those puppy-dog eyes, she was a goner.

“Please, don’t say no. Think it over.”

“I don’t need to think it over,” she answered impulsively. “My answer is no. I have a life in San Antonio, Ayden. I can’t just drop everything because you need me.” She had a home, a job she enjoyed and her best friend, Callie. Why would she uproot her life?

“You haven’t even thought about it,” Ayden said. “Isn’t there anything I can do to entice you? There has to be something.”

The thought continued to nag at her that if she accepted Ayden’s offer, she could help out with her mother’s cancer treatments. Even though they were estranged, Maya couldn't imagine letting her mother suffer when she could have the potential means to help. What kind of person would she be if she did that? But could she go back to working for Ayden knowing her feelings for him weren't truly resolved? "I don't know."

"Maya, we can make this work," Ayden murmured. "With you by my side, we can not only win over Kincaid, but take Stewart Investments to new heights. And with that offer, you would get a share in the earnings. It's a win-win. Please say yes."

"All right, all right, I'll come back."

Ayden couldn't believe the joy that surged through him at Maya's response. Without thinking, he stepped closer. He called himself all kinds of foolish for torturing himself with her familiar sweet aroma, but he couldn't resist. Ayden pulled her into his embrace, squeezing her tightly to him. He felt her breasts pebble against his chest and his groin tightened.

Maya stiffened and Ayden knew he'd done the wrong thing. She didn't welcome his advances. The one night they'd shared had been her attempt to feel loved, coddled, but that was in the past. He mustn't forget that. Still, being in her hotel room was doing funny things to his anatomy again; he pulled away. "I'm sorry. I was just so overjoyed. Won't happen again." He couldn't touch her again. Otherwise, he might lose his head and start to remember what it was like to feel that soft skin of hers as she melted underneath him. He blinked rapidly.

"It's all right," Maya finally said, letting him off the hook. "I guess you were right. It's time I finally stop hiding and return to the life I once loved."

"Do you really mean that?" Ayden quirked a brow. He knew it wasn't entirely true. The report he'd received had told him of Sophia Richardson's health. He knew that the signing bonus was the reason Maya was coming back—she needed it for Sophia Richardson's health costs. He would have given her the money even if she hadn't agreed to come back. Maya was someone he cared about, and if it was in his power to help her mother, he would. He wouldn't want her to experience the guilt he'd felt at not being able to help his mother during her illness. It was guilt he still carried to this day.

"Not the long nights," she added with a smile, "but I did enjoy working with you. We were a good team."

"And we will be again." Once they got back into their work groove, the past would be left behind and they could make a new beginning. He offered Maya his hand. She glanced down at it and Ayden wondered if she was going to renege, but instead her soft fingers clasped his in a firm shake.

"It's a deal."

Ayden grinned. "You don't know how much this means to me."

"Oh, I can guess," Maya laughed. "I suppose there's lots of work piled up?"

Ayden grinned unabashedly. "No. Carolyn is still here for a few weeks, but I wasn't relishing working with someone new. Plus I already had my mind made up that no one but you would do."

Maya Richardson was one of a kind. And although Carolyn had done an acceptable job in her place, Maya was irreplaceable. He'd discovered that when he'd made the mistake of mixing business with pleasure. And speaking of that, it was late. He needed to get out of her room before he did something he couldn't take back. He moved toward the door, but stopped midstep. "How much time do you need to get your affairs in order?"

"A couple of weeks to give notice at my current job. And when I get back to Austin, I'll need some time with Carolyn to get up to speed before she leaves."

He pointed his index finger at her. "I'm holding you to it."

"I've never gone back on my word."

"Very true." She never had and never would, because Maya was a woman he could count on. "I'll see you soon." Ayden left swiftly and closed the door behind him, then leaned up against it.

Closing his eyes, he sucked in a deep breath. It had been dicey in there for a minute. He hadn't realized just how much of a physical tug he'd feel being with Maya again. It had been five years, but the moment she'd opened the door to her hotel room, he'd been transported to that night at his apartment when she'd exploded in his arms and kissed him with a passion unlike anything he'd ever known. Maya had kissed him as if he were a man and not the boss she'd worked with for years. She had aroused him to the point that he'd acted rather than thought about his actions.

For a split second when he'd held her in his arms and their bodies collided, he'd felt compelled to act as he had back then, but in the nick of time he'd managed to do the right thing and move away. He'd just convinced Maya to come back to him and Ayden wasn't about to mess it up because he couldn't keep it in his trousers. He was already the worst kind of scoundrel, having played on feelings he suspected she might still harbor for him.

How did he know?

There had a moment when she thought she'd disguised her true emotions that he had caught a glimpse of something in her eyes. He wasn't positive of how deep her feelings went after all these years, but at the very least, Maya still cared for him, and Ayden had used it to get what he wanted. Which was why he would ensure he kept their relationship platonic going forward—he refused to lose her a second time.

"Are you insane?" Callie stared at Maya in disbelief from across the table of the Starbucks where they'd met the following afternoon when she returned to San Antonio.

"No, I'm not."

"Clearly, you must have lost your mind." Callie reached across the short distance to place the back of her hand on Maya's forehead. "Why else would you agree to go back and work for Ayden?"

"He made me an attractive offer."

"This isn't about money, Maya," Callie responded hotly, "and you know it. You're going because you're still hung up on the man."

"That's not true."

Callie raised a brow.

"It's not. Listen, Callie, I got over Ayden a long time ago, when he nearly kicked me out of his place the morning after we had sex. It made me wise up real quick."

"Well, if that's the case, why go back for more? Why put yourself in harm's way? You know you're not immune to his charms. And I suspect he knows. How else would he have lured you back into his web?"

"I'm not his prey."

"Are you sure about that?" Callie inquired, sipping on her Frappuccino. "Because I suspect you have no idea what you're in for. Five years ago, you opened Pandora's box and found out what it was like to *be* with the man. Do you honestly think you can act as if those feelings never existed?"

"He's offering me enough money to ensure I ignore them."

"I still don't understand, after the way he treated you."

Maya leaned back in her chair and regarded her best friend. She hadn't yet divulged her mother's condition. "Mama is ill."

"Excuse me?"

"Thomas shared with me that she has pancreatic cancer."

"Omigod!" Callie jerked back in her seat. Then she immediately reached across the table and clutched Maya's hand. "What's the diagnosis?"

"They are hoping that, after chemo and radiation, she will go into remission, but the treatments are expensive. Thomas and Raven have been helping out, but with the baby, they are stretched thin."

Callie nodded. "Now I understand why you accepted Ayden's offer."

"The influx of cash will help Mama. Without worrying about finances, she can focus on getting better." Although she and her mother had never seen eye to eye, she was *her mother.* How could she not help out?

"Oh, Maya." Callie's eyes filled with tears. "You are so selfless. Does your mother have any idea of your plans?"

"I called her earlier and told her I was moving back to Austin," Maya replied. "She was pleased that I would be closer, but I didn't tell her about the money. She knows Raven and Thomas have been covering the out-of-pocket expenses, but I don't want her to know that I'll take up the slack going forward. "And promise me you won't tell her."

"Of course not. I would never betray your confidence. But where are you going to live? With your mother? I can't imagine you staying with your sister."

"That's completely out of the question. Although I'm willing to get to know my niece and I accepted Raven's apology, it's going to be a long time, if ever, before we can get back to the sister relationship we once shared. And as for my mother, we're like oil and water. We don't mix. If I stayed with her, all she would do is criticize and compare me to Raven like she did when we were children. It is best if I find my own place, but I'll visit Mom." She'd contacted a property management company who'd forwarded some listings for sublets and short-term rentals until she could find a place she liked.

"All right. I just worry about you, and not only with where you lay your head. I'm talking about Ayden. You're walking into the lion's den with no protection for your heart."

"My heart has nothing to do with the situation. What I felt for Ayden is in the past."

"That's easy to say when you're not seeing the man day and night. I remember the hours you kept before."

"It won't be like that now. He promised. Plus, he didn't want me five years ago, so nothing has really changed."

"Maya…you were intimate with Ayden. Trust me, he *wanted* you."

"For all of five seconds. Anyway, have a little faith in me, Callie. I can do this. I *have* to. Not for myself, but for Mama."

Three

Two weeks later, Maya sat outside her mother's house with the engine of her Honda running. She'd arrived in Austin the day before. Ayden had ensured her sign-on bonus check had arrived within days of accepting his offer, so she'd been able to secure her short-term rental for next six months. She'd put most of her belongings in storage until she was sure returning to Stewart Investments would work out. In the meantime, she'd kept the news of her return to Austin a secret from her family, but now it was time to face the music. Since her relationship with her sister was strained, she'd informed Raven via text of her plans a few days ago. Raven was happy she was coming back home if the emoji that accompanied her texts were anything to go by, but Maya hadn't yet told her mother.

After turning off the ignition, Maya exited the car and climbed the porch steps. The neighborhood looked much the same as it had when she'd left some ten-odd years ago except now the homes appeared older and more worn. Her mother's could use a coat of paint and the lawn needed mowing. Maya was just about to ring the doorbell when the door swung wide.

"Maya?" her mother said incredulously.

"Yes, it's me. Can I come in?" Maya was startled by how thin her mother was. Although it had only been a little over two weeks since she'd last seen her, Sophia had lost another five pounds. Her normally dark hair lay limp on her shoulders and the simple print house shift she was wearing hung off her slender frame. Meanwhile her skin seemed sallow and her eyes had sunk even deeper into her face.

"Of course." Sophia stood back and motioned her into the formal living room. "Would you like anything to drink? I think I have some sweet tea in the fridge."

Maya shook her head. "Nothing for me." She didn't plan on staying long.

Her mother took a seat on the sofa and Maya did the same. "What are you doing here? I thought you went back to San Antonio."

"I did, but I came back."

"So you could start to mend fences with your sister?" her mother offered, folding one leg over the other.

One day, yes, but not now." Although she'd accepted Raven's marriage and her baby niece, Maya wasn't ready to tackle more than that. She had Ayden to deal with.

"Oh, Maya. That's water under the bridge now. You have to let it go and move on."

"I have let it go, Mother," Maya responded. "I came to the baptism."

"Yes, you did. And that was a start."

"Listen, Mama. I didn't come here to talk about Raven.

I came to let you know that I'm moving back home. I've gotten my old position back at Stewart Investments."

"With that good-looking fella you used to work for?" Sophia touched her chest. "Now there was a sight for sore eyes if ever I saw one. That man is gorgeous. Why couldn't you ever snag him?"

Of course her mother would think along those lines. But finding a man wasn't a number-one priority for Maya. She was an independent woman who used her brains to get ahead. "Ayden is my boss, nothing more." And there could never been anything ever again.

"That's too bad. With his looks and all that money, you'd never have to worry a day in your life about how to pay the next bill."

"That's the thing, Mama. I make good money and I can more than help out with whatever it is that you need around the house." Maya looked about the room and noted the peeling wallpaper and loose wood flooring.

Her mother rose to her feet and began pacing the room. "I don't need your handouts, Maya Richardson. I've been doing just fine without you. Raven and Thomas have seen to that."

"I'm sure they have. I just thought—" Her mother might want her help? It was clear Sophia didn't want Maya to know about her cancer.

"That you could come in on your white horse and save the day?" Sophia interrupted. "Well, that's not necessary. We've got it covered."

Maya sighed. "Very well, then." She would just have to tackle her mother's financial woes a different way. She pulled out a slip of paper. "Here's my new address and phone number if you need to reach me since it's clear you're doing just fine without me."

She rose to her feet to depart, but her mother touched her arm softly.

"I'm sorry, Maya. That came out all wrong. I'm glad you're back in town and that you took the time to come see me," she said. "I just don't want to be anyone's charity case, ya hear?"

"Yes, ma'am." Maya nodded and allowed Sophia to walk her to the front door. "I'll stop by again real soon."

"I'd like that."

Maya let out a deep breath once the door closed behind her. What had she expected, that her mother would welcome her with open arms? She and Sophia had never had that kind of mother-daughter relationship. Raven was her favorite child and that hadn't changed. Thanks to her therapy, Maya had learned to accept it and to understand her mother loved her in her own way even though she had a funny way of showing it. But it didn't matter. Maya would figure out a way to help with Sophia's medical bills despite her stubbornness. If there was a will, there was a way.

The next morning, Maya wasn't nervous as she walked through the revolving doors of Stewart Investments' offices. She strutted toward the elevator bank feeling great. She was returning to her old stomping grounds and it felt like home.

She planned on spending the next week gathering as much information from Carolyn as possible. She was so busy running through a mental checklist that she didn't notice Ayden until he was standing beside her.

"Good morning, Maya."

Maya popped her head up and looked at him. "Good morning." She glanced down at her watch. "You're here a bit early, aren't you?" It was a little after seven, and typically Ayden came in around eight. First, he hit the gym for a morning workout before having two cups of strong black coffee for breakfast. Sometimes with fruit and dry toast, other times with an egg-white omelet. She still knew his schedule like the back of her hand.

A chime echoed in the lobby and the elevator doors opened. "Times have changed," Ayden said as they entered. "Since I didn't have you, I've had to adjust."

"And you will need to adjust again because I like having the morning to myself."

Ayden chuckled. "And now so do I."

Maya wondered if she would have time to mentally prepare for working with him again? Apparently not, because here she was being thrown into the deep end of the ocean without a life vest.

They were both silent on the ride to the fiftieth floor. When they reached the top, Maya exited the elevator first. Ayden fell into step beside her as they walked toward the executive offices.

"Not much has changed," Ayden said, "except some of the decor."

The interior offices that were once browns and beige had been replaced with an open concept done in whites and primary colors. The new atmosphere was bright and airy. "I like it."

"I'm glad. I want you to love your working environment since you'll be spending a great deal of time here."

"You promised me that would change," Maya responded.

"I did," Ayden said, glancing down at her. "And I will hold up my end of the bargain."

Despite what she'd told Callie, Maya doubted he would be able to help himself. Some days there would be long hours, but she wouldn't let it consume her life as it once had.

When they made it to the area outside Ayden's office, she placed her purse on what was once her desk and studied her surroundings. It felt surreal being back after all this time.

"Everything all right?" Ayden inquired from behind her.

Maya whirled around. "Yes, of course."

"You can change anything you like."

"Wow! I'm not even out the door and you're ready to replace all semblance of me?" a beautiful blonde said as she walked toward them. She wore a chic knee-length black sheath and to-die for designer pumps. She was nearly as tall as Ayden. "Hey, it's not my fault you want to leave the best job in town to go off and play wife and mom," Ayden said.

Maya could only assume the stunning Scandinavian beauty was none other than Carolyn, Ayden's current assistant. She stepped forward and held out her hand. "Maya. Maya Richardson."

Carolyn shook her hand. "Ah, Maya. I've heard a lot of great things about you. It's a pleasure to finally meet you."

"Congratulations on your pregnancy." Maya tried not to let the envy show on her face that yet another woman was living the life she'd always wanted while she was destined to remain alone.

"It doesn't mean I'm not here for both of you," she said, looking at Maya. "I'm just a phone call away if you need me."

"Hopefully, that won't be necessary if you get me up to speed this week."

"Let's get started." Carolyn made for her desk.

"I'll leave you to it." Ayden disappeared into his office and closed the door.

Carolyn chuckled to herself. "He's not much of talker, is he?"

"Nope. Never has been and never will be."

"I hear you." Carolyn stashed her purse in her drawer and locked it before taking a seat at her desk. "When I first started working here, it took him months to learn my name. I guess he'd gone through so many assistants he couldn't keep up. Eventually, I put my foot down and forced him to acknowledge me. We've gotten along marvelously ever since."

"That's great."

"It wasn't easy filling your shoes," Carolyn continued as she turned on her laptop and punched in the appropriate password. "Ayden thought the world of you and made sure everyone knew it."

"Did he really?" Maya was surprised.

Years ago, she'd learned there were only two avenues a girl could go. The pretty route or the smart route. Her mother had always told Maya her looks were unremarkable, so she'd become a bookworm and excelled in her studies. After college, she'd had options, but had been afraid to branch out. Needing work, she'd become a temporary admin and found she was skilled at multitasking for successful men. That was how she'd come to work for Ayden. Her reputation as the miracle worker had wowed him. It was good to know that her unwavering work ethic had garnered his respect.

Maya spent the duration of the morning going through the dozens of active client files to help her become familiar with all the players. It was well past noon when she looked up from the table in the small breakout conference room she'd relegated herself to and found Carolyn at the doorway.

"You hungry yet?" Carolyn asked. "Because I'm starved. Eating for two has me ravenous all the time." She patted her small baby bump.

"You go ahead. I'm just finishing up and will grab a quick bite later."

Finally she stopped long enough to grab a salad from the building's café only to return to the mountain of paper. Hours later, Carolyn stopped by to tell her she was leaving for the day. Maya hadn't realized it was so late, but she waved goodbye.

She was reading her last file when she felt Ayden's presence. Heat washed over Maya at seeing him again. He'd abandoned his jacket and tie, and had rolled up his sleeves to reveal enormous biceps. Ayden came closer and Maya could swear she felt a light spark inside her when he looked at her so intently.

"Burning the midnight oil?"

"Excuse me?"

He tapped his watch. "It's after six. I thought we agreed that you would have a life outside of this office."

Maya pinched the bridge of her nose. "Well, I intend to. I just finished the last file." She closed the folder and placed it on the table. "Guess I should get on home, or should I say to my short-term rental." She wasn't ready to sign a long-term lease just yet; the rental was affordable and allowed her the flexibility to move quickly if working with Ayden again didn't pan out.

"How about dinner?" Ayden asked, jamming his hands into his trouser pockets. How was it he could look so amazingly good with several days' worth of stubble on his jaw?

"Not necessary. I can pick up some takeout on the way home."

He studied her through hooded eyes. "I wasn't trying anything, Maya. I just thought after a long first day, it might be nice to catch up. And it's not like we haven't shared a meal together before."

He was right, of course. They'd worked late and eaten together on many occasions, though usually it had been takeout, not a formal dinner. But how bad could it be? "All right, I'd like that."

"Let me grab my jacket and I'll be right with you." He was gone for several seconds, giving Maya enough time to regret accepting the invitation. Why was she doing this to herself? Was she so determined to prove that he had no power over her that she would agree to be alone with him? Maybe she was. If they were going to work together, Maya would have to be comfortable spending time in his company. *Alone.*

Dinner on the terrace at the quaint Italian restaurant was exactly that. Ayden didn't make any untoward moves. Instead, he was nothing short of hospitable and caring, holding out her chair, making sure he selected her favorite wine and generally steering the conversation to lighter topics such as movies, books and his favorite sports team. Maya began to relax.

Ayden could be great company. She found herself laughing at his anecdotes and funny jokes. She recalled how he had a sense of humor, but it had taken time to manifest itself. Back in the day, he'd close his door for hours, shutting himself off from the world, only calling Maya on the intercom to do his bidding. In time, Ayden had learned to open up to her and share some of his past, his struggles and his hopes for Stewart Investments. It's why she knew how important securing Kincaid's business was to him. He was more approachable than he'd ever been, and Maya had to admit she liked this new version of Ayden. Perhaps she'd had something to do with him learning to be more open.

When the dessert menu came along, Maya patted her full stomach. "I don't think so."

"C'mon, don't be a spoilsport. Their cannoli is the best."

"Sounds like you know from personal experience?"

"I do." Ayden turned to the waitress, who was still standing near their table. "We'll have the cannoli and coffee."

"Sure thing, Mr. Stewart," the waitress replied, and scurried away.

"This was really nice, Ayden. Thank you."

"You're welcome. I told you things were going to be different this time."

"Yes, you did," Maya replied, "but I wasn't sure."

"I've learned from the past and generally don't make the same mistakes over again."

Maya wondered if that meant becoming intimate with her. She would never know because the waitress returned with their dessert and coffee. Maya watched Ayden pour them each a cup and was surprised when he put three cubes of sugar and a splash of milk in hers. "Thanks." When had he learned how she liked her coffee? Probably the same time he'd discovered she liked to run and kept a journal.

"No problem."

Soon dessert was over and Ayden was walking Maya to her Honda. "Thank you for dinner."

"You're welcome. It's the least I could do since you're working so hard."

"I worked late so I could get up to speed."

"Well, I want you to know I appreciate it. It's good to have you back, Maya. I missed you."

He missed her.

"I missed you, too." Maya didn't wait for his response, and wasted no time hopping into her car and speeding away. She needed distance.

Once she had made it to her apartment, Maya tried not to think about Ayden. She had to focus on something else, anything else, so she called Raven. After her mother's refusal of her help, Maya was going to have to find another approach.

Raven answered on the second ring. "Maya, it's so good to hear from you. Have you made it safely to Austin from San Antonio?"

"I have," Maya replied, "but this really isn't a social call."

"Oh, all right. What's going on?"

Maya heard the disappointment in her sister's voice, but she pressed on. The familial relationship they'd once shared had been shattered. "Thomas told me about Mama's medical bills."

"Really? When did you speak with him?"

"After the baptism, but that's beside the point. I want to help out with the house bills and Mama doesn't want me to. When I mentioned it, she told me you and Thomas had it under control."

"I wish that were true, but with a new baby, it's gotten tight paying for her medications, plus the balance the insurance doesn't cover. Any help you could give would be greatly appreciated."

"Well, I'm here now. Tell me what I can do."

Their call ended soon after, with Raven promising to email Maya with the details of what was outstanding and any upcoming payments. Maya had set aside a good portion of her $25,000 bonus for her mother's care. Feeling accomplished, she retired to bed, but when she did, her mind wandered to Ayden's words. He missed her. She told herself he missed the dependable, efficient assistant who could keep him on task. She knew her job and how to effectively implement the decisions he made. Ayden was no more interested in her than he'd been five years ago. At least now he valued her and liked her well enough to offer friendship. And that was sufficient, because quite frankly she had as much as she could handle on her plate. She was trying to reconnect with her mother while she still had the chance. And maybe she'd even try her hand at dating again. Maya was determined to take back her life, starting now.

Four

The next morning, Maya arrived at the office around the same time as she had the previous day. Neither Ayden nor Carolyn were in sight this time. Maya set about turning on the Keurig machine and making herself a cup of coffee. Although she'd slept through the night, she still felt tired. Probably because it wasn't her own bed in San Antonio.

Wouldn't it be nice if she were sharing it with a certain CEO?

Maya tried to shake the cobwebs from her brain. Why were thoughts of Ayden popping into her head? She'd stopped fantasizing about him years ago. Why was this happening again? Was her subconscious trying to tell her that she wasn't as over him as she thought?

She was heading back to her desk when Carolyn's phone rang. She glanced at her watch. It was early for the phones to start ringing. Maya picked up the receiver. "Stewart Investments."

"Maya, it's Carolyn."

"Carolyn? Is everything okay?" Her voice sounded weak, as if she'd been crying.

"N-no, it's not. I woke up this morning and I was spotting. My husband took me the hospital and we are waiting to see the doctor. Oh, Maya, I don't want to lose this baby."

"And you won't." Maya tried to sound encouraging. "You're a strong, healthy woman, Carolyn. You can do this."

"I hope so, but Ayden..."

"I'll take care of him, don't you worry. You just take care of yourself and that baby."

"Thank you, I appreciate it. But you should know he has a big meeting coming up tonight with a high-profile client. I finished the presentation yesterday. It will just need to be printed out and bound."

"I'm on it. Don't worry. I've got this. If you can, call me later and let me know you're okay?"

"I will. And Maya?"

"Yes?"

"Thank you."

The line went dead and Maya stared at the receiver in her hand. That was how Ayden found her as he approached. "Maya?" He dropped his briefcase and rushed toward her. "Is everything okay?"

She nodded. "Yes, yes, I'm fine. It's not me. It's Carolyn. She's in the hospital. Could be something wrong with the baby."

"Oh, Lord!"

"I know, right?" Tears formed in the corners of Maya's eyes at the thought that Carolyn could lose the baby. Although she'd only just met her, it was obvious how much she wanted to be a mother.

Ayden crouched by the desk and reached for Maya's

hands. "We have to believe that she and the baby will be all right."

Maya nodded and slowly Ayden released her hands to stand up straight. "She told me about a dinner meeting you have tonight with the Kincaid's. That's great. I know how much you've wanted their business."

"Yes, Carolyn was working up a prospectus."

"I'll have it ready for you."

"You mean, ready for us."

Maya stared back in confusion. "I don't understand."

"Carolyn was accompanying me to this dinner tonight. Kincaid is big on family. Although I don't have one to speak of, Carolyn was going to pinch-hit as my plus one. Can you do the same?"

"I suppose."

His brow furrowed and he paused. "Will that be a problem?"

Dinner again with Ayden, except this time she would be his plus one? The evening prior she'd been able to justify it as two people sharing a meal after working late, but this felt different. Maya had to remind herself that this was business. Like Carolyn, she was attending to help him pitch Stewart Investments to his dream client. "No, it won't be a problem."

She hit the ground running the rest of day, working through all the emails, answering those that were urgent and forwarding those requiring Ayden's input. She set up a spreadsheet for his active deals that she'd studied up on yesterday. And thank God she had.

Later that day, Maya wanted to breathe a sigh of relief but fretted over what to wear. Having let her go an hour early to freshen up, Ayden planned on picking her up at 7:00 p.m. and she still hadn't selected a dress. Most of her clothing was still in storage, so her options were severely limited. Maya settled on a one-shoulder body-con dress. Callie had convinced Maya that with her slender figure she could pull it off. It wasn't like she had a lot of opportunities to dress up. Her life in San Antonio had been rather boring up to this point. At least the dress would hug the few curves she had. After adding some chandelier earrings, a spritz of perfume, and some mascara, blush and lipstick, she was ready.

Ayden was already in the lobby speaking with the security guard, which allowed Maya time to survey him. It was impossible to stop herself from staring at him like some love-struck teenager. He was powerfully built, and his suit fitted his broad frame like no other man she'd ever known. Maya felt breathless and her stomach was tied in knots. Ayden had the looks to go with his physique. Those stunning hazel-gray eyes, perpetual five-o'clock shadow and chiseled cheekbones caused her to suck in a deep calming breath.

The truth was, she could have kept looking at him forever, but as if sensing he was being watched, Ayden glanced up and his eyes fastened on hers. He shook the man's hand and walked toward her. Maya's heart rate began galloping at an alarming speed. Her mouth suddenly felt as dry as the Sahara Desert, but she managed, "I'm ready."

Ayden trapped her with his eyes. Helplessly she gazed up into those murky depths, which had suddenly darkened from hazel to something more mysterious. Maya's entire body burned from the look he was giving her. Then he blinked and it was gone, and Maya wondered if she'd imagined the lust she was almost certain was there.

Ayden offered Maya his arm and she took it. "Let's go."

They rode to the restaurant in companionable silence. Neither of them seemed too keen on talking until both their cell phones buzzed, indicating a text message. Maya pulled hers from her clutch. It was Carolyn. "She and the baby are okay," Maya said, turning to Ayden.

He glanced up from the road to reward her with a smile. "That's wonderful news. I'm glad to hear it."

The phone buzzed again and Maya quickly read the message. "But she's not returning to the office. The doctor has indicated her pregnancy is high risk and is putting her on bed rest."

"That's a shame because it leaves you in quite the lurch."

"Not really," Maya said. "I'm more than capable of stepping in, picking up the baton and running with it. I'm just glad I spent yesterday poring through those files."

"So am I, Maya. So am I."

When they made it to the restaurant, the hostess sat them at a table already occupied by Ayden's prospective client. "Mr. Kincaid. Ryan," Ayden said. He offered the elder Kincaid and his son handshakes. "Pleasure to see you both. And is this your lovely wife?"

"Yes, it is." The older man beamed with pride. "Sandy, I'd like you to meet Ayden Stewart…" The petite brunette rose from her seat and Ayden shook her hand.

"Nice to meet you."

"And of course, you know my son. Ryan, Ayden is the man who's going to make us millions."

"Mr. Stewart," Ryan replied, "my father thinks very highly of you. I'm curious to hear what ideas you have for us."

"Of course, but please let me introduce Maya Richardson." Ayden slid his hand to the small of her back and edged her over to the group.

"Ms. Richardson." Mr. Kincaid leaned over and clasped her hand. "You're looking quite lovely this evening. Isn't she, Ayden?"

Ayden's eyes glowed with fire when he looked at her, and Maya felt her belly clench in response. "She is."

"I agree with you, Father," Ryan commented, and Maya's heart started in her chest. There was naked interest in the younger Kincaid's eyes as he searched her face. She wasn't used to being the center of attention, especially from such a good-looking man with his tanned skin, shock of dark hair and stunning blue eyes.

Ayden reached for her then, tugging her forward. A sharp streak of sensation coursed through Maya at his touch. She nearly stumbled into the chair he'd pulled out for her.

Ryan reached for her to assist, but Ayden glanced up at him and said, "I've got her."

"Thank you." Maya hoped her blush wasn't showing at having both men so clearly interested in her well-being. Not that there was any competition. Her nerves had been shot the moment she'd seen Ayden in the lobby. She'd known it was going to be difficult working for Ayden again, but she hadn't realized that she would be thrown into a situation so quickly, especially when she still harbored residual feelings for him.

Before she could even gather herself, she felt the warm strength of Ayden's hand as he patted her thigh, probably in an effort to ease the tension that was no doubt radiating off her. His touch was oddly comforting, even though it made her tingle and brought her entire body to life. A tight coil formed in her tummy and was quickly racing upward toward her breasts, making them feel fuller, heavier. Maya willed her wayward body to relax. She grabbed her water glass and drank generously, hoping the chilled water would cool off her hot flesh.

"So how long have you two been seeing each other?" Mr. Kincaid inquired.

"It's not like that," Ayden quickly responded. "Maya is my assistant. She often entertains clients with me."

Mr. Kincaid wasn't fazed. "My wife was my secretary, too, and as you can see that didn't stop us."

"So you're single?" Ryan's question lingered in the air.

"Um, yes, I am." Maya offered Ryan a small smile.

"It's good to know there's hope for the rest of us mortals," Ryan said.

Was he trying to flirt with her? Because she'd never dated outside her race. She was woefully out of practice in the dating department. It was safer to change the topic. And she did. She discovered that the Kincaids had been married for thirty years and had a daughter, as well.

"Family is very important to me," Mr. Kincaid said. "Stewart Investments is one of the top investment firms in Texas, but it isn't all about money. I want to find someone who values family above the almighty dollar. I used to be all-business in the past and it nearly cost me my wife." He looked at Mrs. Kincaid. "That's why it's so important to work with people who are well-rounded and have work-life balance because, although I enjoy my money, I don't want to be consumed by it, or by the quest to make more. Tell me about your family, Ayden? Are you related to Henry Stewart of Stewart Technologies?"

Maya felt Ayden stiffen at her side, and everyone, including Ryan, seemed to be rapt waiting for his answer. She knew how much Ayden hated talking about his family, much less the father who'd never acknowledged him. It was a touchy subject and one she knew he didn't want to discuss with strangers. The only reason she happened to learn of the connection was because when his mother passed away, an arrangement had arrived from Stewart Technologies.

"He's my father, but we're estranged," Ayden said finally, after several long, tense moments. "I was very close with my mother, but she died about five years ago, so I'm in short supply on family."

"I'm sorry to hear that," Mr. Kincaid said.

Ayden nodded, but Maya couldn't let it go at that. "You won't find another investment firm that is more dedicated, honest and forthcoming than Stewart Investments. Clients are more than just numbers or facts and figures on a spreadsheet, Mr. Kincaid. Ayden cares about you and your family's future and wants what's best to grow your portfolio."

Mr. Kincaid turned to Ayden. "You've got quite the advocate sitting next to you."

Ayden turned to look at Maya. "Don't I know it."

Ayden was stunned by Maya's impassioned speech on his behalf. He'd never had someone have his back, except maybe Luke, and he was an ocean away. He'd always known that Maya was one in a million, but it was more than that. She was a truly exceptional person, and he doubted he'd truly realized just how exceptional up until this moment.

"You have quite the *assistant*," Mr. Kincaid added. Ayden caught his emphasis on the word *assistant*, because she certainly wasn't acting like one.

"Yes, I know." When he'd arrived in the lobby of her apartment, he'd been unable to mask the unadulterated lust that surged through him at seeing her in the slinky red dress. He'd never even seen Maya in color. She usually wore black, navy and beige, but then again, he hadn't seen her in five years. He was supposed to be keeping his distance and maintaining a professional decorum with Maya, but how was he supposed to when she looked sinfully sexy?

The dress showed off her long legs and incredibly fit physique. Running had done her body good. She was tall, graceful and perfectly proportioned. She had long legs, a waist that he could easily span with his hands and two round orbs for breasts. She had an understated beauty and Ayden was having a hard time ignoring her, as evidenced by the tightening of his body. He didn't need this now. Not when his energies had to be focused on securing Kincaid's business. And that wasn't the only problem: Ryan was making no attempt to hide his interest in Maya, and Ayden didn't like it one bit. He reached for his wineglass and drank liberally.

So he switched gears, charming the Kincaids well into the third course. Maya and Mrs. Kincaid were chatting quietly in the dining room about God knows what while he, Ryan and Mr. Kincaid had retired to the cigar room, so Kincaid could try one of the restaurant's Cubans they were known for. Ayden didn't care for cigars, so he opted for an aged cognac.

"There's nothing better than a fine cigar," Mr. Kincaid said, puffing on his cigar.

"I hear they are some of the best in town," Ayden said, and sipped on his drink.

"Speaking of the best...that assistant of yours," Mr. Kincaid responded. "She's a treasure, that girl."

"Yes, she is. And to be frank, I lost her some years back because I didn't appreciate what I had. I don't intend to make that mistake again."

"Is that right?" Ryan smirked. Ayden could see Ryan's mind working on whether that gave him an edge with Maya. It didn't. Maya was *his*. Well, not his, per se, but she was off-limits to the younger Kincaid.

Mr. Kincaid turned to him. "I appreciate a man who

can admit he made a mistake and not let pride come before a fall."

By the end of the evening, Ayden was shaking hands with the Kincaids and wishing them a good night as he sent them back in a limousine to their hotel. Meanwhile, out the corner of his eye, he could see Ryan speaking privately with Maya. He saw him hand her a business card and watched Maya give him a smile. Then Ryan touched her arm as he left. Ayden was not amused. He was thankful when Ryan got in the limo and they drove away. He handed the valet his ticket.

"That went rather well," Maya said. "Don't you think?"

Ayden gave a half smile. "Yes, it did. Thanks to you."

"Me?" Her voice rose an octave. "I didn't do anything."

"Of course you did. You had the Kincaids, each and every one of them, eating out the palm of your hand. I'm impressed and so glad I brought you along."

Maya shrugged and smiled smugly. "What can I say? We make a good team."

Ayden met her gaze. Their eyes locked, held. "Yes, we do."

Desire flared, hot and tangible, between them. Ayden didn't know what possessed him, but he stepped right into her personal space. He wished she hadn't looked at him like that. It heated his blood, and the cool air did little to settle the fever that was coursing through him. He caught her hand and pulled her toward him, compelled to do what he'd wanted to do all night, which was kiss her. He didn't know where this wildness was coming from because he was usually so composed, but Maya's proximity throughout the evening had gotten to him. Her eyes sparked and flared, radiating heat right through him. When she wet her lips with her tongue, Ayden found himself wondering what she would taste like again.

He was bending his head to brush his lips across hers when the valet pulled up in Ayden's Bentley, breaking the trance. He'd been just as enthralled by Maya as Ryan had been, perhaps more so because he knew her, had *been* with her. But he couldn't be again. He'd given her his word.

Slowly Ayden released her. He gave Maya a small smile because in her eyes he could see she'd been anticipating that kiss as much as he'd been. Would it have been light and sweet, or would it have been the frantic passion they'd shared so long ago?

They would never know because Ayden quickly moved to open the passenger door. Maya didn't say a word for several moments. She simply stared at him in confusion. He knew he'd given her mixed signals. One minute he was hot for her and the next he was pushing her away. But it was for the best. When he didn't say a word, Maya finally stepped toward the car and slid in. When she did, the skirt of her dress hiked up and Ayden couldn't resist feasting his eyes on her sumptuous thighs.

When he glanced up, Ayden found Maya watching him. Had she known where his thoughts had gone? If so, her eyes were shuttered and she didn't let on. He closed the door, came around to the driver's side and jumped in. After buckling up, he pulled away from the curb.

The drive to her apartment was fraught with pent-up tension. Awareness rippled through the air, but Ayden ignored it. He had to take Maya back home while he still could. He just couldn't walk her upstairs, because if he did, he'd be asking to come inside. In more ways than one.

They pulled up to the apartment's main entrance ten minutes later. He glanced at Maya. "Thanks for tonight. You did great. Sleep well."

She didn't even look at him as she said tersely, "Good night." Seconds later, she was out of the car without a backward glance. He stared at her retreating figure before pulling away to drive home.

Could he blame her for being angry at him?

He'd behaved horribly earlier, pulling her to him like he was going to start something he couldn't possibly finish. But Maya had been different tonight. He'd seen another side to her. A sexy siren. And it was contrary to what he'd always known about her. That mix had desire ripping through him, igniting a fierce desire to kiss her, claim what had once been his. Because there was no way Ryan Kincaid was going to have his woman. But did he really have a right to think this way? Wasn't this what had led him down the wrong path and caused Maya to leave in the first place? It had taken months to find the right person to replace her, and although Carolyn was awesome, she couldn't read his mind like Maya. He had to back off.

It was simply that talking and laughing with her tonight had caused memories to resurface. There were sparks of desire between them, of that there was no doubt. He would love nothing better than to kiss her, touch her and undress her. But there was no way he would or could allow them to burn as hot as they once had.

Maya had made it very clear that she wasn't interested in rekindling a personal relationship with him. And he had to respect her decision even if his libido didn't like it. And truth be told, she was too good for him anyway. She certainly wouldn't settle for a light and sexual affair, which was all Ayden was capable of. Maya was the kind of woman that you married and made the mother of your children. Ayden wanted no part of that life, and his penance was to go to bed longing for a woman he could never have.

Five

Maya was furious as she stormed through the apartment lobby toward the elevators. How dare he touch her like that? Look at her like that? Who the hell did Ayden think he was? Once again, he was showing that he could not be trusted. He'd told her that their relationship, going forward, would be strictly business, but tonight he'd changed the rules. Back at the restaurant, he'd pulled her to him, like… well, like he wanted her. Her stomach had lit up like a ball of fire, and she'd sparked at the desire that had lurked in those hazel-gray depths. Then, just as quickly, he'd cast her aside as if it hadn't happened.

Just as he had five years ago.

The elevator chimed and Maya entered. Leaning against the wall, she exhaled and closed her eyes. She was trying to force the kick of adrenaline she'd experienced to dissipate. Why had he done it? Stirred up a hornet's nest of emotions that she'd kept buried? For so long, she'd accepted that Ayden didn't want her. Never had. That he'd slept with her that night out of pity. And then tonight, he'd flipped the script, making her wonder if she'd gotten it wrong all those years ago. Had he wanted to make love to her? Had it been more to him? Is that what had scared him off?

No, no, no. She shook her head. She couldn't do this to herself. She'd dealt with this years ago. She couldn't resurrect those feelings of self-doubt. Not again. Maya had gone to therapy to deal with Raven and Thomas's betrayal and her night with Ayden. It had all done a number on her ego and self confidence, but she'd picked up the pieces and finally felt as if she'd let go of the past. She'd faced those demons a few weeks ago when she'd gone to her niece's baptism.

Maya had hoped that taking this job again would not only help her mother financially, but exorcise those buried demons and remind her of her self-worth. She didn't need Ayden's mixed signals and she wouldn't abide it. Not anymore. She wouldn't just accept what Ayden or anyone else doled out to her. He would soon learn that she'd grown and was no longer a doormat.

The next morning, Maya arrived at the office ready to work and full of spice. She was prepared to give Ayden a piece of her mind, but he called to let her know that he had morning meetings and wouldn't be in until later. Maya was puzzled. There were no appointments on his calendar, so she could only assume he didn't want to face her. And perhaps it was for the best. Now she would have time to cool down and regain her composure.

By the time Ayden arrived midmorning, Maya had determined to put last night in the past, like an aberration, and move forward with the job. When he strolled into the office, walking with a lithe, purposeful gait, threading his way toward Maya, she was in control.

And so was Ayden.

"Maya—" he thrust a sheath of papers across her desk without looking in her direction "—I need copies of these immediately." He swept past her into his office and closed the door.

It didn't surprise her that he was ignoring what had transpired last night. He was good at that, acting as if nothing had happened. She would do the same. She did as instructed and made the copies. When she was done, she knocked on his office door. A terse "come in" was issued and she entered.

Ayden's office was as immaculate as the man himself. It held a dark walnut desk along with built-in bookshelves that spanned an entire wall. A sitting area with a leather sofa, low table and wet bar was in the opposite corner.

She headed to his desk. "Here you are." She leaned over to hand him the papers, but he seemed determined to act as if whatever he was reviewing on his laptop was more important than acknowledging her. So Maya dropped the copies with a flop on his laptop. That got his attention and he glanced up.

"Is there anything else, *boss*?" She said the last word with a measure of sarcasm, impossible to ignore.

His brow rose. "Actually, yes. Can you get Kincaid on the line?"

"I'll get right on that." Seconds later, she was slamming his door and returning to her desk. The jerk!

She was smarting over his casual disregard when a delivery man strolled toward her with one of the biggest bouquets of flowers Maya had ever seen. "Maya Richardson?" he inquired.

"Yes, that's me."

"These are for you. Sign here, please." He handed her a clipboard while he placed the fragrant bouquet on her desk. Maya signed for them even though she had no idea who they were from. She was still looking for a card when she heard Ayden's door open behind her, but she ignored him. She was curious who could have sent her flowers.

"Who are they from?" Ayden asked over her shoulder just as Maya found the card.

"Excuse me." She spun away from him, slid the small card from the envelope and read it. *Enjoyed your company last night. Have dinner with me, Ryan.*

A smile spread across Maya's lips.

"Well?" Ayden sounded annoyed when she still hadn't spoken. "Who are they from?"

"Ryan."

Ayden frowned. "Kincaid?"

Maya nodded and then swiveled around in her chair to face the computer. She'd suspected Ryan was interested in her personally, but she'd never thought he'd act on it.

"What did the card say?"

Inflamed, Maya spun back around. First, Ayden wanted to ignore what had happened last night, and now he wanted to play twenty questions with her personal life? "What business is it of yours?"

His face turned red and Maya could see she'd angered him, but she didn't care. "The Kincaids are a client, an important one, so it darn well is my business."

"It has nothing to do with work," Maya replied hotly.

Ayden leaned down. Both his large hands bracketed her desk and made Maya feel caged in. "Did he ask you out?"

Her brow furrowed. "How would you know that?"

Ayden rose to his full height and glared at her. "Because it's what I would do. I saw the way he was looking at you."

"And just how was he looking at me?" Maya folded her arms across her chest. She dared Ayden to say more.

Ayden turned away from her for several moments, and when he faced her again, his features were schooled. "It's unseemly for you to accept dinner with a client."

"That's not fair!" Maya rose to her feet to confront him. She didn't appreciate Ayden implying that she would do anything that would harm Stewart Investments. She'd been a valuable employee for five years. "You know I would never hurt you, I—I..." she stammered. "I mean hurt the company. And you *know* it."

Ayden colored. She'd hit her mark. "I apologize. I didn't mean to insinuate otherwise. So let me rephrase. It's not a good idea to mix business and pleasure."

"Is that a fact?" Her gaze met his and held. There was no mistaking she was referring to last night when he'd almost kissed her. Air bottled up in her lungs as she waited for a response.

Ayden had the grace to be embarrassed and looked away. "Do what you want!" He turned on his heel and slammed his door a moment later.

Maya told herself she didn't care how Ayden felt. She was being given an opportunity to go out with a good-looking, emotionally available man who was interested in her. Why not see where it led?

She glanced at Ayden's door. Because deep down, the man she wanted was closed off to her. Literally.

Ayden stared out his window for several moments before returning to his desk to concentrate on the figures and reports on his laptop, but it was useless. His brain was addled. Never before had he sat at his desk only to discover he'd wasted ten minutes thinking about a woman. And it wasn't just any woman. It was Maya. His Maya. He was imagining her going out with Ryan. Wondering if she'd kiss him. Let him touch her as he once had. He was jealous.

And he hated it.

He had no right to be.

He had no rights to Maya. But the thought of her with Kincaid stuck in his craw. He had seen the lust in the man's eyes when he'd looked at Maya. He had wanted to get to know her all right; he wanted to get to know her intimately! And worst of all, Maya didn't have a problem with it. He suspected she was doing it to give Ayden the finger for last night and today.

And she'd be within her rights.

He was falling back into old patterns. He'd acted as if he hadn't hauled her sensual, soft body against his hard one. Felt the pebbles of her nipples harden in response to their closeness. Heard her breath quicken as she anticipated a kiss between them. But he'd denied her. Denied them both. And now they were both miserable because they, or rather, *he* was trying to forget it happened.

It would have been easy if Maya was in her normal attire of navy skirt and button-down blouse. Except today, she'd chosen to wear a fuchsia-colored blouse that did wonders for her beautiful brown skin. He'd thought Maya returning to Stewart Investments was going to be easy. He had an active love life with plenty of women at his disposal. All he had to do was pick up the phone. There was no reason for him to feel like this; yet, he couldn't get his beautiful assistant out of his mind.

"Ayden?" Maya's voice rang through the intercom. "You have a call on line one."

He sighed. "I'm rather busy right now. Who is it?"

There was silence on the other end. "It's your sister, Fallon."

"I'll be with her in a moment." Ayden let go of the speaker button.

His *half sister*, Fallon. Four years younger than him, they shared the same DNA, but they had different mothers. He hated her witch of a mother, Nora Stewart, who was the cause of the downfall of his mother's marriage to Henry. The wily waitress had made sure she'd gotten pregnant and used it to lure his father away. Ayden had met Fallon a couple of times, but theirs certainly wasn't a normal brother-sister relationship. Why was she calling?

He had to know the answer. Ayden picked up the receiver. "Hello?"

"Ayden, it's so good to hear your voice. How are you?"

"I'm fine, Fallon. But I doubt this is a social call." The last time they'd seen each other had been six years ago when he'd expanded Stewart Investments and bought the building. Fallon had come to the grand opening. He'd been surprised by her appearance, as he was now by her call.

"Wow! I'd forgotten how you like to get to the point," Fallon said from the other end of the line.

"Yes, well, time is money."

"Of course. I was hoping if you had some free time, we might get together for lunch this week."

"I don't know." Ayden kept minimal contact with his half siblings. Although he couldn't blame them for their existence, Ayden still saw them as the chosen ones. The children that Henry deigned to acknowledge as his heirs while Ayden was left out in the cold to fend for himself.

"C'mon, Ayden. It's been several years. Aren't you the least bit curious about me? Dane?"

At times, he was. When he was lonely, Ayden wondered about his siblings and what they were doing with their lives. He knew Fallon ran Stewart Technologies, Henry's baby. Then there was his half brother.

Dane Stewart was an A-list actor in Hollywood. Ayden knew that Dane wanted no part of the Stewart family because he'd said so in several interviews. Ayden was certain there was a story behind Dane's estrangement and Fallon's absolute devotion. He'd even wondered what it would be like to have them as friends, but then he remembered that they'd had different lives. Ayden sighed heavily. "What is it that you want, Fallon?"

"Not over the phone," she whispered. "I need to speak with you privately. Can you meet me on Friday?"

Ayden was curious, so he agreed. "Yes, I'll have my assistant set it up."

"Thank you. I appreciate it. I'll see you then."

The line went dead, but Ayden was still holding the receiver. Exactly what did his sister want, and what did it have to do with him?

By Thursday, Maya was both giddy with excitement for her date with Ryan Kincaid this weekend and perturbed by Ayden's attitude the last couple of days. The only way she could describe his behavior toward her was *chilly.* Ayden was not happy about her spending time with Ryan. His interactions with her were strictly business. Email this. Call this person. There was none of the warm camaraderie they usually shared at the office.

He'd overheard Maya making plans with Ryan for Saturday night after she'd called to thank him for the beautiful arrangement. Since then, Ayden had been acting like a sullen child. He barely spoke to her. He'd been absent the last couple of days and was giving her a wide berth. Maya supposed it was a good thing. They'd gotten too close for comfort the other night. If dating Ryan kept her from obsessing about Ayden and wondering what might happen, it was for the best.

Callie agreed when she called Maya during lunch. Her best friend was happy she was getting back into the saddle and dating again. Maya knew Callie thought she was hopeless when it came to Ayden, but she was over him. Or that's the white lie she told Callie. If Ayden hadn't stopped that kiss, the heat between them would have consumed them. Maya refused to admit Ayden still held any power over her. She would sweep what happened under the rug just as he was doing.

After finishing lunch, she called her mother to check in. As usual, Sophia was saying everything was fine, but Maya knew better. True to her word, Raven had emailed her copies of her mother's outstanding medical bills, and since Raven had been authorized on the account, Maya had been able to pay the clinic directly without her mother being the wiser. She'd also set up a payment plan for future bills. In addition, Raven had sent her mother's schedule, so Maya knew her chemo treatments were every three weeks, but hadn't yet mustered the courage to make one.

When she finally came back from her lunch break, she found Ayden sequestered in his office with the door shut. Maya continued working and filtering calls like she always did. When he was ready, he would come out and talk to her.

Eventually, her intercom buzzed. "Maya, can you make reservations tomorrow for a late lunch with my sister, Fallon, at two p.m."

The line went dead.

Ayden was lunching with his estranged sister, Fallon? How could he just drop a bomb like that and not expect her to ask questions?

One day, years ago, when Ayden had just won a lucrative client that would put Stewart Investments on the map, he'd confided in her about his past and how it had shaped him into the man he was today. Everyone was lauding him as the man with the Midas touch. All except one—his father.

Ayden had shared that deep down, he'd thought he might hear from Henry to say how proud he was of his accomplishments even though he'd done nothing to help him achieve them. Ayden told her that he knew he'd never get his father's love, but he'd wanted his acknowledgment. Despite all his successes, that day never came. And year after year, as Stewart Investments had grown, Maya had watched Ayden's heart grow harder where the Stewarts were concerned, which was why it was surprising he would agree to lunch with Fallon.

Maya worried about him and his well-being. She wanted to know if he'd be okay, but Ayden was shutting her out. Would he ever let anyone in?

Six

The next afternoon, Ayden walked purposefully through the restaurant. He'd made sure to dress for the occasion of meeting his estranged sister, choosing a custom-made suit, red tie and Italian loafers. He'd even gone to the barber to ensure his scalp was smooth as a baby's bottom and his five-o'clock shadow was well-groomed. If the princess of the Stewart family was deigning to meet with him, he had to look his best.

Fallon rose from her chair as he approached, and Ayden was reminded of just how beautiful his sister truly was. With her dark brown hair with honey blond streaks and her smooth café au lait skin, his sister was a knockout. A designer dress revealed her slender but curvy figure.

"Ayden, I'm so happy you agreed to meet me." His sister stared at him through hazel-gray eyes, the same as his. It was a family trait.

"Did I have a choice?" he asked, coming toward her

and pushing her chair in as she sat down. If nothing else, his mother had raised a gentleman.

"I guess I didn't give you much of one," Fallon said after he sat across from her, "but given our relationship I wasn't sure you'd come."

"Curiosity brought me here," Ayden returned, placing his napkin in his lap. "I wondered why you would need anything from me, the black sheep of the family. The son our father can't be bothered to claim."

Sadness crossed her face and Fallon lowered her head. When she looked up again, tears were in the corners of her eyes. "I'm sorry Father has treated you this way, Ayden."

He shrugged. "What's it to you, anyway? You're his heir."

"And you're still my brother," she responded with a ferocity that shocked him.

"Now you want to claim me?" He smiled sardonically. "Why, Fallon? It's never been that important to you before."

"That's not fair, Ayden. I reached out to you when I went off to college, and you shot me down. You weren't interested in a little sister then."

"And I'm not interested in one now."

"Ouch." Fallon took that one on the chin, but bounced back, her eyes narrowing as she looked in his direction. "Despite having grown up away from Father, you're just like him. You know how to hit below the belt."

Ayden sucked in a deep breath. He deserved that. He hadn't meant to be unkind, but it was a little late to play brother and sister. That time had come and gone. But, at the very least, she deserved to be treated with respect like any human being. "I'm sorry."

She raised a brow.

"I am," he insisted. "This is all a bit disconcerting."

Fallon gave him a half smile, and Ayden felt a kick in the gut because it warmed his cold heart to see it. "It is for me, as well. It wasn't easy calling you for help, but I did."

"Help?"

"I'm in trouble, Ayden."

Ayden sat upright in his seat, training his gaze on her beautiful facial bones. "What kind of trouble? What can I do to help?"

"Careful, Ayden," Fallon said with humor to her tone. "You almost sounded like a big brother there."

His eyes narrowed. "What do you need, Fallon?"

"I don't know if you knew, but I'm CFO of Stewart Technologies. Have been a few years now."

"I'd heard."

"Have you also heard that the company isn't doing well? We've been in trouble for several quarters now. I've been doing my best to contain the damage, but bad investments and poor project planning have crippled the company. I've tried my best to turn it around, but there's little hope of saving it now."

Ayden frowned. He didn't like the direction this conversation was heading, but he was here now and he had no choice but to listen. It would be rude of him to get up and walk away, even though that's exactly what he wanted to do.

"For years, I tried to get Father to listen to me, but he's stubborn and pigheaded. Determined to do things his way, and now we're in a bind. We need a bailout."

And there it was, Ayden thought. The catch that had brought Fallon to contact him out of the blue. She needed money. "And what is it you expect me to do?"

"Ayden." Fallon reached across the table, which seemed as wide as an ocean, and took his hand. "I've heard great things about you. Everyone's calling you the miracle worker. If anyone can help turn this around it's you. And..." She paused as if searching for her words. "With some of your financial backing we could save the company."

Ayden stared at Fallon in disbelief. He glanced around the room to see if anyone had heard, because he wasn't sure he'd heard right. Fallon, Nora's daughter with Henry, was asking him, the son Henry had cast aside, to save *her* father's company. Surely, she had lost her mind. "And why would I want to do a thing like that?"

"Because it's our family business."

"No, Fallon. It's *your* family business. Stewart Investments is *my* business."

"But..."

"There's no buts. Henry chose to divorce my mother and walk away from us, and that's fine. That's his choice, but when he did, he washed his hands of me and subsequently any allegiance I had to this—" he made air quotes with his hands "—family."

"Ayden, I know you're upset with Father."

"Upset?" His voice rose and when it did, several patrons looked in his direction. "*Upset* is acting as if we had a minor disagreement, Fallon. I'm not upset. I *hate* him. I hate him for how he treated me, but most of all for how he treated my mother. He left her with nothing, even though she helped him start that damn company."

Tears sprang to her beautiful eyes—so like his own. "Wh-what? I thought—but my mother said..."

"Your mother lied, Fallon. Lillian Stewart was the woman behind the man, working two jobs to get Henry through college so he could work on his degree, helping build the capital necessary to open Stewart Technologies. And when he became successful, he kicked her to the curb for a younger model and cheated her out of her rightful share of the company. So Fallon, there's not a snowball's chance in hell I would ever help that man or his company and, unfortunately, that affects you." Ayden rose to his feet.

"Ayden," Fallon rushed out of her seat and placed a firm hand on his arm, stopping him before he'd taken two steps past her. "Please don't leave this way. I had no idea about what happened to you and your mother. I wasn't even born. Surely, you can't blame me?"

"I know that, Fallon, and I don't blame you. Henry's mistakes are his and his alone. I came here today out of respect for you even when I didn't have to. I heard you out, but there's nothing left to say." He glanced down at her hand on his sleeve, but she held on firmer.

Her eyes implored his and he saw the fear in them. "I need your help."

"I'm sorry, but the answer is no. Let the company crash and burn because, quite frankly, that's exactly what Henry so richly deserves." Ayden wrenched his arm away and spun on his heel. His heart was thudding loudly in his chest and his pulse was racing. He quickly threaded his way through the tables until he made it to the door. Once he was outside, he leaned against the building's facade and inhaled deeply.

Rage was coursing through his veins. Not at Fallon, but at Henry for ruining the company his mother helped build. Ayden wanted to punch something, *someone*, but instead he walked. And walked. He would walk back to the office so he could cool off and let calmer heads prevail.

Maya glanced down at her watch. It was well after five o'clock and the office was starting to clear out, but Maya couldn't leave. She hadn't heard from Ayden all afternoon and she was worried. He hadn't returned from his lunch with his half sister. Maya was dying to know how it went and if he was okay, but he hadn't so much as called to check in for messages.

It was nearly six when she finally gave up and began packing up her belongings. She was turning off the lights when she saw Ayden walking toward her from the reception area. Instead of his usual long and confident stride, his shoulders were hunched over. As he drew closer, Maya could see anguish etched across his face.

"Ayden?"

He glanced up, but looked straight through her and walked into his office. Maya was rooted to the spot as conflicting emotions tore through her. Should she go after him? He appeared so forlorn. Lost even, if she had to put a name on it. Or she should she go home and let him figure it out alone? They'd agreed to have a purely business relationship. Getting involved would complicate things.

But she couldn't leave him like that, could she?

Making a split decision, Maya threw down her things and headed for his door. She was surprised to find it ajar. He was sitting on the couch with his head hung low, a bottle of liquor on the table in front of him. A glass of dark liquid was in his hands. Maya suspected it was the aged cognac he kept on hand for celebrating a victory or sweet deal. But today was different. He was drowning his sorrows, whatever they may be.

She walked toward him quietly. He didn't say a word when she sat beside him. Instead, he continued drinking. When he'd finished the first glass, he poured himself another. They sat in silence for an eternity before Maya spoke. She was dying to know what happened. "Ayden?"

"Hmm…?"

"Are you okay?"

"No." He took another sip of his drink.

Ayden wasn't talkative by nature, but when he was in this mood, he would be even less forthcoming. "Did something happen at your lunch with Fallon?"

He turned to glare at her. The full force of his piercing hazel stare rested solely on her, and Maya squirmed in her seat at the intensity. "What do you think?"

Maya swallowed. She had to push and break through the barrier Ayden had erected to protect himself. She understood because she'd done the same thing herself. "What happened?"

"I don't want to talk about it."

"Perhaps if you didn't hold it inside, you might feel better," Maya offered.

"Feel?" Ayden huffed. "I don't want to feel anything."

Maya blinked several times, but tried again. "Ayden…" She touched his arm and he shrank away from her. Jumping to his feet, he made for the window on the far side of the room.

"Don't touch me, Maya. Not right now. You should go home." He turned away from her to face the window.

"I can't go home and leave you like this. You're hurting and I want to help."

He spun to face her. "You can't help me, Maya. No one can. Unless you can erase the last thirty years and make my father love me, want me—" he beat his chest with his fist "—acknowledge me as his son. His firstborn. The rightful heir to Stewart Technologies."

"Oh, Ayden."

"Don't!" He pointed his finger at her, tumbler still in hand. "Don't you dare feel sorry for me! I won't have it."

"Okay, okay." Maya held up her hands in surrender as she walked toward him. She took the glass out of his hand and placed it on a nearby table. He watched her with keen eyes, his chest rising and falling. "You don't have my pity. But I'm here for you, Ayden."

Heavy awareness surged through her as she locked gazes with him. Maya swallowed, but her mouth felt dry and parched. She inched forward until they were standing a breath away from each other. Something fundamental changed as they stared at each other, something that electrified the airspace. Maya was afraid to speak, afraid to break the interlude.

Maya touched his arm and when she glanced up, Ayden's gaze had turned from tortured to hot and burning. She should move away and get out of the office fast, but she couldn't seem to stop herself. There was so much tension inside him. Tension she wanted to help relieve. As if pulled by some imperceptible thread, her body moved closer to his. Maya felt the heat of him in her lower half as their bodies brushed once, twice. Then Ayden's hand flew to the small of her back and pressed her forward, clamping her tight against him.

Air whooshed out of Maya's lungs, but that didn't stop her from tipping her head upward and peeking up at him from beneath her lashes. She shouldn't have done that because with that movement, she swayed into his space. Ayden leaned forward until they were chest to chest, and then he kissed her. Their lips touched slowly, hesitantly at first, as if they were both unsure of whether they should continue, but then Ayden shifted, and Maya felt the strain of his erection against her middle and the kiss erupted.

Her mouth opened under his and he swept her into his embrace, kissing her deeply. Before she knew it, Maya's back was hitting the window, but she scarcely noticed because she was coming alive under Ayden's skillful mouth. His hands were threading through her hair and his mouth was devouring hers. Hunger coursed through her, and she thrust her hips involuntarily against his as an ache began to claim her lower region.

Ayden grasped her hips and tightened his arms around her, tipping her head to just the right angle so he could stroke his tongue with hers. Over and over again, he stroked her, deeper, harder and faster until he had Maya moaning in pleasure. She cupped the back of his neck and his hands roamed over her. When he found her breasts, he molded and kneaded them with his palm. He was luring her into a dark pit of need and Maya was drowning. She felt his hands snake under her dress, felt him touch her thigh.

Please, oh God, she wanted him to touch her there. She tilted her hips in silent invitation, begging him to do whatever he desired.

And just as his hands began inching to the damp place between her thighs, a knock sounded on the door. "Housekeeping."

Maya jumped back as if a bucket of cold water had been thrown on them. She glanced at the door and then back at Ayden. His face was a storm of desire and Maya licked her lips.

"Do that again and I'll have you on the desk and to hell who sees us."

Maya blushed and, without saying a word, rushed for the door, swung it open and fled from the room. She ran past the stunned cleaner standing just outside the door, grabbed her purse and made for the elevator. She didn't dare look behind her because she couldn't look at Ayden. Not after what had just happened between them. If that cleaner hadn't knocked on the door when she had, who knew what would have happened.

Maya knew exactly what would have happened.

She would have allowed Ayden to make love to her again. And then where would she be? Back at square one.

* * *

Ayden slammed his fists down on his desk. He hadn't meant for that to happen, but Maya had gotten too close to the sun. And if she wasn't careful, she would get burned. That was exactly how he felt right now. Like scorched earth. Seeing Fallon had resurrected his demons. Ayden didn't talk about his family *ever* except the one time with Maya. She was the only person who knew he'd been abandoned by the great technical genius Henry Stewart.

But it wasn't exactly true. Ayden could remember a time when he was younger, before the divorce, when his father had been in his life. He'd been about five years old. He recalled his parents together, happy, but then Nora had come into the picture. Ayden had vague recollections of his mother and Henry arguing. His mother accusing Henry of being unfaithful. Ayden remembered finding Lillian crying in her bedroom because his father had asked her to leave.

Leave *her* house. And she had. She hadn't fought for what was hers—what was due her after she'd helped him build the company. Instead, she'd allowed that evil witch Nora to play lady of the manor in their home while he and his mother had been kicked out. Ayden blamed Henry for all the hardships they'd endured, the mental and physical abuse at Jack's hands. So there was no way in hell he would bail that man out of trouble. Let the company crumble. It was what Henry had coming. He was sorry Fallon was caught in the crossfire, but she was a grown woman and it was her decision to run the company. She would have to figure her own way out.

But Maya. Maya was another story. She'd only been trying to help, to lend a sympathetic ear, and he'd taken advantage of her. *You're weak.* The nasty voice of his conscience called him out. He'd let himself indulge in her when he'd given her his word that he would behave. If he couldn't keep the promises he'd made, he was no better than his louse of a father Henry, who hadn't kept his marital vows.

Ayden closed his eyes, but it did little to erase the imprint of Maya from his senses. He could still smell her sweet scent in the air. How in the world was he going to be able to forget how she tasted and go back to a professional relationship?

Seven

The next morning, Maya awoke feeling more exhausted than she'd been before going to bed. When she'd arrived home, she'd paced, unable to sleep because she couldn't get the kiss with Ayden off her mind. So she'd pretty much clock-watched the entire night, and time had seemed to stagnate.

Throwing back the covers, Maya showered and threw on her gear to go for a run. When she was in a mood like this, running was the best cure. She waved at her building's security guard and started for a nearby park about half a mile away. Maybe she could lose herself on the trail and feel invigorated afterward.

An hour later, Maya felt no better. In fact, she felt terribly silly for making a mountain out of a molehill. It was just a kiss. But was it?

Ayden wasn't just *any* man. He was the man of her dreams. The man whose face she had been unable to forget for five long years. And now, during her run, he was all

Maya could think of. The kiss had stirred up past feelings Maya thought she'd resolved. It had been earth-shatteringly passionate. It had rocked Maya to the core and made her wonder whether she could continue working for Ayden.

Maya realized that they'd never really resolved what happened five years ago. Instead, they'd acted like it was a one-time thing because she'd been upset over Thomas. She'd thought it had been pity, but now she realized that was a lie. If they'd both been bold enough, they'd admit there was something *there.* An attraction simmering just below the surface. Under the right circumstances and conditions, they combusted.

How else could she explain why Ayden had kissed her last night and she'd kissed him back? She'd been a willing and active participant in that kiss. Her heart thundered with excitement at how passionate Ayden had been. She'd felt the full force of that unleashed energy and doubted they would have stopped if not for the well-timed knock on the door.

Knowing that she felt this way, there was no way she could go out for dinner tonight with Ryan. Not when she had these swirling emotions surrounding Ayden on her mind. Once she made it to Starbucks for a coffee, Maya went to a quiet corner to make her call.

Ryan answered after several rings. "Maya, good morning."

"Good morning, Ryan. How are you?"

"I'm excited for our date this evening."

"Listen, about that—"

"Don't tell me you're canceling?" Ryan interrupted.

"I don't think it's a good idea that we go out," Maya said. "I really can't handle anything other than friendship right now. I have a lot going on in my life."

"Friendship sounds like a great start. Let's scratch dinner. How about attending a polo match?"

"Polo?" Maya had never been to a match and understood nothing of the game.

"Yes, polo. You can put on your Sunday best, well, in this case, your Saturday best, and meet me at the Austin Polo Club."

"I don't know...." Maya recalled that Ayden loved the sport. He used to talk about how he and Luke had played it during undergrad. Was he still playing for this club? But what if he were? Did it really matter? With all the people attending, it was highly doubtful he would even notice her.

"Do you have other plans?"

"No, but..."

"I'll see you at two then." Seconds later, the call ended and Maya was staring down at her phone. Ryan had hung up without giving her a chance to change her mind. Very sneaky of him. But she didn't have any plans, and if Ryan was okay that all she had to offer was friendship, then why not? She hadn't been out with anyone other than Ayden since she'd returned to Austin. It would be nice to have some male companionship, even if was a non-date. And who knows? Polo could be fun.

Ayden needed physical exertion to help clear his mind and give him some perspective on why he kept screwing up royally with Maya. He'd already gone to the gym this morning for two hours and was happy he had a polo match scheduled for even more punishment.

All morning as he'd hit the treadmill, weights, even the boxing ring, his mind kept wandering to Maya. And how he'd been greedy for her last night. He'd wanted to feel her skin against his. Had wanted to kiss her, touch her, and if that knock hadn't interrupted them, he would have taken her everywhere—up against the window, the desk, the floor, the couch in his office. He wouldn't have cared, because she'd spiked a need in him he couldn't recall feeling in...well....in five years. When that very same need had rocked him to his core and caused him to push her away.

Ayden hadn't understood it then and darn sure didn't understand it now. Maya was his assistant, his friend, yet she was the only woman who fired up a lust in him that was so profound he lost all thought or reason. She made him impulsive rather than cool and in control like he usually was in sexual encounters.

He had to get himself back on track, and today's match at the Austin Polo Club would help. After the gym, he'd gone home to shower and get ready for the game. He'd donned his usual ensemble of well-worn riding boots that fit just below the knees, white riding breeches and a black polo shirt with the number 3 for his position in the polo club. He liked being the attacker. And today, there was a tournament against a club out of San Antonio and he was ready for battle.

When he arrived at the club, he hopped out of his Bentley, gave his keys to one of the many valets and grabbed his gloves, kneepads and helmet with chin strap. He was looking forward to running his polo pony, a beautiful Thoroughbred he'd purchased some years back. He could thank Luke for introducing him to the sport in New England, because it had stuck. Ayden had found the polo club and been a member ever since. He typically tried to play twice a month to ensure he and his pony were one on the field, which in this case was the size of six soccer fields.

When he arrived at the stables, which housed two hundred Thoroughbreds, his team was already getting ready for the tournament. Ayden wasted no time saddling up his pony, and braiding and wrapping its tail. Once he was ready, he swung his leg around and into the stirrups. A club hand was on board to help, handing him his helmet and mallet.

"You ready to give those San Antonio boys a whooping and send them home?" Eddie, a venture capitalist and one of his team members, asked when he was mounted.

"Heck, yeah!" Ayden responded.

The first chukka went supremely well with Austin making the first goal. Ayden was really getting into the game. And when the umpire threw the ball between the two teams on the second chukka, Ayden took off after it with a fury, challenging the opposing San Antonio team member by riding him off. It worked. It moved his opponent away from the ball and out of the play so his teammate could score a goal.

"Good job!" Mateo, another of his team members, yelled as they began leading their ponies back to the equestrian facility for a break.

"Thanks, I was in the..." Ayden's sentence was cut short when he spied Maya and Ryan stepping out on the field to stomp the divots. What was she doing here? And with Ryan of all people?

Ayden was furious. Uncaring of who was watching, he began riding his pony across the field in Maya's direction.

"Having fun?" Ryan asked as he led Maya onto the green so they could stomp the grass.

"Oh, yes," Maya said, smiling from ear to ear. "Thanks for suggesting this." She hadn't the foggiest notion what to wear to a polo match. The only other time she'd seen one was when she'd watched Julia Roberts in *Pretty Woman*.

Did she need a big hat? She hadn't brought one with her. After rummaging through the closet, Maya had found a lace-embroidered off-shoulder white jumpsuit with wide leg pants. She'd matched it with some chunky wedges and large hoop earrings. She thought she looked pretty good. And when she'd met Ryan he'd agreed by giving her an appreciative whistle. He looked equally casual in a pair of Dockers, a polo shirt and a blazer.

"My pleasure." Ryan's mouth curved into a grin. "To be honest," he said, stomping the green with his foot, "I'd be happy with any time I got to spend with you."

Maya glanced up at him and there was no mistaking the interest in his gaze. Ryan wanted more than friendship, but that's all she had to give him. Her relationship with Ayden was too complicated for her to bring someone else into the picture, no matter how great he might be.

She wanted to say more, but then she heard hooves, and when she glanced up, she saw Ayden barreling down on them. Ryan grasped her by the waist and pushed her behind him as Ayden barely stopped his horse in enough time in front of them. Maya sucked in a deep breath at the near miss and noticed the lethal glint in Ayden's hazel eyes.

"Ayden, in God's name, man, you could have killed us," Ryan lashed out.

"Hardly," Ayden said, hurtling himself over the pony and pulling the animal forward by the reins. "I take care of what's mine."

The possessive look he gave Maya caused her stomach to knot up and her throat to suddenly become very dry. Was he talking about her? Because she wasn't his. She never had been and doubted she ever would be. He didn't do commitments. She'd always known that.

"What are you doing here?" Ayden inquired. There was an edge to his voice that Maya didn't understand.

"You invited me, remember?" Ryan replied. "At the restaurant."

"Ah yes." Ayden nodded and his voice became mellower. "I forgot. Though I had no idea you were bringing Maya." He glanced in her direction again, his gaze traveling from the wedges on her feet to the one-piece jumpsuit showing off her bare shoulders.

Maya finally found her voice even though her throat felt parched. "It was a last-minute thing, but I'm glad I came."

"Is that so?" Ayden's brow furrowed.

The level of tension between them ratcheted up and Maya's nerves were stretched tight. "Yes, that's right." She didn't appreciate his tone. He was acting as if she'd done something untoward when she'd only accepted a simple invitation to a polo match. *During the day.* It wasn't as if they were on a date. But weren't they? Even though Ryan had suggested it under the guise of "just friends," she knew he wanted more. But he also hadn't given her the chance to say no, having hung up before she could respond.

"Glad you're enjoying your date," Ayden said. "Be sure to watch me on the field." He jumped onto the back of the horse with ease and, after a swift kick, they were gone.

Ryan turned and eyed her. "What the hell was that about?"

Maya shrugged as if she didn't have a clue, but she knew. Ayden was jealous. Jealous over the fact that she was here with Ryan on what he thought was a romantic date when they were just friends. But why not let Ayden stew on it? He had no claims on her, and it would be good for Ayden Stewart to eat a little humble pie.

Ayden was angry. He didn't like how cozy Maya and Ryan were. Didn't like the level of intimacy he'd witnessed between them. Not one bit. He'd arrived back at the equestrian facility to cool the pony down and have a refreshment.

Although he didn't want a relationship with Maya, he

didn't want Ryan to have her, either. Which was totally unfair. Maya deserved someone better, who would treat her well, marry her and father a gaggle of babies. It's what she'd always wanted and thought she might have with the knucklehead who'd married her sister. Instead, she was in limbo with Ayden because he kept giving her mixed messages. They had a professional relationship one day. And the next, he was kissing her senseless and muddying the waters. Ayden couldn't make sense of it. He knew his jealousy was irrational, but he seemed powerless to control it.

"Are you going to keep daydreaming, Stewart, or are you ready to win this thing?" Eddie said from above him.

Ayden glanced up and found his team was already back in the saddle. "Yeah, I'm ready. I'm ready to pummel them." He hopped back onto his pony and they headed onto the field. He was going to win this thing. He had an audience and wanted to show Maya how skilled he was at polo. Of course, there were other skills he'd rather show her, which included the two of them on a bed or whatever surface was available.

He blinked. *Get your head out of the clouds, Stewart*, he reminded himself as the umpire threw the ball. Ayden took off down the field.

Unfortunately, the San Antonio team must have regrouped during halftime because they came back stronger than ever and won the third and fourth chukka, forcing a draw. Now they had to play another chukka, and the first team to score would win. Ayden wasn't playing his best and he knew it. Every time he got a chance, he was looking across the field, trying to find Maya, wondering what she was doing with Ryan. It was driving him crazy.

All four team members had gathered for a pep talk. "Come on, guys," Mateo commanded. "We've got to win this, otherwise we don't get to the Centennial Cup. So let's do this."

"Let's do it!" they all yelled.

Fired up, Ayden went all in. As soon as the ball was in the air, he rode toward his man. Ayden bumped the other player with his shoulder while simultaneously attempting another maneuver to hook his mallet when his opponent hit the ball. But their mallets got tangled together and both ponies began to get agitated. Before he knew it, Ayden was hurtling through the air and hit the ground with a loud thump.

Ayden had a splitting headache. Furtively he glanced around the room and that's when he realized he was at the hospital. The last thing he remembered was getting tangled up with the opposing player at the polo match and flying through the air. How long had he been out? He couldn't remember, he just knew he hated hospitals. That was where his mom had died. He tried to move, but felt immobile. Glancing down, Ayden saw a compression wrap around his ankle.

He couldn't afford any broken limbs. He led an active life and had a full workload. He wiggled his ankle. Thankfully, he could move it, but it was definitely swollen. He pressed the buzzer for a nurse. Several minutes later, one walked in. Dressed in blue scrubs and a white jacket, the young brunette came toward him to take his vitals.

"Ah, you've awoken from your slumber," she said.

"How long was I out?"

"For a while. You have a mild concussion, a contusion on your left eye and a sprained ankle, but otherwise, you'll be fine."

"Is that all?" he asked snarkily. "When can I get out of

here?" He used the remote to lift the bed upward into a sitting position. He hated feeling helpless.

"Not tonight," the nurse replied. "We're keeping you overnight for observation, but I'm sure the doctor will release you tomorrow into the care of a loved one."

The care of a loved one. He didn't have anyone here because Luke was across the ocean. His mother had been the only family he'd ever had. And as far as Fallon or Dane, he doubted either of them would come to his aid. The only person he could think of, the only person he would want taking care of him, was Maya. Maya cared for him and would be willing to help. And what better way to ensure she stayed away from Ryan than keeping her close by his side.

Oh, yes, Maya was the right person for the job.

Eight

Maya anxiously paced the hospital waiting room. How long was it going to take for them to tell her something? She'd been waiting for hours to hear about Ayden's condition and no one would tell her anything because she wasn't family. Ryan had stayed with her, but eventually she'd told him to go home. There was nothing he could do and she wasn't leaving until she could see for herself that Ayden was okay. Ryan had understood and advised her to sort through her feelings for Ayden.

When she thought about the accident, her heart turned over in her chest. She'd gasped in horror when Ayden had fallen from the horse. Immediately, she'd run to him, uncaring of how it might look to Ryan or anyone else. She'd just known she had to get to Ayden. He'd been lying motionless on the green and was unresponsive until the ambulance had arrived. He'd opened his eyes briefly on the ride to the hospital, and she hadn't seen those beautiful hazel-gray eyes since.

Once they'd arrived, she'd been treated like a second-class citizen and sent to the waiting room because she wasn't family. No one would talk to her until finally she'd pleaded for any word. They'd told her he was stable, but nothing more.

"Ms. Richardson?" a female voice called out from behind her.

Maya spun around and rushed toward the nurse. "Is there any news on Mr. Stewart?"

"Yes, ma'am. He's awake and asking for you."

Thank God! Maya closed her eyes and said a silent prayer. "Take me to him."

"Follow me."

The nurse led her into a private room. Ayden was sitting on the bed, fully awake with his ankle wrapped. He had one black eye, and a bandage was wrapped over the other side of his head, covering his left eye. Maya rushed toward him and, without thinking, flung herself into his arms. He clutched her to his hard chest.

"It's okay." Ayden patted her back as if he were comforting a small child. "I'm all right, Maya. I have a concussion and a sprained ankle, but other than that, I'm fine."

Inhaling, Maya counted to three and slowly rose to her feet. She'd overreacted and shown her true feelings. "I'm so relieved." Then she reached across the distance and swatted his arm. "Don't ever scare me like that again."

Ayden gave her a sideways grin. "Hey, I'm sorry. Didn't mean to give you a scare. Or sprain any ligaments." He nodded downward toward his ankle.

"Serves you right for those moves you pulled," Maya replied. "Ryan told me not many people try both those moves together."

"I had to do something. We were going to lose."

"And now look at you. You're going to have to take it easy. Maybe use the time for a much-needed vacation."

"I don't vacation," Ayden responded. "I have a business to run. I just need someone to help me while I'm..." He searched for the right word. "Incapacitated."

"Good luck. You're not an easy man to deal with."

"I don't need luck. I just need you."

"Me?" She hadn't been prepared for such a blunt, matter-of-fact statement.

"I need a nursemaid who can take care of me and help me navigate the next week, and I can't think of anyone more qualified than you."

"A-Ayden, that's crazy. I'm no nursemaid. I'm just your assistant."

"True, but you know me. You know what I like and dislike better than any other person," he replied. "You can do this, Maya. Unless there's a reason you can't?"

"What are you talking about?"

"I'm talking about Ryan Kincaid. You were with him at the polo match. In that outfit." He motioned toward her jumpsuit, which showed off her figure and a small swell of cleavage. "I know he's interested in you. Is the feeling mutual? Is that why you can't do me this favor?"

So he was jealous of Ryan. She knew it! But what would make Ayden think she could possibly get involved with another man after the kiss they'd shared last night? Ryan was just a friend, but Ayden didn't know that. It served him right that he was jealous. Over the years, she'd listened to him expound on plenty of other women.

Ayden's behavior didn't make any sense. He'd had a chance with her five years ago. But Ayden hadn't wanted her then. So what had changed?

Why now?

"Well?" Ayden was looking at Maya and waiting for an answer.

"I don't have to justify my actions to you or anyone, Ayden."

He glared at her and she could see he wanted to say more. She'd read between the lines with him long enough to know he was biting his tongue. He contemplated her for several long moments, his gaze scraping her from head to toe. It was a standoff that Maya intended to win.

"You're correct," he said, his voice softening. "I have no right to interfere in your personal life. I was out of line. But I am asking you for your help. You know me—and my needs and wants—better than anyone else. I want you."

Those words sank her. Her belly somersaulted in the air and did a triple axel like an ice skater, but she mustn't let it. She couldn't do this. There was no way that in spending time with Ayden, day in and day out, her true feelings for him wouldn't be exposed. "I'm sorry. I can't." Maya turned away. She couldn't look at him because doing so was playing tricks with her emotions.

"Maya, please," Ayden implored from the bed. "I'll double your salary. Whatever it takes. I *need* you."

Maya reminded herself to stay strong, but when she swirled around to face him, the pleading look in his eyes stopped her cold. There was no way she could deny this man anything even though it wasn't in her best interests. "Okay. Okay, I'll do it."

A large grin spread over his gorgeous face despite the bandage across his eye. "I knew you wouldn't let me down," he said smugly. "You should probably get back to the rental and pack up your things. I'll have a driver bring your belongings to my mansion."

"Your house?" she squeaked.

"Of course. You can't possibly take care of me from

your apartment. You'll need to move in, temporarily that is, until I get on my feet."

"I can't move in with you, Ayden."

"Why not?"

Because I'm in love with you. Because we kissed last night and almost had sex in your office the night before. Maya's face grew hot with a blush and she responded, "It's just not a good idea."

"Rubbish. It makes the most sense for you to be close by. So run along and collect your things and I'll have my driver meet you in a couple of hours."

"You can't just run roughshod over me, Ayden."

"I'm not trying to, but you must see how ridiculous it sounds for you to be my nursemaid from your apartment."

When he put it like that, it made Maya appear silly for suggesting such a thing. "Fine. Fine," she agreed begrudgingly.

"Good. I'm glad that's settled. Make yourself comfortable at my place. Feel free to choose any room you like. And then be back here tomorrow morning because that's when they're releasing me."

"Is there anything else, boss?" Because that was exactly the tone he'd used with her. Not the sexy way he said her name last night in the heat of passion.

"I'm sorry. I didn't mean to sound so formal, Maya. I really appreciate you doing this for me."

She nodded and before she could put a foot in her mouth again, Maya left the room. She needed some air anyway. Ayden had used her affection for him to lure her into his home. Now they would be sharing close quarters. How on earth was she supposed to keep her cool?

It didn't take long for Maya to pack up her meager belongings. And as promised, the driver called her when he arrived at the apartment building. He and the bellhop helped put all her suitcases into the limousine. Maya got in and leaned back against the buttery soft leather interior. It wasn't her first trip in a limousine. She'd accompanied Ayden on many occasions when they'd worked together. But it was quite different to be treated to this kind of luxury on her own.

Leaning back, she closed her eyes. Maya couldn't believe she was doing this. Not only had she accepted her old executive assistant position, but somehow she'd allowed Ayden to convince her to serve as his nursemaid *and* move into his home? It was insanity. But it had been impossible to deny him, especially after he'd said he needed her. *Wanted* her.

Of course, she knew he hadn't meant it like he had last night. That had been a moment in time, when he'd been in pain and reached for the nearest person to comfort him. She'd been convenient. She was a woman and he was a man. A man used to getting sex. Ayden had wanted to escape his past and she'd been willing. Like any red-blooded man, he'd accepted what she was offering.

She searched her purse for her phone. She'd called Callie after Ayden's accident and been beside herself. Callie had calmed her down, but would still be worried.

"Maya." Callie picked up on the first ring. "How is Ayden?"

"He's okay. He has a concussion and a sprained ankle, but he's okay."

"Thank God! I had no idea polo matches could be so dangerous."

"From what Ryan told me, they usually aren't, but Ayden was playing aggressively and making bold moves."

"Sounds like Ayden was jealous seeing you with another man. Do you think he was showboating to garner your attention?"

Maya was silent for a moment as she drank more of her champagne. "It's doubtful. He just wasn't exactly happy that I was with a client."

"A client? You mean another man?"

"I dunno," she fibbed. Because she'd thought the same thing. And she just had to spit out why she'd called. "Anyway, you should know I've agreed to move in and help Ayden around the house and at work until he's back on his feet."

"Sweet baby Jesus!" Callie retorted. "Out of the frying pan and into the fire. Don't you ever learn, girlfriend? What on earth possessed you to agree to such a thing?"

"He needs me. Please, be supportive, Callie. I need you to understand."

"Oh, Lord, Maya. I'm just scared that you're going to get hurt."

"I'll be okay. I can handle this." Or at least she hoped so, because if not, Callie was right. Ayden had the power to truly devastate her, so much so that she might never recover.

Nine

"Comfortable?" Maya asked once she'd settled Ayden in his master bedroom, fluffing his pillows and tucking the covers around him. She'd arrived late that morning to pick him up from the hospital. She'd come prepared with a change of clothes for him consisting of a tracksuit.

He smiled. He was more than comfortable. He was on cloud nine because Maya was here with him. Truth be told, when he'd made the outrageous suggestion, he'd expected her to turn him down flat. She'd put up some resistance, but in the end, he'd persevered and convinced her to move in with him. And with her tending to his needs day and night, there was no way she would have time to see Ryan Kincaid.

Was he really that jealous of his client?

Yes.

He hadn't liked seeing Maya spending time or having fun with another man. Her smile was reserved for only him.

"Yes, I'm comfortable, Maya. Thank you," he finally answered.

She'd been busy since last night. She'd placed crutches nearby to help him get around on his own. He could see her touches in the room, too. There were freshly cut flowers on the nightstand. His favorite spy books had been neatly stacked beside them along with a bottle of water and some pain pills. She'd filled his prescription. She'd literally thought of everything.

It was why he'd wanted her here with him.

Or at least it was one of the reasons. If he was honest with himself, it went deeper, beyond a friend caring for another friend, but he couldn't think like that. She was just doing him a favor.

"Is there anything you'd like?" Maya inquired.

You, Ayden thought as he peered at her through thick lashes. Today, she was dressed in slim-fitting jeans that showed off her sweet behind along with a long-sleeved sweater that had cutout shoulders. She was hardly wearing any makeup other than some mascara and some type of gloss that made her lips shine. He wanted to lean over, grab her by the waist and kiss it off. Although she might appear plain to some, Ayden thought she'd never looked lovelier. Lord, he was in a world of trouble.

"I'd like to go through any outstanding proposals including the Kincaids' to make sure they don't need tweaking before you send them out."

"You want to work?" Maya inquired with a frown. "For Christ's sake, you just got out of the hospital and are recovering from a concussion. Not to mention it's a Sunday, Ayden. I don't work on the weekends. So if you want this arrangement—" she pointed between the two of them "—to work, then you're going to have to remember those parameters."

"All right, what would you suggest we do? I can think of a few." Even with a bum leg, he had a few ideas, but they were certainly not PG-13.

"How about a movie? Or we could marathon a television show on Netflix."

"I don't watch TV."

Maya rose from her seat. "That's too bad because I'm going to find an activity for us that doesn't require the use of a bed."

He bowled over with laughter as he watched her scoot out of the room.

Maya was happy for some breathing room. She knew what other ideas he had because her mind immediately went to imagining the two of them naked, sprawled out over his sumptuous covers, kissing and making wild, passionate love. She'd felt her cheeks grow warm. Had Ayden sensed where her mind had wandered?

Probably not.

She was just a means to end, taking care of his immediate needs while making sure the office ran smoothly in his absence. Would he ever see her as more? Did she want him to?

Her mind was swirling as she set about locating the butler. She had to find some activity to keep the two of them busy on her day off. Because she was sure, come tomorrow, Ayden would be ready to get back to work, sprained ankle or not.

She found the butler downstairs in the kitchen talking to the chef about dinner. "Good afternoon, Ms. Richardson. Is there anything I can help you with?" he asked.

"First, you can call me, Maya." When he began to interrupt her, she held up her hand. "I'm going to be staying here while your boss recovers, so please call me by my first name."

"Very well, Maya. And second?"

"Do you have cable, internet, Netflix, anything to amuse us?"

A half hour later, Maya was armed and ready to entertain. The butler had secured a television and DVR on wheels and brought it into Ayden's master suite. Ayden had always told her he much preferred reading a good book or engaging in extracurricular activities with the opposite sex to watching mindless television. The butler had also found several board games like chess and dominoes and Taboo to keep their minds occupied until dinner. Meanwhile, she'd thrown some popcorn she'd found in the pantry into the microwave.

"What's all this?" Ayden asked when they brought in all the goodies.

"Your education on being an everyday joe," Maya said with a smile. "We're going to watch movies, eat popcorn and veg out all day."

"Really?"

"That's right, and you're going to love it."

And they did. While munching on popcorn, Maya joined Ayden on his bed—*above the covers*—and made him watch *Pretty Woman.* And instead of going downstairs to a formal dinner in his dining salon, dinner was served to them on television trays. Afterward, they ended up playing a game of chess. Ayden absolutely killed her.

"No fair," Maya said when the game was over. "You're a master at this. When did you learn how to play?"

Ayden shrugged. "I learned chess at boarding school. We didn't have much else to do. Thanks to my stepfather, I knew how to hustle those rich kids out of their money.

For them, it wasn't a hardship, but for me it ensured I had spending money because my stepfather didn't allow Mom to send me any money at school. He was just glad to be rid of me."

"What happened during school breaks?"

"I usually begged to go to friends' houses. Sometimes it worked. Sometimes Jack tolerated me coming home, but he made sure I knew that I was only there on his sufferance."

"That's terrible, Ayden. I'm sorry you had to endure that."

"I survived. And I don't want to end our fun evening on a sour note," Ayden said. "Plus, it's late and I'd like to get some rest so I'm ready for work tomorrow."

"You don't intend on going to the office, do you?"

Ayden shook his head. "No, not just yet. I'll work from home. At least until I get the hang of those." He nodded toward the crutches lying against a nearby chair.

"Those are easy. I taught Raven how to use them when she broke her leg in middle school."

"Have you spoken to your sister since the baptism?" Ayden inquired.

Maya greeted him with an icy stare. "I thought we were forgoing heavy talk?"

"I was just curious. I know how much she meant to you."

"My sister used to mean everything to me, but as you know, times have changed. We've spoken about my mom's care, but that's about it. You mind if we change the subject?"

"Okay," Ayden said. "I was just trying to be there for you like you've been there for me."

She offered him a smile. "Thank you, and I'm sorry if I bit your head off. I appreciate you caring. It's been a long night, and I'm going so you can get some sleep," Maya said. "I think you've done enough for today."

"I had fun. I can't remember the last time I honestly said that, so thank you." He leaned over and wrapped his arms around her in a hug. It should have been quick, but it lasted a little longer than was necessary. Maya felt her nipples instantly harden into bullets. Had he noticed she was turned on by a simple embrace? When he released her and she glanced up at him, Maya's heart stopped.

He'd noticed. His eyes were liquid, bottomless and filled with desire. She heard his breathing change ever so slightly and a throb of awareness coiled through her. He smiled and ran the back of his fingers down her cheek, and she shuddered. How had they gone from the friend zone to a heat flare in a matter of seconds?

"Ayden..." She didn't get the chance to utter another word because he closed the gap between them and sealed his mouth hungrily over hers. Maya responded to his kiss as every ounce of pent-up frustration from spending the day with him surged through her. She moaned and opened her mouth up to the onslaught of his kiss. She was just as eager as he was to taste, to lick and to twine her tongue with his. She drew him closer and he pushed her backward. Maya felt the pillows at her head as his torso pressed against hers, crushing her breasts against his magnificent bare chest.

Their mouths and bodies aligned perfectly and Maya parted her lips, inviting him in. Ayden took the cue and delved deeper. He took his time exploring, stroking his tongue back and forth against hers.

"This needs to come off," he said, and began tugging at the hem of her sweater. She obliged and tossed the offending garment over her head, revealing her breasts. Moaning, she captured his lips in a savage kiss, clattering her teeth against his as she sought more. Understanding her need, Ayden drew her closer against his body, settling her against his impressive erection. Maya tilted her hips back and forth and began rubbing shamelessly against his rigid length.

"Ayden…" she moaned.

His sizzling eyes sought hers and held. Then he began thrusting upward to meet her hip rolls. A fierce longing gripped Maya's insides. She knew she should slow things down, think about her actions, but she was powerless to fight the carnal desire he incited in her. She wanted to remove every stitch of her clothing and let Ayden make love to her, but she knew it would mean more to her than him. For him, it would just be a release and he'd treat her the same as before.

He sought her face with his hands and brought her closer, diving in to kissing her more thoroughly. Maya could feel herself losing control especially when he pushed his hips forward and ground his erection against her. And when she felt his hands at the zipper of her slim jeans, she didn't stop him. One of his hands snaked lower inside and she laced her fingers with his to guide him to her nub. When he dipped inside her and began stroking her inner walls, Maya was lost as pure pleasure raced through her.

Soon she was gasping and trembling and her muscles clutched his fingers as her climax rolled over her in waves.

"Did that feel good?" Ayden whispered as his lips left her mouth to nuzzle at her neck.

His words woke her up from the haze of desire she'd been under. Embarrassment flushed over her at how wantonly she'd behaved with him. She sat upright, pulling on her sweater as she went.

"Maya?"

"Please don't!" she exclaimed, scooting off the bed. "This…this should never have gotten this far. I told you it was a mistake for me to come here." She ran for the safety and cover of her bedroom. With a sprained ankle, Ayden wouldn't be chasing after her. She had to get some distance and figure out how she'd let the situation get so out of control.

Ten

Frustrated, Ayden sat upright, staring at the door Maya had just run through. Jesus! He rubbed his head. He'd really done it this time. The kiss in his office had been one thing, but tonight they'd had such a wonderful evening together talking, watching television and playing board games that it made Ayden realize just how much he wanted Maya. The heat between them was off the charts, so much so neither of them could deny the sparks when they were in such close quarters.

So he'd kissed her, not thinking about the complications of his actions. The sight of her half-naked body had jolted him. She was so beautiful, from her soft brown skin to her small breasts. She was exquisite and all he wanted to do was slake his thirst for her. Taste her very essence. He wanted to take those dark nipples into his mouth, to sink into her slick heat and let the passion between them explode. But he hadn't gotten the chance because Maya had run away from him *again*.

He wanted to go after her and bring her back to his bed, but he couldn't. Maya was skittish and he didn't blame her. He'd messed up last time when he'd appeared unaffected by their night together even though he'd been far from it. In fact, the desire he'd felt had scared him and he'd tried to marginalize it, brushing it off as good sex and nothing more.

It was certainly the best he'd ever had. And he wanted more. More of Maya. But how did he convince her to explore this side of their relationship when he'd hurt her before? Add the fact that he wasn't keeping the promise he'd made to her to keep their relationship professional and no wonder she was upset. Usually Ayden was a man of his word. He prided himself on it. But when it came to Maya, he didn't think with a level head. He'd been so convinced that night five years ago had been a fluke that he'd simply imagined how intense the attraction between them had been, but he was wrong. Years ago, he'd deceived himself, refusing to admit how much she meant to him, and now look at where they were.

Ayden glanced at the clock. It was after midnight and he was in no mood to sleep. His mind was racing, as he kept reliving the moment she'd come and the sounds she'd made when his fingers had been buried inside her. Jesus! Didn't she understand that she couldn't fight this attraction any more than he could? Because as sure as the sun rose in the morning, it was inevitable that they would fall into bed again. The chemistry between them would no longer be denied. It had probably always been there. Five years ago, they'd opened that door and there was no going back. Ayden had found the one and only woman who made him want to go back on his word.

Maya awoke the next morning knowing what she had to do. She had to leave Ayden, the job, Austin, all of it. Money be damned. She'd figure out a way to help pay her mother's cancer treatment bills. She was bright, and qualified assistants were always in high demand. She would find a job.

Throwing the covers off, Maya went to the bathroom. After brushing her teeth, showering and dressing, she packed up her minimal toiletries. Heading back to the bedroom, she pulled the suitcase out of the closet. She hadn't had time to unpack because she'd been so focused on caring for Ayden yesterday. Maya placed the luggage by the door and paused because she wanted to smell the flowers outside her balcony one last time before she left. When Ayden had said she could make herself comfortable, she'd chosen the room above the gardens. Opening the door, she walked to the railing and looked out over the colorful plants in full bloom, taking in the fragrance wafting in the air around her.

Her arrangement with Ayden was untenable. She couldn't continue doing the same thing and expecting a different result. Ayden was her Achilles' heel and she had to face it that being his nursemaid would undoubtedly have her winding up in his bed. Maya accepted that she had no willpower when it came to resisting him. Callie was right. She was in over her head.

She heard a creak behind her and turned to find Ayden on crutches behind her. Maya didn't speak and turned back around to stare at the garden.

"Maya, I recognize that last night the situation got out of control."

"You mean that boundary we crossed, that *you* said wouldn't happen again?"

She heard his sharp intake of breath. It wasn't fair to blame him entirely for what had happened. She'd played an active role. She whirled around. "I'm sorry. That was unfair."

He shook his head. “No, you’re right. I promised to keep my hands to myself, but failed miserably. And if we’re being honest, I can’t promise that I’m not going to touch you, not kiss you, and not make love to you.”

All of Maya’s tingly parts came alive at his bold declaration. “So then you’re in agreement that we can’t work together and it’s best we terminate this agreement.”

“Far from it.”

“Pardon?” She didn’t understand. He’d just said that he wasn’t going to keep his promise for their relationship to remain professional.

“I think we need to acknowledge there is something between us and *act* on it. Stop denying it exists and just see where it goes.”

“Straight to your bed,” she countered. “Because we both know where it will lead.”

“And is it so wrong that we enjoy each other?” Ayden asked, hopping toward her until they were a few feet apart. “Don’t you think it’s high time we started acting like adults and admit we’re attracted to each other?”

“Ayden…”

“You want me. Don’t you?”

Maya lowered her gaze. She couldn’t believe they were having this conversation. Right now. He was putting everything out in the open and pulling no punches. When she didn’t answer, she felt him throw the crutches to the ground and move over to the railing until he was inches from her face.

“I dare you to say you don’t.”

Maya rolled her eyes upward. “Yes, I want you. There. Are you happy? I admit it.”

“No, not really because you’re too far away from me to kiss you properly.”

Maya leaned over and Ayden rewarded her with a hot,

deep kiss. She moaned softly, opened her mouth, allowed his tongue to dip inside and mate with hers. W*hat was she doing?* Maya wrenched herself away and when he leaned in again, she put her hand against his hard chest. "Are you sure about this?"

"Yes. Don't deny us this pleasure when we both want this."

She did want him more than she had any other man, and he was offering her the opportunity to have unfettered access to him. But what did it all mean? What happened once he tired of her?

"Stop thinking, Maya. For once, just feel, allow yourself to let go and be *mine*."

His words startled her. Be his. They'd only been together once and it had been the most amazing sexual experience of her life. If she allowed herself to go there again, Maya was afraid she'd never be the same again. The first time she'd been completely devastated and had had to move away because she couldn't stand to be near him. What would happen this time?

"Come away with me."

She frowned in consternation. "Where?"

"To Jamaica. You were right. I never take a vacation and now, with this bum ankle, it's a prime opportunity to take some time off and explore us." He wound his hands around her neck and pulled her closer, bringing her into his air space. He leaned his forehead against hers. "Come away with me."

"I don't know, Ayden." She pulled away. "You're moving too fast. You want me to fly to Jamaica at a moment's notice? I have responsibilities now. You know I want to be here for my mother's next treatment."

"Of course, I understand that. It would be a short getaway. Plenty of time for you to get back, but enough time for us to discover our feelings in paradise without any outside influences."

Maya was torn. She did want to go with Ayden, but she was also afraid to jump into the deep end of the ocean without a life vest. Even though he'd admitted his desire for her, Ayden had the power to hurt her because she still had unresolved feelings for him. Feelings that went deeper than lust. Yet, if she didn't take this opportunity she would always wonder what could have been.

"All right, I'll go with you."

Maya couldn't believe she was on a recliner in a living room–style cabin of a private plane on her way to Montego Bay with Ayden. Once she'd agreed, Ayden had contacted his pilot to file a flight plan. In her wildest dreams, she would never have imagined that he would want to spend time alone with her or that she'd readily agree. But one devilish yet sinfully sexy look from him had her abandoning her principles and packing a suitcase for Jamaica. And she knew full well what was in store during their stay—mind-blowing, toe-curling sex the likes of which she'd never experienced except with him.

Maya was both excited and terrified. She was by no means a virgin, but she'd only been with a handful of men. And none of them had ever made her feel the way Ayden did. One look, one touch from him set her on fire. She didn't want to disappoint him.

A lump formed in her throat. She regarded him from across the aisle where he lay sprawled out on the couch with his ankle up, playing with his tablet. He seemed perfectly content, as if he didn't have a care in the world. Was he used to whisking women away on getaways to paradise so he could wine and dine them and take them to bed? Or maybe there would be no wining and dining, just sex. Full stop.

She hazarded a glance at him and found his eyes on her. "What are you worrying about, Maya? I hope you're not regretting your decision to come with me."

She shook her head. "I'm just wondering what you have in store for me."

He chuckled, showing off his winsome smile and perfect white teeth. "If you're asking if I intend to let you come up for air after I've had my wicked way with you, the answer is yes. We're going to Jamaica on vacation. I may not be able to do everything like climbing Dunn's River Falls, but we can certainly take in the sights and enjoy the culture."

Maya smiled brightly. "All right, that sounds good."

"You're too far away over there. Why don't you come over here." He gave her a wink and patted the empty seat beside him.

"Ayden Stewart, I have no intention of becoming a member of the mile-high club. Plus, the crew is just in the other room." She inclined her head toward the front of the cabin where the pilots and flight attendant were assembled.

"I promise to be good."

"I highly doubt that."

"Come here," he commanded. The tone of his voice had Maya rising from her seat and moving to him, but she stopped a few inches away from him. It forced Ayden to sit upright, grasp her arm and haul her forward. "This is much better," he said when she was in his lap. "And this will be even better." He lowered his head and brushed his lips across hers. She was fast becoming addicted to his kisses. He used everything in his arsenal to make her his willing captive.

When he finally lifted his head, he smiled as he looked

at her. "You look thoroughly kissed. Every man will know that you're with me."

He sat her upright and for the rest of the flight wouldn't let her leave his side. Maya supposed she should be flattered by all this attention, but what happened at the end of their vacation? Where did they go from there? She shook her head. She wouldn't think of the future, only the here and now with Ayden for the scant time she had with him.

They arrived in Jamaica later that afternoon and were met on the tarmac by a limousine. A driver took care of their luggage and his crutches while Ayden leaned on Maya for support to help him to the limo. Soon they were leaving Montego Bay and heading through the countryside. Maya peered out the window taking in the sights of the island country.

"You look like a kid in a candy store," Ayden said.

Maya turned away from the window. "I'm sorry, am I being too gauche? I've only been out of the country once during spring break when I let Callie talk me into going to Cancun."

"And how did that go?"

"Terrible. Callie was wasted half the time and when she wasn't, she was curled up next to several guys. I spent much of the time reading on the beach. The best part of that vacation was the fact that I was of legal drinking age and could partake in the cocktails."

Ayden stared at her for several long moments. "Have you ever done anything out of your comfort zone?"

"This," she responded. "I'm running off to an island to have an affair with my boss."

"Is that all I am to you—your boss?" Ayden asked.

His question startled her. She hadn't meant to offend him. If she had, it was a bad start to their journey. "No, of course not." She moved away from the window. "I'm sorry, you're more than just my boss." She took a deep breath and said what she truly felt. "You're about to become my lover."

He grinned and the light returned to his eyes. "That's right. And I intend to ensure I satisfy your every need."

"I can't wait."

They arrived at a beautiful villa built on the side of the mountain. It was the epitome of romance. The home was surrounded by long clinging vines, bougainvillea, fragrant flowers and dense green trees. There wasn't another house for miles. They would be secluded in this love nest. Tucked away from the world. Just the two of them.

Once their bags were taken inside, Ayden grabbed the crutches and showed Maya the grounds. "You've stayed here before?" she asked.

He nodded. "I come here sometimes when I need to be alone."

Maya wondered if he'd ever made peace with what happened, but chose not to ask. She just followed behind him. The inside of the home was white and clean with modern furnishings. The large kitchen and living area were open to the great outdoors which overlooked a terrace that had a luxurious infinity pool for their use. "I can't wait to slip into my bathing suit and get in."

"Who says you need a bikini?" Ayden replied, "We're the only ones here, Maya. You can feel comfortable in your birthday suit."

She turned away and began walking down the corridor to see the rest of the home. He wanted her to walk out in the open completely nude? She could never do that. She'd feel too self-conscious. Raven had always had the rocking body with curves for days that men liked, while Maya had always had a slightly boyish figure. Thank God, she'd finally gotten boobs.

Ayden caught up with her at the master suite, which housed a raised platform bed with a silky duvet in deep red and loads of cream pillows strewn over it. Swaths of fabric hung from the ceiling, draping the bed. They were gauzy and sexy. It clearly wasn't a bed made for sleeping.

"Maya!"

"Hmm?"

"Sit." He motioned to the bed and Maya took a seat so they could be eye to eye. "You have nothing to be ashamed or embarrassed about. You have a beautiful body."

"You don't have to say that, Ayden. I know that I'm not like the curvaceous women you usually date."

He cupped her chin, tilting her head so he could peer into her eyes. "Maya, I love your body."

"You do?"

"Yes, and I can't wait to show you just how much."

"When?" she asked expectantly, eagerly.

He gave her a wolfish grin. "Later, after dinner."

"Promise?"

"Oh, it's a promise I intend to keep all night long."

Eleven

Ayden ignored the jolt of arousal that had been surging through him from the moment they'd arrived. He wanted to give Maya the romantic evening she deserved rather than immediately throwing her down on the bed and thrusting inside her wet heat until she called out his name. It was crazy to think that for years he'd been blind to her beauty until that night five years ago opened his eyes. Ayden always had boundaries and each person had their proper place, but he'd been unable to put Maya back into the box he'd had her in. Instead, all their time together was marked by sexual tension and awareness.

Tonight was no different. After arriving, they'd both showered—*separately*—and were now in the living room having a drink before dinner. Ayden had arranged for a local catering company to drop off meals for them during their stay. A candlelight dinner was set up on the patio along with a bucket of champagne so he and Maya could eat underneath the stars. When they were ready, all they had to do was pull the food out from the warmer on the counter. Soup was in a heated container nearby and salad plates were already in place.

But he wasn't sure he wanted dinner. He wanted to devour Maya. Her beautiful dark brown hair was stylish, sleek and straight. She'd changed into a print sundress with spaghetti straps that stopped at the knee, giving him an unfettered view of her long legs.

It wasn't easy navigating, but he managed to pull out her chair. "Thank you," Maya said once she was seated.

Ayden shuffled to the other side, tossing down his crutches. "You're looking exceptionally lovely this evening, Maya."

She blushed. "Thank you."

"Would you like some champagne?"

"Love some."

He took care of pouring the bubbly into their glasses and, once filled, leaned both elbows over and held up his flute. "A toast."

"To us."

"And unexplored territories," Ayden finished, sipping his champagne.

Maya drank her champagne, regarding him from under mascara-coated lashes. He noticed she wasn't wearing much makeup and he liked that about her; she was comfortable being herself. He wanted her to feel that way, but he sensed her tension from across the table.

So he began talking about the fun things they were going to see and do in Jamaica while he ladled soup into the bowls on the table. "I've hired a tour guide for the day after tomorrow. Thought he could show us around the island. You can take some photos."

She smiled as she accepted her soup bowl. "I'm looking

forward to it. Hopefully, we'll get to eat some authentic jerk chicken. I hear Jamaica has some of the best."

"I didn't realize you liked spicy food."

"Then you need to catch up on all things Maya. Starting with how I like my pizza."

Ayden appreciated this feisty side of Maya, and over the next hour as they tucked into their dinner of Caribbean-style fish with grilled pineapple, shrimp and vanilla-rum butter sauce, he learned even more about her. He knew she loved running but didn't know she listened to Audible during her runs. Or that she had a fear of heights due to falling off the monkey bars when she was six years old. In his prior relationships, if he could call them that, he'd never taken the time to get to know their likes and dislikes, but Maya made him want to go deeper, know more.

By the end of the evening, they'd adjourned to a large chaise and removed their shoes to stargaze. They'd imbibed the entire bottle of champagne, along with a fair share of wine with their meal. They were both feeling relaxed, so it was only natural when Ayden leaned over and brushed his lips across Maya's. Hers were soft and sweet like the creamy custard of the crème brûlée they'd had earlier for dessert.

She tasted so good he dipped his head for another taste. Maya wound her arms around his neck and he pressed his body against hers. Feeling her against him was electrifying and he slid his hands down her bare arms to her breasts. He caressed the small mounds and felt her nipples pebble to his touch. And when she shuddered, he knew Maya was ready to take their relationship to the next level.

He rose up on one arm and looked down at her. "Why did you stop?" she asked, looking up at him in bewilderment.

"I just want you to be sure, Maya."

"I'm sure, Ayden. I want you. So stop talking and make love to me." She clasped his head and brought his mouth down on hers. He tried to keep it gentle, but the kiss deepened and desire bloomed. He wanted to explore her, taste every inch of her. His mouth left hers and found a path to her shoulders. He kissed the soft blades, sliding the straps of her sundress down as he went until her dress was lowered to her waist and he could feast his eyes on her breasts.

He bent down and closed his mouth over one round globe. Maya nearly jackknifed off the chaise as he sucked it deep into his mouth, swirling the rock-hard tip with his tongue. He alternated between sucking and licking and tugging the sensitive nipple with his teeth, causing Maya to squirm underneath him. The fact that she was so turned-on pleased him tremendously and he intended on giving her a lot more pleasure. He splayed his hand across her stomach to keep her down, so he could lean over and palm the other breast and give it the same ministration.

While his mouth played havoc with her upper body, his hands roamed lower, aiming for the place between her legs. His fingers slid underneath her dress, which had shifted up to her waist with all her squirming. He snatched the tiny scrap of fabric from her hips and tossed it aside, then plunged deep inside. Ayden found her deliciously hot and wet. He was thrilled with the knowledge that she was ready for him. His groin tightened in anticipation of what was to come.

"Ayden," Maya cried out when his fingers teased her, stroking in and out of her core.

"I want to taste you," he said gruffly. He moved lower to kiss her abdomen and stomach until he came to her hips and thighs. He splayed them open with his arms, pushing them wider to make room for what he wanted to do. He teased her first not giving her what she wanted. He licked the inside of both of her thighs, the back of her knees, even kissed her feet before he came back to her core. He licked the seam and Maya let out a sob of pleasure that only made Ayden want more. His tongue slid in farther, teasing the sensitive nub with soft flicks and licks. Her legs began to shake and she began to shiver uncontrollably.

She was close.

"Please," she begged him. Her moans and mews were driving Ayden crazy. He knew what she wanted, but he wasn't about to give it to her. Not yet. If he did, he wouldn't be able to hold himself together and would climax almost immediately because that's how hard his erection was. He needed to sate her first. Otherwise, if he took her now, it would be over too quick.

"Easy, love," he whispered, and returned to feverishly stroking her with his tongue until her entire body spasmed and she clutched around him. Her honeyed taste filled his senses and he lapped her until she eventually subsided.

Maya couldn't believe she'd just let Ayden make love to her out in the open. She'd always been somewhat of a prude. It was like she was outside her body, but couldn't stop herself. The man made her wanton and greedy for whatever he had in store. And if she allowed herself to think about it, she'd stop, and she didn't want to. She was enjoying being with Ayden and exploring this side of herself.

"Are you all right?" he asked, glancing up at her as he eased upward to kiss her.

She could taste herself on his lips. It was heady stuff. She ached to touch him, but she wanted to do so when they were skin to skin. She rose onto her knees and quickly threw off her sundress, tossing it to the floor.

Ayden grinned as she sat before him, completely and

unabashedly naked while he was still fully clothed. "So beautiful." His eyes darkened and Maya felt the words through every part of her.

She leaned forward and began unbuttoning his shirt. He shrugged it off his broad shoulders, bringing into view his beautiful torso along with his muscular biceps and trim waist. Her fingers tingled to touch more. She moved to his belt, loosening each loop, until finally she could unzip him. He stood and dropped his pants and they fell to the floor by her dress. Then he worked off his boxers to reveal the most spectacular erection she'd ever seen.

He was beautiful and *large*.

She would gladly take all of him inside her because she'd wanted this for so long. She hadn't thought it would ever be possible to be with Ayden again, yet here she was. He crawled onto the chaise beside her, covering her body with his, and Maya lost all coherent thought except that she was exactly where she wanted to be. In the moonlit darkness, Maya felt it was safe to say exactly what she wanted. "Please, Ayden."

"Please what?"

"Make love to me."

He gathered her in his arms and claimed her mouth. His fingertips caressed her all over with feather-soft strokes, up and down her side and then lower until his fingers slid along her crease. He teased her core, testing her yet again, making sure she was wet. And when he locked gazes with her, she knew he was seeing if she had any last-minute regrets. But she didn't have any. Then she watched as he retrieved a condom from his pants pocket and sheathed himself.

Soon she felt the ridge of his shaft, notching at her entrance. He eased forward inch by delicious inch and she gasped. But she wanted him even deeper and lifted her knees to help guide him in farther. He braced himself on his elbows and in one fell swoop surged inside her.

"Oh, yes," Maya moaned. It felt right to be joined with Ayden this way.

"You feel so good, Maya. And so tight," he panted as he began moving inside her. "Why did I ever think I could resist you?"

Maya didn't have an answer because she too had been denying the pull between them. But he'd been right. It was inevitable that they would end up like this. And so she gave into the moment, wrapping her ankles around his back and lifting her hips to move to the rhythm he set. Ayden flexed his powerful body and she sensed he was struggling for control because he began thrusting frantically. She parted her thighs wider, wanting him to fill her as completely as only he could.

"Maya..." He rasped out her name and his hold tightened around her as he pumped faster and faster.

"Yes," she cried as tension began building inside her. She could feel her body begin to tremble and she grabbed his buttocks and clutched him closer to her. And when he pulled back, only to thrust in again, she greedily met him as he pushed their pace. When her climax hit, she became undone and screamed his name.

He continued pounding into her until, moments later, she heard a loud groan rip from deep inside him and he fell on top of her. Maya tried to suck in air, but it was impossible. She gasped for breath as he rolled to her side.

Maya lay still, afraid to look at him, staring at the stars overhead. Had he felt the intensity of their coupling as she had? They'd been frenetic, more intense than five years ago. Yet it had been a totally sublime experience that she couldn't wait to relive over and over throughout their days in Jamaica.

"That was over much too quick," Ayden said softly from beside her.

With a small grin, she turned to him. "It was sensational."

"I'm sorry. I'm usually more in control, but with you..." His voice trailed off.

"With me what?"

"I can't seem to find it anymore."

She was happy that he felt he could be honest with her. "I've felt the same way for a long time."

"How long?"

"C'mon, Ayden, are you saying you didn't notice that I pined for you for years before I met Thomas? Maybe even after..."

He rose up on an elbow to look at her. "No, no, I didn't. I've always been aware of you, Maya—" he stroked her cheek "—but you were always so composed and buttoned up. And then when you came to me upset and brokenhearted, I don't know, something snapped and all I wanted to do was make you feel good. Special. Adored."

"You did that then. And now," she whispered as the warmth of his words enveloped her. She was eager for him to tell her more. Instead, he reached for her, closing the gap and sealing her mouth hungrily with his. She reciprocated, responding to him with abandoned enthusiasm. His arms wrapped tightly around her and Maya felt the hard ridge of his shaft against her middle. She couldn't believe he'd recovered that quickly. Or that she was just as desperate to feel him inside her again.

A maelstrom of unbridled lust and passion that only Ayden could quench took over. She crawled up the length of his body and straddled him, settling against his bulge. Ayden's gaze was dark and intense and filled with desire. He reached for yet another condom and rolled it on. She watched him, spellbound. And when he grasped her hips firmly, she sank down on him, drawing him in. He filled her in the best possible way. "Yes," she purred.

She enthusiastically began grinding hard against him, eager to feel his powerful body pressing against hers. Her hair fell into her face, but she didn't care. She put her hands on his chest for leverage and adjusted the angle, taking him even deeper inside her. And when she found the right rhythm, she rode him.

"Damn it, Maya." Ayden stared up at her, his skin glistening with sweat. She could feel him trying to slow down the pace, but she kept undulating against him. That's when he began to devour her, holding her more tightly as he nudged his hips higher, thrusting harder and faster into her. When her orgasm struck, her back arched like a bow, and only seconds later, a loud guttural groan burst from his beautiful lips. He thrust one final time and her entire chest constricted as yet another tidal wave of pleasure surged through her. All Maya could see was a flash of lightning as she closed her eyes and fell forward, drifting into another dimension.

Twelve

Maya stirred awake the next morning on the platform bed in the master suite as light streamed through the windows. How had she gotten here? Then she recalled that sometime during the night, Ayden had scooped her into his arms and carried her to the bedroom where he'd proceeded to make her come again and again. But where was he now? When she glanced over at his side of the bed, he was gone and the sheets were cool to the touch.

Last night had been an incredible night of lovemaking and snuggling next to Ayden. He'd been voracious in his appetite for her. Her underutilized muscles were slammed while several intimate areas felt sore, but she welcomed that if it meant Ayden wanted her as much as she wanted him.

Determined to go find him, she sat up, threw off the covers and went in search of something to wear. She was rummaging through her suitcase when Ayden returned carrying a tray laden with food and coffee mugs.

"Where do you think you're going?" he asked.

"To find you." Maya grabbed her silk robe and slung her arms through it, knotting it at the waist.

"Did I say you were allowed to get dressed?" Ayden asked as he laid the tray on the bed and took a seat.

She grinned. "I can't very well walk around naked."

"Why not?"

Maya flushed. She didn't answer him; instead, she walked toward the bed and sat beside him. "What do you have here?"

"Some omelets, toast, fresh squeezed orange juice and coffee."

"You made all this?"

"Oh, heck no, the catering company stopped by this morning."

"Did they? I didn't hear them."

He grinned. "That's because you were exhausted."

"I wonder why."

He rolled to his side and leaned over to kiss her. "I can think of a number of reasons, but you need to eat. And I'll draw you a bath. I suspect you're a bit sore this morning." He searched her eyes for confirmation. "We, were, um, very vigorous last night."

Maya flushed. He was right. He hadn't been gentle, but she hadn't wanted him to be. Nevertheless, she'd never spoken so openly about intimacy with another man. "Thank you. That would be lovely."

He hopped off the bed and headed for the en suite while Maya continued nibbling on toast and the delicious Denver omelet. She heard the tap running and smiled at his thoughtfulness. When she was done eating and Ayden hadn't returned she went to the bathroom. He had not only drawn a bath, but he was in it.

"Are you coming in or do I have to come and get you?"

"That won't be necessary," Maya said, relieving herself of her robe and sinking into the steaming water. She leaned back against Ayden, pressing her backside against his shaft. He was semi-erect, but that was quickly changing. She opened for him, letting him take any liberties he chose, but he didn't. Instead, he washed her thoroughly and then eventually swaddled her in a towel and carried her back to the bed.

Maya was a bit disappointed. She'd thought he would gather her against his chest so she could straddle him and go for another round, but instead, he laid her down on the bed. Desperate not to lose the connection, she circled her arms around his neck. He kissed her then, openmouthed, with such raw passion that her brain short-circuited. Heat pooled at her core, making her want him all over again. "Ayden..."

"Hmm..." He'd moved from her mouth and was nibbling at the sensitive spots on her nape and neck. When he dipped his tongue inside her ear, Maya moaned.

"Feel good?"

"Yes..."

"I'd like you to feel even better." He shifted down her body and Maya parted her legs, letting him in.

He glanced up, his eyes locking with hers momentarily before he began to pleasure her. He teased her with his tongue and fingers, arousing her so much so that she thrashed and begged him to take her, but he didn't. Instead, he licked her until her orgasm struck hot and fierce and she came apart. Her entire body trembled and he kissed through the aftershocks until lethargy took over and she closed her eyes.

But as she drifted off, the truth hit her hard in the chest. Maya had allowed herself these moments to enjoy Ayden and all he could offer because deep down she knew it wouldn't last.

Ayden hadn't made any promises. He'd only offered her this week, this moment in time when it was just the two of them away from the world. She'd taken it and she wouldn't surrender to regret now.

She was here in Jamaica with Ayden, the man she loved. Oh yes, that was the truth. There was no denying it.

She loved him.

Ayden stared down at Maya's sleeping figure. Her mass of hair was spread across the pillows like a fan. He gently lifted a strand and breathed in the fresh citrus scent. It smelled like Maya, and his chest felt tight and his breathing became harder. He rubbed his forehead.

He'd thought coming to Jamaica would help clear up this insatiable need he felt for Maya, but it appeared he'd only stoked the flames. Waking up with Maya by his side should have been alarming because he typically never stayed the night with other lovers. Once his lust was sated, he left and returned to his own home to sleep. But, with Maya, he felt like he was home. And when he'd turned to her during the night, she'd welcomed him with open arms, all too eager to please.

And she had pleased him immensely.

With each orgasm, her tight, slender body had blown his mind into a million pieces. He'd watched her responses, heard her cries and moans as he'd extracted every ounce of pleasure he could from her pert breasts to the thatch of hair between her thighs. She was his fantasy come to life and he'd made sure to taste every inch of her.

Just now, he'd wanted to take her again and she'd been willing, but he'd needed to regain some composure. He felt off his game. Felt as if he was diving into the deep end of the ocean without knowing how to swim. They would have to get out of this house tonight. If they didn't, Ayden feared he'd keep her naked and writhing on the bed for the entire length of their stay.

Eventually, Maya did awake and he arranged for them to go to Rick's Café, one of the famous bars in Jamaica. They arrived before sunset so they could see the brave souls willing to jump off the highest cliff into the Caribbean. They'd dressed casually for the night out; he was wearing linen trousers and a matching button-down shirt while Maya had opted for a filmy dress that left her shoulders bare.

"We're here," the driver announced when the limo stopped.

"Ready for a fun night?" Ayden asked, squeezing Maya's hand, which had been resting in his for the entire drive from the villa.

"Absolutely."

The well-known bar was alive with activity, full of bikini-clad and bare-chested patrons. After a well-slipped tip, the host was able to find them a table overlooking the West Cliffs. The view was spectacular, and Ayden was looking forward to the sunset as well as time spent with the woman across from him.

"This is great, Ayden. I'd heard about this place and always wanted to come."

"Are you feeling adventurous?" He inclined his head toward the top of the cliff divers were jumping from.

Maya shook her head. "No, thank you. I'll leave it to the daredevils. But I'll cheer them on from here."

"My kind of gal."

He appreciated Maya even more when instead of ordering a cocktail, she got a Red Stripe like a local and indulged in jerk chicken and Jamaican beef patties. The woman was full of surprises. He doubted any of the well-coiffed women he usually dated would be caught dead in an establishment like this. For them, it had to be five-star all the way, but Maya was content with just being normal. Ayden didn't realize just how much he'd been missing out on until now.

They didn't stay and close down Rick's Café. After watching the colorful and vibrant sunset and dancing hip to hip to reggae music from the live band, Ayden was horny as hell. When Maya had put her rear to his groin and begun grinding her hips to the rhythmical music, he'd been in both heaven and hell. Hell because he was getting turned on by a dance in front of too many people and heaven because it would take hours to get back to the villa so they would have plenty of time to enjoy each other in the limo.

After finding the condom in his wallet, he knew he wasn't even going to try. Once they were seated in the limo, he hauled Maya into his lap and crushed her mouth to his. He indulged himself in her with long sweeps of his tongue, thrusting and stroking until eventually he had to come up for air. All he could think about was touching her, kissing her. He leaned his forehead against hers.

"I want you," he murmured.

"We're in a limo." The blacked-out divider had been lifted as soon as they'd entered.

"I don't care." He lifted her so she was straddling him. Then he ran his hands through her hair and brought her mouth forward to his. And when he'd tasted his fill, he bent his head to suck her through the fabric of her dress. He reveled when she arched to meet him, pressing her nipple into his mouth so he could take a nip. Ayden reached underneath the dress to find the thong, the only piece of underwear he knew she was wearing. He was delighted to find it damp with desire and, with a tug, ripped it from her body. Then he plunged a finger inside her.

"Ayden..."

He stopped her cries by closing his mouth over hers and let his hands do all the talking. He began feverishly stroking her and she bucked against him, her breathing coming in short gasps, but he had no intention of letting her climax without him. He reached between them and tugged at the zipper on his trousers until he got himself free, then lifting his hips, he shoved them down with one hand while holding Maya in the other.

"Maya," he groaned, and handed her the condom. "Put it on."

She looked at him, her eyes glazed with desire, and complied. Once he was sheathed, he kissed her again and thrust inside her.

"Oh, baby, you feel so good," he said, before withdrawing slightly and slamming back in again. He repeated the process over and over and Maya lifted her hips to meet him as he went as deep as he could. But this couldn't be just about him and his release. Slipping his hand between their bodies, he found her sweet spot and pressed his thumb there. Maya's entire body began to shake, her muscles contracting around him.

Ayden was lost and all he could do was continue pumping inside her until he felt the familiar tension build in his body. He stiffened and then exploded inside of her, triggering yet another orgasm for Maya. She collapsed against him, clutching his shoulders and circling her arms around his neck.

Neither of them spoke for the remainder of the drive. They just tidied themselves up as best they could until the driver eventually pulled up in front of the villa. Ayden glanced over at Maya. Her hair was unkempt and her dress was wrinkled with damp spots at her nipples. There was no denying she looked as if she'd been made love to. And even though he'd just had her, Ayden wanted her again.

He was in big trouble. If this was how he felt after a few days with Maya, how was he going to feel when their short time in Jamaica was over? He was quickly losing his head to this beautiful, amazing woman, and it scared the living daylights out of him.

Maya sat across from Ayden as they played a game of dominos on the deck outside the villa. She'd enjoyed these lazy days in Jamaica with Ayden. Waking up and going to sleep, making love or just lounging by the pool.

When she had time, she'd called her sister to check in on their mother. They didn't talk long, only enough for Raven to inform her that Sophia was lethargic and nauseous, but otherwise hanging in there. Maya wished there was more she could do, but they had to allow the chemo to do what it was designed for. After the call, she was down in the dumps, so she was especially excited when Ayden had told her they would tour the island and visit Dunn's River Falls.

Ayden hadn't been able to climb the falls with a bum ankle, but he'd waited for her at the bottom while she'd soldiered up the cliff. Afterward, however, he'd been sore and achy from the hiking and she'd had to give him a foot rub and put him to sleep. That hadn't lasted long and he'd woken up in the middle of the night as hungry for her as he'd been that night in the back seat of the limo. She blushed thinking of the encounter.

She lifted her fingers to her lips, recalling the feel of his mouth and how magical his kisses were.

"And what are you thinking about?" Ayden asked as he moved another domino.

"Oh, nothing. What are we going to do on our last night here?"

"Anything you want."

"How about we find the nearest hot spot and hang out with the locals?"

"You sure?"

"Why not? Could be fun."

"I'm game if you are."

Just then Ayden's cell phone buzzed beside him. He glanced down at it but didn't answer, as he'd done for several days now. Although she wanted to ask him who was trying so urgently to reach him, she was afraid to delve too deep.

"Important call?"

He shook his head. "Yes…no…maybe so."

"Which is it?"

Ayden shrugged again and she could see his shoulders stiffen as if he didn't want to answer, but he did. "It's my sister, Fallon. She's been trying to reach me to convince me to help her."

"But you can't."

"*Won't* would be a more accurate word." Ayden made another move. "I won."

Maya glanced down and, indeed, he had, but her mind hadn't been on the game. It had been on him. "Maybe you should talk to her."

"It won't change my mind, Maya. I'll give the Stewart family exactly what they gave me. Nothing. I owe them no allegiance."

"True, but she is your sister."

"In blood only. And why are you pushing this anyway?" He glared at her. "You more than anyone know how my mother and I were treated by Henry Stewart."

Maya was surprised by the icy glare Ayden was giving her. She knew it was a touchy subject, but she was trying to help. She cared deeply for this man and his well-being. "Yes, of course I do."

"Then why?" he pressed.

"Because..." Her voice trailed off.

"Speak your mind, Maya. You obviously have something to say."

"I just want you to be happy, and settling things with your family might bring you the peace you crave."

"I *am* happy," he replied. He reached across the distance between them, grabbed her arm and pulled her into his lap. "Here with you." He grasped both sides of her face and kissed her hard on the mouth.

Maya could see what he was doing. He was effectively ending the conversation and shutting her out like he always did. And she let him because it was what he needed. But some day—some day soon—there would be a reckoning that he wouldn't be able to turn away from.

Thirteen

About an hour before arriving home in Austin, Ayden looked out the window of his private jet and reflected. He had enjoyed Jamaica and spending time alone with Maya, but it was time for him to get back to work. He'd never been gone this long from Stewart Investments. It was his baby. A dream he'd accomplished on his own with no help from Henry Stewart.

Which was why Fallon's request was so misguided. She had to have known he would turn her down. Ayden had been estranged from the Stewart family for decades. Had it really come as a surprise to her? It must have, because she'd been trying to reach him on and off for the last three days.

He glanced across the cabin at Maya, who was lying on a reclining chair sleeping soundly with her Kindle in her lap. He'd been banking on having a little fun while airborne and seeing if he could convince her to become a member of the mile-high club. Over this week, she'd not only been an extremely passionate lover, she'd been open to trying new things, like when he'd pulled some silk sashes from his luggage and tied her hands… Christ! He needed to get a grip. They were going back to Austin to work. Now that his ankle was starting to feel better, he wouldn't need any help at home. Maya could go back to her apartment if she wanted. The problem was, he didn't want her to. His emotions had become entangled and he wanted her with him. But for how long? He didn't know, but surely they could figure out something. He sat up straight, frustrated by the circumstances.

She stirred in the recliner and glanced over at him. "How long was I out?"

"Not long." He closed the report he'd been reading on his tablet. "We'll be landing in another hour."

She rubbed the sleep from her eyes. "Great. That will give me time to freshen up."

"You look beautiful, as always."

"If you say so."

"Maya, I would think after a week in Jamaica with me that you know I find you utterly ravishing."

A grin spread across her face. "Yes, I suppose."

"Suppose? Why don't you come over here and I'll convince you."

She shook her head. "Oh, no, you don't. The limo was bad enough, but not the airplane."

He laughed. "All right. You can't blame a man for trying. So listen. I think we should discuss what happens when we get back."

Maya's eyes grew large and he saw genuine fear in their depths. He would have to tread carefully because he didn't want to hurt her. Not now. Not ever.

"Yes?"

"You're moving in with me."

Her mouth turned down in a frown. “Is that a question or a statement?”

“The latter.”

“I don’t recall being asked.”

“You agreed to take care of me,” Ayden replied, annoyed by her response.

“And now you’re healed.”

“Are you saying you don’t want to come back home with me?” Ayden wasn’t ready to let her go, not by a long shot. She’d come to mean more to him than just a lover. She was his friend.

“Of course not, but we hadn’t really discussed it.”

“We’re discussing it now.” Why was she being so noncommittal? This wasn’t like her. Now that the shoe was on the other foot, was she done with him? He couldn’t believe that. He’d been with her, he knew Maya cared a great deal about him. Surely this wasn’t the end of the road?

She sighed. “Yes, we are. I just wasn’t sure of what you wanted. I just assumed that Jamaica was Jamaica, and I would move back to my place.”

Ayden couldn’t believe he’d misjudged the situation so entirely. Unbuckling his seat belt, he walked over and sat beside Maya. He grasped her delicate hand in his. “I’m sorry if I wasn’t clear about what I wanted and how absolutely hot I am for you. I want you to come back with me to my home. Please say that you will.”

Maya stared into his hazel eyes. Any girl would jump at the chance to have what he was offering, but she was hesitant. She knew Ayden didn’t share her feelings. He hadn’t said he was in love with or even that he was falling for her. He’d said he was *hot* for her. Meaning that as long as she was willing to be his bedmate, he’d happily have her. But again her mind went back to that age-old question: *how long?*

"Maya?" He sounded unsure. It saddened her that she was making him feel this way, but she also had to protect her heart.

"Maybe it's best if I go back to the apartment. I mean, you're better now and you don't really need a nursemaid."

"Or a lover?" he asked coldly, pulling his hand away from her and rising to his feet. "Are you saying you've tired of me after one week?"

"No, that's not what I'm saying at all," Maya responded hotly, jumping to her feet. "Don't put words in my mouth, Ayden Stewart."

"Then what? Why are you turning me down? I know it's not because you didn't like the sex. I lost count of your orgasms."

Tears sprang, stinging her eyes. How could he speak to her this way after the week they'd shared? She spun away from him and began walking to the lavatory, but he called after her. She couldn't face him because she feared he would see the tears fall.

"Maya, wait! I'm sorry. I shouldn't have said that." He reached her with two long strides and caught her at the door. "I'm truly sorry. You didn't deserve that. I guess I don't know how to do this." He rubbed his head in frustration.

"Do what?"

"Be casual with you about sex. You're not like the other women I've been with. You're Maya."

"And that's a bad thing?" Her voice cracked when she looked at him.

"Yes. No. God! I don't know, you're making me crazy." He began pacing the cabin.

"See." She pointed to him. "You don't know how to do this any better than me."

"I know I want you with me."

"So Ayden gets to have everything he wants. Me at the office. Me in your bed. What about what I want?"

"C'mon, Maya. That's not fair. I rewarded you handsomely to get you back at Stewart Investments, and as for being in my bed, you wanted me as much as I wanted you."

Maya turned away from him. He was right. It was unfair of her to put her expectations on him. "You're right. There. Are you happy?"

He stared at her intently. "Not in the slightest. Not unless you're agreeing to come back with me."

"For tonight, yes," she countered. "All my stuff is there."

"And after?" he pressed.

"We'll just have to see."

Have to see? Ayden was still reeling from Maya's words earlier on the plane as he got ready for bed. She'd refused to give an outright yes or no to his request for her to stay with him. Or had he meant *live* with him? He hadn't really defined what he meant. Was that why she was unsure?

Since they'd returned from the airport, he'd been busy catching up on phone calls and emails in his study. There were several from Fallon, as expected. Maybe Maya was right. He should call her, if for no other reason than to make sure she was okay, because despite what he'd said, he did care.

As for Maya, when they arrived, she'd immediately gone upstairs to unpack. Or pack? Ayden didn't have a clue. Just like he didn't know where to go from here. It was all so confusing. Maya was confusing. Bringing her back to Stewart Investments was supposed to be straightforward. He needed an assistant and with a little coaxing she had become available. He'd never anticipated that the attraction he'd felt for her so long ago would rear its ugly head. He'd thought he'd worked through those feelings. It had been a one-time thing because she'd been hurt and he'd wanted to console her. He'd moved on with his life, dated other women and relegated that night to an indiscretion not to be repeated.

He'd never anticipated becoming so taken with her that he'd whisk her off to paradise and make love to her day and night. Or that he would feel a deep yearning to commit to her in some form or fashion.

No one could have foreseen it.

Or could he have? If he'd just dealt with the insatiable lust he'd had for her back then, maybe it would have fizzled out and they'd have gone their separate ways. Now it was complicated because he knew what it was he'd been missing out on all these years. Now Stewart Investments needed her—or rather, *he* needed her—and he'd do anything to keep her.

With renewed purpose, he strode to his library door and took the stairs two at a time until he reached the second floor, where Maya's room was located. The door was ajar and he watched from the doorway as she *unpacked* her suitcase. Surely, this must mean she'd decided to stay? His heart began thundering in his chest, but Ayden refused to analyze what it might mean. "Knock. Knock."

Maya whirled around on her heel to face him. She was holding a sexy little teddy that she'd worn for him in Jamaica, though it hadn't stayed on her long. "Come in."

Ayden smiled as he came toward her, only stopping when he was in her personal space. Maya stepped backward, dropping the teddy, and he advanced. He loved this dance between them. It was a sort of foreplay he would never get tired of. "You're unpacking."

"No, I was just getting out something to wear for tonight..."

He grinned. "Oh really? Well, what do you say you leave that teddy here and come to my room? Because you won't really need it for what I have planned." He circled his arm around her waist and led her out of the room.

"What about dinner?"

"I'll have dinner sent up."

Maya felt oddly out of sorts Monday morning as she went through her usual routine of getting Ayden's calendar settled for the week. Could it be because her sinfully sexy boss and the best lover she'd ever had in her life had kept her up half the night doing wicked things to her? Although she hadn't agreed to move in with him, she had enjoyed the last few nights at Ayden's with unadulterated relish. She even had the whisker burns on her thighs to prove it. Maya blushed. She knew she was expected to jump back into work even after a week and multiple nights spent in Ayden's arms.

He didn't seem to have any problem getting back into the swing of things. She glanced at his door, which had been closed for most of the morning. Ayden had one meeting after another with department heads after their vacation. Eventually the door opened and he emerged. He was wearing a charcoal suit that made him look every bit as powerful as he was. Several other men departed after him.

"Maya, can you come into my office?" He went back inside.

She picked up her tablet and followed him. Ayden was standing by the floor-to-ceiling windows staring out over Austin.

"Close the door."

She did as instructed and when he spun around to face her there was only one thing she saw in his stare. Red-hot desire. She swallowed.

"Come here." He breathed his command.

Maya battled with herself—her pride demanding that she deny him. He'd already gotten his way by having her stay at his house. She couldn't give him everything. But her own lust for him won out.

She stepped toward him until she was close enough for him to grasp her waist and pull her against him. She arched her neck and glanced up into those eyes she always got lost in. He lifted his hand and curved it around her neck, bringing her face closer to his. Then he bent his head to kiss her until she softened against him. She felt powerless and gave in to the passion he aroused. His lips were firm and sure and took everything. When they broke the kiss, their breathing was shallow and unsteady.

"I've been dying to do that all morning," Ayden said. "I've been in those damn meetings thinking of nothing but kissing you." He stroked her already swollen lips with his thumb.

"We can't do this here." Maya tried pulling away, but Ayden wouldn't let her go.

"You're right. I'm sorry. I should have been more discreet."

She let out a sigh of relief. "Thank you. I don't want everyone to know we're an item." She glanced behind her at the door. "They'll think I got this job back because we're sleeping together."

"But you and I know that not's true. You're back as my EA because you're the best."

"Even better than Caroline?" she asked with a smirk.

His dark eyes stared back at her. "You know the answer to that."

"Good, because this assistant needs to leave early today. My mother is trying a new treatment and I'd like to be there." When they'd been in Jamaica, she'd shared her mother's condition with Ayden.

"Of course. You didn't even need to ask. I wish I had been there when my mom was ill. Take whatever time you need. I'll see you back at the house later?"

She nodded. "Thank you."

He kissed her on the forehead and released her.

After finishing up some last-minute items for Ayden, Maya drove to the cancer center where her mother would be getting her treatments. When she arrived, she found Sophia, Raven and Thomas sitting in the waiting room. They all rose when she approached.

"Maya, I'm so glad you could come," Raven said. "Mama, aren't you happy Maya's here?" Her sister looked up at her and smiled for the first time in a long time.

"You told her about my condition?" Her mother turned to Raven. "I thought you had it covered?"

"Of course, I told her. She had a right to know," Raven responded. "It can't all be me mom, you have another daughter."

"I didn't want Maya burdened especially starting her new job. Or should I say her *old* job." Her mother attempted a laugh, which turned into a coughing fit that required Thomas to help her into a nearby chair.

Maya immediately rushed to her side, kneeling in front of her. "Are you okay?"

"Why are you all hovering over me?" Sophia huffed, coughing again into a handkerchief she pulled out of her purse.

"Because we care," Raven said from beside her. "We all do." She glanced in Maya's direction. "And it's about time you know how much."

Her mother frowned. "What do you mean?"

"It means Maya has been helping pay for your treatments since she returned to Austin. They were too expensive for us to manage with a new baby, and we needed her assistance."

Tears sprang to Maya's eyes. She couldn't believe Raven was taking up for her when she never had in the past.

"So *you're* paying for my continued therapy?" her mother asked, staring at Maya.

"Yes, Mom. I am." Maya wiped away a tear with the back of her hand. "Is that a problem? Or would you rather your favorite daughter and son-in-law continue to struggle?"

"Of course not," Sophia stammered, with tears in her eyes. "I just never thought you cared."

Maya rolled her eyes upward and prayed for strength. She couldn't stand on the sidelines while cancer ravaged her mother. And the monetary assistance wouldn't help only her mother—it was about healing herself. She truly needed to let go of the past. "You're my mother. And although we don't see eye to eye and never have, I do care. I love you."

Tears filled her mother's eyes. "Thank you. I know I may not deserve it, but I'm glad you're here." She squeezed Maya's hand back.

"Good, because you have both your daughters here to support you." Maya glanced over at Raven, who gave her a reassuring smile. They were a long way from reconciliation, but they'd get there. And for the first time in years, Maya was open to it.

A nurse appeared several moments later to take her mother away for the treatment. When they advised that one person could come with her, Maya fully expected Sophia to ask for Raven, but she looked at Maya.

"Would you come with me?"

Maya rose to her feet. "Yes, Mama. I will."

Fourteen

Ayden prowled around his enormous house, glancing at his Rolex every few minutes. It was after eight o'clock and he hadn't heard from Maya. He knew she'd gone to be by her mother's side, but that had been hours ago. She hadn't called or texted and it was driving him crazy. She didn't answer to him after hours, but the least she could have done was let him know everything was all right.

Eventually, after working through the evening, he flopped on the couch and made himself comfortable by turning on the television and flipping through the channels. He never watched TV; it was just noise. Even though he knew his staff was down the hall, he felt lonely without Maya. His voracious hunger for her was not subsiding; he wanted her more than ever. He loved the way she stood her ground, telling him off when she didn't agree with him. Or the way she found joy in the simple things in life like playing dominos or drinking a Red Stripe.

He'd tried to ignore his feelings for Maya, but they kept resurfacing. She was smart and funny and beautiful, with her sexy, tight body. He recalled how she'd looked in a bikini with her skin sun-kissed from the Jamaica sun. He was craving her something fierce and he knew she felt the same, but she was erecting barriers between them. She hadn't agreed to permanently move in with him and had kept her short-term rental. Why was she holding on to it? Was her coming to San Antonio only temporary? It brought a pang to his chest to think of her leaving him. It reminded him of the loss he'd felt when his mother had moved him away from his father, from the only place Ayden had known as home, into a sad one-bedroom apartment. He didn't want to lose Maya. She made him feel alive. Ayden felt like he could do anything when he was with her, like he was worthy. But, more importantly, he'd never been this content or this relaxed with another woman.

He drew a deep, ragged breath. Ayden couldn't remember the last time he'd been truly happy like he'd been these last couple of weeks with Maya. Before her, he'd worked around the clock, stopping only to eat, work out or have the occasional dinner with any number of nameless, faceless women, then leave their beds in the middle of the night. None of them had held a candle to Maya. He stayed with Maya *every night*. He looked forward to drawing her close and spooning with her. And when he did, it was the best sleep of his life.

Eventually, he retired to the master bedroom to shower and get ready for bed. He'd changed into black silk pajama bottoms when he heard Maya's car pull into the driveway. He waited for the click of her heels on the marble floor as she climbed the stairs. Her steps were silent on the plush carpet in the hallway, but he finally sensed her outside his room. Was she trying to decide if she should come in? He hopped off the bed and padded barefoot to her room. "Maya?"

She jumped. "You—you startled me."

"I'm sorry." His gaze swept over her face as he looked for signs of distress. Her eyes were glassy. "Is everything okay? "

She looked downward and when she lifted her head back up, he could see tears staining her cheeks. It made him feel as useless as a rag doll to see her so upset. "Maya, Maya." He pulled her to him, grasping the sides of her face to make her look at him. "Did something happen today?"

She shook her head. "No, it's just..." Hiccupping, she tried to speak through her crying. "I can't..." Her voice trailed off, and she leaned into him and began softly sobbing.

"It's okay." He held her firmly, desperate to give some of his strength to her. "I'm here for you."

When she finally quieted, she spoke softly. "The treatment they're giving Mom is aggressive. Very aggressive. But it's the only way they can try to rid her of the cancer. It didn't seem real when I found out, but today... There was no denying that my mother could die."

"But she's not going to," Ayden murmured in her ear. "Because of you, she's getting the best treatment available."

"I know that, but it's still so scary. I—I could lose her. And even though we haven't been close, I've always known she was there. And if something happens to her, I'll be all alone because I don't think Raven and I can ever go back to being sisters again, not after her betrayal."

Without hesitation, Ayden said, "You won't be alone, Maya. You'll always have me."

As soon as he said the words, he wished he could take them back.

He wanted them to be true because he cared deeply for Maya, but he couldn't guarantee her that their relationship would always be like this.

He didn't do commitments because there was too great a risk of getting hurt.

Had he just doomed their relationship by telling his first white lie?

You'll always have me.

Ayden's words kept replaying in Maya's head the next day even though she tried to keep her mind on work. Ayden had left hours ago, leaving her to her own devices and thus giving her plenty of time to recount last night. After making love, she'd slept in his embrace as he held her, unable to sleep because his words were in her head like a nursery rhyme she could never forget. She knew he didn't mean them. Couldn't possibly. She didn't have a future with Ayden. She'd been living in an alternate yet blissful universe while ignoring the obvious.

Ayden was an attractive, wealthy man whose interests lay in making money. But it was inevitable that Ayden would return to his former ways. She had to look on their time as the precious gift that it was. He'd made her feel beautiful, sensual and desirable, and she would always be grateful. She would remember their time in Jamaica fondly. The time they'd shared, however, had an expiration date.

Maya was steeling herself for that moment when Ayden would want her to go back to being only his trusted assistant instead of his lover. When he looked to her to make appointments and spreadsheets rather than being desperate for their next kiss or lovemaking session. When she'd have to go back to her boring life in which no other man would ever measure up to Ayden. She knew that when that time came, she'd leave again. There was no way she could see him day in and day out after the time they'd shared. Except this time, she wouldn't go far. Her mother needed her.

She'd started over once. She could do it again. She just didn't want to. She'd set aside most of her sign-on bonus to help with her mother's treatments. There was some left over in her savings, and with her new salary and generous stock options, she could make it until she found a new position.

"I'm back." Ayden startled her as he strode toward her desk.

"How was your meeting?"

"Successful. I convinced Kincaid to bring his portfolio over to Stewart Investments." He grinned from ear to ear. "It was a big day for me."

"That's wonderful, Ayden." She was happy he'd finally landed the elusive client.

"I want to celebrate. What do you say we take off early for a night out on the town?"

Her eyes fixed on his beautiful face and her heart began galloping in her chest. "Why, Ayden, are you asking me out on a date?"

He smiled wolfishly. "Well, ma'am, it appears I am." He rubbed the perpetual five-o'clock shadow on his chin. "Would you like to accompany me to dinner?"

Ayden's infectious mood was catching and Maya felt herself getting excited. "I would love to."

An hour later, Maya was staring back at her reflection in a dressing-room mirror. Rather than navigate the Austin traffic during the middle of rush hour, Ayden had driven her to a stylish boutique where he'd given her her own *Pretty Woman* experience complete with a designer dress purchased right off the rack. Maya had balked at such an outrageous gesture. She had plenty of dresses back at the house, but Ayden wasn't taking her back home. The saleswoman had been happy to assist when he'd pulled out his platinum credit card and told her price was no object.

Now Maya was in a teal halter dress that clung to her slender curves and did wonders for her complexion. She'd touched up her makeup with subtle eye shadow, mascara and lipstick she carried with her. The clerk had insisted she add shoes and a bag, so Maya was ready for the night with a clutch and beaded sandals with straps that wrapped her delicate ankles.

Ayden was waiting for her at the curb, having stepped out to take a phone call earlier while she got dressed. "You look stunning." He whistled as she approached the Bentley.

"You should know. You paid an outrageous sum for this dress."

"I wanted you to not only look good, but feel good."

His words put a smile on her face. "I feel like a million bucks."

"Good." He opened the passenger door and pulled her inside. "Get in."

Ayden took Maya to a popular restaurant known for its wealthy clientele. It was the first time they were going out in public as a couple. Since they'd become lovers, they hadn't been seen by anyone other than the housekeeping staff at the villa in Jamaica and his estate.

Did this mean Ayden might want more from her than a short-lived affair?

Maya didn't want to be hopeful, but it was hard not to read between the lines when he was going out of his way to impress her. First with the couture dress and designer shoes, and now with a fine dining experience. Upon arrival, he showered her with the most expensive bottle of champagne and treated her to the finest meal she'd had in a long time. Each plate was a tiny work of art created by a master chef. Maya felt like she was floating, weightless, carried away on a tidal wave. She knew what was happening. She was falling deeper and deeper in love with Ayden.

Her mind warned her to be cautious, prudent even, to not outwardly portray her true feelings, so she focused on the easy, undemanding conversation they had a tendency to share. She loved the melodic sound and timbre of his deliciously masculine voice. Every now and then she would glance up, only to find his eyes fixed on her, and she was helpless to tear away her gaze.

When the exquisite meal was finally over and they were drinking cappuccino with their intricately conceived desserts, someone called his name. “Ayden!”

Ayden turned and smiled, then rose to his feet to greet half a dozen suited gentlemen coming toward them. It was late, but clearly they’d just had a business meeting. He shook the men’s hands. “Good to see you. You enjoyed your dinners?”

“Of course. This place has the best duck in Austin,” one of the men answered.

Several of them glanced in Maya’s direction and Ayden motioned her over. “Gentlemen, I’d like you to meet Maya Richardson, the best executive assistant in all of Austin.”

“Is that why you’re taking her out to a meal here?” There were snickers.

Ayden cleared his throat. Maya could see he was uneasy with the conversation, yet he was allowing it, feeding into it. “You misunderstand. We’re colleagues.”

Maya was stunned and stared at Ayden in anger and bewilderment. Tears pricked the back of her eyes, but she refused to let these Neanderthals see it. He hadn’t even defended her when they had snickered. And she couldn’t believe Ayden had just told these men that she meant nothing to him. He might as well as have put a neon sign on her that read Booty Call. Maya had to get away before she said something that embarrassed them both. "Excuse me. I need to visit the ladies' room."

She heard several of the men laugh behind her. "Does she know, Ayden, that you're not the settling-down kind?"

Laughter followed her as she left the dining room, Ayden's included.

Maya nearly slammed the door against the wall as she pushed the door to the restroom open. Not only had Ayden not introduced her as his girlfriend, but he'd laughed about it. Hell, she would have even accepted his describing her as his date, but his *assistant*? Clearly he valued these men's opinions so much that he wasn't even willing to acknowledge she meant more to him than someone who just worked for him. She was furious!

She clasped both her hands to her face and inhaled, trying not to cry. She couldn't make a scene or fall apart. Not here. Not now. Damn! Why did she still care about his reputation after he'd just treated her so shabbily? Because she loved him, and despite everything, she wouldn't embarrass him like he'd just done her. She glanced at herself in the mirror. Her makeup was still intact; she'd held it together. *Just barely.* Now all she had to do was get out there. She just hoped the other men were gone.

As she entered the dining room, she saw Ayden sitting alone. Thank God.

He stood when she approached. "Maya…"

"I'm ready to go." She didn't bother sitting down. "I'd like to go now."

Ayden nodded. "I figured as much and have already taken care of the bill."

Maya didn't wait for him to continue and strode toward the door. She wanted to get away from him as soon as possible. Go back home and lick her wounds. But she wasn't truly going back home. She was going to Ayden's, where she wouldn't have a moment alone to process what had happened.

He must have followed her because he slid beside her at the valet counter, handing the attendant his ticket. Maya folded her arms across her chest and waited for them to fetch Ayden's car. Surprisingly, he was silent beside her. Maybe he knew she was peeved and was in no mood to talk. She did have one question for him.

Why?

Why bring her to a fancy restaurant?

Why romance her at all if all she was to him was a damn good assistant that he just happened to sleep with?

The Bentley arrived at the curb and she didn't wait for Ayden's assistance. She opened her door herself and slammed it shut. He took the hint and walked around to the driver's side. Once it was just the two of them, he turned to her. "Maya. About earlier… I'm sorry."

"I don't want to talk about it."

"Please don't let what happened ruin a great night."

"You did a fine job of that all by yourself."

She heard him suck in his breath. Score one for her. But she really wasn't interested in winning a battle of wills with Ayden. The real reason she was upset was because he didn't love her. Never would. And she was fooling herself to think otherwise. It was the same as she'd done with Thomas all those years ago. She'd foolishly thought he loved her. When, actually, he'd been sleeping with her sister behind her back. It was humiliating and she'd felt those exact same feelings tonight standing by Ayden's side when he relegated her to nothing more than the help. She couldn't look at him, much less talk to him.

The ride back to his mansion was fraught with tension. As soon as the car stopped, Maya hopped out, but

Ayden was hot on her heels. He caught her in the foyer and snagged her hips to him, but she refused to be *handled.* She knew exactly what Ayden would do: he would try to brush aside what had occurred at the restaurant. Make it appear as if she was blowing it out of proportion. And because she was so weak, when it came to him, she'd succumb and he would carry her off to bed where they'd have sex all night long. But then where would they be? Exactly where they'd started.

She continued twisting and turning in his arms in an attempt to get away, but all she did was spin herself around until her backside was against his swelling erection.

"Stop fighting me," he whispered, clasping his arms around her.

"Let me go." Her steely tone must have soaked through his brain, because he released her and they faced off. His hazel eyes were searching her face. For what? She wasn't sure. She just wanted to go to bed. *Alone.*

"I'm going to bed." She grasped the railing of the staircase and started to ascend.

"Maya, I don't want to end the night like this. Can't we talk? Please?" he implored.

She stopped on the staircase. "Talk? About what? That after nearly two weeks spent in bed together that there's nothing between us? Is that what we're going to talk about?"

He frowned. "That's not fair, Maya. Some of them are my colleagues as well as clients. Did you honestly expect me to tell those men that we're an item? To spill my guts to them and tell them how I truly feel?"

She descended the stairs until she was back facing him. "Actually, I did, Ayden. I expected you to acknowledge that I *meant* something to you."

"You do. You know that. I wouldn't have been with

you this entire time, giving up work and obligations, if you didn't."

She felt confused. "But yet you couldn't bring yourself to tell those men that you were *with* me, *dating* me. But I get it, okay? What we do in the dark is supposed to be for our eyes only and no one else. What I don't understand is why take me out for dinner? Why not just keep me in the house to service you at your beck and call?"

His eyes blazed fury and she could feel the anger emanating from his every pore. "That was a cheap shot, Maya."

"But well deserved." She spun on her heel and ran up the stairs, but Ayden refused to let sleeping dogs lie and she heard his footsteps behind her. When she made it to her room, she slammed the door, shutting him out. She heard the latch give way on the door and sensed Ayden's presence behind her as much as she heard the door click closed behind him. She didn't want to look at him. He'd hurt her. She just wanted to go to bed and forget. To block out the pain until morning, when she would be forced to face reality, which was that Ayden was never going to love her.

When Maya began unzipping her dress and it stuck, she let him come behind her and help. He stilled her by placing his hands on her shoulders. Then he easily slid the zip down until he reached her bikini panties. Despite the tension between them, she stepped out of the dress, removed her undies and turned around to face him, naked.

Desire and hunger shot through her as it always did when she looked at him.

Maya didn't speak and neither did he. Instead, she allowed him to tug her toward him until she was lost once again in the bliss she always found in his arms.

Fifteen

The next morning Ayden was gone from her bed before Maya woke up. She was thankful because last night shouldn't have happened. She'd been so upset with him for how he'd treated her in front of his colleagues. How could she have allowed him to make love to her afterward? He must think her a fool, ruled by her libido rather than her head. She'd allowed the physical pull Ayden had on her to make her go completely left when she meant to go right.

After showering and dressing for the day, Maya packed her things. It was time for her not only to get out of Ayden's house, but out of his orbit. She should never have allowed him to convince her to come back to work for him, not with the feelings she'd had. Knowing that he'd desired her, too, did little to soften the blow that Ayden wasn't the type of man she was looking for. And there was no way she could lie or pretend otherwise. If she did, she wouldn't be true to herself and it would suck away her soul.

Maya felt like a raw and open wound. The time they'd shared in Jamaica had been real, so real that it had changed *everything*. Ayden had made her want more than he was capable of giving to her, plain and simple.

Her task was complete in under a half hour because she hadn't brought that many belongings to Ayden's. She called downstairs and the butler ensured her luggage was taken to her car. When she inquired where Ayden was, he informed her he was in the morning room having breakfast. Maya saw no better time than the present to let him know her plans.

She had to do this for her own self-respect and self-worth. Somehow, she'd survive this, just as she had when he'd crushed her spirit five years ago.

She found Ayden reading the newspaper, a cup of coffee along with a half-eaten plate of food on the table in front of him.

He glanced up when she walked into the room. "Good morning." He put down the paper. "I didn't want to wake you, so I came downstairs. I hope you don't mind." He eyed her warily as she sat down next to him.

She shook her head.

"Would you like some breakfast? I can have Cook whip you up something, an omelet perhaps or some crepes. He makes the best crepes you've ever had in your life."

Again, she declined with a headshake. Was Ayden Stewart nervous? Because he was babbling about breakfast when he had to know there was more to be said between them.

"We need to talk."

He chuckled quietly. "Whenever a woman says those words, it can't be good."

She stared at him incredulously.

He held up his hands in defense. "Don't bite my head

off. It was just a joke to lighten the mood because I suspect I'm not going to like this conversation very much, am I?"

He fixed his gaze on hers and Maya reminded herself that she'd made up her mind and there was nothing he could do to change it. "I'm leaving and moving back into my apartment."

He nodded. "I suspected as much when I saw your bags were brought down."

"You know why?"

"You're upset about last night. You feel like I disrespected you and this is your way of punishing me."

Maya rolled her eyes in frustration. She wanted to strangle him because he wasn't getting the point. "I'm not trying to punish you, Ayden."

"Then why?" He pounded the table with his fist, startling her. "Why isn't what we have good enough? Why are you leaving me? I know you like it here. *With me.* I know you want to be here and I don't want you to go. So why leave, if not to punish me?"

"Because I want *more*, Ayden. And I'm not willing to take whatever scraps of yourself you're willing to give me."

"I don't understand. What is it that you want? Whatever it is, I'll give it to you."

"Don't you see? You can't. You and I are on different pages. Yes, I've been happy here with you. Cut off from the world in our idyllic little slice of heaven. But it was never real. It was never going to last. I know that and so do you. I want marriage, babies and a white picket fence. I want a family."

"A family?"

"Yes, I've always wanted one. When I was with Thomas, I thought we were headed in that direction. But he went and married my sister and gave her all the things I've always craved. Especially someone to love me." There, she'd said the word aloud. The *L* word that she hadn't dared to speak or make mention of, but she had to now. She couldn't go on making the same bad decisions. Something had to give.

"I wish I could give you all those things, but I can't."

"You mean you *won't.* Because you're not capable of anything more than immediate gratification. And like an idiot, I went along with it, accepting less than what I wanted because I wanted to be with you. Because I never truly got over you the first time." She shook her head. "Why did I do this to myself? Maybe it's because I've never felt like anything special. I never have been for any other man, so why should now be any different? My own mother said as much for most of my life. And as for you, I'm a convenience who just happens to be compatible with you sexually."

"Don't say that!" Ayden shot to his feet. "I don't ever want to hear you say that you're nothing special, Maya. Because you are. You are to me."

Then why won't you love me? She wanted to scream at him, but instead she stared back at him and felt the tears of unrequited love trickle down her face.

"Maya, please don't cry…"

He reached out to touch her, but she bunched her shoulders and moved away. She couldn't let him touch her. Not now. Not when she was weak and vulnerable. He would use it to his advantage to pull her back into his web. She barely had enough strength to have this conversation and demand the things she wanted, whether he was able to give them to her or not.

"It's okay. I walked into this affair with my eyes wide open. I knew who I was dealing with."

He frowned in consternation. "What the hell is that supposed to mean?"

"Nothing." She rose to her feet and began to walk toward the doorway. "I've said what I have to say and it's best I left."

"Oh, no, you don't. You're not getting the last word. At least not until you tell me what you meant."

"You want to go there, Ayden?"

"Yes," he stated unequivocally. His eyes blazed a fire through her.

"All right then. How about we start with the fact that you've never had a serious relationship a day in your life. You flit around from one affair to the next."

"That's because I haven't had the time. I've been building Stewart Investments."

"Rubbish. It's because you're scared. Scared of getting close to anyone or anything because you're afraid of getting hurt. But guess what, Ayden? I'm equally scared, but I'm willing to put myself out there on the off chance that one day—one day—I might find someone who loves me just as much as I love them. And I know that's not you."

"Maya..." His tone softened, "I—I'm just not capable of anything more. I wish to God I were because you're an incredible woman, deserving of happiness. But I just don't believe in happily ever after."

"That's because you're still holding on to the past and the anger you have toward your father. Until you make peace with your family, you'll never be able to move forward."

"You know nothing of my family, not really, other than the few tidbits I told you."

"You're right. I only know the scraps you've chosen to share with me or that I've garnered from working with you all these years, because you've closed yourself off, Ayden. To the world. To your sister, Fallon. And most of all to me. I can't just be the woman you sleep with anymore, no matter how pleasurable that might be. I want more. And I *deserve* it."

"Yes, you do," Ayden said finally in a quiet, defeated tone. "You deserve more than I could ever give you and that, my precious Maya, will be my greatest regret."

Maya nodded and then quietly left the room.

Ayden stared at the doorway Maya had departed through. He'd been sitting there for the last hour in utter shock. She'd walked out on him. He'd woken up this morning with a deep sense of foreboding of her departure, but he'd told himself it couldn't possibly be true. Maya, *his Maya*, would never leave him. During breakfast, he'd told himself that Maya was upset. Understandably so. He could have handled last night better, but at the time, he just hadn't known what to say.

Were they on a date?

Was she his girlfriend?

They certainly hadn't discussed the ramifications of becoming intimate. Seeing his colleagues had caught him off guard. He'd been that way from the moment she'd walked out of the boutique. She'd looked sensational. Beautiful. Stunning. But mere words did little to describe her. Unfortunately, he'd behaved like an utter jerk. He'd hoped making love would be a salve to her tender spirit, but it hadn't been, even though for him it had been magical. He couldn't recall another time in which he'd felt so connected to another human being.

This morning he'd planned on asking her to make their living arrangement permanent. It was the best he could offer when he didn't do commitments, but for Maya he'd been willing to make an effort. But he hadn't gotten the chance to even ask, because she wanted marriage and babies. And a darn white picket fence! Why did women always want the moon and the stars? Why couldn't she let him have his say and just move in? It might not be exactly what she was looking for, but at least it would have given her some kind of commitment.

But marriage?

Babies?

Oh, hell, no!

Ayden didn't ever plan on getting hitched. He'd seen how married people, supposedly in love, treated each other. When the dust settled, the only ones hurt were the babies, the innocents that had been pulled into their parents' unholy matrimony.

No, thank you. He was content with the single life.

Or at least he had been until Maya had come roaring back into his world with a vengeance.

Now what was he supposed to do? Was she cutting him off entirely? Although, it would be devastating not to make love to her again, he supposed he could get through it if he buried himself in work. But what of Stewart Investments? The last time she'd left him, it hadn't been just him, but her position. It had taken him nearly half a year to find someone. He couldn't go through that again. He *wouldn't* go through that again.

He'd lived with his father's betrayal all these years, accepted he would never be acknowledged as his son. But he couldn't bear it if Maya turned her back on him, too. Because this time, it would destroy him, and Ayden wasn't sure he'd ever recover.

Ayden didn't know what to do. They couldn't go back to their working relationship. They couldn't be lovers anymore. And he doubted she wanted his friendship. There was nothing he could offer her that would entice her to stay and that was the greatest travesty of all.

Maya hated the letter she'd just penned to Ayden and sent by courier. Once again, she'd resigned her position as his executive assistant. The only difference was that this time she was offering her services via virtual assistant until he could find someone permanent. She was prepared to draft his presentations, handle his schedule, make appointments and take his calls *remotely*. She'd thought it through and, logically speaking, they didn't need to see each other. She could do her job without ever laying eyes on him.

It was the best she could come up with on short notice. She knew he was working with several important clients, especially Kincaid, and she was invested in his success. So she was willing to listen to his voice over the phone giving her instructions or read an email with his name on it so long as they had no interaction face-to-face.

She was weak when it came to Ayden. If she were in the office, he'd use every weapon in his arsenal to break down her defenses, and Maya knew herself. Knew she would crumble. So she was offering this olive branch. Either way, the signing bonus was hers free and clear according to the offer letter she'd signed.

She wondered how he would react when he received her resignation. Would he blow his top? Or would he be thankful because she was out of his hair and he wouldn't have to worry about dealing with her demanding any more of him?

Maya found out when her cell phone rang nearly an hour later.

"What the hell is this?"

Maya knew exactly who was on the other end of the line and what he was referring to. "Ayden, you must have received my letter."

"Yes, I did. And I don't accept it."

"C'mon, Ayden. You know it's best if we keep our distance. As a virtual assistant, I can still assist you with the important deals on the table, giving you plenty of time to interview and find my replacement."

"I don't want to replace you, Maya."

She sucked in a breath. "Well, those are your options. You can take them or leave them." She held her breath as she waited for his response.

"I will leave them. Thank you very much. If you want away from me so bad, go ahead, but I warn you, you signed a contract."

"An offer letter," she corrected. "Besides, when I signed, you stated our relationship would be professional only. We crossed that line, Ayden, and no court in the land would uphold that document if they heard what went on between us in Jamaica."

"Damn it, Maya. Don't do this."

"I'm truly sorry, but it's the only way. We both want different things out of life. You're content with the status quo. Me in your bed. While I, on the other hand, lose out on finding my happily-ever-after. Well, no more, Ayden. I'm going to chase after what I want until I find it. Don't stand in my way."

He sighed heavily. There was silence for several long moments in which she heard his slow and controlled breathing before he said, "I will miss you."

"I—I'll miss you, too." Then Maya ended the call. She had to. It was torture to both of them if she let it continue. She would forgive Ayden the same way she had Raven and Thomas, because he was her past and she had to look toward the future. A future that included a husband and children someday. The problem was, her heart was breaking in two and only Ayden could put it back together again. But he wasn't willing or able.

Sixteen

Ayden sat at his desk befuddled. He'd lost ten minutes because he'd been daydreaming about Maya. He told himself it would get better.

But it didn't. The ghost of Maya was everywhere. In his bed. At the office.

He still wanted her, in his life, in his bed, but she wanted marriage and babies. Ayden couldn't give her that. Yet he didn't want to live his life without her. So he'd let her walk away when he didn't want her to go. Did it mean he was in love with her? He wasn't sure. He'd never been in love before. But if there was anyone he wanted to love, it was Maya. He thought about her day and night. And with each passing day, he missed her more and more. Nothing eased the ache in his heart. Not even work, which had been his cure-all for loneliness. The sense of loss was so acute it physically hurt to breathe.

It had been nearly two weeks since Maya had left the mansion, calling him out on his failure to commit. They had been the worst weeks of his life since his mother passed away. Back then, he'd felt alone in the world and emotionally battered. He felt the same way now.

And work was going horribly.

He wished he'd taken Maya up on her virtual assistant offer, but he hadn't. The recruiter had sent a candidate who had emailed the wrong proposals to two different clients earlier in the week. And when he'd yelled at her for the mistake, she'd left the office crying, vowing never to return. The second temp hadn't been much better, but at least she'd lasted a few days. Could no one handle the simple requests he made of them? It was late Friday evening and he would have to muddle through on his own.

Ayden reached for the phone on his desk and called Luke. He didn't care what time it was in London. He needed a sounding board.

"Do you know what time it is?" Luke said.

"No, I didn't look," Ayden responded.

"Well, it's past midnight here," Luke said groggily.

"Sorry."

"No, you're not. So what's going on? I haven't heard from you in over a month so I assumed everything was going swimmingly."

"It was."

"And now it's not?"

Ayden sighed heavily. "Far from it."

"What's happened?"

"Maya left me."

"I could have told you that was going to happen," Luke replied. "It's barely been a month and I bet you ran the poor girl ragged. I warned you about easing up."

"That's not the reason she left."

Silence ensued on the other end of the line before Luke said, "Don't tell me you shagged her again?"

Ayden snorted. "We had a consensual and mutually gratifying relationship. But she still left me. Can you believe it?"

"Are you daft or what, mate? The woman came back because she's had the hots for you, probably did from the get-go, and the first thing you lead with is sex? You don't offer her any kind of commitment other than a good shag—even though you know she's the settling-down kind? Instead, you choose the easy way out? And for the life of me, I don't understand why she went along with it. But go figure. Love is blind."

"Love? No one said anything about love."

"Oh, bloody hell, Ayden! The woman is in love with you. She wouldn't have agreed to come back otherwise. Not after the way you treated her after that one-off five years ago."

"I offered her a lot of money, which she needed to take care of her ailing mother."

"And that might have played a role in her accepting the job, but you and I both know that she came back for *you* and only you. Because deep down she wanted to see if there was a chance for a future with you, and you blew it!"

"Luke, you know I don't believe in love and marriage and all that crap."

"That's a real shame, Ayden, because you're going to miss out on the best thing that ever happened to you, mate."

"Luke..."

"The next time you call me in the middle of night, at least be ready to take my advice. 'Cause right now I'm telling you to sod off," Luke growled.

"Thanks a lot."

"You know I love you like an adopted brother, but I'm going back to bed. Call me tomorrow when you gain some common sense."

Ayden hung up the phone and leaned back in his chair. He felt like all the energy had been zapped out of him. If anyone could give it to him straight and he would listen, it was Luke. With the exception of Maya, Luke was the only person Ayden implicitly trusted.

Was he right?

He'd spent the last fifteen years of life not only surviving, but trying to meet some expectation in his mind that if he was smart enough and rich enough, Henry Stewart would give him the time of day. He had to face facts: Henry was never going to love him. He had to stop looking back on what could have been, *should* have been. It was time to look at what was right in front of him.

Maya.

He'd kept up a shield with every other woman he'd ever been with, keeping them at arm's length, never allowing them the chance to get close—but not with Maya. He couldn't pretend with this woman. She saw straight through him, not just to his triumphs and successes, but to his failures. She knew he liked his coffee black with two sugars, but she also knew his deep, dark secrets, which made it impossible for him to deny that there was something between them. Something strong and powerful had been forming, but because of Ayden's hang-ups, they were dead in the water. Like Luke, Maya had told him that he needed to resolve his past. Make peace before they could have a future.

Maybe they both had a point.

Ayden knew exactly what he had to do to get started.

Ayden arrived unannounced at Stewart Technologies. He wasn't interested in seeing Henry Stewart, but he was determined to see his sister. After her repeated phone calls, texts and emails had gone unanswered she'd stopped contacting him. And he couldn't blame her; he'd acted like a complete ass toward her. He couldn't give her the financial bailout she needed, but at the very least, he owed her an apology for ignoring her.

When he told her assistant that he was her brother, however, the woman politely said, "Nice try." Fallon had one brother and that was international superstar Dane Stewart. But Ayden hadn't budged from the spot until she'd finally agreed to tell his sister he was standing outside her door.

In time, Fallon emerged from her office in an elegant red pantsuit. Her blond-streaked brown hair was flat ironed and her makeup was flawless. She was the epitome of class and sophistication. She stood in the doorway and regarded him. "I'm shocked you've deigned to darken my doorstep, Ayden Stewart."

"I deserve that," Ayden said, walking toward her, "but I'd like to talk if you have a moment."

Fallon glanced at her assistant. "No interruptions, please. My brother and I have some unfinished business."

Ayden couldn't resist a smirk as he passed the woman, whose mouth hung open in shock. He strode into the room, and Fallon closed the door behind him. Then she folded her arms across her chest and stood rooted to the spot.

"I have to admit, big brother, I'm surprised you've come into enemy territory. Because that's what I am to you, right? Your enemy. So what gives? Why are you here? And what's happened to you? You look god-awful!"

Ayden knew he looked tired and there were lines under his eyes. He hadn't slept in the weeks since Maya left him. He answered her first question. "You're not my enemy, Fallon."

She rolled her eyes upward. "You could have fooled me, Ayden. Your actions speak louder than any words. And, trust me, those were enough. I know my mother did yours wrong and you blame my family for every bad thing that happened in your life. But guess what, Ayden? I didn't harm you. I wasn't even born when all that went down. Yet you blame me as if I had some control over the past."

"You're right."

"Excuse me?"

"I said you're right," Ayden replied, raising his voice. "I was wrong to blame you, Fallon. You and Dane are innocent in this." She nodded but didn't speak, so he continued. "Our parents are to blame for what went down back then, and I'm sorry that I put you in the middle of that. You've tried to extend an olive branch to me and I've never wanted to take it."

"Because you're angry that I got the life denied you?"

"Yes." Ayden was man enough to admit that. "You and Dane not only got my father—" Ayden beat his chest with his fist "—but you got the good life. The houses, the cars, the travel, the fancy clothes and schools. While I had to work my butt off for everything I've ever achieved."

"But I bet it's all the more sweet," Fallon replied.

"What do you mean?"

"I know you had a hard life," she responded. "But my life hasn't been a picnic, either. I admit I've had every material possession, but you want to know something? I've also had a disinterested, self-absorbed mother who couldn't be bothered to raise the two children she had in order to keep our demanding father. And Henry Stewart? He hasn't been an easy man to love, constantly pushing me to excel. I've had to bust my tail for years to prove I'm the best person to run this company. I've always been in Dad's shadow, unable to run Stewart Technologies how I see fit without constant input and criticism. And right when I make it to the top, I see my whole life's work on a weak foundation and the sand is crumbling underneath my feet."

Fallon walked over to the couch and sank down onto it.

Ayden rushed over. "I had no idea how hard it's been on you."

"Father wanted Dane to take over the company, but my baby brother is only interested in making movies. He's never wanted to be a businessman, much to father's chagrin."

"So he pushed you."

"Yes. And don't get me wrong, I love what I do. And I love this company. It's why I came to you for help."

"And I turned my back on you," Ayden replied. "I'm sorry for that, Fallon. It's just that…"

She reached for his hands and grasped them. "It's okay. I had no right coming to you. Not after what father did to you. But I felt I had no choice and was out of options. The reason I called was to let you know I'd had it out with my mother and she admitted to ensnaring father. I only wanted to say that I was sorry."

"Thank you for that," Ayden said. Hearing that Nora had admitted to part of the blame was something, but what about Fallon? "What are you going to do about the company? If you really need the money, I could loan it to you. Not to the company directly, but as a personal loan with a good interest rate."

"Ayden, that's very generous of you considering the circumstances, but I could never accept, not knowing how Daddy treated you and your mother. This isn't your cross to bear. It's mine."

"But you're my sister."

"And I will find a way and might already have. Anyway, the fact that you've come here today—" her voice caught in her throat "—you have no idea how much this means to me."

"It means a lot to me, too, Fallon. I've been alone for a long time. Hell, since before my mother even passed.

And, well, I've felt adrift without a family, but if you and Dane are willing... I'd like to try to have a relationship with you both." He was never going to forgive Henry for abandoning him or his mother, but he could try to forge a bond with his siblings.

A warm smile spread across her lips. "Ya know, I wouldn't mind having a big brother. Someone I could look up to. Maybe even call for advice?"

Ayden returned her grin. "I'd like that. I'd like that very much."

Fallon glanced down at her watch. "Now I have to get to a meeting, so let's plan on having dinner sometime soon, okay? I won't push. We can do this in baby steps."

"Baby steps." Ayden laughed. He opened his arms and, after several seconds, Fallon came into his embrace, returning his hug. It was a small gesture, but meant everything to Ayden.

After leaving Stewart Technologies, Ayden felt a heavy burden had been lifted off his shoulders. Clearing the air with Fallon and agreeing to start anew as a family was one the best decisions he'd made in a long time. He hadn't realized just how much the hatred and anger was eating him up inside and taking up room in his heart. To acknowledge that he needed Fallon and Dane was a big step for him. He was used to being on his own, staying in control, feeling nothing, but being with Maya had changed him.

He'd been pretending for years that Maya was just an assistant, a friend, even a lover, but she was more than that. She was everything to him. He had to talk to her. Tell her that he was a fool. Tell her that he loved her. Tell her she was his other half, his soul mate, and pray that she would take him back. He was prepared to lay down every vestige of his pride, *do anything*, if she'd just give him another chance.

* * *

It was essential that Maya keep her mind occupied. It was time she got settled and moved on with her life. It had taken a couple of weeks, but she'd found a permanent apartment in an area of Austin she liked and given up her short-term rental. Callie had driven from San Antonio to help her unpack her belongings from storage over the weekend so it would feel like home.

Maya had to admit the added benefit of being in Austin was that she was closer to Sophia. She'd already been able to make it to her mother's last couple of treatments.

This time she wasn't running from her problems. She was sticking around to spend time with her mother and develop some semblance of a relationship with Raven. Just that weekend, she'd met up with her sister at a baby store to shop for baby clothes and they'd gone for coffee afterward, which allowed Maya to coo over her niece. It was a small step toward mending their relationship, but one she never would have taken if she hadn't come back home.

She wasn't desperate for money, and was keeping herself busy until she could find a new job. Busy cleaning and decorating her new home. Grocery shopping to fill her refrigerator. Running in the early-morning hours. Focused on the books she read. Any activity she could think of that would take up room in her mind. Because if she didn't, the memories would arrive. And what purpose was there in reliving the nights she'd spent making love with Ayden. Because that's exactly what it had been. It hadn't been sex.

She was in love with Ayden and had given him a part of herself, but he didn't love her back. What was wrong with her? Why couldn't she find a man who would love her? She'd thought Thomas had, but he'd chosen Raven over her. And now Ayden. He was everything she wanted and could ever need. She wanted to be his wife, the mother of his babies, but he didn't want her forever. Just right now. It made Maya realize that she'd never really loved Thomas because he paled in comparison to Ayden, the man she'd secretly loved for the last decade. And she had to face the facts: she couldn't force him to love her back. She had to accept that he was never going to love her like she loved him. Heck, he didn't want to even try. She understood he'd been hurt, but would he ever allow love in?

Thoughts of Ayden were still invading her subconscious on Monday morning when she started a temp job a headhunter found for her. Maya tried to block Ayden from her mind and concentrate on typing. Tap, tap, tap on the keyboard. She could and would do what was necessary to move forward by keeping focused on the spreadsheets and reports she was assigned.

The elevator door chimed and Maya didn't know what made her look up. Maybe it was the powerful force field surrounding Ayden that required her absolute attention. Because there he was, striding toward her desk. Maya's stomach hollowed at the sight of him. She tried to quell the feeling, but there was no point. The effect of seeing him after weeks of going without was too much.

Ayden was standing in front of her in the flesh!

The man she'd loved, who'd once held her in his arms, kissed her passionately, made love to her tenderly, cuddled with her quietly was here. He'd been her entire universe that week in Jamaica. She would have probably continued to carry on their affair, grateful for whatever piece of himself he was willing to give her. Who knew how long she would have gone? "How did you find me?"

"An investigator."

"Why? We're over, Ayden. There's nothing left to be said."

"I disagree. I need to talk to you," he whispered.

She chuckled to herself at his arrogance, but why should she be surprised? "It's always about you, isn't it? Well, no more, Ayden. I choose me and my happiness. You should go."

"That's fair, but I'm not leaving. If I have to, I'll camp out until we have an opportunity to talk. I miss you, Maya."

A tear slipped down her cheek at his honest admission. "All right, we can talk."

She moved from behind the desk and walked toward the elevator. Ayden's hand closed around her elbow.

"I miss you, too, by the way," Maya commented, giving him a sideways glance, "but that changes nothing."

Ayden snorted. "It changes everything, Maya. It means there's still a chance."

"A chance for what?" She sniffed.

"For us."

They were silent as they waited for the car. Maya didn't know what to say. She had no idea why Ayden had come. She still wanted love and commitment, marriage and children. The whole enchilada. And she wasn't willing to settle for less.

The elevator arrived and Maya stepped in. She stole a glance at Ayden and found his eyes fixed on her. Watching her. She didn't want to look too closely at him. She would hear what he had to say and then leave. The car dinged again and several more people entered, forcing Ayden to move closer. Far too close for her liking. Her breath tightened in her lungs at his nearness.

The ride ended several moments later. Maya walked quickly through the lobby toward the revolving doors and across the cascade of steps that led to a large courtyard housing a green space where workers came to eat their lunch. Since it was still late morning, it was deserted.

Maya broke away and sat on a nearby stone bench. She needed to put distance between them. It hadn't been long enough for her to become immune to being near him. As it was, she'd had a hard time in the elevator because she'd felt his hard chest pressed against her back as it became overcrowded.

"What do you want, Ayden? I thought our conversation at your mansion and then again over the phone was pretty clear."

"Not quite," he responded, taking a seat beside her. "There's a lot I need to say to you and you need to hear."

She shrugged. "All right, I'm all ears."

He turned to face her. "For years, I was used to not having any emotions because feelings equaled weakness. If my stepfather saw me have any kind of emotion whatsoever when he was verbally abusing my mother or smacking us around, he'd hit us harder. Yell louder. So I learned to control my emotions to show none. Become impenetrable so I wouldn't get hurt."

"I'm sorry, Ayden. I can't even imagine how horrible it was. But I still don't understand what this has to do with us."

"A lot, if you'll give me a chance to explain. When you walked into my office ten years ago, I sensed you were something special, someone different from the other women I'd met. You weren't looking for anything from me, so you fit perfectly as my assistant. But as the years went on, you became less of an assistant. You became my friend." When she began to speak, he held up his hand. "I know I made your life hell back then. Having you send flowers and gifts to my dates. I think in my own way I was trying to test you to see if you would crack and throw yourself at me, but you never did. You just quietly let me be myself. Soon, I was opening up to you about the childhood I'd endured. I know it wasn't everything, but it was more than I'd told anyone."

"I remember I was surprised when you shared your story with me."

"You listened. You didn't judge or offer platitudes. It meant the world to me. And I think part of me knew that I had to keep you at arm's length. Otherwise, I would fall head over heels for you."

"But you didn't, Ayden."

"Five years ago, you cracked my armor when you came to me distraught over Thomas. I honestly never meant for anything to happen between us. I wanted to comfort you. Make you see how beautiful you were inside and out. And then you kissed me. Leading to the most spectacular night of my life up to that point."

"Yet you still showed me the door," Maya pressed. She hadn't forgotten the hurt she'd felt.

"Because I was scared. Scared of the feelings you'd evoked in me. Feelings I'd never felt before with another woman. So, of course, I did what I knew best. I pushed them down. Acted as if they didn't exist. I hurt you immeasurably and you left, with good reason. But then you came back, and all those old feelings resurfaced, Maya." He leaned in to cup her face with his large hands. "Don't you see they'd never really left? They'd been buried this entire time. But that week in Jamaica brought them to the forefront. It changed everything. I could no longer hide how much I wanted to be near you, mouth to mouth, skin to skin. I finally had you in my life and didn't want to let you go."

"Neither did I. You made me ridiculously happy in Jamaica and afterward. I thought surely you must feel something. Maybe even love me, just a little. But then you were willing to let me walk out the door, out of your life."

"I'm sorry, Maya. I was afraid I wouldn't be able to give you everything you might need. Marriage? Children? It terrifies me because I never wanted to do what my father did to me, Maya. He ripped me apart. Destroyed our family. Took away my home. Abandoned me. Gave away *my* inheritance to his new family. Never acknowledged me."

She touched his cheek with her hand. "Then don't be that man, Ayden. Be better than him."

He nodded and she saw tears glistening in his eyes. "It's why I'm here. I took your advice. I met with Fallon and we talked. We're going to try to make a go of this brother-sister thing. Hopefully, Dane will be on board, too."

"And your father?"

He shook his head. "That ship sailed a long time ago, Maya. And I can live with that. What I can't live without is you. I love you, Maya. And if you'll have me, I want to be your friend, your lover, your partner, your *husband*."

A sob worked its way upward and she let it out. *Had she really heard him correctly?* "Husband?"

"Yes, I want to spend the rest of my life with you, Maya. I don't want my life to be consumed with work. I want it to be full and rich. I want someone to share it with. I want you. Please tell me it's not too late. Though even if it is, I'm going to try my best to win you over."

She placed her palm flat on his chest. "You don't have to try to win me over, Ayden. You've had me from the moment I stepped foot in your office ten years ago and every moment thereafter. I love you. I always have and I always will."

Her entire body swayed toward his and Ayden swept her into his arms, kissing her fiercely, passionately. His faint stubble teased her skin and she moaned at the realization of a dream come true. When they finally parted, he reached into his suit pocket, and before she knew it he was down on one knee, pulling out a ring box. "Will you marry me, Maya? Will you make me the happiest man on earth by agreeing to grow old with me and have lots of babies that look just like you?"

With the back of her hand, Maya wiped the tears that were sliding uncontrollably down her face. "Yes, yes, yes, I'll marry you, Ayden."

His mouth moved over hers, slow and warm. "I promise I will treasure you for the rest of our lives."

"As will I. You won't be alone anymore, Ayden, because we're family."

"And you, my dear Maya, are my home. I love you."

Epilogue

"I can't believe I'm going to meet *the* Dane Stewart," Maya said when she and Ayden sat down to dinner at an exclusive restaurant in Austin known to cater to the wealthy. "And that we'll be related!"

"That's right." Ayden smiled. He couldn't wait to make Maya his wife. She would be his and vice versa. Since they'd gotten engaged several weeks ago, he'd been eager to get started planning their wedding. He was just sorry he'd wasted so much time, taking five long years before he'd finally admitted that she was the best thing to ever happen to him. But they were together now and that's all that mattered.

"Are you nervous?" Maya asked, peering up at him from under thick lashes.

Maya was intuitive. She must have noticed him tapping his foot underneath the table. "I would say I'm anxious," Ayden responded evenly. "Fallon has always been open to accepting me as her brother while Dane, up to this point, has steered clear of the family, same as me. So I don't know what to expect."

"You can expect that I won't judge you for our parents' shortcomings," a deep male voice said from behind him, "like you did Fallon."

"Dane!" Fallon muttered from behind him, swatting him on the arm. "You promised to behave." She wore a scowl that didn't match the vibrancy of her orange midi-dress, which was tailored to perfection on her slender figure.

"I was just joking," Dane said, laughing as he turned to face her.

Ayden rose to his feet and faced his baby brother. Dane Stewart was as tall as Ayden, well over six feet, with an athletic physique hidden in all-black attire: jeans, T-shirt and leather jacket. He had the same caramel complexion as Fallon, but didn't share Ayden and Fallon's eye color. His were dark brown and mischievous. Ayden could see why he was America's favorite actor.

"Dane." Ayden offered his hand and Dane snorted.

"We're brothers, Ayden. I think a hug is in order."

Ayden was stunned when Dane walked toward him and wrapped his arms around him in a bear hug. He'd never had a family before. Never thought he'd ever have one. Or even needed one. But now that they were here, Ayden wondered how he'd ever survived like that. He patted Dane's back. "Yes, we are. Yes, we are."

They parted, and a surge of emotion welled in Ayden. He could feel tears at the back of his eyes. Sensing he was overcome, Maya came and stood beside him, sliding her hand into his. It was a simple act, but meant the world to him. He smiled down at her and she rewarded him with a beaming grin.

"Where's the champagne?" Dane glanced around for the waiter. "I believe there's an engagement to celebrate."

"Bring it on," Fallon concurred with a grin. "It's time we welcome Maya into the family."

As champagne soon followed, Ayden sat back in his chair and thought about how thankful he was to finally get to know the brother and sister he'd once refused to claim, with the woman he loved by his side. Life couldn't get any better.

* * * * *